Binary Agent

Rod Johnson

ISBN-13: 978-0-578-35815-4

DEDICATION

To my brother-in-law, Thomas S. "Rod" Brasfield, the inspiration for Master Sergeant Tom Lechler. Rod was my hero and a patriot. He lied about his age to enter the Army at sixteen, giving a homeless person a fifth of whiskey to sign his dad's name on the enlistment papers.

Rod was fighting in Korea on his seventeenth birthday and spent two tours with the Army Special Forces in Vietnam, part of that time detailed to CIA's Phoenix Program and a member of an actual Green Light Team as described in *SPIRITs of Retribution* and in this book. He participated in countless special operations around the world with his A-Team and upon his retirement, Rod had devoted twenty years of his life to serving his country.

Rod collected Ford Mustangs and was passionate about the University of Alabama Crimson Tide. He loved his Green Beret brothers, too. But more than anything, he adored his wife – my late sister Jerene – and their two daughters, Kate and Beth.

He was the baddest of bad-asses and as with all the real ones I've ever met, downplayed his military service with humility, counting himself lucky to have done so.

Rod passed away June 1, 2021.

I love you, Rod. Rest in peace.

ACKNOWLEDGMENTS

I would like to acknowledgement the immeasurable contributions of my editor and biggest supporter, who also happens to be my wife. Without Amy's tireless efforts with my manuscripts, I would never be able to bring them to completion.

PROLOGUE

"Hit." A couple of seconds elapsed.

"Hit" preceded another interval of about the same length.

"Hit" followed the final shot.

Josh Morgan removed the magazine from his Daniel Defense, Model DDM4 V3 AR-15, confirmed it was empty of all thirty of the rounds the former CIA Officer had started with, checked the extractor to ensure it was likewise clear, and set the carbine on the shooting bench.

Newly retired Army Special Forces Master Sergeant Tom Lechler leaned away from the spotting scope through which he had observed the impact of the 5.56 MM NATO bullets and removed his ear plugs.

"Dang, son. That's some stunning gunning."

Morgan stifled his smile, though inwardly he was pretty proud of himself.

"Well, I'm not Chris Kyle, but I'll take it," he said.

The two men exchanged a fist bump, and Morgan removed his own hearing protection and shooting glasses.

Lechler stepped away from his position while the native Texan took his place behind the Vortex Diamondback spotting scope and examined the results of his latest volley on the red and white Redfield Target. The one foot by one foot sheet of paper had a large diamond in the center with a smaller one in each corner. Morgan had shot six rounds at each of the five separate patterns. Looking at the lower right grouping that he had ended with, he saw a satisfying collection of all six in an area of under a two-inch diameter. While he never acknowledged his friend's compliment further, he nevertheless considered it high praise from a former Green Beret.

Morgan's Golden Retriever Biscuit trotted alongside the two shooters as they walked the two hundred yards to the wooden target frame in front of the dirt berm that served as a backstop for the shots.

It was a glorious Autumn Sunday, one of those Wyoming days that made people forget how bitterly cold it could get in the winter. The aspens had displayed their brilliant hues of gold, orange, red, and yellow a few weeks before and had subsequently dropped their leaves. So, the sun shone through the bare limbs, casting long shadows in the late afternoon.

Some eighty yards to the side, a coyote watched from the far edge of Morgan's property just outside Jackson Hole.

"Many of them around?" asked the former soldier.

"Yeah, a good many."

"Ever shoot 'em?"

"Nah. I don't have livestock or poultry to worry about. And they've always left Biscuit alone. So, I leave them alone. Figured they were here before I was."

The wild animal lowered its head and took tentative steps toward the two men, but as they stopped and turned to face it for a longer look, it scampered away.

Lechler said, "Yeah, I agree. Live and let live."

Morgan considered the irony that each held that philosophy, given that each had dispatched a few living, breathing human beings in the recent past. But they would each maintain that, in a perfect world, they would have preferred that their actions had never been necessary.

Morgan knew that Lechler had, as a career warrior in the service of his country, seen more than his share of armed conflict, and that it probably seemed to him like a dozen lifetimes.

For his part, the ex-CIA Officer had taken his first human life in self-defense many years before in the small Latin American island country of Terrador. He had killed again protecting himself and his late friend, Trent Weston, former President of the United States, just over two years ago. But that time, on a pier along the Texas Gulf Coast, he had shot National Security Agency Deputy Director Everson Blake in cold blood.

He had similarly executed an unarmed man who was pretending to be a U.S. Secret Service Agent about six months ago, not far away, just outside of Jackson.

In Qatar Morgan had also killed the man behind Weston's assassination while that man was defenseless. The first men he had killed out of fear for what they might do to his fiancée and others that he loved. But unlike those actions that he felt to be preemptive, in Doha he had poisoned the eighty-two-year-old solely out of revenge.

He felt no remorse for any of the killings, but as time put distance between him and his acts, despite the necessity he continued to believe justified them, he knew that the deeds had damaged his soul. Morgan had no idea whether it could be repaired, especially since he had one more killing that he was hellbent on carrying out.

As the former CIA officer tore the paper target away from the frame, he admired his groupings again.

"So, you and Maggie really done?" inquired Lechler.

Josh Morgan let out a deep sigh as he cast an irritated glance toward Lechler and put a fresh target in place.

"Hey, just asking."

"Yeah. I mean, probably. I don't know what we are."

"Have you talked to her?"

"Not since I left D.C. and came back home."

Lechler's muted whistle underscored his comment before he had even made it. "Wow. Five months?"

Morgan didn't answer and turned to begin the walk back to the shooting bench.

"Why don't you call her?"

"Why don't you mind your own business?"

Tom Lechler held up his palms and tilted his head. "Sorry, pal." He continued with, "But you…" before thinking better of it and falling in behind Morgan. Out of the younger man's sight, though, the ex-soldier shook his head and whispered quietly enough that his words couldn't be heard. "But you're an idiot."

Josh took his seat behind the spotting scope. Lechler sat down and prepared his Bravo Company Manufacturing Mod4 AR carbine. The two men donned their glasses and placed their hearing protection in their ears. Lechler attached the magazine to his rifle, charged the first round, and settled the weapon on the gun rest. Morgan peered through his scope while the Master Sergeant aimed through the Steiner PX4i 4-16×56 mounted atop his carbine.

The former Green Beret's training took over – he held his breath and sensed the interval between heartbeats to minimize motion as he squeezed the trigger. As soon as he completed the first shot, the scope's reticle settled back onto the target.

Morgan heard the report, muffled by his ear protection, and simultaneously saw a slightly less than quarter-inch hole appear in the very center of the largest centermost diamond on the paper sheet, two hundred yards distant.

No sooner had the spotter shouted, "Hit," than a second black dot showed on the target, slightly overlapping the first.

The third round pierced the target about one quarter of an inch from the first two, the separation barely distinguishable, even through his high-quality optics.

"Hit!" Morgan confirmed loudly. But in a hushed tone, he followed with, "Damned showoff."

CHAPTER 1

Twenty-two Days Later
DAY 1 – MONDAY

As he was almost every morning and night, Edmundo Solis sat in front of his computer. Single and therefore unencumbered by the demands that a relationship would bring along with it, he spent his time monitoring developments in his homeland of Nicaragua. In his mind, the brutal regime of *el Presidente* Sergio Zamora was a blight like no other on the planet. Solis researched the atrocities and distilled the facts into briefs that he posted on his own blog.

El poder salvador de la verdad never had many readers. Almost none, to be exact – until recently. Suddenly, for reasons unknown to Solis, there was a surge in visitors to his site and subscribers to his blog. And though most were from Nicaragua, many of the new readers were from around the world. He believed that *The Saving Power of the Truth* was becoming a vital voice in the Central American country and a source of hope for its people in the face of oppression.

Edmundo Solis had escaped Nicaragua – at least that was how he saw it, even though his departure wasn't challenged – when he was seventeen. He lived in Mexico for four years before immigrating to the United States. Solis began the process of becoming a naturalized citizen of the U.S. immediately after attaining his fifth year as a permanent resident, the minimum amount of time legally required.

The overwhelming majority of Nicaraguans living in the United States settled in Florida and California. Initially Solis had made Miami his home. Later however, he relocated to Richmond, Virginia, until ultimately moving to Norfolk.

Now, as a never-married thirty-year-old, Eddie Solis was as proud a flag-waving American patriot as existed in his adopted home. And he used his treasured right to free speech to cry out against the atrocities rampant in his native land. The dictator Zamora was more ruthless than Daniel Ortega, the president of Nicaragua before Solis' birth, had been. Zamora assumed the role of leader of Nicaragua when Eddie was ten, so the native of Managua had witnessed the dictator's terrorization of his homeland for seven years before leaving for good. And as a student of his country's history, he was certain that no man had operated with as much savagery as the current despot.

Solis looked at the time on his computer display. He had just enough time to fire off his daily email to his contact in Washington, D.C. He typed the update furiously, clicked on "send," shut down his computer, and left for work. He felt a sense of satisfaction because this day's correspondence was different. Rather than merely providing a summary of the state of things in Nicaragua, it carried a promise of real information of a real operation being carried out by Zamora's operatives in a foreign country. He had no knowledge of the identity of the country or the nature of the mission yet, but his source in Managua had assured him that it was nefarious.

Edmundo Solis' sense of accomplishment came from the fact that, in his heart, he believed he was becoming a prominent enough voice to make a difference in his native land.

♦

The outgoing White House Press Secretary hugged her successor.

"I've never left a job that I didn't worry about who was taking over – until now. Maggie, dear, I couldn't be happier. I honestly believe I'll be able to enjoy my retirement, knowing you're in my office… Well, *your* office."

Incoming White House Press Secretary Margaret Loughlin beamed at her predecessor. "I hope I can make you proud, Marie."

"Of that, I have no doubt. You've already demonstrated your ability. You were meant for this. During the whole time I was out, you were flawless."

A tall, sandy-haired woman placed a hand on the retiree's shoulder. "Will you give us a moment, Marie?"

"Of course, Madam President."

Maggie Loughlin watched as Marie Ginnetti left to visit with others in attendance at the noon celebration. Ginnetti was able to walk without a cane, but her gait was slow and uneven, with a limp from the injuries she received from the assassination attempt on President Sandra Hendrickson. The explosion that shattered the front of St. John's Episcopal Church on the Chief Executive's Inauguration Day had killed her Vice-president and others and had badly injured an additional number, among them her son, Adam, Jr.

The Press Secretary was still inside the chapel when the bomb exploded from within one of the massive exterior columns. The effect of the blast was lessened somewhat by the wall that stood between her and it. The President's staffer had suffered a collapsed left lung, a broken left arm, major trauma to her left side, and a concussion. Oddly, all signs of those injuries had faded, but a piece of shrapnel from the church's wall had torn into her left leg. And though it was perhaps the least of her injuries, it was the one that had a lingering visual impact.

Maggie wondered if the limp would ever go away. POTUS interrupted her thoughts.

"Maggie, I wanted to tell you how thrilled I am to have you take over for Marie. I'm confident that you'll measure up to the high standard she set."

"I'll certainly do my best, ma'am. Secretary Ginnetti has certainly set the bar high."

"Maggie, I wanted to let you know that I've consulted with Secret Service Director Cortland, and we've decided to take the almost unprecedented step of assigning you Service protection."

"Ma'am?"

"In light of everything that happened last Spring, we think you should have agents assigned to you; at least for the foreseeable future."

Maggie knew that the only Press Secretary to have ever been given Secret Service protection was President Trump's Sarah Huckabee, after she had been angrily confronted at a restaurant by another diner.

"Ma'am, I don't think…"

Maggie's objection was cut off by the President's raised hand.

"Already done, Maggie. Now go enjoy the rest of the reception. I have to get back to my desk."

"Anything I can help you with, Madam President?"

POTUS waved off the offer and laughed. "I know where to find you. Things will get busy for you soon enough."

Despite trying to refuse the offer of a Secret Service detail, Maggie was quietly relieved. Only a few months ago, she and Josh Morgan, who were engaged at the time, were in Jackson Hole to visit Maggie's friend, Curtis Jones. Jones had taken over management of Maggie's public relations firm, Image Quest, when she moved to Washington to work in the West Wing. He was seriously injured in a car wreck that Morgan discovered was a murder attempt. A group of individuals, working at the behest of billionaire philanthropist Linus Schwartz, had targeted Morgan and everyone close to him to settle an old vendetta.

The group had assassinated Former President Weston and had subsequently abducted Maggie. So, Maggie accepted that having some agents around her would be a good thing.

She turned to greet one of the members of her staff and determined that she would put all the unpleasant memories out of her mind. Maggie would do as President Hendrickson had suggested and return to the reception and enjoy the celebration of her promotion and her predecessor's retirement.

♦

Central Intelligence Agency Director Elizabeth Parnell was growing impatient.

Over five months earlier she had reached an agreement with Josh Morgan to work for her. He was adamant that he wouldn't return to CIA as a Case Officer. He had been there, done that. Going to work for the Agency right out of college, Morgan had successfully completed *ad hoc* assignments in his cover as a photojournalist until he found himself at the center of an unsanctioned operation to assassinate the president of the small Latin American country of Terrador.

The CIA officer had eventually discovered that the plan's sole purpose was to reinstall a man as dictator who had enabled a rogue network to line its members' pockets through drug and human trafficking. The organization was made up of corrupt operatives from the National Security Agency and the Central Intelligence Agency who worked with South American cartels and the dictator of Terrador before he was voted from office in that country's first free election.

Notwithstanding the fact that Morgan had upended the plot, he was booted from the Company. During the years afterward, the ex-CIA officer had rescued a kidnapped former president and discovered evidence in Russia that helped prevent a war between that country and the United States. More recently he had also brought down a billionaire who was planning to resurrect the illegal operations in Terrador.

The tycoon also had his sights on Morgan and the people he cared about. The NSA Deputy Director whom Morgan had killed, Everson Blake, was the billionaire's son. As he had the son, Morgan had eliminated the father. But the construction magnate's fixer, Oskar Lammers, had escaped. He had been the point man of the scheme. Through surrogates and his own direct action, Lammers had overseen the assassination of the former President, had Morgan arrested for murder and then treason, abducted Morgan's fiancée, and tried to kill Morgan.

Morgan obviously hated Lammers. So, it made perfect sense that, among his nonnegotiable demands that were conditions for working for

Parnell, Morgan had required the time and support to go after Lammers first.

But it was approaching a half year since the DCI and her new contract employee had reached their agreement. Morgan had turned down two operations from the Director and had yet to take care of Oskar Lammers.

Josh received a monthly stipend, a retainer, of sorts. Parnell never actually expected much in return. It was mostly a means of providing some financial support to the man who had done so much for his country. But it would become increasingly difficult to justify the payments if Morgan never made it into the field.

However, with all her frustration at the lag between her agreement with Morgan and his carrying out any actual assignments, Parnell was certain that the situation was nearing a resolution. It had been three weeks since the CIA Chief had heard from the man. And the onset of the break in communication had coincided with Parnell's providing him Oskar Lammers' location in Venezuela.

♦

With the celebratory reception for her in the West Wing ended, newly sworn-in White House Press Secretary Margaret Loughlin took her seat behind the desk in her new office. She had previously occupied the office when she had filled in for Marie Ginnetti during her hospitalization. But now the office was officially hers and she had conflicting emotions.

The professional in Maggie's makeup knew that the position constituted what many viewed as the career pinnacle for anyone in the public relations field. Consequently, she felt great pride and an eagerness to excel. On the other hand, only a few months ago, she had sat at a table in a restaurant not far from the White House waiting for her fiancé whom she had broken up with. Maggie was prepared to leave her job in the West Wing and move back to Wyoming with Josh or do anything else it would take to reconcile with him. She had been completely undone at Morgan's actions throughout the ordeal that saw him charged with murder and then treason, herself kidnapped, and Former President Trent Weston assassinated. Maggie had witnessed Josh shoot a defenseless man in cold blood, and she had come to find out that it was at least the second time he had committed such an act. She had first thought he was a different man than the one she loved, but finally decided that the violence she had seen him inflict wasn't a sign of some inner demon that was ever-present. Instead, she had become convinced that it was evidence of such devotion in Morgan to those he loved that he would make whatever sacrifices were necessary and take whatever actions were required to protect them.

Sitting then at the lunch table at McCormick & Schmick's, waiting for

Josh to arrive, she had been certain that he was the same man she had loved for so long. Maggie had come to believe that, to keep her safe, he was prepared to violate whatever personal morals he possessed and damage himself physically and emotionally to any extent that resulted. Maggie was ready to walk away from her job to make things work out. She was convinced that all would turn out well; that their relationship would be restored.

But when Josh had arrived, everything turned upside down. He broke things off for good, saying that he couldn't put her through what he believed would be a perpetual string of violence and conflict in his life.

Now Maggie was committed to regaining some happiness and peace to her life. She thought of Josh Morgan every day, and while the pain was easing slowly, she held on to a small hope that one day they would reunite.

The flash of the "new mail" icon on her computer screen ended Maggie's momentary indulgence in her memories and hopefulness. She had long since turned off any audible notification of new messages. She received so much email that the string of alerts would sound like a disjointed tune.

"Might as well take a look at what's already in my inbox," she decided.

Press Secretary Loughlin sighed at the substantial amount of electronic mail. With nobody yet hired for her former position as Principal Assistant Press Secretary, the current missives belonged solely to her. Of course, she would delegate to her staff, but until then the process of doing so, as well as sorting out what of the messages were pure garbage, was all hers.

CHAPTER 2

The smile on Maggie Loughlin's face was instantaneous as she saw the "From" on her email. Why this person had fixed his attention on her was a mystery, but fixated he was. She had received an email every morning and most nights for some time. Their inception seemed to generally coincide with the beginning of her role in the daily briefings concerning the recent crisis with the Russian Federation.

Perhaps Edmundo Solis saw her as more accessible than other West Wing officials when he started sending the updates. After all, at the time she was only a *Deputy* Secretary and not the real thing. She never read the emails anymore. They consisted of the same thing every time – accounts of atrocities that the Nicaraguan government was committing.

Most of Solis' narratives sounded like the stuff of conspiracy nuts. They added little to what was commonly known and reported by the media. The communiques were short on details and long on diatribe. But they were no doubt penned by a man driven by a genuine passion for the Latin American country. Maggie had even personally answered one of the earlier emails, rather than let the automatic reply from her email account suffice as her response. The then-Principal Deputy Press Secretary had thanked the man for his correspondence and assured him that she would forward his email to the State Department, which she had.

Maggie had come to regret having sent that personal note now because Solis had come to think of her as a sort of pen pal. He had even begun "signing" the emails with only his first name – Eddie.

But Maggie felt that every American needed to feel like he had a voice. Perhaps it was for that reason that Maggie could never bring herself to delete the emails. So, she smiled again and moved the unread message to an archival folder simply titled, "Eddie."

♦

"He looks frailer than the last time I saw him. His injuries and extended stay in the hospital have taken their toll."

MSG Tom Lechler, U.S. Army, Retired, had never seen Oskar Lammers so he had no frame of reference from which to make such a characterization. So, he simply grunted at Morgan's observation.

Lechler had recently retired from the U.S. Army and another of Morgan's nonnegotiable demands for returning to work on a contract basis for Parnell at CIA was that she bring Lechler into the arrangement as well.

The two CIA contractors sat in their vehicle watching Lammers walk slowly down the street in San Cristobal, Venezuela. The man carried a bag of groceries with one hand and had a rolled-up magazine tucked under his other arm. Through the Nikon binoculars, Morgan could see enough of the print on the cover of the magazine to note that it was in the German's native language.

"We could take him out from here when he gets to a place a little less public," Lechler suggested.

Morgan replied, "No, I want him to know it's me."

A couple of minutes elapsed before Lechler spoke again. "You know, Josh, it's never a good idea to make this sort of thing personal."

Morgan didn't remove his eyes from the binoculars, but his partner could see him cut his eyes toward him from behind the eyepieces.

"Already is."

Lechler drove at a slow pace to avoid overtaking the German. He knew that any operative of the caliber Morgan insisted this man to be would make them, but this is what he wanted, so they crept along. Staying back as far as they did created problems. Lammers could make a turn, enter a store with a back exit – anything to shake them off his six when he spotted them. And again – assuming that the man was as capable and experienced as Morgan swore he was – he would have checked out every building, every route, every possible way to escape in a familiar area that he frequented. If he did anything other than walk obligingly along the sidewalk, the pair following him would have to continue the pursuit on foot or lose him – possibly to never pick him up again.

"He can't be that unaware," the retired soldier said. And after a pause and a glance in his partner's direction, "Can he? I mean, he's either a dumbass without a clue that we're here or… or he knows we're here and doesn't care."

Morgan cut his eyes from the binoculars again.

"Damn, Josh, you think he's on to us?"

Morgan nodded. "Possibly."

"If he does, you think he knows it's you?"

"I hope so."

"Then why doesn't he make a run for it?"

"Not his style."

♦

"Ms. Loughlin…"

Maggie looked up from her work to see a tall, lean figure whose face was familiar.

"Hi, Agent Marchman." She stood to shake the Secret Service Agent's hand.

"It's good to see you again. Congratulations."

"Oh, thanks." Maggie returned to her seat and ran both hands through her auburn hair. "Part of me wonders what I've gotten myself into. No, really, I'm thrilled. Thank you. Sit down. Please."

"No, ma'am. I'll stand. I just stopped by to let you know that I've been assigned to your detail. I'll be on your daytime shift, which really means from the time you start your day until you end it. Others will take the night shift."

"Well, it's nice to have someone I know."

Macarthur Marchman and his senior partner, Joy Griffith, had been pulled into the protective detail of everyone around Former President Weston when he had fallen ill with what was at first believed to be a stroke.

"Yes, ma'am. My assignment is only temporary until they get a permanent team assigned."

"Regardless of how long it is, I appreciate you watching over me. Sure you won't sit down?"

"No, thanks. There is some coordination that needs to be sorted out. Good to see you, Secretary Loughlin."

"See ya, Mac."

Maggie's gaze lingered on Agent Marchman as he walked away.

"This might not be so bad," she thought.

The Press Secretary's examination of her new but temporary security agent ended abruptly with the sound of her mobile phone. She shifted her eyes to her caller ID and saw the name of Michael Driessen. The just-retired U.S. Navy Captain had come on board in the last week as the new Deputy Director at the National Security Agency. Since the death of Everson Blake, the position had been filled by two Acting Directors. The more recent one seemed to be headed for the position full-time until a diagnosis of leukemia forced him to withdraw his name from consideration.

Captain Driessen's Naval career had largely been in the Navy Cyber Warfare Development Group. NCWDG served as the Navy's center for cyber warfare innovation.

Earlier in his career, before his eight-year stint as the Deputy Commander at NCWDG, Driessen had served three years in the Second Fleet as the Cryptologic Resource Coordinator. As CRC he was responsible for management of cryptologic assets, cryptologic coverage and tasking plans, and other duties and procedures.

But it was the four-year period between those Navy duty stations that the former Naval Officer learned his way around the NSA. Driessen's Joint Assignment was a liaison between the NSA's efforts and cyber warfare within the U.S. Navy. Recently contemplating retirement and with the position of Deputy Director still open, Driessen applied for the job, was selected, and resigned his commission after twenty-two years as an officer in the United States Navy.

"Captain Driessen, was our call scheduled for today?"

"No, Secretary Loughlin. Tomorrow. But something has come up that you might be asked about. We just discovered that a Chinese rocket has failed to reach orbit."

"Geez… Another one? Does the press know yet?"

"Not as far as we can determine. Beijing hasn't made anything public yet. NSA picked up some transmissions, but we were also monitoring the launch with our satellites."

"What can I say publicly, Captain?"

"Nothing yet, Secretary Loughlin. Just didn't want you to get blindsided."

"Okay. Thanks. And it's Maggie."

"Only if it's Mike, ma'am."

"Deal. I'll let you know if anybody brings it up."

"I'd appreciate that, ma'am."

"Can I brief my staff, Mike?"

"We'd prefer to limit it to only those who might be in direct contact with the press corps."

"Got it. Thanks for the heads-up, Mike."

The line went silent.

"Hmmm…"

In May of 2021, the Chinese Long March 5B rocket had tumbled out of control in low orbit for several days. The event caused serious concern throughout the world that some debris might survive reentry into Earth's atmosphere and fall into a populated area. At twenty-two metric tons, it was among the largest objects to ever reenter Earth's atmosphere uncontrolled. Fortunately, the remains fell harmlessly into the Indian Ocean near the Maldives.

An earlier launch of the same rocket type had also failed, and pieces fell in Africa.

As in the United States, Beijing was attempting to open up its space endeavors to commercial participation, largely without success. The Chinese company iSpace had two of its Hyperbola-1 rockets fail within a six-month period in 2021.

Accusations from NASA and the European Space Agency that China had cut corners and that their practices were irresponsible had created tensions with the Communist nation. That friction had continued to the present and had spilled over into other areas of relations between China and other countries, but with the United States, in particular.

Maggie felt the likelihood of the booster hitting a densely populated area was small. After all, over seventy percent of the earth's surface was water. But crafting a response that was critical but wouldn't aggravate the already heightened sensitivity of the Communist regime about its space program would be Maggie's responsibility, at least as far as the White House's reaction was concerned.

"You never know what kind of things will come up on a given day," Maggie muttered quietly. Then she got back to work.

CHAPTER 3

The White House Press Secretary had notified the President's Chief of Staff, Noah Chandler, about the situation with the Chinese rocket. Of course, he already knew. Maggie rarely surprised Chief Chandler with anything. A large part of his job was to get out in front of anything and everything that his boss might face. He had already given thought to an official reaction when Maggie called him. The pair worked out a draft and Chandler presented it to President Hendrickson for her approval.

It was a good thing they were prepared. The first question in the very late afternoon press briefing that dealt mostly with Hendrickson's itinerary for the next couple of days concerned the wayward booster.

"Emery," the President's Press Secretary said to call on the first of the networks' White House Correspondents.

"Emery Sorensen, QNN," the middle-aged reporter announced. "QNN has learned that another rocket launch by the People's Republic of China has failed to achieve its intended course, leaving the booster tumbling in a low orbit. What is NASA's assessment of the danger and what message does the President have for Beijing?"

A few hours had passed since Captain Driessen had informed Maggie of the situation, and Xinhua, China's state media outlet, had reported the event. In typical fashion Xinhua had underplayed any potential danger and quickly moved away from the announcement to other stories. So, while knowledge of the matter among the journalists wasn't a surprise, the fact that the first question concerned it was.

"Slow news day, I guess," Maggie thought. Then she dove right into the prepared statement. It was a non-answer, really, as many of her responses to the media were. But one of the arts necessary for a public relations expert was to make it *sound* like an answer.

"There is no reason at this time to expect any worse an outcome than in the other failures of China's rockets."

The opening remark sounded passive enough but embedded in it was a reminder that this was merely the latest in a string of malfunctioning launch vehicles.

"Certainly, the President is disappointed in the China National Space Administration's lack of success in addressing their repeated inability to launch their space vehicles safely. But this is not something she wishes to communicate publicly. The President is monitoring the situation and has already been in touch with the NASA Administrator and DoD personnel to assess the matter as it develops. She will provide her comments to Beijing privately, rather than publicly. Next question."

A follow-up on the same topic and then another both failed to elicit a more substantive response, so the Press Pool moved on.

◆

Eddie Solis had just ended his workday, and as he always did, stopped in at *Nicaragua Genuina* for a bite to eat and a beer – one beer. He never allowed himself the indulgence of more than that because he needed to remain clearheaded for what he considered to be his *real* job, or jobs – editor/head correspondent/chief blogger of *El poder salvador de la verdad* as well as public servant and resistance fighter.

Genuine Nicaragua had opened just a few years earlier and was the only restaurant of its type in the Norfolk area. Eddie enjoyed the place because, as suggested by the rather uninspired name, it reminded him of his favorite eatery in his hometown of Managua. The small *restaurante* did little business and those who did frequent the establishment worried that it might not survive much longer.

Eddie always sat alone, though he had struck up a friendship with Carlos, the owner, and even carried on a few flirtatious encounters with the man's daughter. He felt that Ana liked him, never realizing she was just humoring him. Ana was genuinely fond of Eddie, but he wasn't her type. Her "type" was the man – almost any man – who could deliver her from her job working for her father and spirit her away to another, better life far away from Norfolk.

Eddie would've asked Ana out, but for the same reason that he never drank in excess, he wouldn't allow himself a social life. Eddie was a man on a mission, but his devotion couldn't prevent him from loneliness. So, whenever he got the chance to speak with others in the restaurant who had fled the brutality of Nicaragua for lives in the United States, he was thrilled. All, like he, were condemning of the dictator ruling their native land.

A pair of men sat at the table next to his, chatting idly without so much as a glance in Solis' direction. That is, until one of the men rose to visit the *baño.* The remaining diner ordered another *cerveza* and gazed around the interior of the dining area of *Nicaragua Genuina.* Finally, his and Eddie Solis' eyes connected. Both men smiled meekly and nodded. Each looked away but the eye contact was long enough that it would've been awkward not to speak.

"This is a nice restaurant," opened the first man.

"Yes, it is nice," replied Solis. "The food is very authentic. The owner is also a native of my country."

"Luis Gutierrez," said the fellow Nicaraguan, standing and offering his hand.

Eddie extended his hand, "Eddie Solis. Nice to meet you."

The conversation carried on in Spanish for a moment until the second diner returned from the men's room.

"This is my brother Santos." Then looking to his sibling, "Santos, this is Eddie."

After the opening pleasantries ended the men moved and congregated at Eddie's table, where the conversation continued. Eddie even allowed himself the luxury of a second *cerveza.*

"So, do you live in the U.S.?" the new acquaintance asked.

"*Sí.* And you?"

"*Sí.* We have just arrived and are looking for an apartment."

Eddie provided local information and offered suggestions about possible living quarters for the new arrivals. The men continued to chat amiably about their homeland, life in the U.S., and other topics of common interest until Santos asked, "What do you do, Eddie?"

Though his real passion and, in his mind, his real job, was blogger, Eddie always answered that query with his full-time, paying job.

"I drive a delivery truck for UPS. What do you do?"

Luis answered for both.

"We are mechanics. We worked in the same shop in Managua until we grew tired of the political climate. We have saved money to try to open our own shop here, but we are afraid it won't be enough."

More conversation ensued until Luis excused himself for a restroom run. As he left, Santos said with more than a hint of regret, "We feel very isolated from Managua. We don't get any in-depth information."

That was Eddie's cue to introduce his new friends and fellow countrymen to *El poder*, but before he could, Santos continued.

"The only place we can get information that seems to be reliable is a blog called *El poder salvador de la verdad.* If you haven't seen it, you should take a look."

Eddie's cheeks and forehead flooded with a wash of red.

"That's my blog," he blurted. He would've preferred to have been a little less exuberant, a little cooler. But he'd never had anyone give such an endorsement who didn't already know of his involvement with the social media content. A total stranger's familiarity, no less approval, of his work gave him a sense of validation for what he'd been doing to provide a voice for those oppressed under the Sergio Zamora regime.

"Eddie Solis? *Edmundo* Solis? You're that Edmundo Solis?!" Santos thrust his hand across the table to grasp Solis' and began to shake it vigorously. As he did, his brother Luis returned and sat at the table.

"Do you know who this is, *hermano*? Edmundo Solis!"

"Of *El Poder*?" Luis asked enthusiastically.

"*Sí!*"

The younger brother practically ripped Eddie's hand from Santos' to shake it himself.

"This is a great honor, *amigo*! Edmundo Solis! *Es verdad*?"

Solis couldn't quite bring himself to make eye contact. His head lowered, he bobbed it up and down a couple of times.

"This is a great privilege, *amigo*! A great privilege indeed! Waiter, *por favor*, bring three more cervezas. No… rum! You have *Flor de Caña*?" Getting the affirmation, Luis continued, "Then, *tres Flor de Cañas*!"

Eddie Solis started to refuse – he'd already had one beer more than his self-imposed limit – and he hadn't had anything harder than *cerveza* in years. But he was overjoyed. He had just met two of what Americans called "fans." And besides, *Flor de Caña* was an exquisite rum. "So," he thought, "Why the hell not?"

After all, it felt like a celebration.

Partly because he felt as though his blushing was embarrassing but mostly because he really needed to take a piss, "world-famous" blogger Edmundo Solis excused himself for a trip to the men's room.

♦

It was 11:45 PM in San Cristobal, Venezuela, and Josh Morgan and Tom Lechler stood outside the apartment where Oskar Lammers stayed. They had followed him throughout the day and had seen him with no one who appeared to be a contact. In fact, during their surveillance, the pair hadn't seen the German speak to a soul aside from a clerk in a grocery store. Satisfied that he had no associates or support, they had followed him to his flat.

In addition to his anxiety, Morgan felt a sense of excitement. It had taken a long time for Director Parnell to come up with a location for the man. Vindication for a great number of transgressions by this enemy was at hand, he was sure. While Lechler stood watch, looking down the hallway for anyone who might stumble into the operation, Morgan placed a small device over the door peephole and viewed the live feed on his smart phone. Distorted though the image was, he could clearly see Oskar Lammers sitting at the dining room table some distance from the door.

"He doesn't seem to be aware of anything," Morgan thought. And he believed that his presence in the visible part of the apartment should make it easier to catch their target by surprise than if he were in another room. He lifted his index finger to signal to Lechler that, at least as far as he could tell, there was only the one person in the apartment and that he had eyes on him.

The plan was straightforward. In that he'd had more experience with this type of breach, Lechler would make the incursion. But he was under strict orders – if you could call it that – that he was under no circumstances to take out Lammers himself. That was Morgan's job, and he would enjoy it. Once they were inside, Morgan would take a few minutes to have a conversation with the man who had been an integral part of the plot that killed former President Trent Weston, and who had kidnapped Maggie Loughlin, and tried to kill Morgan himself.

Morgan had considered torturing the man but had decided that he needed to maintain what little of his morality that he believed remained, so he would simply state his case and do away with him.

The ex-CIA Officer stuffed his phone with the peephole reverser into his pants pocket. He gave Lechler a thumbs-up and examined his weapon again. Unlike previous confrontations when Morgan had what were basically stock, publicly available handguns, this time he had something more in line with what a special operator, as he seemed to have become, required.

For the close-quarters encounter Morgan and Lechler had anticipated, the former Master Sergeant had recommended and acquired a handgun he assured Morgan fell in the category of an oldie but a goodie. The Heckler & Koch MK23 began production in 1993 and was chambered in a .45 caliber. It was a match-grade pistol with a laser pointer and a suppressor. Morgan pulled back the slide just enough to assure himself that a round was present. Then he and Lechler reversed roles. Morgan assumed watch down the corridor while his associate fixed his attention on the relatively flimsy-looking door.

A deadbolt was just above the knob, which also had a keyhole, so there were two points of security. The former Green Beret aimed and delivered a front kick that placed the heel of his right foot to the side of the doorknob and the deadbolt, at a point midway between the two vertically. The door was as weak at it appeared and broke apart as it crashed open.

Lechler stepped forward, his H&K at the ready. Morgan followed him in and, to his irritation, had to step around his partner whom he thought should've moved to the side. An apparently unsurprised Oskar Lammers looked at his two "guests" with an almost bemused expression. Morgan looked to Lechler and noticed an odd body language. The former soldier's shoulders were slumped, and his gun slightly lowered.

Morgan turned his attention again to Lammers, with his .45 raised and ready for action. Lammers began to stand, palms facing toward his intruders and arms raised. Morgan recoiled slightly and stretched his arms somewhat toward the man he so desperately wanted dead.

"Mr. Morgan, aren't you going to introduce me to your friend?"

The German's smirk grew to a full grin, which unsettled Morgan. He looked at Tom Lechler, whose gun hand was now hanging at his side.

"What?" demanded Josh Morgan.

The former Army Special Forces operator smiled, sighed, and shook his head.

"I guess you didn't hear the click."

♦

Edmundo Solis – he felt more like "Edmundo" than "Eddie" right now, given his fame with Luis and Santos Gutierrez – returned to the table where his admirers waited. They stood, each with a glass in his hand, and nodded in a show of reverence. Santos handed a glass to Eddie, who took it with a great deal of anticipation. Not only was *Flor de Caña* a highly regarded rum in his homeland, but he also knew that the occasion was intended as a tribute to him.

"To Edmundo Solis and *El poder salvador de la verdad,*" said Luis.

"*Sí!*" agreed Santos.

An embarrassed, and thrilled, Solis nodded humbly. The three raised the glasses aloft briefly before taking sips of the reddish amber liquid.

The owner/bartender of *Nicaragua Genuina* and his daughter smiled their approval as they watched through the window to the small patio where the three new friends had moved so they could smoke. They conversed for quite some time.

"*Sí*, I have many contacts in important places, both in Nicaragua, and elsewhere," Solis exaggerated. He leaned forward and drew on the cigar that Luis Gutierrez had given him. "In fact…," – Eddie spoke in a near whisper now – "…one of my contacts works for the U.S. President. She is in the White House." He drew on his cigar again and with a wave of his hand, said, "We correspond every day."

Solis nodded his head and leaned back.

"No!" said Santos. "Who is it?"

Edmundo waved the hand holding the cigar. "No. No, I cannot," he protested, though he knew he would milk the disclosure for effect a while longer before finally disclosing the identity. The name would surely impress.

"*Por favor*, Eddie," Luis agonized "You're killing me."

"I can say this much." Eddie blew a smoke ring. "I have given her very sensitive information about an operation that I have uncovered by the bastard *presidente* Zamora. She has told me that she will sit on the information until I have more details – the complete story – and then she will pass it along to her boss, *La Presidenta de los Estados Unidos de America*: *La Presidenta* Hendrickson!"

Solis took another satisfying draw on his cigar and leaned back. The Gutierrez *hermanos* giggled like schoolgirls.

"*Por favor*, Eddie!" Luis clasped his hands together and pled again. "*Por favor*."

After a few more minutes of the Gutierrez brothers piling on the praise and Edmundo Solis basking in it, the founder/blogger/editor of *El poder* put his hand to his forehead. The more than usual amount of liquor, combined with his giddiness at the unrestrained adulation from his drinking companions, was taking its toll. He smiled at the men opposite him and let out a deep sigh.

"My contact is the new Press Secretary for the American President. Her name is Margaret Loughlin. I tell her what I have uncovered about Zamora's activities and she in turn, tells me what the U.S. administration knows from their side. Confidentially, of course."

The expressions on the Gutierrez brothers' faces affirmed that the disclosure had hit its mark. They *were* impressed.

Edmundo Solis leaned back in his chair, blew another smoke ring, and insisted, "That's all I can say."

Solis had always done his work on his blog out of patriotism, but now he felt like a celebrity, of sorts. And it felt good.

♦

"Well, shit," lamented Tom Lechler, former U.S. Army Special Forces soldier. "This sucks."

Ex-CIA Officer Morgan still didn't know what his problem was.

"Mr. Morgan, your associate has stepped on a pressure plate that is attached to an explosive device." Lammers shifted his attention to the compromised operator. "Not the sort of thing normally used indoors, is it?"

Lammers returned to his chair beside the small wooden dining table.

"Oh, I've been certain since our last phone conversation that you'd come for me. Your problem, Mr. Morgan, is that you take these matters far too personally. That will be your downfall. Had you let it go, you would've never heard from me again. But you couldn't do that. It's against your very nature."

Lechler turned his eyes to Morgan. "Sorry, Josh."

"I can't take you anywhere," the former spook said with a wryness he didn't feel.

"Guess not." Lechler shrugged his shoulders and smirked.

Morgan understood that if Tom stepped off the plate, which was hidden under a rather large area rug, the improvised explosive device would detonate, killing both Lechler and him.

"You know this would kill you, too, Lammers."

"I've considered that. But in my recent, lengthy hospital stay that you helped arrange, I received the unfortunate word that I have an inoperable tumor on my brain stem. Grade 4, I'm afraid. So, my death, should it occur now, will have only been hastened by a few months; perhaps weeks. It might be preferable to die now, in fact, by the IED or at your hand."

"Shoot the fucker, Josh."

Morgan's head was clouded with scenarios that were in conflict with what he had planned for the German. He wouldn't have tortured Lammers, but to simply shoot him seemed to be so… well… anticlimactic. It occurred to Morgan that, perhaps, by shooting the bastard, he might actually be doing him a favor, given his condition. The sudden death would preempt a more miserable one, possibly coming only at the end of unspeakable suffering. The thought of that type of demise appealed to Morgan, but he didn't want to deprive himself of the vengeance for all the man had done to him and his loved ones.

"Morgan, shoot the son of a bitch, or I will. Then we'll deal with my situation."

"Quiet, Tom." Josh Morgan kept his gun trained on Lammers but rubbed his forehead. Finally, he addressed his adversary.

"What prevents me from doing you right now? The idea is kinda growing on me."

Oskar Lammers tipped his head toward and past Morgan.

"He does."

Morgan felt the pressure of a gun barrel on the back of his head. Tom Lechler turned to see a uniformed policeman with a gun pointed at Morgan. He was afraid to make a sudden move for fear of detonating the IED. He had faced similar situations before and was prepared to face death, but he knew the explosion would kill his partner, too. And besides, the policeman clearly had the drop on Morgan.

"Please drop your gun, sir," Lammers said to Lechler.

"How 'bout I just hand it over? This thing I'm standing on may be a little sensitive."

"As you wish."

The ex-Green Beret handed his gun over his left shoulder to the gunman behind Morgan.

"And now yours, Mr. Morgan."

The planned vengeance would have to wait, Morgan decided, if it even happened at all. He handed his H&K to the policeman.

Oskar Lammers gave the policeman an envelope with a generous stack of money.

"I should withhold a great deal of that for cutting things so close," he said sternly. "But I suppose everything worked out."

"*Gracias*, *Señor* Lammers."

"Toss your phones to me." The men complied. He tossed the ex-soldier's on the table. Then he removed the peephole device from Morgan's and stuck it and the phone in his pocket.

"We find ourselves in a familiar situation, Mr. Morgan," Lammers said, referring to the time when he had Morgan similarly at bay in Qatar before the American turned the tables on the German. During the turn of events at that time, a CIA Officer stationed in Doha had shot Lammers, believing he had killed him.

Morgan smiled, "And how'd that work out for you last time, Oskar?"

Lammers sneered his reply. "I'm afraid you have no such cavalry to ride to your rescue here… Josh."

♦

"Good night, Mac," White House Press Secretary Margaret Loughlin said to Macarthur Marchman, as he opened the door of her apartment for her.

"Night, ma'am," replied her Secret Service escort, handing her the key.

"Please. Call me Maggie."

"Can't ma'am. Not allowed. And not appropriate."

"Why? We are going to be working together."

"No, ma'am. *I'll* be working. *You'll* be safely going about your normal routine."

"Whatever you say… *Agent Marchman*." Maggie snapped off a silly salute.

The protector and protectee smiled.

"There'll be someone outside all night."

"Okay. Goodnight, Mac. Thank you."

Maggie walked into her apartment. It was smaller than the one she had shared with Josh. She had no need for the extra room. Still, she couldn't quite bring herself to part with the apartment where she and Josh had lived. She mainly left clothing and furniture there that she had no room for in her new place. She had joked with friends that the old apartment had to be one of the world's largest walk-in closets or the most expensive storage unit. She rarely went there, and when she did, she never lingered, not wanting to reminisce about her life there.

Secretary Loughlin's first full day in her new post had been a long one. It was after 10:30 PM in Washington. She set her briefcase on the dining table and opened her laptop with the intention of working a while longer. But after a mere five minutes of staring at the screen with no progress, she closed the lid and went to the kitchen to pour herself a glass of red wine.

Maggie sipped at the vino and decided she was eventually going to need more. With the bottle in her left hand and the glass in her right, she moved to the couch and turned on the television, as she often did. Only these days she didn't have Josh's shoulder to lay her head on in the time before she inevitably nodded off.

Moments later, with her still full wine glass resting next to the bottle of cabernet on the coffee table, Maggie Loughlin was fast asleep.

♦

"You know, I might just step off this thing and blow you to hell," Lechler warned.

"But alas, you will not because it would also kill Mr. Morgan."

"That's the only thing holding me back, asshole."

"As for you, Mr. Morgan, I can assure you there will be no repeat of our last encounter. I made the mistake of getting too close to you and allowed you the opportunity to take advantage of the blunder. I will make no such mistake this time. I will keep my distance.

"And though my injuries and, yes, my cancer, have robbed me of strength, a .45 caliber bullet will cover the distance to your chest before you can take one step. You know, Mr. Morgan, during my time in the hospital, I gave a great amount of effort to researching you. My contacts in many of what your President Hendrickson's administration would call rogue governments, gave me quite a bit of information. I've developed a very impressive biography on you. You've been busy over the last few years."

"Well, I try."

"Ah, Mr. Morgan, you do amuse me. Sarcastic till the end. But, let me continue, the Saudi Arabian government in particular has a keen interest in gaining access to you. It seems you've run afoul of them on two occasions; once with regard to their desire to put your President Weston on trial for war crimes, and secondly, when you interfered with their operation to put your nation at war with the Russian Federation."

Morgan's anger burned at the mention of the Saudis.

"They're paying me a handsome sum to deliver you to them. I have no idea what need I have of the money, given that I'll die soon, but the thought of turning you over to them pleases me. And I certainly won't do that for free."

The ex-intelligence officer's eyes drilled into the weak-looking man aiming the gun at him.

Lammers' stare was equally intense and filled with hatred. "I told you that nothing I had done was personal – just business. And I advised you to not allow it to become personal with you, either."

"And I told you it was too late."

"Yes, Mr. Morgan. Yes, you did. Well now it's personal for me. You've chased me for what? Retribution? Vengeance?"

"Seemed like a good idea. Still does."

"Well, now the tables have turned. I'm not a religious man, by any means. But I must admit to praying to whomever or whatever might be out there, that I would see your end."

"Thought you were giving me to the Saudis."

"Oh, I am, but I will be going along. I wouldn't miss what they are going to do to you."

"So, what now?"

"We wait a while."

"Can I sit down, Lammers?"

"No. Like your friend there, you may stand." The German looked at his watch. "I thought you'd come later. It will be some time before our transportation arrives."

CHAPTER 4

DAY 2 – TUESDAY

Nearly three hours had passed since Tom Lechler and Josh Morgan had stormed through the door into Oskar Lammers' apartment.

Morgan was amazed and even had a grudging respect for the German, especially given his poor health. Lammers had sat, gun at the ready the entire time without speaking a word. Even when he had tried to engage him in conversation or provoke him into a mistake with his usual taunts, Morgan had realized no success.

Another two hours passed with equal silence, when Lammers' phone chimed.

"Yes, we will meet you downstairs now." He disconnected from the call he had received and stood.

Oskar Lammers motioned toward the side of the room with his gun, and Morgan reluctantly obliged and moved away. The captor began to back toward the door to exit first so that his captive wouldn't have any use of the hallway for an advantage.

The former sergeant felt powerless. At first, he was sure that Lammers was going to shoot him, but then he realized the German couldn't because he might fall off the pressure plate and detonate the explosive device. And for the same reason, Lechler had no option to make any sort of move. A wrong move and he would kill not only Lammers and himself, but almost certainly his friend. It was as complex a standoff as it could be.

"So, what about me?"

The German sized up the ex-Green Beret's situation.

"Tell you what. You get out of that, you deserve to live." With that, Oskar Lammers poked his head through the opening where the door had been. He looked both directions and, seeing no one, backed into the hallway, motioning Morgan to follow.

Lechler and Morgan exchanged a frustrated glance.

"See you later, Tom."

"Count on it, Josh."

♦

Eddie Solis began to stir. He had an immobilizing headache, and he realized he had pissed his pants. Furthermore, as his awareness improved, he grasped that his hands were tied and that he had a hood over his entire head. Once he was fully alert – more or less – it occurred to him to cry for help.

It was nearly 9:00 AM, but Eddie Solis had no idea of the time.

"Where am I? Someone… please."

The intensity of his cries became more extreme.

"Where am I? Answer me. PLEASE!!! Somebody… ANSWER ME!"

But no answer came.

"HELP!!!" he cried even louder. "Who are you? Why are you doing this?"

Edmundo Solis had no recollection of falling nearly unconscious at the Genuine Nicaragua Restaurant. Or being helped to his feet and on his way by a cheerful, obliging pair of Nicaraguan brothers. Or completely passing out in the back of an unremarkable Ford van.

He had no idea where he was or why he had been brought there. Edmundo Solis began to weep.

♦

Morgan and Lammers had been gone mere seconds and though Lechler was confident he'd find a way out of his predicament, he had no clue what the solution was going to be. The former Master Sergeant knew his fitness and mental toughness would enable him to stand for a very long time. He'd already stood for nearly five hours, keeping pressure on the plate that had activated the IED and afterward had kept it from exploding. But Lechler also understood that time was of the essence if he was going to be able to help his friend.

The former SpecOps warrior knew that there were various levels of sophistication with such devices as the one that had him stymied. Some exploded as soon as pressure was applied by anyone stepping on it. This one obviously wasn't of that type. Otherwise, he would have already been killed, along with Morgan. The German would've died, too, which made a pretty compelling argument – from his perspective – against the man constructing the device for an instantaneous detonation.

Another type of pressure activated IED would detonate with any change in pressure in the form of weight of the person trapped on it. In other words, if the pressure decreases, as in the case where the target steps off – boom!

Likewise, if weight were added, the IED would also explode. Lechler couldn't help but remember the scene early in Raiders of the Lost Ark where Indiana Jones had to estimate exactly how much sand to put in the bag that he would substitute for the golden idol. Jones failed, of course, mostly because there was no way a few pints of sand would weigh as much as a solid gold idol, Lechler always figured. Still, the former sergeant thought, the *Hovitos* Indians must've been pretty sophisticated at building their traps.

The type of detonating trigger that the ex-sergeant felt was most likely for the one under the welcome mat on which he was standing was very low-tech. Once pressure was applied, it activated the IED. It would only explode when all, or at least a significant amount of weight was removed.

Tom Lechler hoped that that was the type of bomb he was dealing with, because it was the only type he had any chance of defeating – and surviving. Unlike Indiana Jones, he didn't have to substitute an equal amount of weight as his – only enough to keep sufficient pressure applied.

The answer, then, was simple. The execution, however – and the former soldier regretted the choice of word in his mind as soon as he thought it – was problematic. As Lechler surveyed the room, there wasn't a single thing he could reach that weighed enough to keep an adequate amount of pressure on the IED.

♦

Edmundo Solis was groggy enough that sleep seemed to not be that far away, but the panic of being a prisoner more than kept slumber at bay.

Eddie struggled for an answer as to why the Gutierrez brothers had taken him. He had no family and no money of his own for a ransom.

"If only I hadn't passed out," he thought. "They wouldn't have had the chance."

Solis' reasoning was interrupted by the creaking of a door opening. Through the bottom of the bag over his head he could see – sense, more accurately – a trickle of light. It was bouncing around, so he knew it had to be a flashlight. Then the blackness of the cover over his head became a dark gray as a light was apparently turned on in the room where he was.

A hand grabbed the bag, along with a fistful of hair, and ripped it off his head.

Before him stood Santos and Luis Gutierrez. None of the three spoke for several seconds.

"Why have you taken me? I have nobody who will pay a ransom. I have no money," Eddie Solis finally begged.

The brothers shook their heads as tears began to well up in their prisoner's eyes.

"When I began to pass out, at first you tried to help me. Then you took advantage of me!" Eddie continued.

Luis spoke for both of the captors. "You are an idiot, Solis."

The sudden, awful truth that should have been obvious to him when he first began to awake, now struck him like a sledgehammer.

"You drugged me!" His mind raced, but the facts were still the same. He wasn't someone who would yield a great amount for ransom.

♦

Master Sergeant Lechler, U.S. Army, Retired, sized up the objects in the room, estimating in his mind which would be the heaviest. He came to the unfortunate realization that none of the objects weighed enough to be of any use. Never mind that he couldn't reach any of them.

He studied the walls beside the door, as he had several times before. Not only couldn't he make it through the open doorway before the device exploded, but even if he did, the flimsy walls of the old apartment building would offer no protection from the blast.

Lechler looked at the room's furnishings again. About ten feet away was the sofa. Upon a closer inspection, it appeared it might be a sofa bed. That would be heavy. But would it be heavy enough? And how to get it to him?

The ex-soldier took off his tactical belt. Lechler's waist was thirty-five inches, but his belt doubled back considerably after passing through the buckle, so it was about forty-six inches. That was less than half the distance he needed. Still, the D-ring buckle might be of use. There was a gap between the arm of the sofa and the upright back. Lechler thought he might be able to toss the belt edgewise into the gap and then pull back to wedge the buckle securely. It just had to be longer.

Lechler unfastened his pants and let them drop to the rug beneath him that covered the pressure plate of the IED. Physics told him that he weighed the same whether on two legs or one – that his entire weight would transfer to whichever leg was supporting him. Enough pressure would remain on the detonator if he was on one leg or both, but he still felt better when both feet were on the floor, if for no other reason than stability. After several hours of standing, he might be a little wobbly. Gingerly, Lechler slid his feet out of his shoes. Then he raised his right heel, lowered his pants carefully, and slid the waist underneath his foot. Then he raised his toes to free the right leg of the garment. He duplicated the process with his left foot.

With his pants free, the trapped man unclipped his knife from the edge of his pants pocket. Lammers had felt no need to have him empty his pockets. The German had the gun.

Lechler began to cut the pants legs into strips. He wished he was wearing his tactical pants. The ripstop fabric would be much stronger than the cotton slacks he had on. But he had what he had.

He quickly braided strips each into several lengths of cotton rope, enough that the combined length would reach the sofa. He tied the braids together with an Alpine Butterfly Bend. Then Lechler cut a hole in the tongue of his belt large enough to pass one end of the improvised cotton rope through it. He secured it with a Bowline knot.

Finally, the former Green Beret tossed the buckle toward the rear of the arm of the couch. A miss.

After seven more misses, the belt's edge slid down in the gap between the sofa's arm and its back. He tested its strength and security with a few tugs and, satisfied, began to pull. The couch was as heavy as he had hoped and reluctantly began to slide across the wooden floor.

Suddenly, the belt came free. The sudden lack of tension caused the buckle to fly past Lechler's face. Worse, the resulting slack caused him to begin to fall backward. Like a kid trying to keep his balance on a log across a creek, the man's arms were flailing like a windmill. Then he thrust both arms forward as counterweights to his backward momentum. His motion stalled and he collected himself.

"Better not shit my underwear. That's all I've got on," he muttered.

Once he regained his composure – or at least as much composure as you can have when standing on a bomb – Lechler tried again to snag the piece of furniture. It took him several more tries than it had at first, but the buckle finally caught in the slot. He lowered his end of the makeshift rope to a shallower angle for better purchase on the couch and began to pull.

The sofa began to creep toward him. Lechler could hear the cotton material stretching and he was sure he could hear tearing, but after what seemed an eternity, the end of the sofa rested next to the mat beneath him.

The former Special Operator squatted and felt through the rug to determine the edges of the pressure plate.

Lechler wanted to move as slowly as possible. He had also decided a little-bit-at-a-time strategy was better than an all-at-once effort.

He leaned over to grab the arm of the sofa. It wasn't as heavy as he'd first thought. Holding his breath, he lifted one end and cautiously set it on the mat. Then he looked at the other end of the couch. Then Tom Lechler realized there was a flaw – possibly a fatal one – in his plan. The couch sat on four legs, onto which the weight was distributed. And due to the length of the sofa, he couldn't get all four legs onto the pressure plate at the same time. Resting only on the two legs of the closest end probably wasn't going to be heavy enough to maintain adequate pressure on the IED.

"Stupid!" he labeled himself aloud. "Only one solution," he continued.

Lechler lifted the end of the couch closest to him and slid the far end closer. Finally lifting the entire piece of furniture end up off the floor, he set it on one end on the pressure plate. But in doing so, he lost his balance and stepped off the plate.

Lechler braced himself for an explosion, though realistically, by the time he'd had the awareness to do so, it would've been too late.

He sighed heavily. The ex-operator had successfully replaced his weight with that of the furniture. And no explosion!

However, as he began to release the sofa, he realized that it was terribly unstable. He dared not wiggle it around to find a good position, but it sure as hell wasn't going to stay put as it was.

Lechler took the remaining pieces of cloth that were once part of his pants and kneeled to stuff them under the end of the couch that was now resting on the pressure IED.

He eased one hand away from supporting the couch. It teetered. He adjusted a piece or two of the cloth he was using for shims. It seemed steady – well, steadier.

Lechler remained by the upright piece of furniture for a moment and decided he could let go. He would like to have looked around in Lammers' apartment for some pants, but decided it was more prudent to get the hell out of Dodge. Besides, he had more clothes in his vehicle.

He reached down with his right hand to pull his right shoe back on, keeping his eye on the unsteady sofa. Then he pulled his left shoe on.

As Lechler took his first step away from the sofa, the unsteadiness of the old wooden floor caused the couch to shift slightly. The ex-MSG grabbed his phone from where Lammers had left it on the table. The floor creaked again. He paused briefly and then sprinted into the hallway and to the stairs. He flew down the steps, taking two and three at a time, expecting the explosion at any moment. He burst through the exit to the sidewalk and ran several yards before he finally paused.

"Well, how about that!" he thought, as he looked toward the building he had fled.

Simultaneously with that thought and his relief, a tremendous boom erupted, accompanied by a shower of bricks and sheetrock from the second-floor apartment into the street around him.

Lechler pulled his arms over his face and fell away from the blast. Flames and smoke poured from the gaping opening in the wall. With the sound of debris landing not far from him, the man looked back at the building and the extent of the damage.

"Wow! He wasn't kidding!" he exclaimed out loud.

CHAPTER 5

The zip ties on his wrists behind his back were terribly uncomfortable, but Josh Morgan had much more serious concerns. His position between the two Saudi operatives in the back seat of the sedan was cramped and left little opportunity for any direct action.

Oskar Lammers sat in the passenger seat in front. He never spoke to his fellow passengers, nor to Morgan. In fact, Morgan believed the German had dozed off a couple of times.

"The cancer must be taking its toll," the captive thought.

Morgan wondered about his partner. Did he find a way off the IED? Or…? The former intelligence officer didn't want to think about the alternative.

"Hell, he could still just be standing there," he thought.

Morgan could tell by the road signs that the vehicle was headed to the airport. They had left Venezuela and were in Colombia in the town of Cúcuta. While there was an airport in San Cristobal, it was small and unlighted. This airport, *Aeropuerto Internacional Camilo Daza,* was a larger, grander facility. Morgan was confident that the aircraft that his abductors would whisk him away in was larger than the small San Cristobal airport could support. The ex-CIA Officer knew that if his captors succeeded in getting him on a plane, he was toast.

♦

She didn't remember exactly when she had moved from the couch to her bed. She discovered that she hadn't taken time to remove her makeup or put on the t-shirt she usually slept in. Maggie awoke with only her panties on. Her clothing and her bra were on the floor beside her bed. She looked at the clock on the nightstand.

5:55.

The alarm on her phone would sound its regular wakeup call in five minutes, so there was no use trying to recover any time for additional sleep. She rose without energy and moved to the bathroom. The woman reached into the shower and turned the faucets' handles. She waited for the water to warm, removed her panties, and stepped in and turned her back to the spray of water. The hot water cascaded over her head and shoulders, pouring over her breasts with a mild splash as it dropped to the tile flooring.

Maggie resolved, as she had on many other days, that this was the day that she put Josh Morgan behind her. But just as they had on all those other days, her eyes misted with the tears that betrayed her intentions as lies.

Maggie showered longer than usual – certainly longer than she should've given that she generally tried to be at work by 7:30. The blessed comfort of the warm water flowing over her body evaporated with the barely audible sound of the doorbell.

Abandoning her shower, Maggie grabbed her robe and headed for the door. Still wet, through the peephole, she saw her guardian and ride to work. Even through the contorted, wide-angle view of Mac Marchman, she could see that he was ever alert. His back was to the door and his head was on a swivel, surveying both directions of the hall.

As she dried her hair with a towel in one hand, without so much as a second thought, Maggie opened the door. Agent Marchman turned around. His shock at seeing his charge in only a robe was heightened when he looked to see her cover gaping enough to show one of her breasts. Maggie was embarrassed, but as was her practice, chose to dismiss it with some humor.

"Come on, Mac. Don't you have sisters?"

Secret Service Marchman took a bit longer to look away than he should have. When he did, his face reddened and he answered, "Yes, ma'am, I do. But you're not one of 'em."

Maggie returned to her bathroom to finish getting ready for work, she was – despite her embarrassment – a little excited. It had been a while since a man had looked at her like that – that she knew of anyhow.

On the way to the White House, Agent Marchman never spoke to her, nor even turned to look at her. Maggie, for her part, never spoke either, but she did frequently look in the rearview mirror to see if Mac occasionally looked back.

He never did.

♦

The sun was just peeking over the horizon.

Morgan was pleasantly surprised at the lack of cruelty in the treatment he had received from Lammers and the Saudis up to this point. Of course, he knew that the absence of brutality was temporary. How temporary, he didn't know, but he was certain that his future held extreme violence.

The former CIA Officer speculated that the men escorting him were merely delivery boys. He was also reasonably certain that, unless things changed dramatically, he was destined for Saudi Arabia. With that thought, his memories turned to his late friend, Trent Weston. The former President and he had developed an unshakable bond born during the time when Weston, as Morgan currently was, had been kidnapped to be delivered to the leaders of the Holy Islamic Kingdom of Saudi Arabia. Where the despots had intended to put the once leader of the free world on trial in front of the entire planet for war crimes and other alleged atrocities against Islamic nations, Morgan knew he warranted no such public drama. They would torture him, simply for the pleasure of it, and then kill him.

The ex-spy likewise knew that he was a target of the terrorist regime precisely because he had intervened in their plot against Weston and had rescued him. Then sometime after that he had also disrupted a Saudi plot to put the United States and the Russian Federation at war with each other. Simply put, Morgan was a thorn in the side of the Saudis. And while the subsequent assassination of the Saudi president at the hands of U.S. Army Green Berets had left the nation's leadership in turmoil, the hatred Morgan knew they held for him would transcend any change in power in the Saudi government.

Morgan wondered again about the fate of Tom Lechler, whom he had met during the U.S.-Russia crisis. He was worried, but not as much as he felt he should be. He knew if anyone could get out of the mess that the ex-Green Beret was in, it was Lechler. That confidence of the operator's skill eased his concern. And that was good, he knew. He had his own dilemma to deal with; one that was escalating rapidly as the vehicle which transported him pulled into the airport. The car stopped for a few minutes and the driver chatted with airport security. That no paperwork was completed and the car wasn't searched seemed to confirm his suspicion that the goons transporting him had diplomatic immunity; that or deep pockets.

♦

The White House Press Secretary sat at her desk poring over the emails that had come in overnight, and which continued to accumulate at a frenetic pace even as she read. Maggie entertained a fleeting doubt as to why she had taken this job before she smiled, shook her head, and leaned back in her chair. She looked at her phone for the time and said aloud,

"That's odd."

She leaned in toward the computer display and looked at her inbox. Maggie filtered the increasing list to show only unread emails and scrolled through them.

"Nothing there," she confirmed. But to make sure she hadn't missed it, the auburn-haired Wyoming native typed five letters into the search window of her email program. Then she clicked on the small magnifying glass icon to start the search through the correspondence.

"Wow… that's *really* odd," Maggie said softly. She thought back and couldn't remember how long it had been since she had failed to receive a note from this person.

"Maybe you've finally got yourself a life, Eddie." She smiled and returned to her work.

♦

Edmundo Solis slumped in his chair, his pain from the beating compounded by the cutting pressure of the restraints on his wrists as they pulled against the arms of the chair. Above him, the single bulb in the abandoned warehouse illuminated him somewhat. That was why his abductors had placed him there. The rest of the building remained dramatically dark.

"I don't know why you are doing this," he whispered through swollen lips. "I don't know what you are trying to get me to say."

The remark brought a blow from Luis' fist as he swung it into Eddie's left cheek.

"Who have you been getting information from, you sorry bastard?" His partner swung his left fist into the man's right jaw with a hammer blow.

"Somebody in our government has been feeding you information. If you don't tell us who it is, you're of no use to us," Santos warned. He took a semi-automatic pistol from his waistband, pulled the slide back to rack a bullet into the barrel. The Nicaraguan lifted Eddie's chin.

"Dammit, Solis, we want a name now!" screamed Luis.

Santos pressed the barrel of his handgun into the sweaty, dirty, bleeding forehead.

Edmundo Solis began to weep again as he had off and on through the ordeal.

"I don't know who it is," he cried. "I get anonymous texts with this information. I really don't…," he started, and then he passed out.

Luis and Santos Gutierrez looked at each other. Luis' rage manifested in a scream while Santos threw up his hands and spun away from their prisoner.

"*Carajo*!" Santos shouted. "Fuck! Fuck! Fuck!" He turned to face the unconscious man and pointed the gun to his head. As he began to squeeze the trigger, his cohort pushed the gun down and away from the intended target.

"Not yet, Santos. Not yet."

♦

Former Army Special Forces Sergeant First Class Tom Lechler watched the flashing blip on his monitor and was closing ground quickly. His target had paused for a short time at what appeared on the electronic map to be the entry to Camilo Daza International Airport before moving to the hangar area of the airport. He didn't know why they had stopped. Perhaps a security checkpoint or something, he figured. Lechler really didn't care. Any delay – no matter how brief – gave him additional precious time to catch up. He had come to suspect that the airport was his associate's destination and now that it was confirmed, he drove frantically to get there to be of some help.

He realized the good fortune for him and Morgan was that Oskar Lammers, for whatever reason had put Morgan's phone in his own pocket rather than discard it. That allowed him to track the hostage and his captors with what he thought of as a sophisticated version of "find my phone." However, had Lammers tossed Morgan's phone, the ex-Case Officer had another device in the sole of his shoe that would be locatable on the application. The problem was that it was more susceptible to interference and loss of signal. So, tracing Morgan's route by his phone's signal was preferable. Lechler had his own phone, but instead of following Morgan on his own device, Lechler was using a very precise tracking monitor acquired courtesy of Director Elizabeth Parnell at the Central Intelligence Agency.

♦

The Saudi Arabian operators that Oskar Lammers had handed Josh Morgan over to dragged him roughly out of the sedan.

"I need to take a leak," Morgan insisted.

"You'll be on the plane soon. If you can't wait until then, piss your pants," countered one of his escorts.

Morgan smiled slightly. He knew the ruse wouldn't work but he was in "anything's worth a try" mode. Ahead of him was a smallish private jet with markings in both Arabic and English. An Arab pushed him toward it.

As he approached the airstair descending from the jet, Morgan looked for a place to escape to, or some means of overpowering his captors. No luck.

The five men reached the aircraft. The pilot waited beside the plane for his passengers to board. He would enter last and close the hatch.

One of the Saudi operatives ascended the small stairway built onto the plane. Then Lammers followed and finally the two remaining Saudis nudged Morgan toward the steps. Upon reaching the top step Morgan delivered a back kick to the man most closely following him. He knew it wouldn't change the outcome, but he wasn't going quietly. The blow to that man's chest knocked him forcefully into the one behind him, who twisted awkwardly, his head crashing onto the lowest step and knocking the pilot to the ground as well.

The man already onboard yanked Morgan onto the plane and pistol-whipped him repeatedly until he dropped to the floor of the cabin. The Arab Morgan had kicked rose and rushed up the airstair in two bounds. He was about to deliver a few blows of his own when he realized the man he had crashed into wasn't following. The Saudi turned and found his associate still lying on the tarmac, head turned at an awkward angle. Spreading from the back of the man's head was a pool of blood. He was gasping for air desperately, agonizing with what was an obviously broken neck, one which momentarily proved fatal.

The pilot was slowly getting to his feet and moved some distance away, determined to stay out of the fray.

From his place on the floor, his hands still bound behind his back, and face mashed against the plane's floor by the first Arab's foot, Josh Morgan managed to observe the lucky result of his desperate kick.

"Wow… that was unexpected," he said dryly. As he watched the man he had kicked consider futilely how to assist the dying man, the Saudi's head suddenly came apart in a spray of red mist and white chips of his skull.

"Lechler," Morgan realized.

Seeing the passageway to the plane blocked, the fear-stricken pilot bolted away from the jet toward a nearby pushback tractor and knelt behind it for cover.

Without regard for the fate of the two men lying limply on the black surface of the tarmac and not realizing the pilot had deserted them, the remaining Saudi Arabian thug on the plane began to frantically pull at the stairway to close it for takeoff. His head swiveled as he looked around for the sniper.

Morgan thought, "Paid off once," and kicked the man, who collapsed clumsily as the gangway fell back open. He tumbled to the floor of the jet's cabin and began to rise to a sitting position as his head, too, exploded from the impact of a .308 caliber round from Tom Lechler's rifle.

Inside the jet, Oskar Lammers slammed his handgun into Josh Morgan's head, dazing him and fled to the flight deck. Outside the plane former MSG Lechler was making a wild dash toward the aircraft, which had begun to taxi away with the airstairs still dangling from the fuselage. The aircraft pulled about a hundred yards away from the ex-Green Beret, where it spun around to put the open doorway on the opposite side from the gunman who had taken out two of the Saudis.

Oskar Lammers rushed from the cockpit to the opening in the fuselage and with all the effort a dying, cancer-stricken man could muster, lifted the stairway to a closed position and secured it. The German returned to the pilot's seat and resumed taxiing toward the runway. Without clearance from the tower or any other communication, Lammers began to accelerate the craft. The jet lifted from the runway. The German henchman was an accomplished pilot in all manner of aircraft, but he hadn't remotely anticipated that he would be flying now. He figured he would just get airborne and then figure out a plan.

Suddenly the German remembered that he had left Morgan unattended. He flipped the switch that put the plane on autopilot to return to his adversary.

As he rose from the seat, he turned to receive a kick to the groin from the man he had left semiconscious in the rear of the plane. He stumbled backward in agony against the copilot seat and into the instrument panel. The jet lurched to starboard from the impact to the wheel before the autopilot corrected and resumed lifting the craft from the airport runway. Lammers reached into his jacket pocket for his gun. He would just take care of Morgan right now once and for all. He would deliver the body to the Saudi Arabian government in the hopes they would still make good on the bounty they had promised for the American's delivery. He wanted to send the money to his sister. But if the Arabs refused, what the hell? He was dying anyhow.

♦

Far below and receding into the distance, Tom Lechler fired multiple rounds toward the small jet's engines, but to no effect. He could only hope he had evened the odds a bit for Morgan. As it was, his only reasonable course of action was to try to get out of the area and save his own neck after killing two men in broad daylight at a federal airport.

He retreated to his vehicle and sped for the exit.

"I'll see you when I see you, Josh. Give 'em hell!"

♦

While the German had been distracted getting the plane off the ground, Morgan had come to and fumbled around in the pocket of the dead Arab lying beside him and found a knife. Before Lammers could retrieve his pistol, the ex-spy, hands free now, hammered the side of the German's face with his fist. Lammers fell backward again and dropped the gun.

Morgan reached for it, only to get Lammers' left foot to his jaw. As Lammers lunged again for the gun, Morgan grabbed him by his shirt and pulled him forward. Morgan fell onto his back with the German atop him.

Morgan was astonished at Lammers' strength and resolve. After all, he was near death, but still fought like a healthy man half his age.

The pair grappled on the floor for a few moments before the American gained a superior position on the German. With one crushing smash to the face, the fight ended.

Josh Morgan gathered in the handgun from the floor beside the pilot's seat. He walked calmly to where Lammers lay and was stirring. Now that the fight was over, Morgan thought, it seemed that any adrenaline-fueled strength and will that Lammers had summoned had evaporated in defeat. He pointed the barrel at the man on the floor of the aircraft.

The American former CIA Officer began to squeeze the trigger. But despite that he had killed three men in cold blood over the last couple of years, he couldn't bring himself to finish the act. It wasn't because he had a sudden attack of conscience. It was that Morgan felt he was letting Lammers off the hook too easily. The man was, after all, dying. Morgan felt that simply shooting him was the compassionate equivalent of putting a beloved pet down when it had a terminal illness.

And there was also the matter of flying the plane. Morgan's only experience in piloting something of the sophistication of this aircraft was "flying" Microsoft Flight Simulator on his computer back in Jackson Hole.

"Why don't you finish me?"

Morgan watched as Oskar Lammers rose and took one of the passenger seats on the private jet. Ever aspiring to be a gentleman, despite his professional ruthlessness, Lammers straightened his collar and jacket. He took a handkerchief from his pocket and dabbed the blood from his face.

"Shut the fuck up," came the American's reply. Morgan turned to go to the cockpit but pivoted to face Lammers again.

"And, go to hell, you son of a bitch."

♦

White House Press Secretary Margaret Loughlin stepped from the dais after the morning briefing and began the walk to her office. Mac Marchman fell in behind her.

"You know, I think I'm pretty safe in the West Wing, Agent."

"Yes, ma'am," replied her Secret Service escort, "I'm sure you are. But you can't be too careful."

Maggie never turned as her protector trailed behind her, but she could feel his smile. And she was sure he could feel hers, too.

♦

In his time at CIA, Morgan had acquired quite a gift for reading people. It was certainly a requirement of field personnel to size up what individuals were thinking, feeling, and planning, but he was especially adept at it. And everything in him told him that Oskar Lammers was done. Still, he kept looking over his shoulder from his place in the pilot's chair.

He had received several transmissions from the control tower of the Camilo Raza airport. And while the easiest thing would've been to respond and ask for assistance, the jet was flying northeast. He knew he was over Venezuelan airspace and Venezuela was after all, a less than friendly country to his own. So, he had decided to continue with the jet on autopilot and give some thought to exactly where he should fly. He knew he was going to turn the plane around to head back to Colombia, but that was the extent of his strategy. He wasn't even sure how far into Venezuela he was.

Surprisingly, the controls were very similar to those on his computer simulator app at home. He studied the instrument console at some length, knowing that in short order, military fighters would most likely arrive to "assist" him to a safe landing under their direction to a location of their choosing.

♦

Maggie Loughlin thought again about the lack of an email from Eddie Solis. She didn't know why it bothered her, but it did. Arriving at her desk from the press briefing, she looked again at her Inbox. Still nothing. As much as she tried to laugh it off as his finally getting a clue that they weren't pen pals and that he had hopefully moved on, there was this inner tugging. She recognized it as the same sixth sense that Josh had always seemed to have when something was wrong. She thought about calling him but realized two things. First, she was just being silly. Secondly, it was really just going to be an excuse she had manufactured to justify talking to her ex-fiancé.

For the first time since she and Josh had broken up – or more accurately, he had broken up with her – Maggie Laughlin felt a real commitment to moving on.

♦

Josh Morgan received the message from the control tower that "safety escorts" would arrive soon to accompany him while the air traffic controllers gave him instructions where to land. And he was damned sure the jets would be from the Venezuelan Air Force and would direct him to an airport in that country.

Morgan wanted to call Betsy Parnell, but not only did he suspect that the call would be intercepted, he knew there was little she could accomplish from her office at CIA when he was over an unfriendly country. So, he turned the wheel to port to complete a one-eighty. That would at least get him headed back to Colombian airspace.

He had flown – rather the plane had flown itself – over Venezuelan space for only a short time, so Morgan felt sure he was within a couple of hundred miles of the border. No escorts had shown up yet, and he had no idea where they would be coming from. But at the instant that he had the thought, two Russian-made Sukhoi Su-30s of the *Aviación Militar Nacional Bolivariana* arrived, one on each side of his plane.

While he was occupied and his attention diverted from his adversary, he sensed a presence approaching from behind. Oskar Lammers had apparently gotten his second wind and nearly knocked Morgan out with a blow to the head with a pitcher he had found in the galley of the jet. Morgan fell forward into the wheel that thrust forward and pitched the plane into a mild descent. He turned and put a knee into the German's privates. Lammers dropped to a kneeling position in the aisle behind the flight deck. His strength was waning, but he was determined to fight on.

The former U.S. Agency spook lowered a shoulder and dove into his opponent. Lammers fell backward with Morgan atop him.

Morgan pummeled the German repeatedly on the head and in the chest until the man succumbed to the brutality.

Morgan bolted for the cockpit. The jet had fallen into a steeper descent. He pulled back at the wheel with negligible effect. He looked out the cockpit windows to see the jet fighters still escorting him as his aircraft fell toward the earth. He stole a glance toward Lammers who lay motionless in the aisle. He would've preferred to somehow coerce the man into flying the plane. But Lammers seemed to be out, and the American didn't have time to waste trying to revive him. He was certain Lammers wouldn't cooperate anyhow.

There was no way that Morgan was going to avoid going down. The best he could hope for would be to have some semblance of control when the plane reached the ground. He continued to pull back on the wheel and, despite there being some leveling of the craft, he *was* going down.

Morgan thought back to his time on Microsoft Simulator. He looked and found the throttle. He eased it back and the aircraft slowed noticeably. Suddenly, the jet began to stall, so Morgan pushed the throttle forward. He regained some control.

There was no time to refer to maps, so he looked at the terrain below. The plane leveled and slowed. He watched the airspeed and the horizon on the gauge. As the plane began to respond favorably to Morgan's efforts, he considered regaining altitude and waiting for help. But he decided he had to land at some point.

Josh Morgan looked ahead toward the horizon. Villages and towns of varying sizes dotted the landscape. More importantly, he saw a decent-sized highway before him. He didn't know what country it was in but all he could think of at the moment was getting down safely.

Looking ahead for the straightest stretch of the highway, he banked hard to his left and felt the plane slip in that direction and lose altitude. He pulled the wheel to level his flight. He fine-tuned his glide path to line up – he hoped – with the road. He eased the throttle and pushed the wheel forward. His approach looked good, at least in comparison with the Microsoft equivalent of things. His altimeter read 200 feet, but that really wasn't news to him. The ground was coming up to him frighteningly fast.

Then suddenly, an alarm sounded.

"Shit! Shit! Shit!"

Morgan looked desperately for the lever to lower the landing gears. He felt he was already committed to landing, but he would prefer to do it with wheels down. To his right, he found the control and pushed it forward.

He was a scant sixty feet above the ground when the gears began to lower. They weren't fully engaged when the plane made contact with the highway.

Morgan pulled at the wheel and worked the aircraft's pedals, trying to aim it for the center of the highway. However, the impact, since he wasn't belted into his seat, threw him off the pilot's chair into the instrument panel and onto the floor. He felt the plane collide with the pavement and veer to the left.

Morgan fell back to a seated position. When the private jet bounced again, he lurched forward. Engines shut off, the plane assumed a position where it faced to the left, although it was still sliding sideways down the highway. It began to rotate clockwise until it was facing the center of the highway again. Morgan managed to get into the pilot's seat, but it was of no real advantage in that he had no control over the direction of the aircraft. In desperation, he finally abandoned any attempt at controlling the plane and directed his attention to securing the safety belt.

As the plane slid down the highway, it veered slightly to starboard and then a little to port. It slid into a car, causing it to roll off the highway.

The grinding of the metal against the asphalt was overwhelming and distressing. The noise overpowered Morgan's senses. The jet plowed into another car.

The craft slid sideways, sparks flying up past the copilot's window. Morgan felt the left wing break away as it clipped a tree on the side of the road that was much narrower than it had looked from the air. The sudden loss of balance caused the plane to roll in that direction, almost flipping over. Finally, the momentum of the aircraft ended, and it came to rest in the middle of the highway. Cars and trucks had slammed on their brakes at the sight of the oncoming tons of metal.

Morgan took a deep breath. His sigh was loud and powerful. He unbuckled the harness from the pilot's seat and stood. But as he rose, Oskar Lammers stood facing him in the aisle with the gun he had somehow retrieved pointed toward him.

"I guess this is where things end."

"Go to hell, you German son of a bitch!"

But without so much as the slightest expression, Oskar Lammers turned the gun to his own temple.

"Goodbye, Mr. Morgan. You'll always know that you didn't beat me."

"NOOOOOO!" Morgan screamed as he ran forward toward Lammers. As he reached the man, the gun went off. But the impact of Morgan's charge had redirected the barrel so that the bullet only grazed the man's scalp.

Morgan grabbed the semiautomatic and pointed it at the prone Lammers.

The German smiled and said, "You know, you're really just doing me a fav…"

Oskar Lammers' final taunt was interrupted by the report of the handgun in Morgan's hand. The bullet lodged deep in the man's chest. He looked at the American with significant disbelief.

"Decided I don't care," Morgan concluded. He stepped forward and put a final round in the forehead of Oskar Lammers.

CHAPTER 6

"Geez! You've got to be kidding me!" an exasperated CIA Director practically shouted. Betsy Parnell pushed her hands through her hair, turned off the speaker of her phone and lifted it to her ear. "Any idea where they've taken him?"

"No, ma'am," admitted Tom, who had driven away from the airport following his shootout. He was parked on a small road about thirty miles southwest of Cúcuta.

"Damnation," Parnell muttered.

The CIA Director's attention turned to one of the four TVs she kept in her office, always on and tuned to major cable news networks. One's display showed a private jet sitting in the middle of a highway, one wing missing and emergency personnel scrambling on top of and around the crashed craft.

"I'll get back with you, Lechler." Parnell raised the remote and increased the volume as two of the three remaining displays switched to the same feed as the first.

The voice over the images admitted that details were sketchy but proceeded to babble on anyhow. The male voice stated the location as being about twelve miles north of Cúcuta, Colombia, on Cúcuta-Puerto Santander Road. The nation's top spy turned to her desktop computer and launched the Company's maps application. It wasn't real-time, so in that regard it wasn't much better than Google Earth. However, the resolution was orders of magnitude better than the tech giant's since it was captured by NSA satellites.

As Parnell typed into the search field, she was sure that this was the plane Morgan had been taken away in, given the crash site's location in the general vicinity of where Tom Lechler said it had taken off.

"At least you're in friendly territory, Josh." Then she added, "Sort of."

The Director typed in the first few letters of Cúcuta, and a dropdown filled with various matches materialized. She selected her desired location from the list with her pointer. Instantly overhead imagery appeared, centered on Cúcuta, Colombia.

With a left click, her pointer grabbed the image, which she dragged so that a point she estimated to be twelve miles from the city took center position on the map. Then she zoomed in on the image to a more appropriate view. Lining the road were alternating stretches where it was open land on one side or dense forest on both sides, and various combinations of open land opposite treed areas.

"Well, no doubt you'd head for the trees… if you're alive."

Parnell turned her attention back to the televised news report as she heard the reporter's account.

"At least one person survived the crash and has apparently fled the site," the disembodied voice of the journalist relayed. In the background of the live feed, in the midst of vehicles scattered about the road, some people who were probably their owners conversed with uniformed law enforcement officers. All were pointing animatedly to the more densely forested side of the road between Cúcuta and Puerto Santander.

"I hope that's you, Morgan," Director Parnell said, though in her heart, she knew it was. She shook her head, smiled, and pressed the number in her "Recent Calls" list that would reconnect her with her contractor.

"Lechler, I know where Morgan is."

♦

The Gutierrez brothers sat in chairs a few feet from where Eddie Solis slumped in his, muttering and groaning in pain.

The pair had used every tool they could think of, and they were masters at extracting information from even the best trained, intelligent operatives. Solis was neither. The brothers were at a loss. The only decision that remained was whether to kill their captive now or later.

The only bit of information that might prove useful was the blogger's disclosure at the café that the current White House Press Secretary was his "contact" in Washington. And even that claim, as Santos had elicited from Eddie during the torture, was exaggerated. Still, the Nicaraguan brothers couldn't chance a loose end who worked for U.S President Hendrickson.

"So, what do you think?" Santos asked.

Luis stroked his chin and raised his gun toward Solis. Santos believed Luis was going to end the man's life then and there. Instead, his brother simply said "bang" rather softly, feigning recoil as he did. He stood and placed the gun in his waistband.

"I think, Santos, that we let him live a while longer while we get some rest."

Because Santos had lost the note with its address, it had taken the pair longer than expected to find the vacant warehouse where they had deposited their prisoner. Immediately afterward, they had searched his apartment, but they found nothing of use. And even though neither was a topnotch hacker, both were fairly adept at getting past unsophisticated software security. They had been surprised at the complexity of Solis' cybersecurity. So, they had taken his laptop when they tossed his apartment and his mobile phone when they had abducted him.

"We can turn his computers over to experts in our embassy. Looks like we're going to Washington anyhow," Luis offered. "In the meantime, we leave Solis here and, if he dies…"

"Or *ratas* get him," Santos interjected.

"*Si*, or rats get him," Luis repeated, "then it is no huge loss. But if the need arises to question him again, hopefully he has survived."

"*De acuerdo*," Santos agreed.

♦

After finishing her call with Tom Lechler, the CIA Director returned to the satellite images on her computer. She zoomed out for a broader view. About forty miles to the north of the crash site and Morgan's apparent location was the city of Tibú.

"That'll do," she said aloud.

Parnell looked up a number in her online directory and called the U.S. Embassy in Bogotá.

"Ramirez… Director Parnell. I need you to send some people to run an errand for me."

After a short conversation in which Parnell gave her instructions with very little helpful information, Colombian CIA Station Chief Felipe Ramirez called his personnel embedded with a small contingent of the U.S. Army's 82nd Airborne and passed along their assignment.

♦

Josh Morgan had fled the crash site into a thickly wooded area on the left side of the road. At least it was on the left when he started his desperate attempt to land the jet. He had remembered to retrieve his phone from the late Oskar Lammers' pocket before he did. He had also gotten a look at a highway sign as he ran from the ripped fuselage. It had said, *Puerto Santander*. Unfortunately, he had no way of knowing any further where that meant he was. Morgan wasn't even sure what country he was in. Had the jet managed to cross the border back into Colombia? He didn't know.

What the former CIA Officer knew was that if he was still in Venezuela, it would be only minutes before investigators arrived on the scene. It was a foregone conclusion that the pilots of the fighter jets escorting him would've relayed word that the civilian craft had gone down – and where.

If he had crossed into Colombian airspace before going down, Morgan felt the arrival of officials would be delayed, but only by minutes. He looked at his phone. No service. However, there was still one benefit to having the device with him. The same app that had led Lechler to him at the airport worked by GPS, not cellular service, so maybe someone would have looked for him electronically through that technology.

But another glance at his phone's display alerted Morgan to a problem worse than the lack of cell service. Its battery was almost dead. That presented a choice. He could leave his phone on until the last bit of life faded away and hope someone would lock in on it before it did. Or he could hope that someone who was already tracking him, specifically Tom Lechler himself, would follow the protocol the pair had previously worked out together.

Reluctantly, the former CIA Officer turned contractor turned his phone off. He would power it up again at twenty-minute intervals, beginning with seven minutes past the hour. Lechler and Morgan, based on the very unlikely possibility that someone else was able to track him via his phone, had agreed to stay away from logical times to go online – on the hour, ten-minute or fifteen-minute increments, or the bottom of the hour. They had arbitrarily chosen seven because it was supposed to be a lucky number. And they had selected twenty-minute intervals to be "live" for as little time as possible. Morgan looked at his watch. It was six minutes past 9:00.

"So, I'm supposed to turn it on in one minute? Hell, I just turned it off."

Morgan decided he would forego the first designated mark and activate his phone twenty-one minutes later at 9:27, then again at 9:47, and again at 10:07.

"If I live that long," he thought.

Morgan didn't like his odds trying to evade officials in the forest. On the other hand, he believed he had gotten away from the scene of the crash without anyone getting a good look at him. And he wore fairly nondescript clothing, so perhaps he could simply try to make his way back to the highway and blend in with onlookers to the sight of a jet in the highway.

No, he decided, he would try to escape detection among the trees. Yet, that posed another problem. When he turned his phone on at the prescribed times, *if* someone picked up his location, by the time they got there, Morgan wouldn't be there anymore. He would've had to keep moving. And *if* someone managed to locate him, who would it be? How would he know who it was safe to disclose himself to?

The former Case Officer finally decided he was trying to figure out the answer to problem number ten when he was only at problem number one. And that was evasion. He decided his best alternative was to get three or four hundred yards distance from the highway and move, as best he could figure, parallel to it. He tried to remember which direction the closest town had been. He hadn't exactly been in a position to spend a lot of time surveying his surroundings beyond the immediate area where he was going down.

So, the American moved diagonally away from the road – due south – and then headed more to the southwest. He was sure that was the direction of Cúcuta, and he might come to a smaller village sooner than that.

♦

Former Green Beret Tom Lechler ended his call with CIA Director Parnell.

"Cúcuta, huh? So, Josh, you made it back across the border and survived a crash? I'm on my way, buddy."

Lechler needed to feel like he was doing something to help his friend, despite the realization that he probably wouldn't get there in time to do Morgan any good. Besides, the personnel that Parnell had dispatched from Tibú would certainly get to Morgan before him. Still, the ex-soldier couldn't just wait around twiddling his thumbs. He put the stick in "drive" and headed toward Cúcuta, where he and Morgan had entered Colombia only a couple of days earlier and where he had just seen the jet depart with his friend.

♦

Less than ten minutes after receiving instructions from the head of CIA, Station Chief Ramirez had Case Officers Valentina Herrera and Jeronimo Mosquera driving south from Tibú to look for a needle in a haystack named Josh Morgan.

The United States had deployed members of the 82nd Airborne Division of the U.S. Army to Colombia years earlier and had maintained a presence of varying sizes and for various reasons ever since. At the time of the initial arrival Colombia's top government officials had stated that the purpose of their presence was to assist in anti-drugs trafficking operations, since the flow of drugs from Colombia into the U.S. was a critical issue.

Of course, opponents of *el Presidente* Ivan Duque at that time and continuing since, particularly the *Polo Democrático Alternativo*, or Democratic Pole party, believed that the real purpose of the Americans' presence was to apply pressure to Venezuela, which had been a thorn in the side of the U.S. for years. The opposition leaders objected to what they believed to be an illegal deployment of foreign military on the basis that the Colombian Congress hadn't approved the agreement.

The American soldiers were based in the most prolific drugs-producing regions around the nation. They were primarily stationed in Nariño in southwest Colombia, in the south in Meta, and in Norte de Santander on the northeast border of the nation with Venezuela.

Of course, wherever U.S. military personnel were present, so were CIA operators. Their job was not only to gather intelligence to assist the anti-drug trafficking missions, but also to develop assets and run those agents in collecting intelligence in the northern countries of South America, most notably Venezuela.

Herrera's and Mosquera's duty stations were with the U.S. Army near Tibú, a municipality in the department of *Norte de Santander*. They had a photo of Morgan. Period. Their Station Chief, Emmanuel Ramirez, had told them that they didn't need to know anything else. Their only job was to make contact and bring him to the Embassy. Herrera and Mosquera were relatively new to CIA but incumbent with their jobs was the understanding that they had to operate under the "need to know" guideline and not worry about *want* to know. So, they didn't.

Their primary order was that under no circumstances were they to engage military or civilian authorities, even if it meant losing Morgan.

"ETA thirty-five minutes," Herrera figured.

"Sounds about right," Mosquera agreed.

♦

Edmundo Solis lay sleeping in the abandoned warehouse. The Gutierrez brothers had locked him in a side room that had apparently been a storage area of some sort. It was in one corner of the main area of the warehouse, so it shared two walls with the exterior of the building. The remaining two walls were comprised of a substantial metal mesh that rose completely to the ceiling about twelve feet above.

The door to the supply room had a lock but the thugs didn't have the key. So, they used a chain and padlock to secure the door.

When they had departed, they had left a couple of loaves of bread, a pound of unsliced pastrami, and a few bottles of water.

Solis awoke with a start to the sensation of something on his left arm. In horror, he shook off the rat that was nibbling at the dried blood on his forearm. Growing up in Managua, the Central American had seen enough rats to not be afraid of them. But none of those had been licking or gnawing at his flesh.

Eddie arose and stumbled to the door of the tiny room. He twisted the knob. It wasn't locked, but when he pushed against the door, it was instantly stopped by a chain.

The only light was from a rip in the metal sheeting that made up the wall of the building. Solis knew that when night fell, he would be without light. And that meant, he also knew, that the rats would cloak themselves in the dark to go about their business.

For the first time since his ordeal began, Edmundo Solis gained some resolve. He determined to make a plan. In the dimness of the little available light, he examined the rest of his clothes. All of them appeared to have blood on them.

"*My* blood," he thought.

He took off his shirt. Then he removed his pants and piled them together in a corner of the room. Even his undershirt had blood on it that had soaked through his UPS uniform shirt. So, he removed that, too.

Next, he dampened a dirty rag that he found lying in the room with a sparing amount of the water that his captors had left. Without benefit of a mirror, Solis scrubbed every inch of his head – his face, neck, scalp; everything. He could only hope he got all of the blood off and that he was no longer bleeding.

With his body clear – he hoped – of blood, perhaps the rats would leave him alone when their time came, the darkness of the night. His shoes and socks had blood on them, but he dared not remove them. He had heard horrific stories of people's extremities being ravaged by the rodents. There was also blood on his underwear that had penetrated his uniform pants. But he left them on as well. There was no way he would leave that extremity vulnerable.

Light was fading in his "cell." Eddie felt it was too early for the sun to be setting, though he had no clue about the time of day. So, he believed the sun was simply moving to a point above the warehouse away from the gash in the metal. In the remaining light he had, the Nicaraguan activist used the rag to try to remove as much of the blood from his underwear, shoes, and socks as he could. Hoping he had cleaned them enough, he replaced his damp undershirt and pants.

Then Eddie considered his food. The Gutierrez thugs had left a bucket in the room to, Eddie supposed, use when nature called. He decided he would instead relieve himself on the floor in a corner and placed the bucket upside down over his food to keep the rats away from it. Before doing so, he removed the bucket and gnawed off a piece of the pastrami and a couple of slices of bread. After thinking about it for a moment, he decided he needed to ration his fare. After all, he had no idea how long he would be there and, without the presence of the traitorous brothers to intimidate him, Eddie was determined to survive this mess. He reduced the amount of food he had taken and placed some back with the rest.

With the bucket in place with pieces of scrap metal atop it to weigh it down, Edmundo Solis took bites of the bread and meat. He didn't feel like eating, but he wanted to maintain what little strength remained after his beating.

He was suddenly motivated by the realization that his tormentors must work for Zamora. They were a part of the atrocities he was striking out against.

So, Solis steeled himself for a long, frightening ordeal.

♦

The ex-Special Forces Operator looked at the time on his phone. He had been driving for about twenty minutes. It was 9:25 and he was traveling through Cúcuta. He knew, or rather hoped, that Morgan would follow their agreed-upon protocol and turn on his phone in two minutes and that he would leave it on for two. Lechler pulled out of the traffic so that he could devote his full attention to the same monitor he had used to track his friend to the airport in Cúcuta earlier.

He watched the time. It felt like it took ten minutes instead of two, but 9:27 appeared on the display. He tapped the touchscreen icon repeatedly to refresh the screen. But nothing appeared but the blue dot that indicated his own phone's location.

"Nothing! Dammit, Josh!"

Lechler refreshed another time and a red dot appeared in addition to his own.

"There you go!" he shouted.

But as soon as the dot had appeared, it was gone. Lechler left the display as it was. The center of the screen had been the location of the red dot – and therefore Morgan's – and was at a spot off the highway that the former sergeant estimated to be about twenty minutes away. If Morgan was on the run, he would move between now and then. But he would also turn his phone back on in twenty minutes and Lechler would get a current fix on the man's position and direction of travel.

With a spray of gravel from his tires, Tom Lechler sped from the highway's shoulder and accelerated into the sparse traffic. As he did, he placed a call to Betsy Parnell on his satellite phone.

CHAPTER 7

Case Officers Mosquera and Herrera knew they were approaching the crash site when the traffic began to back up. Herrera turned off the highway onto a side road and parked.

"Better call Felipe," she said.

Mosquera entered the code to wake the phone up and tapped the number on the display that represented Ramirez's and the sat phone dialed the number. He spoke for a minute and ended the call.

"Okay, so here's the deal. Felipe says that Director Parnell is personally involved in this thing. And before you ask, we still don't 'need to know.' The Director told Felipe that she has an operator coming from the other direction and that he has a way to track Morgan."

"So, exactly why are *we* here?" Herrera wondered aloud.

"I don't know. Moral support, I suppose," Mosquera cracked. "No, the way Felipe explained it is that Parnell wants to do everything possible to ensure that the first face this Morgan fellow sees is a friendly one."

"If you say so, Jeronimo. If this guy coming our way…"

Mosquera looked at notes he had scribbled. "Lechler. That's the only name Felipe gave me."

"If this Lechler has a way to find Morgan, that means Morgan has a transponder. Why don't we just tune into his frequency and go get him?" Valentina Herrera asked, reaching for their own monitor in the back seat.

"Can't. Ours won't work. Apparently, this is something the two guys cooked up."

Herrera rolled her eyes. "Great. Do-it-yourselfers."

The two CIA officers sat in silence momentarily.

"Tell me, Jeronimo, do we at least have a way to identify the other guy – you know, the not-Morgan one?"

"Lechler? Yep." Mosquera held up his notes to show the make, model, and license plate number of the vehicle. "And ETA is about fifteen minutes."

"Not even time enough for a good nap."

"Nope."

♦

Tom Lechler wanted to pull over to watch his monitor more closely but decided to press on. But he knew he was in Morgan's area because, in addition to a line of backed-up traffic, over the roofs of the vehicles he could see the outline of a plane's vertical stabilizer.

The ex-warrior shook his head in disbelief at his own ignorance. Despite all his years in planning for every contingency, Lechler had failed to anticipate the traffic jam – even on this remote road – that kept him from Morgan. And with Morgan possibly not expecting him, there was no way his partner would be able to come to him. Lechler put the shifter in "Park" and rubbed his temples.

Parnell had told him on their phone call that news reports were that authorities had found at least one body in the plane. Not surprising, the ex-sergeant had remarked to the CIA chief. It was, after all, a plane crash. But Parnell cleared that up in a way that didn't surprise the former Special Operations soldier. The deceased had been shot.

"Must be Lammers," Lechler had thought. He had wondered why Josh hadn't just turned himself in. But now he realized that the questions that would arise from Parnell's disclosure explained that. Colombia and the United States were friendly enough – but not *that* friendly. They would want to investigate a homicide on their own soil themselves. And despite the cordial, if cool relations between the two countries, much of the Colombian government was very touchy about U.S. interference in their affairs.

"If only I could get in touch with Josh," Lechler thought.

The former sergeant slapped his forehead.

"Wait! He probably knows I'm coming. I mean, our tracking app works both ways."

Right at 9:27, the red dot representing Josh's phone appeared. The tracking wasn't active. It only showed locations at a moment in time. So, Lechler waited about thirty seconds and refreshed his screen.

Morgan's dot reappeared. And it was closer! Josh was moving toward Lechler.

"He's been tracking me the whole time, too. Smart boy, Josh."

Suddenly, the red dot disappeared. The former Special Forces soldier thumped his finger on the display in the way that aviators used to do with analog gauges, but which was utterly pointless with a digital display. Lechler looked at his watch. Morgan should've been online for about another minute if he was following protocol.

"What the hell?"

Lechler scratched his head.

♦

Josh Morgan had checked the location of Tom Lechler each time he powered up his phone. He, too, was troubled by the sudden loss of location for him. But he knew the reason why. His phone's battery had finally died. Morgan had realized he could check to see if help was on its way – at least, help in the person of Tom Lechler. He was certain Lechler would be tracking him and note that he had moved in the direction the ex-soldier would be coming from.

The plan would be to risk leaving his phone on longer than their established methodology so that Lechler could follow his movement. He would move away from Lechler's direction momentarily so that it would be apparent to the ex-Green Beret that he was aware of his presence. But then Morgan would resume moving in his original direction toward Lechler. He had hoped his battery would live long enough to signal his friend an exact location to meet. Morgan couldn't risk going directly to Lechler on the road. Even briefly reversing course as he had back toward the general direction of the crash site had been risky enough. He would continue toward some spot that was still off the highway. He'd have to figure out how to locate Lechler.

The former Case Officer figured he would most likely be captured. Evasion in unfamiliar territory without a map or assistance was almost impossible. And the failure of his phone's battery likely removed the word "almost" from his odds.

♦

"Yes, Director Parnell," former MSG Lechler confirmed. "The signal just disappeared from my screen. It could be a glitch. Or… it could mean he's been captured."

"Or it could be something simpler. Maybe his battery went dead."

"Yes, ma'am. That's certainly a possibility."

"So, how do we communicate with him, Sergeant?"

There was an extended silence as the two tried to come up with options.

"Director, you said you had some officers in the area.'

"That's correct."

"I think we should get them to communicate with Josh. I'm leaving my van and heading into the trees to track him. I've had some experience in that."

In spite of the dire situation, Parnell smiled. "I bet you have, Tom."

"But even with my training, I can use some help."

Tom Lechler explained his plan to the CIA Director.

♦

Val Herrera couldn't believe what she was hearing. "They want us to do *what?*"

"Swear to God, Val."

"And what do we do when we're confronted – and we *will* be confronted – and asked to explain what the hell we're doing?"

"Felipe said the Director's exact instructions to us were: 'Think of something.'"

The partners laughed.

Mosquera commented, "Aren't you glad we have Diplomatic Immunity?"

"Yeah. Just hope we don't have to play that card."

And with her comment, Case Officer Valentina Herrera put the sedan in reverse and moved onto the highway.

Then she laughed aloud and asked her partner, "Ready?"

Mosquera only nodded.

♦

Somewhere in the middle of an unnamed forest, frustrated by the inopportune timing of the demise of his phone's battery, Josh Morgan heard the repeated blaring of an automobile horn.

"What the…?"

The distraction of the din notwithstanding, Morgan returned to considering his options. He was almost to the point of surrendering and hoping for the best.

"If only I could communicate with Tom," he wished. Then he continued with, "Oh, surely not. It's in the wrong direction."

Morgan sat on a fallen tree trunk and thought things through, finally deciding that, if he surrendered, did it really matter where?

He rose and turned in the direction of the infernal constant blasting of the automobile horn.

"I hope I'm right."

♦

At the sound of the car horn commencing its wail, Tom Lechler jumped from his car and walked slowly toward the trees on the right side of the highway, unzipping his fly as he proceeded. He figured people would be so disgusted by the sight of a man walking toward the privacy of the trees to piss that they would pay him little mind.

"On the other hand, I know very little about the customs here, what I'm doing may be commonplace. Hell, folks may pull out binoculars for a good look," he cracked silently.

Lechler moved to a spot where several trees stood in close proximity and positioned himself behind them. He proceeded to urinate.

"Might as well go now. Who knows when I'll have another chance?"

Zipping his fly up, Lechler hoped people would be distracted by the persistent honking of the car horn. And he hoped Morgan would understand it to be a beacon.

MSG Tom Lechler, U.S. Army, Retired, broke into as rapid a sprint as he could while still maintaining full awareness of his surroundings.

♦

CIA Officers Herrera and Mosquera finally saw a pair of surly looking officials moving toward their car. One was desperately moving his hands up and down with palms facing downward to demand they quieten down.

The other moved his closed index finger and thumb across his lips in what was clearly a universally understood signal to zip it. His other hand rested on an exposed handgun in a holster.

Herrera paused from her horn-blowing briefly and asked her partner, "You don't suppose he'd really shoot us, do you, Mosquera?"

"I would."

The two laughed and Val Herrera began pressing the center of the steering wheel again.

When the two men finally reached the car, they took positions on either side. Herrera stopped her honking but couldn't resist one last toot. The officer on her side of the sedan failed to see the humor in her defiance.

The man practically shouted. "What do you think you're doing?" he demanded.

♦

Morgan couldn't help but notice when the noise from the vehicle stopped. But in the ensuing silence, he heard on the fallen leaves the footfalls of at least two men.

"This is over," he thought, and resigned himself to the inevitability of being captured. "Might as well give it up."

♦

The presence of the two officials at the car made the situation significantly less humorous than it had been.

Mosquera began to speak, "You see, officer…" he began before Val Herrera interrupted.

"It's my fault, sir." She took her fellow Case Officer completely off guard when she placed her right hand on his knee – the inside of his left knee. She sold the meaning with a look of desire at her partner. She returned her attention to the officer outside the car, while Mosquera tried to manage a smile of his own.

"Officer," Herrera said in Spanish with a Colombian accent, "we've had a romantic getaway planned for weeks and something has always gotten in the way. We've had to postpone it… I don't know. How many times, darling?" She looked at Mosquera to perpetuate the ruse.

"Uh, ten… sweetheart. …I think."

"Ten!?" Herrera exclaimed in her own mind. She patted Mosquera on his leg again and said with a giggle, "Well, it certainly seems like it."

Out of sight of the two officers, she shot an "are you an idiot" look at her "lover."

"I'm really sorry, sir. Surely you can understand the, uh, needs of two young people. If we promise to keep quiet and turn around and head back home, can you overlook our indiscretion?"

The lull in the one-sided conversation dragged out to the point that both CIA Officers were beginning to worry. Finally, the officer nearest Herrera said, shaking his index finger at her, "You can go. But only because I have more important things to do than deal with your horny nonsense. I have a murderer to catch."

The two Americans' faces never registered their surprise, but it was the first thing they had heard about murder."

"Yes, you're right, officer. We're sorry… I'm sorry. Our actions were unforgivable."

The officer started to leave but returned for one last remark.

"Go. And I mean now. But if you don't and you make another sound, my partner will shoot you both!"

The partner's expression signified "Why me?" But he fell in behind his superior.

"I, uh… I didn't know you felt that way about me, Val… sweetheart."

Herrera slammed the back of her hand into Mosquera's chest. It stopped his laughing, but only momentarily.

Herrera put the gearshift in reverse.

"And ten? TEN? Seriously? Moron!"

"Hey, you put me on the spot. I didn't know what to say. Sorry, Val."

"I mean, really… ten times you've put me off. Not very committed, are you, Jeronimo? I'm going to have to rethink the nature of our relationship."

Herrera and Mosquera laughed, and the car began to roll backward to turn around and head for the side road on which they had been parked earlier.

♦

Tom Lechler was making rapid progress through the trees. He managed to avoid any contact with the people searching for Morgan. However, he hadn't seen one sign of his friend. The car horn/distraction/beacon for Morgan had stopped a few minutes earlier. Hopefully, if the former CIA operative had caught on at all, he had continued in the direction of the racket from the automobile.

Finally, he saw a broken limb. The peculiar thing was that it wasn't just bent. It was completely broken off its small sapling. Even stranger, it was lying on the ground a short distance from the small trunk. It was even resting directly atop a footprint that was more deeply embedded into the soil than others.

Lechler considered what he saw: a small branch appearing to be deliberately severed sitting on a footprint that seemed to be made to be deliberately obvious.

"Well, I'll be," he thought before heading off in the direction the limb was pointing. "*Might* be pointing," the ex-soldier corrected in his mind.

CHAPTER 8

If he gave himself up, Josh Morgan knew he would have to answer a lot of questions about what had happened on the crashed jet, given that there were bodies on it – bodies of men who didn't die from injuries in the crash. And the plane had caused multiple vehicles on the highway to crash. He hoped no one was injured in the pileup. But he was tired. The rush of adrenalin that he'd experienced in the fight with Oskar Lammers and the crash had long since evaporated.

Morgan knew that Colombia was basically on friendly terms with the United States, but he wasn't sure that would be enough to keep him from answering for shooting Lammers and the plane crash. Still, he was coming to the conclusion that he would take his chances.

Hearing the footfalls of searchers nearby, Morgan made his decision. He began to step into a clearing to surrender when he saw a pair of men at the far edge moving away from him.

"Shit!" he thought. "That's not good."

♦

Tom Lechler heard the footsteps of someone moving quietly through the grove of trees just beyond a small clearing ahead of him. If what he heard was his partner, then Josh was in trouble because there were two sets of feet making the noise.

Crouching behind a bush next to a large tree trunk, the operator tried to determine what the situation was. Suddenly, a hand reached around to cover Lechler's mouth. Reflexively, training took over and the former Green Beret drove his right elbow into the chest of his visitor. He spun around to see the man toppling backward; first onto his ass and then fully onto his back.

Gun aimed at the figure on the ground, Lechler was surprised to see Morgan with a grimace on his face. Slowly, the ex-CIA Officer raised an index finger to his lips and groaned, "Shhh."

Lechler spun around to see if the commotion he had caused had alerted the men ahead of him to his presence. To his relief, though they seemed to have heard the disturbance, they weren't approaching. He turned back to Morgan, who was getting to one knee and rubbing his sternum.

"Damn, Tom."

"Don't ever sneak up on me, Josh," the former sergeant growled in a hushed tone.

"First, I shouldn't have been able to sneak up on the mighty Tom Lechler. And secondly… shhh." He raised his index finger to his lips again.

Lechler helped Morgan to a position that provided better cover, where his friend plopped back onto his butt and sat with his knees pulled up, still massaging his chest.

Morgan's eyes suddenly grew wide. He tapped his eyes with his index and middle fingers and then pointed in the direction he wanted Lechler to look. The former soldier had already turned in that direction, having heard the same sounds Morgan had. He crouched lower and Morgan shifted so that he, too, was better concealed.

At the edge of the small clearing, two men crept stealthily along. They wore black tactical clothing and carried semi-automatic submachine guns. The weapons had suppressors. The men were Middle Eastern.

"They're not part of any search party," Lechler whispered.

"You think? That's what I was trying to tell you."

The two men were on full alert. They had heard Morgan fall when Lechler laid him out with his elbow and were moving in on the pair's location. The retired warrior retrieved his handgun from his waistband. Not figuring to get into a gun battle with the searchers looking for Josh, he had left it holstered while moving. He had pulled it out briefly when Morgan had surprised him but had put it away again. Now he knew there was no way to avoid encountering the men. They were coming straight toward him and his partner, guns raised at the ready.

Former MSG Lechler had noted that the adversaries were wearing body armor. Lechler pointed to Morgan and then at his gun.

"No," Morgan mouthed.

Lechler rolled his eyes and gave his friend a look that communicated how stupid he thought he was to not have a gun.

He thought to himself, "Gotta make these count."

Lechler decided to let the men get as close as possible before taking action. He watched for any sign that they were on to him and Morgan and were about to fire. The men were less than ten feet away when the closest one finally caught sight of the two Americans. He was moving his finger into the gun's trigger guard when Lechler's suppressed .45 caliber bullet struck him in the center of his face.

Before the first had even begun to fall, Tom Lechler sprang to his feet and fired his second round, which entered the other man's head through his left eye socket.

Lechler surveyed their surroundings.

"If there are others, they're not close by," he told Josh.

He dragged the bodies into denser brush and moved back to Morgan.

"Here," he said, handing Morgan his cellular mobile phone.

"No signal here, Tom."

"No, dipshit. You're not supposed to call anybody. You're going to use its compass app. Go north-northwest. In about three hundred yards, you'll come to a gravel road. There will be a car there with two CIA spooks in it. Parnell sent them from their station near here, so they're expecting you."

"What about you?"

"Heading back to the van. There's some stuff in there I need to get my hands back on, if the authorities haven't searched it and found the gear already."

♦

New White House Press Secretary Maggie Loughlin's day wasn't nearly as chaotic as she had feared and expected. She had finally gotten into the mindset that she had when she filled in for her predecessor in her absence. Maggie just took things as they came, trusting her organizational skills to stay ahead of demands on her time.

The knock on her door only halfway broke her intensity on the briefing she was preparing.

"Yes?" she answered over her shoulder.

"Can we interrupt for a sec?"

Maggie looked up to see Mac Marchman with another man she didn't know. She stood and extended her hand to that man while smiling at Mac.

"Secretary Loughlin…" – the title would take some getting used to – "this is Special Agent Andre Maddox. Andy… uh, Agent Maddox and I have known each other a while. We worked together in the New York Field Office."

"Pleased to meet you, Agent Maddox."

"Thank you, ma'am. My pleasure."

Andy Maddox was about the same height and build as Marchman, but he looked about ten years older. Still, it was hard to tell. Marchman looked several years younger than his age. And Maddox seemed to have a more serious demeanor than Marchman. Well, all Secret Service Agents had a serious demeanor. It was just that Mac seemed to lose some of the hardness when he was in the West Wing.

There was an awkwardness with the silence that followed. Finally, Agent Maddox said, "I'm Agent Marchman's replacement."

Marchman had a moment of genuine embarrassment.

"Oh, yeah. Right. I… uh… well…"

Maddox spoke again, "Well, I'm not really taking his place. I'm just assuming his responsibilities where you're concerned, ma'am."

Maggie looked at Mac and her stomach knotted slightly. She didn't like change, despite that she managed it well. And she didn't like working with people she didn't know. And she really didn't want to lose Mac.

"Oh… Already?"

"Yes, ma'am. It happened sooner than any of us expected," Marchman said when he had finally regained full composure.

Maggie noticed that not only did Marchman not seem bothered by the change, but he also appeared upbeat.

"Agent Marchman has filled me in on your typical schedule. We'll work the details out as we go."

"I'm sure you'll do fine," Maggie said, realizing she had spoken as if Agent Maddox was some understudy stepping up into a role that might be over his head.

"I'm sorry. I mean… I have full confidence in you," she said, hoping that she hadn't insulted Maddox.

"You're in great hands, Secretary Loughlin," Marchman said, concluding the introduction.

Agent Maddox turned for the door, looking back over his shoulder to see his friend and associate lingering.

"Go on ahead, Andy. I've got to cover a couple of things with the Secretary about the handover."

Maddox wondered what details Mac needed to cover with Secretary Loughlin that he shouldn't hear also, in that he was taking over as her protective detail. But instantly he knew.

"Okay. Catch up with you later," he said. Then he thought, "You dog."

♦

While Tom Lechler was off recovering the van he had driven to the crash site, Josh Morgan had made his way to a dirt road. He peeked through a stand of trees along the road that intersected the small highway on which he'd crash-landed the jet. About seventy yards away sat a small SUV with two people in it. Morgan retreated farther into the trees, walked parallel to the dirt and gravel road until he was even with the vehicle. He emerged with his hands away from his body.

"I hope this is them."

Mosquera looked at the photo of Josh Morgan and compared it to the disheveled figure walking toward him and his partner.

"That's Morgan, Val," he said, motioning to his fellow CIA operator with his right hand while checking out the road ahead of him through binoculars.

The ex-CIA officer turned contractor entered the back seat of the SUV hurriedly and slumped to the floor as his "chauffer" put the vehicle in gear and started moving forward. Not a word was said until the trio were on the paved road and headed north toward Tibú.

Once they were a few miles safely on their way, Morgan rose from the floorboard and took a seat. Mosquera reported to the Bogotá Station Chief that they had their passenger.

Herrera's phone rang. She gave Jero a surprised look, accompanied by, "Yes, ma'am." Val handed her phone to Morgan. "It's for you."

Morgan listened for a couple of seconds and then greeted his caller.

"Hi, Betsy."

Morgan assured the Director of the Central Intelligence Agency that he was fine. He learned from Parnell that Lechler, too, was on the way to Tibú. When traffic was allowed to proceed around the plane, he had passed without incident.

"Yeah, I know, Betsy. I owe you."

He listened while his caller explained to him in detail the degree to which he owed her.

"Thanks, Betsy." And the call ended.

Finally, the three occupants exchanged introductions.

Val Herrera said, "You know the Director? You keep some lofty-ass company."

Then they maintained a silence that lasted all the way to Mosquera's and Herrera's base near Tibú.

♦

Secret Service Agent Mac Marchman asked the Press Secretary, "May I sit?"

"Of course," Maggie said, motioning to a chair beside her desk. As her guest sat, Maggie noticed he was wringing his hands.

"Uh… and I don't even know if this is appropriate, but now that I'm not on your detail anymore, I wondered if… uh, maybe…" The Secret Service Agent paused and exhaled.

Maggie looked at him, leaned forward with a puzzled look, and repeated, "Maybe… what?" Then she shrugged.

"Would you have dinner with me?" Marchman's question flew out of his mouth at lightspeed. He pursed his lips and raised his eyebrows. He tilted his head and shrugged.

"You know, dinner?" he said again.

Maggie was stunned. She leaned back in her chair.

"Oh, gee… uh, dinner…" Maggie's pulse raced, and her stomach flew up to her throat.

"That's okay. I understand," Mac said as he stood to leave.

"I'm just not sure that's a good…" Maggie stopped in the midst of her refusal. Her kneejerk reaction was to be faithful to her and Josh's relationship, but reality set in that there was no "relationship" anymore. So, in her mind, Maggie Loughlin thought, "Why not?"

"Wait, Mac. You know, dinner sounds lovely. What'd you have in mind?"

The pair worked out the details and the date was on.

CHAPTER 9

United States Secret Service Agent Mac Marchman saw the other agent's smile from the car where he sat outside the entrance to Maggie Loughlin's apartment. The man was the night shift to Marchman's former day shift, now covered by Agent Andy Maddox.

When the man offered a silly wave and blew Marchman a kiss, Mac returned the gesture with a middle-finger salute. But as soon as he turned away, he smiled at the good-natured camaraderie.

Mac had on the same suit he had worn at work, minus the tie. Still, he pulled at his collar as though he had one on as he stood before Maggie's door.

He pressed the doorbell.

In an instant, his date opened the door.

Maggie Loughlin wore black leggings and black stiletto heels. Her dark gray ruffle back blazer covered a low-cut cotton/spandex camisole. Her auburn hair hung more casually than the style she wore in the West Wing. And the white stone necklace was the perfect accent.

Mac was briefly without words.

"I'm speechless. You look amazing."

Maggie's face flushed ever so slightly.

"Thanks, Mac. Well, I'm ready if you are."

"Sure. Let's go."

The pair walked out the door of Maggie's apartment complex to see Spencer Oakley, the Secret Service Agent assigned to the Press Secretary for the night shift, holding open the door to his Service sedan.

"Ma'am."

Mac stalled in the walk toward his own car, stopping Maggie with him.

"What's going on, Spence?"

"Waiting to take my protectee and her date to dinner."

"I… uh…" Mac paused to look at Maggie, who didn't look surprised, and then back to the agent before them.

"I didn't know that… well, that you'd be driving us."

"Not only driving you, sir." Oakley smiled slightly. "Where she goes, I go."

"That's not necessary, Spence. I'll watch over her."

"Can't do that, Mac. You're on a date." He smiled again. "Not at work. I'm on duty, so…"

Mac Marchman noticed that Maggie seemed to be enjoying his surprise, dismay, and embarrassment at the development. Finally, she spoke.

"I told Agent Oakley of my plans tonight so he could be prepared. It makes sense. You know, in case you're distracted."

"Of course. It makes perfect sense. And I do intend to be completely distracted tonight," Mac said with a grin, trying to salvage some control over the turn of events, and his ego. "Shall we go then?"

Maggie entered the car, followed by Mac. But before her former agent followed her into the sedan, while he was out of her sight, he delivered some daggers from his eyes to his fellow agent. Oakley shrugged and winked, reserving his muted laugh until Mac got into the back seat and closed the door.

Agent Oakley surveyed the surroundings as he moved to the driver side. Once in, he fastened his safety belt and spoke into his wrist.

"Bluebird on the move."

The United States Secret Service had given Maggie Loughlin the code name Bluebird when she was Acting Press Secretary. Even though she didn't have constant overwatch at that time, she was occasionally in the company of President Hendrickson or other officials who did have such protection. Therefore, she needed a short moniker so that references to her could be made without using her real name. The staff who came up with Maggie's had thought it especially clever, owing to her auburn hair and blue eyes. Both the Eastern and Western Bluebirds of the U.S. had rust, or auburn color in front of the brilliant blue of their backs and wings.

Agent Oakley pulled away from the parking lot. All of his pleasure at the awkwardness of his fellow agent had vanished. He was in full business mode.

♦

Secret Service Agent Spencer Oakley parked his sedan. It was unusual to have only one agent on an outing like this. And it presented a couple of weaknesses in his protection. He couldn't drop his passengers at the door to the restaurant and leave them alone while he parked. Nor could he use valet parking, which would leave his Service automobile in the hands of a civilian. The safest solution was to park the car and walk with the Press Secretary and fellow Secret Service Agent Macarthur Marchman across the parking lot to the *Fiola Mare's* entrance.

He felt awfully exposed.

Oakley walked through the door being held open by one of the hosts, held up his credentials, and took a couple of steps into the dining area. He looked behind himself and past his charge and her date. Finally, he allowed Maggie and Mac to walk past him to their reserved table.

The last time Maggie had eaten at *Fiola Mare* was one of the final times she and Josh had dined with Former President Trent Weston and his wife Alicia. The attention she and Mac were receiving because of their security escort wasn't on a par with what they received when they were with the former First Couple. She felt awkward then, as now. A wave of nostalgia swept over Maggie. She missed Trent and Alicia. And she missed Josh.

"Something wrong, Maggie?"

Mac's date snapped out of her trance and smiled.

"No. Nothing at all. Just some memories from this place."

Mac Marchman knew of her relationship with Josh and correctly supposed that the recollection included him.

"We can go somewhere else, Maggie. Really. It would be no trouble…"

"No, Mac. It's fine."

Maggie took Mac's hand and resolved to enjoy the night without the ghost of her ex-fiancé haunting her.

♦

"I saved your ass – again!"

"Bullshit," Josh Morgan answered. "All you did was even things up for me. Just a little. You really didn't do shit for me."

Tom Lechler smirked, "You're so full of it."

"Yeah," challenged Josh Morgan. "I fought it out with Lammers on a plane that was going down. I kicked his ass."

"You mean the guy who was dying of cancer? Right! That took some doing." Lechler rolled his eyes.

"And I landed the goddam plane."

"Landed? You forget that I saw the plane on the highway. I don't think that qualifies as a 'landing,' Josh."

"I walked away, didn't I?"

"Point taken."

The two had flown in a U.S. Army Blackhawk from the outpost at Tibú to the U.S. Embassy in the Colombian capital of Bogotá. A driver transported the pair to *El Dorado Luis Carlos Galan Sarmiento International Airport*, also known as *El Dorado* International, where they were on their way mere minutes after arriving.

Josh Morgan smiled as he leaned back in the seat of the Learjet that Betsy Parnell had sent to retrieve her contractors.

Both men were silent for a few moments until Morgan said, "Thanks, Tom."

"Don't mention it, Josh. Besides, you did the hard stuff. I sat about a hundred meters out and pulled a trigger. You did the heavy lifting."

There was an interlude of silence.

"But I still don't think what you did qualifies as a 'landing,' Morgan."

"Whatever you say, Tom." Morgan smiled again and nodded off.

♦

"That was nice. Thanks, Mac."

Maggie had enjoyed the dinner more than she thought she would. Beforehand she had thought that having Agent Oakley along would be the equivalent of having a chaperone. She had considered him as a sort of barrier between her and Mac that would prevent her date from thinking of the dinner as something more than it was. Maggie had felt some misgivings about the outing anyhow. Despite that there wasn't a man in her life anymore, she didn't want to go too far past platonic at this stage of things.

But during the dinner, she came to wish the tagalong agent wasn't around, keeping watch. She hadn't changed her mind about the nature of the date. She simply felt uneasy at having someone who knew and worked with Mac watching everything that transpired. She had genuinely desired some privacy, more intimacy than a chaperone allowed.

But standing here, outside the door to her apartment, Maggie felt the awkwardness come rushing back.

"I enjoyed it, too, Maggie."

Maggie nodded. Spence Oakley had stayed behind while Mac had walked his date to the door. He figured he could manage to be both date and agent for that short amount of time.

It was clear from his lingering, but not really saying anything, that Mac was waiting to be invited in. Finally, he said as much.

"Got time for a nightcap?"

"Oh, gee, Mac. Uh, not tonight. I have an early morning and lots on my schedule. But thanks for a really great evening. I wasn't sure I was ready to get out, you know. But I had a great time."

"Sure. I understand. You're right. It's late. I ought to get going myself."

Then he leaned in for a kiss. Maggie didn't recoil, but she managed to take control of the situation by making it a brief peck on the lips, then turning her head to the side and laying it on his chest, turning the moment into more of a giant hug.

"Goodnight, Maggie."

"Goodnight, Josh," she said. Her head still against Mac's chest, she squeezed her eyes tight and clinched her teeth. There were no words for a full three seconds before she finally separated from her date.

"Oh, God, Mac. I'm so sorry. I don't…" The auburn-haired woman dropped her head and put both hands to her face. "I can't believe I said that. I really didn't think about him all night…"

Mac Marchman reached up and stroked his chin and sighed.

"I'm making it worse, aren't I?" Maggie admitted without looking up.

Mac held up his thumb and index finger with a gap of about a half inch between them.

"Maybe a little," the man said. He managed a small smile. He took both of Maggie's hands in his.

"This has been a great night." He reinforced the comment with a more sincere smile than the previous one. "I understand you were in the relationship with *him*…" It was as if he couldn't say the name. "…and so, this had to have been difficult."

Mac lifted Maggie's right hand and kissed it gently.

"So, let's just forget about it."

"Thanks, Mac. I'm sorr…"

Before she could finish, Mac put his index finger to her lips.

"Forgotten. Okay?"

Maggie closed the door behind her and leaned against it, dropping her purse on the floor. She put both hands over her face.

"Great, Loughlin. Really great."

She slumped to the floor, back still resting against the door, and remained there for some time. Finally, she rose. She put her handbag on the coffee table and started for her bedroom. Halfway there, she did an about-face and walked to the kitchen. She poured a half snifter of Brandy and resumed her march to her bedroom.

"Idiot."

♦

Outside Maggie's apartment building, Mac Marchman walked quickly past the sedan where Agent Oakley was sitting. Spence lowered his window and said slyly. "You weren't gone long."

"Bite me." Marchman never slowed down nor turned to his friend, who raised his window and smiled.

CHAPTER 10

DAY 3 – WEDNESDAY

It was well after midnight. The flight had gone quickly for Josh Morgan and Tom Lechler. Both were exhausted from their ordeal of the last thirty-six hours of confrontation with Oskar Lammers and the days of surveillance before then. The luxury of being in a secure place where there was no need to suspect danger was lurking about had made sleep easy and blissful during the flight.

The CIA's private jet completed its rollout. Gears were chocked and the airstair was lowered while the two men gathered their meager belongings.

As they walked down the gangway to the tarmac, Morgan couldn't resist one more dig at his friend about his escape from the pressure activated IED in Lammers' apartment.

"So, you really used your pants as a lasso?"

Lechler didn't answer.

"I said…"

"Yes, Morgan. More of a cord, but yes… I did," the ex-soldier mumbled.

"Glad I wasn't there to see that."

A raised middle finger answered the observation.

"Seriously, I might've shot myself rather than see that. I mean, how do you unsee something so pitiful?"

"*I* might shoot you now."

"I think we're both glad you had extra clothing in the van."

This time Lechler ignored the comment. The former CIA officer knew he'd taken things as far as he needed to.

"We survived another one, huh, Tom?"

"Yeah, we did, partner."

The CIA contractors exchanged a fist bump.

"Kinda getting to be the norm for us, Josh."

Josh Morgan didn't answer. He only nodded. But in his mind, he was afraid Lechler was right.

As the two men went separate ways. Josh thought about the apartment he had shared with Maggie. He missed her and considered calling to see how she was. But he knew it was best to let her go.

He and Lechler left Andrews Air Force Base, the airfield portion of Joint Base Andrews for the hotel where rooms had been reserved for them. After an early meeting with CIA Director Elizabeth Parnell, Morgan would board a commercial flight to Jackson Hole Airport and home. He wondered how long he would be there before Parnell sent him and Lechler to do the Agency's bidding in some far-away locale.

♦

Edmundo Solis lay on the floor of the room in which he was imprisoned. It was bare except for a handful of rags he had found scattered about that he used for a pillow.

It was deathly quiet, so he knew he was nowhere near an active, busy business area. The only sounds interrupting the stillness were the scratching of the mice and rats as they scurried across the dirty surface of the floor or pawed at the bucket under which Solis had placed his bread. The rodents no doubt smelled the pieces of the only food that he had and seemed intent on getting to them.

The limited knowledge the native of Nicaragua had of behavioral psychology came from attending night college in Miami during his first years in the U.S. He had taken a couple of Psychology courses to better understand human nature. One prominent psychologist's work came to mind. B.F. Skinner's theories were being confirmed as Solis tried to sleep. Unrewarded, the rats eventually began to give up. At first, they were extremely persistent, but slowly, their efforts became less frequent. Still, after some period of time, they returned to try again, with the intervals between attempts increasing as reinforcement was continually denied.

Psychologist Skinner had maintained that free will was merely an illusion. All creatures behaved as they did because they had been conditioned to do so. Eddie Solis didn't understand what conditioning had placed him in this position, but he certainly possessed no free will to exercise at the moment. And certainly, he had no control over the matter.

The rodents' clicking on the floor didn't frighten Solis, as it might've others. As a child in Managua, he had slept with his siblings on mats on the floor of his family's apartment. He knew that, if you created an unrewarding environment and kept yourself clean to avoid becoming a temptation yourself, they would generally leave you alone.

Solis knew that he was here because the Gutierrez brothers, acting under the orders of *Presidente* Zamora, directly or indirectly, were concerned about a series of blogs he had written about an operation being carried out in another country. And while Luis and Santos didn't believe him at first, it was true: Solis didn't know the source of his information, the country where the op was occurring, or any real details.

Solis also knew that, had he known and revealed his source, he would already be dead, instead of merely battered. And that source would likewise suffer a brutal beating before a merciless death.

Edmundo Solis understood that he wasn't a brave man. It wasn't personal courage that had created his resolve to escape this torment. Solis was determined to live for the love of his country. He wanted to survive to uncover the final details of Zamora's operation, to see it destroyed, and to bring to light the evil that was in the very soul of the Nicaraguan dictator.

He believed that the Gutierrez brothers would never return unless they needed something additional from him. That was unlikely. Solis knew no other facts and he was convinced they had come to believe him. So, he would try to sleep through the pain and the tumultuous thoughts spinning through his mind. When morning came, perhaps the little tear in the exterior metal wall of his makeshift cell would allow him enough light to assess his situation more accurately and let him develop a means of escape.

CHAPTER 11

After not much sleep, former CIA Case Officer Josh Morgan and ex-Master Sergeant Tom Lechler waited outside the Director's office.

"I never asked, Josh. What got you into CIA?"

Morgan recounted the story of his being recruited right out of college.

"Your Russian professor. No shit? Was it something you'd thought of as a kid? You're younger than me, but with all the spy shows on TV…"

"Didn't even know what CIA was back then."

"So, what *did* you want to be when you grew up? I guess I could ask you the same question now: What *do* you want to be *if* you grow up?"

Morgan simply smiled. "I guess that depends on when you would've asked me. It changed almost daily. I loved the simple life of farming. I adored my grandfather. One of the things I always noticed was how happy he always was. As I grew older, I realized that it was because he was satisfied with his life and content with who he was."

"Not much of that going around nowadays," Lechler lamented.

"No, there isn't. Then when I was about eight, my grandmother gave me a camera. She was quite gifted as a photographer, even though she only took photos of our family, vacation pics – that sort of thing. She was completely self-taught but the portraits she took of us and her friends… They're still some of the finest I've ever seen."

Lechler nodded as his friend continued.

"I was hooked immediately. Not just the craft but the bond with my grandma. What about you, Tom? What did you do before Special Forces?"

"Chopper pilot. Blackhawks. I lied about my age to get into the Army at age sixteen."

"No kidding. I never knew that."

"Yeah, gave some wino some everclear to sign my dad's name to the enlistment papers."

"Your dad didn't want you to enlist?"

"Actually, he wouldn't have cared. Just didn't know where he was at the time. We eventually reconnected and became real close."

"So, how'd you end up wearing the Green Beret, Tom?"

"I was doing an extraction in… Well, I'm not supposed to tell anyone where. Anyhow, it went to hell. Three of the twelve on the A-Team were shot up really bad. Another three were wounded less seriously. Was supposed to do a rope extraction but some of the meat-eaters couldn't manage it. Landed my craft and ran out to help get 'em while the rest of my crew shot the hell out of the bad guys."

Morgan was surprised at the nonchalance of Lechler's account. He was also shocked that he was telling it at all. Josh had always noticed that Tom never initiated a battle story. But if you asked him, he'd tell you.

"Anyhow, we got out okay. Made some contacts with those guys and blah, blah, blah. Next thing I know, got invited to test. And, well, here I am."

"And the legend was born," Morgan teased.

Lechler, despite the good-naturedness of the remark, didn't care for it.

A few minutes later, the pair sat across the desk from the CIA Director.

"So, it sounds like mission accomplished," Parnell said.

"I suppose," Morgan answered.

"How do you feel?"

"Oh, I can't say it's really satisfying. But I do think it's just."

"So do I, Josh."

"Thanks, Betsy. And thanks for letting me get this behind me."

"It was one of your demands. 'Non-negotiable,' as I recall."

"Yeah… well, thanks just the same."

There was little more in the way of debriefing. After all, the matter with Oskar Lammers wasn't an Agency op.

Parnell asked the question that was the basis for the early morning meeting.

"You ready to get after it, Josh, Tom?"

"Whatever you need, ma'am," the former Green Beret answered quickly enough that Morgan wondered if he even wanted time off.

"I'm ready, Betsy. I… I think I'm suited for this now. My soul… well, I'm not sure I have a soul, Bets."

"I'm not sure any of us in this line of work does, Josh. At least, not one that matters."

There was a pause of several seconds before the Director of the Central Intelligence Agency spoke. "Tell you what, Josh. You've been through a lot. Take some time. I'll call you in a couple of weeks and we'll get you engaged. But no saying 'no' this time. Deal?"

"Deal. Thanks, Betsy."

Lechler's response didn't sound quite as enthusiastic, Morgan noticed.

Morgan and Lechler left the CIA boss' office in the Headquarters of the George Bush Center for Intelligence without much conversation.

Lechler dropped Morgan back off at his hotel, where he would rest a while before heading to Reagan National Airport. The former soldier got out of the car and walked to his partner.

"Well, I guess I'll see you when I see you, Josh."

"I expect so, Tom."

The pair grasped hands and pulled each other into a hug. Josh waved at Lechler, who raised his right index finger to his forehead in a kind of faux salute before retaking his seat behind the rental's wheel.

Josh got to his room and rubbed his eyes. He'd had plenty of sleep on the plane from Colombia and a bit more in his hotel room afterward, but he remained weary. He had been consumed by the need to find Lammers for months. Morgan had prepared physically and sharpened his skills with weaponry. Now that the matter was over and his need for revenge satisfied, he felt weak without the adrenaline and thirst for vengeance that had fueled his quest. He dropped his single bag onto the floor by the bed and opened the sliding door to the patio off his room and sat.

After a few minutes of gazing over the cityscape of the District of Columbia at nothing in particular, he pulled up the address book on his phone and tapped the entry for "Maggie." His finger hovered over her name on his phone's display momentarily before finally pressing the button on the side of the phone that shut it down.

♦

Maggie Loughlin was in her office in the West Wing, beating herself up over her slipup in calling Mac Marchman by her former fiancé's name. She considered calling Mac but decided to just leave it alone for the day and wait to see if he called her. The problem was compounded by the fact that she'd had a great evening with her date and hoped to see him again. She wasn't ready for anything serious but dating again – well, it had been nice.

Maggie turned her attention back to her work, tackling the massive amount of email that awaited her. She had scanned only a handful when she became curious. She clicked to place her cursor in the search field for the inbox of her email app and typed in a few letters.

"No results," she read and admitted to herself that she was actually worried.

"Okay. This is just silly," Maggie Loughlin proclaimed to herself. "I don't even read his emails. He's obviously obsessed with his blog… and maybe with me. So, why is this even a thing?"

The White House Press Secretary searched her new emails again. There was nothing from Eddie Solis.

She thought, "I have no reason to even think anything is wrong."

Maggie leaned back in her chair and tapped her fingers together. She reluctantly decided to get back to work, but it was only a few minutes before the thought of Edmundo Solis came to the forefront again.

Maggie clicked on the folder labeled "Eddie." The latest email was three days old.

"Why haven't you emailed, Eddie?" she mused.

Maggie double-clicked on the last email from Eddie.

"Something very important," she read. "I'll tell you more tomorrow," the note had said.

"Why didn't you contact me, Eddie?"

The Press Secretary clicked "Reply" on Eddie Solis' last email and typed.

"Didn't receive your email regarding the 'something very important,' Eddie. Looking forward to reading it."

She lingered as she read and reread her message. She struck the last sentence and hit "Send" before she could talk herself out of it.

Her attempts to get to work failed again. Maggie returned to Eddie's email and looked below the content. Even though Solis always signed his emails "Eddie," below his shortened name was his full email signature identifying himself as editor/head correspondent/chief blogger of *El poder salvador de la verdad.*

Guessing that the phone number he listed was a mobile, she hurriedly texted, "hope all is well" and tapped the send icon. Maggie realized that she'd just given her "correspondent" her private mobile number, but there was nothing she could do about it now. Just as suddenly, it occurred to her that, since Edmundo Solis didn't have her number, he wouldn't even know who had sent it.

Maggie began to retype the text.

"Oh, hell," she whispered to herself and typed the number from Eddie's email onto her phone keypad and touched the green circle with the icon of a phone handset.

"Straight to voicemail," she recognized. As she heard, "You've reached the voicemailbox of Edmundo Solis and *El Poder…*," she touched the red circle and disconnected.

"Where are you, Eddie?"

♦

Walking down the concourse at Reagan National Airport, Josh Morgan paused to check the monitors. His flight to Jackson Hole Airport in Wyoming was listed "On time." He couldn't wait. He'd left his Golden Retriever with his friend Scott Taggart. He was excited at the notion of sitting on the porch swing at his log home with Biscuit, drinking some iced tea, and watching the world of his property with no demands on his time. He had nothing to do for at least the two weeks that Parnell had promised.

He had arrived at the airport well before his flight departed so he grabbed a coffee and sat down to read the latest Brad Thor novel on his phone. He laughed to himself that he was living out some of protagonist Scot Harvath's adventures – on a smaller, less significant scale, of course – yet here he was reading a spy novel as a means of escape.

He laughed again. This time out loud.

♦

Maggie Loughlin had reached the end of her patience and took her phone. A couple of taps on the screen and the phone number appeared: "Josh."

Maggie tried to tap the phone number, but her finger wouldn't cooperate. She put the device down and stared at it for a split second before seizing it quickly and initiating the call.

She instantly regretted it, but she was committed.

♦

Josh Morgan couldn't keep his mind on his reading. His thoughts were dominated by the prospect of being home with Biscuit without a care in the world when his phone chirped the announcement of an incoming call.

"Maggie," the display showed.

The phone continued to beep and vibrate while Josh stared at it with much indecision.

"Maggie. Shit."

Finally, Josh tapped the icon on the display to connect the call. But it was too late.

♦

In Washington, D.C., in the West Wing of the White House, Maggie Loughlin heard, "Morgan. Leave a message."

Maggie disconnected. The only thing worse than calling him was having to leave a message. She was in the middle of saying, "Damn it," when her phone rang. The Caller ID said, "Josh."

"Hi, Maggie."

"Hi, Josh."

There were a few seconds of silence until finally, "Sorry I missed your call. I'm at the airport and I, uh, well…"

"No problem, Josh. Going somewhere?"

"Home actually. I'm at Reagan."

"Oh…," Maggie said weakly. Her heart sank and her stomach churned as she thought of his having been so close and she hadn't seen him. She wondered why he was there and what he was doing. However, logic and detachment caught up with her emotions and she continued.

"How have you been? How are things? How's Biscuit?"

Maggie knew she tended to ramble when she was at a loss for words.

"We're good. We're both good. How're you, Mag?"

"I'm okay. Well, good, I guess. Did you hear about…"

"Your promotion? Yeah, I heard. That's amazing, Maggie. I'm so proud of you. But you know, you deserved it. You were made for this."

The awkwardness of the seconds that elapsed was felt on both ends of the phone call.

"Well, I… uh…," Josh started.

"Josh, I need your help."

Realizing this wasn't just a social call, Morgan replied, "What is it, Maggie?"

"First, Josh, I know this is nonsense but…"

Then Maggie Loughlin related the entire story of how Edmundo Solis had first contacted her when she was the Assistant Press Secretary, had continued to contact her every day, and how he had suddenly failed to do so. She said that she was worried mostly because he seemed excited about some important new information he had and had promised to email her the following day.

Josh managed to stifle the laugh that almost came out. Fortunately, his smile and the rolled eyes were invisible to his ex-fiancée.

"Maggie, sweet…" Josh cut off the term of endearment and started again. "Maggie, I'm sure it's nothing. I'm sure he's – What's his name?"

"Eddie."

"I'm sure Eddie's fine. You gotta admit, it's a little silly for a grown man to latch onto you this way. A little creepy, too, if you ask me."

Maggie hung her head on the other end of the call. She knew Josh was right.

"But let's say everything is just as innocent as he says. Maybe he's finally got a life."

Hearing her own thoughts echoed back to her brought Maggie back to the conversation.

"I know. That's exactly what I thought, too."

"Maybe he's got a girlfriend and doesn't need to contact you every single day."

"You're right, Josh. I'll drop it. It's no big deal. Probably nothing at all. It's just that… You know how you've always had this ability to sense things? You know how you've always had these instincts about things and said you always trust your gut? Well, right now that's how I feel. But I'm being silly. I'm sure I'll hear from him soon. Or maybe not. Who knows? Thanks anyway."

The former couple spent another few seconds in a difficult attempt at small talk, punctuated with awkward intervals of silence. Finally, they hung up.

Josh Morgan looked at his watch and realized that his plane would be boarding at any moment. At that very instant, the attendant at the counter beside the gate announced that to be true.

He took up his backpack and started for the departure gate. He was fourth in line, so he didn't have to wait long for his turn to head down the ramp to the plane that would take him home. When the attendant reached for his boarding pass, Morgan paused and drew it back.

"Sir?" the airline employee said.

Morgan stared at the man.

"Sir, you can board now." This time the statement was absent the smile. "People are waiting."

"Oh… Sorry."

♦

In the office of the Press Secretary of the President of the United States, its occupant answered her call, uncharacteristically without looking at Caller ID.

"Maggie Loughlin."

"Okay, Mag. Send me everything you've got on this Eddie Solis."

Maggie stiffened in her chair and put her free hand to her mouth.

"Josh, are you sure?"

"Hey, it's me. When do I have to be sure about something to do it anyhow?"

"Thanks, Josh."

"Yeah, well, you owe me," her ex-fiancé answered with his usual reply to an expression of gratitude. He immediately regretted it. Considering how things stood between him and his former fiancée, it felt odd.

In the West Wing, Maggie immediately began to delegate some matters so that she could set about collating all she knew about her Nicaraguan pen pal.

Once she was sure she had everything ready to transmit to Morgan, she called him.

"Hi, it's me. How do you want me to get this to you? It's a lot for a text. Should I email it? Or do you want me to get it to you at your hotel?"

"Well, that's the thing. I can't get my room back or another one at my usual places."

There was a lengthy delay before Maggie spoke again.

"I don't know how you'd feel about this, but I still have our old apartment." She winced at his lack of an immediate reply.

She continued, "You'd have it all to yourself."

"You don't live there?" Josh inquired, simultaneously wondering why she still had the place if she didn't live there.

"No, I, uh… I live somewhere else."

Josh wanted to ask if she lived with someone but knew it was not only none of his business, but that he wasn't sure he wanted to know the answer.

"Sure you wouldn't mind?"

"No. The place is empty."

"Well, that gets me out of a jam. And I'm sure I'd only be there a day or two while I try to find Eddie."

"That's fine, Josh. I'll bring the information over to you. It will be good to see you again."

"Thanks, Maggie."

She was about to hang up when she heard Morgan continue.

"I'm sure he's fine, Maggie. You know, I think it's really nice that you're concerned about him like this. I always loved your tenderheartedness."

Maggie was touched and embarrassed.

"Well, I… You know,"

"And now that you're this super-bigshot, it's gracious of you to still be considerate of us little people."

"Turd."

Both smiled at each other invisibly across the cell signal.

"I'll find him. You know I was a journalist? Right?" Josh said sarcastically. "I'm good at finding things… and people."

"I know, Josh."

Neither spoke again and disconnected the call.

Maggie Loughlin held her phone to her chest and closed her eyes momentarily. When she opened them, she saw Mac Marchman retreating from her office doorway and wondered how much of her conversation with Josh he had overheard.

♦

At Reagan Airport, Josh Morgan waited his turn in the rental car line.

"This is ridiculous, Josh," he reprimanded himself.

But as he stepped forward to the counter to see if he'd have better luck getting a car than he'd had getting a hotel room, he continued, "But, this is Maggie."

CHAPTER 12

Edmundo Solis had limited light peeking through the gash in the metal wall of the building in which he was being held. But at least there was some. However, it didn't provide any illumination relative to a means of escaping his predicament.

The Gutierrez brothers were still MIA. Eddie believed that was a good thing, but it might actually be a mixed blessing. If they returned, it would probably mean he was in for additional tortured interrogation. But if they never came back, it could mean he would die of starvation alone in this dingy, smelly building.

He had eaten a small piece of his bread. It had taken all his of will power to resist scarfing down the whole piece. But he had no idea how long it would have to last. The same was true of his water. He knew his captors had only left it to allow him to live a day or two in case they needed to return and question him some more.

Eddie was bruised and battered from the beating his fellow Nicaraguans had delivered. He was sure they had gifted him with broken ribs. One eye was swollen nearly shut. And some of his lacerations and scrapes most likely should have had stitches.

During the night, a couple of cuts had opened slightly and had begun to bleed. He discovered that because rats had licked at them. He had awakened in a panic and swatted them away. And to try to prevent it from happening again he knew he needed to clean the wounds. He dared not use his precious water for that purpose, so he decided to use his saliva. His dehydrated state from thirst and his condition made it nearly impossible to come up with any but he had managed to spit on the dirty rag he had used earlier.

Eddie had thought he might be able to wave the same cloth through the hole in the wall, but there were two problems. First, even if he stood on the metal bucket under which he had hidden his food from the rodents, he couldn't reach the gash.

In addition, he hadn't heard any noise that might convey human activity nearby. There would be nobody to see his distress flag. In the early morning the blogger had heard the sound of motor vehicles, but they were far distant.

Solis realized he could try to hold out as long as possible and hope help miraculously arrived. Or when he was certain that no one was coming and that he could hold out no longer, he would end things on his own terms.

The only thing he saw that would serve the purpose was a piece of metal bending inward from the metal mesh interior wall of his cell. As he wondered if he would have the courage to take his own life, he also wondered if the metal would be sharp enough.

As he considered the possibility of cutting his wrist, he said to himself, "I hope it's sanitary. Wouldn't want it to get infected."

Edmundo Solis smiled for the first time in more than a while at his gallows humor. His attempt at making light of his situation quickly faded and he found himself having to fight off tears again.

"I'm not going to do this. I can't."

He struggled but finally stood, despite the aches and stabbing pain from his beating.

♦

Maggie and Josh had agreed to meet at the townhouse they once shared at The Wharf, a development not far from the National Mall. He arrived first and waited dutifully in the hallway. Fortunately for him, the doorman had remembered Josh and had let him in the building.

Memories flooded the former CIA Officer's consciousness. He recalled the times they stood gazing out their window over the cityscape of D.C., embracing and not making a sound, just taking in the beautiful view. It was especially pretty when it snowed, both during and afterward.

Josh also recalled his and Maggie's almost nightly ritual of sitting on the sofa. Her head was on his shoulder and his leaned on hers. And though the television was usually on, they rarely paid any attention to it.

Another recollection that sprang to mind was the occasional large breakfasts that he would make for them. Neither he nor Maggie were normally big breakfast eaters, so the occasional weekend calorie binge was a treat.

However, one memory wasn't as fond. It was from this very apartment that federal agents and District police officers had whisked Morgan away to try him for murder and then treason.

The apartment's former occupant considered what a jumble of

memories he had of this place, and what a jumble his life had become over the last couple of years.

Josh looked at the time on his phone. Although he always wore his watch, the phone was as easy to look at. Maggie was running late. As the man jingled the keys in his pants pocket, a curious thought occurred to him.

He pulled out the ring with a small number of keys on it and placed one in the deadbolt of the door. Morgan paused momentarily and turned it. The bolt retracted from the doorframe.

Morgan smiled. "Maggie never changed the locks."

He desperately wanted to get out of the hallway to avoid any uncomfortable encounters with former neighbors, but he turned the key in the opposite direction and relocked the door.

He thought perhaps Maggie might have changed the security code on the alarm system and he didn't want to activate it. But there was another reason – the real one – that he didn't go in. Given the way things stood between him and his ex-fiancée, he felt it would be a terrible invasion of her space, regardless that she didn't live there.

Josh returned his keys to his pocket and called up the novel he was reading on his phone. He had barely got past the first page when he heard the voice that he had heard daily for so long.

"Josh."

Josh Morgan looked up to see the woman he still loved approaching, followed by a serious-looking man he didn't recognize.

Josh and Maggie embraced, and though it felt awkward at first, they lingered as if neither wanted to be the one who ended it. Finally, Josh separated from Maggie. He looked past her to her unknown companion and thrust out his hand. The man didn't respond with his.

"Oh, Josh, this is Special Agent Maddox. The President thought it wise to assign Secret Service protection to me for a while because of all the things that… Well, you know."

Pangs of guilt invaded Josh's mind. He knew that all those things that had happened to Maggie that necessitated the bodyguard had been his doing.

"I'm glad, Maggie. Relieved."

"Why didn't you go in? Same key; same alarm code." She inserted her key, unlocked the door, and marched in. She was eager to get out of the watchful gaze of Agent Maddox. And though she couldn't know for sure, Maggie suspected her ex-fiancé was, too.

Josh followed Maggie in and closed the door.

Secret Service Special Agent Andre Maddox took up a watchful position in the hallway, thinking to himself, "Mac, old friend, you're going to hate getting this news." Maddox wondered how long the former couple would be inside.

Maggie set her purse and briefcase on the coffee table.

"I like what you've done with the place, Maggie."

Bewildered, Maggie glanced at the apartment and then at Morgan with a puzzled expression.

"It, uh, looks just like it did when we…," she started, but cut off when she saw Josh beginning to smile.

"Ass!" she said in response to his tease.

"It's good to see you, Maggie."

"It's nice to see you, too."

The pair was motionless, until Josh finally moved his eyes away from Maggie's.

She looked down and mumbled, "So…"

"Yeah. What have you got for me?"

"I printed out a few things, but most of what I have for you is on this thumb drive. It has copies of every email Eddie Solis has sent me. There is also a document with a link to his blog."

Josh picked up the printed documents and began to flip through them.

"There's also a profile on Eddie. When it became clear that he was maybe a bit… well…"

"Obsessed with you?"

Maggie blushed somewhat and said, "Yes. Anyhow, I had a background check done on him."

"Smart. And?"

"Honestly, Morgan, I think he's as harmless as he comes across."

Josh Morgan smiled at Maggie's use of his last name. They each used to do that a lot when they were a couple.

"Ever talk to him? You know, by phone?"

"Never."

"So, that's everything?"

"Yeah. In a few minutes you'll know everything about Edmundo Solis that I do."

Morgan didn't look up. He opened his backpack to retrieve his laptop.

"I really appreciate this, Josh. It's silly, I know."

Josh assured her, "Not at all," though he believed it was.

"Well, I, uh…"

"Yeah," Josh whispered.

"I need to get back to the office."

Morgan's acknowledgement was a soft, "Uh-huh," as he turned his attention to the task Maggie had given him.

In a way, it felt like old times to Maggie. When Josh was in "mission" mode, he often became so absorbed in it that he tuned everything out. But the inattention wasn't as irritating as it had been "back when." Maggie collected her belongings and was about to head for the door.

"Maggie…" Josh had followed her toward the door.

She turned and faced him. Each reached tentatively for the other, but this hug was deliberately shorter than the earlier one. Still, in that brief moment, unknown to the other, each closed their eyes.

Maggie left the apartment without looking back.

"I'll be in touch soon, Maggie."

Maggie Loughlin's auburn hair bounced as she nodded without speaking. She felt tears welling up but put them at bay instantly.

♦

Luis and Santos Gutierrez watched from their rented SUV as a tall, intense man surveyed the area surrounding his sedan while he held the door open for a very attractive woman. They had traded in their van for the more comfortable vehicle and had driven straight through from Norfolk. While they drove, President Zamora's intelligence department had worked up a profile of the current White House Press Secretary. In a stroke of good fortune for the operators, the address that the dictator's staff had come up with was the woman's old address. In addition, the intel stated that she shared it with a man who was a professor at Georgetown University. When Morgan had come to Washington with Maggie, he was originally going to teach Journalism at Georgetown.

The two men had unwittingly come to Maggie's and Josh's old townhouse at The Wharf while she was coincidentally there. They had arrived moments after Maggie had so they hadn't seen Morgan show up before her.

Before heading to where they believed Maggie and Morgan still lived, the Nicaraguan brothers had made a detour to a D.C city park. Luis had sat on a bench looking at his phone, with Solis's computer and mobile phone beside him. Another man joined him on the bench. The two never spoke or otherwise acknowledged each other. But when he left, the younger Gutierrez brother left the laptop and phone behind. A short time later, the second man picked up the abandoned computer and cellphone and left. The devices were safely in the hands of Nicaraguan Embassy staff who would have more success unravelling their secrets.

Now Luis looked at the photo they had downloaded from the White House website, then held it up for his brother.

"That's her," observed Santos.

"*Sí*, but that's not him," Luis replied. He held up a photo of Josh Morgan that they had found on the Georgetown University web page.

The brothers' eyes followed their target's escort as he closed the door behind her and walked to take the driver's seat. He had the look that all seasoned operators would recognize. He was dressed in a suit, but was obviously very fit, and had a very serious demeanor about him. Even the sunglasses added to their characterization of him as security personnel.

"*Hermano*, I didn't think the person in this position had a protective detail."

Luis's reply was a simple shake of the head. Then he spoke the same conclusion that his brother had reached.

"Santos, this is going to be much harder than we thought."

♦

As a former intelligence officer whose cover was that of a journalist, Josh Morgan had the research skills that was a prerequisite for both of those professions.

He had started with the missing man's website, figuring he might as well get a sense of what the man said about himself and what his labor of love entailed before moving on to what others had surmised about him.

Solis was obviously enraged about the atrocities being carried out in his home country. He railed on Nicaraguan Dictator Zamora with a fury that he never attempted to hide.

And even though the posts were surprisingly well-written and testified to an extremely intelligent man, Morgan still had come to an assessment of Edmundo Solis. He saw him as one of many who believed that just because they had the ability to answer the minimal questions it took to open most social media accounts, they had simultaneously become profound pundits about any and every topic.

Josh recalled a joke that Maggie had once told him. She had said that when she was younger, she was insecure because she didn't feel like she was an expert on anything. Then, in her words, "I discovered social media. Suddenly, I was an expert on everything."

The researcher leaned back in his chair at the kitchen table where he worked. He stretched and arched his back. Josh decided he needed caffeine.

Looking around the kitchen counter, he found that the coffee maker was gone.

"No reason Maggie wouldn't have taken that with her," he realized.

Josh continued to the built-in refrigerator and opened it to find it empty, feeling foolish for even thinking there might be a soft drink. He looked at his watch.

"1:40."

He wanted to call Maggie but realized that he had nothing that would justify reaching out to her and decided he should just let things lie. Instead, he put his computer in his backpack and slung it over his shoulder.

"No reason I can't continue this elsewhere."

In the hallway, Josh Morgan locked the door to his once-apartment, thinking again that it was somewhat odd – but nice – that Maggie hadn't changed the locks when they broke up.

♦

Santos Gutierrez said, "Doesn't look like a teacher, does he?"

His brother didn't reply but continued to compare the man wearing the coat and tie and sporting neatly combed hair in the photograph with the one walking across the parking lot of The Wharf. This man was dressed casually and needed a haircut. The sunglasses made confirmation a little difficult, as well.

"That's him, though, *mano*," he concluded, and handed him the photo of Georgetown University Visiting Professor Joshua Morgan.

"*Sí.*"

♦

Maggie knew that Josh's emotions had been stirred, just as hers had at their meeting. What she didn't know was what his expectations were of what would come from the encounter. She didn't even know what she wanted to come of it. She thought of one thing that might provide a little clarity and picked up her phone and tapped a number.

"Hi. It's me."

♦

The Nicaraguans drove past where their quarry had parked. Some distance past Morgan, Luis paused in the street. Seeing the man go into a coffee shop, the driver paused to let his brother out.

"Call if you need me to come get you, Santos. Or anything else."

Santos nodded and walked back in the direction they had seen the Press Secretary's boyfriend enter.

The ex-CIA Officer entered Swing's Coffee, at the corner of G St. NW and 17th St NW.

"Josh Morgan! As I live and breathe!'

His deceased best friend and CIA analyst Ben Reid had first introduced Josh to Swing's many years before and Josh had made it a point to get his brew there as often as possible ever since. Polly had been a barista since long before he had ever heard of the place.

Polly hurried around the bar and gave her infrequent customer a very long hug.

After a rather extended catchup conversation, Josh ordered the double-shot espresso to deliver the jolt he felt he needed. Then he would switch to a 12-ounce Latte.

Outside, being that Swing's was west of the White House complex just across from the Old Executive Office Building, Santos Gutierrez felt very conspicuous. He was certain surveillance cameras would capture his every move, especially if he lingered too long in one place.

Finally, the Nicaraguan thug felt so exposed that he called Luis to pick him up on G St. NW a little bit west of the coffee shop.

Getting in the car, he hurriedly explained the predicament and the *hermanos* agreed that they would return to the couple's apartment and resume their surveillance there.

♦

"Maggie," Mac Marchman answered. The coolness of his greeting was understandable but stung just the same.

"Mac, are we okay?"

"Why wouldn't we be?"

Maggie hated the attitude and tone of voice that men often adopted when they were trying – too hard, in her opinion – to appear unaffected by certain circumstances. But she passed it off as a "guy thing," held her tongue to stifle the retort that almost came and continued.

Mac had heard from his friend Andy Maddox, who was Maggie's daytime babysitter, about her meeting Josh Morgan at their old apartment. If he hadn't already questioned where he stood with her, that piece of news would've prompted it.

"What are you doing later, Mac?" Maggie noticed an immediate alteration in the man's disposition.

The two arranged to get together for drinks after Maggie left her office. She had warned him that it would have to be brief; that she had a special project she had to work on. She didn't tell Mac that her special project was actually one Morgan was working on for her. And she wasn't aware that he knew she had met Josh at the apartment they formerly shared. He suspected that the special project had something to do with her old fiancé, but that was okay – sort of. Things seemed like they might be back on track with Maggie Loughlin.

♦

Josh reread every syllable of Edmundo Solis' social media presence. What he decided – again – was that the man was something akin to someone who ran a radio station from his apartment with a signal that covered a meager number of city blocks. His ramblings were part conspiracy theory and part retreads of real news organizations' stories.

Solis, Morgan thought, had some delusions about the significance of what he was doing, if not about himself, as well.

"Why would anyone care what he was doing or saying? Certainly not to the point of doing something to him." And that was, after all, what Maggie was worried about, even if that possibility remained unspoken.

"Who would get worked up by him?"

"What did you say, Josh?" inquired Polly, who was clearing the table next to her customer.

"Oh, nothing. Just reading the news."

The barista smiled and returned to her place behind the counter.

There were a few things that puzzled the former spy/photojournalist.

First, Solis had, as Maggie had said, emailed her at least daily for months. Much of the time, it was twice each day, morning and night. For it to suddenly stop without an explanation to Maggie did indeed seem strange.

Secondly, he had said specifically in his last email to Maggie that he had big news, something important, and that the big reveal would come the following day. It was possible, Morgan knew, that he had made it up and was suddenly on the spot by not having anything significant to deliver. But Morgan wondered why Solis would've set himself up to look like such a fool.

No, Morgan was sure the man had something that he believed was important, whether it really was or not.

How Josh analyzed those things was largely in the context of Eddie's relationship with Maggie, even if it existed only in his mind. But there were a couple of things of real substance; factual things that gnawed at Morgan.

Eddie Solis' blog had almost no hits for its entire presence on social media. At least that was what the federal background check that Maggie had requested stated. But in the last while, the number of his followers had exploded. Well, Morgan realized, "exploded" relative to his historically paltry number of readers.

And that surge coincided almost exactly with the time the blogger began to suggest that he was onto a clandestine operation by President Zamora's regime. According to Eddie, it was in another country and the interference was intended to wreck the economy of that country and topple its government.

Within two days of first reporting that discovery, Eddie's clicks skyrocketed, by his standards, with hits occasionally reaching over two hundred per day.

And that did bother Morgan. How did so many people find out so quickly? You'd expect, Morgan thought, that the readership would climb along a curve that grew as word of his theory spread. Instead, the increase was almost a vertical spike on the graph of his traffic. It was as if a lot of people, or maybe a few people checking in repeatedly throughout the day, had a very particular interest in his tease of some new revelation.

Edmundo Solis had stated that his source was from "high in the Zamora regime."

"Could he have really stumbled onto something?"

And for the first time since Maggie had told him about the missing man, Morgan's gut began to get in line with hers.

♦

Maggie Loughlin and Mac Marchman enjoyed a single glass of wine and a brief conversation that Maggie hoped would put him at ease without leading him to think she was interested in anything serious.

When her phone chimed that she had a call, she wanted to ignore it, but when you work in the West Wing, that was frowned upon. She looked at the caller's name.

"Shit," she thought.

Maggie connected and said, "Hi. Oh. Nothing. Just having a drink with a friend." She smiled at Mac and knew it couldn't have appeared more forced. She also knew from the expression on his face that he suspected it was her former lover.

"Maggie, I can't believe I'm about to say this, but you might be right about Solis. Can you meet me at our apartment?" He knew the "our" slip was uncomfortable but decided to let it go.

Maggie smiled her artificial smile at Mac again and said, "Of course."

"Your special project?" her date asked and signaled to the bartender to close their tab.

Maggie knew she had upset Mac again but couldn't deal with it at the moment. She hugged Mac briefly around his neck, avoiding the clumsiness of whether there should be another kiss and what kind it should be.

"I'm sorry, Mac. I've got to go."

CHAPTER 13

Nicaragua became an independent republic in 1838 after gaining independence from Spain in 1821. Its history was marked by instability and brutality and through the years the government was almost perpetually corrupt and manipulative, interfering in every aspect of its citizens' lives.

Opposition to the corruption became violent. The oppressed citizens across all socio-economic classes united under the Marxist Sandinista movement and revolted in 1978. The brief uprising toppled the government. Daniel Ortega Saavedra, who had led the guerrillas during the revolution, assumed power in 1979, but as with many things, the cure turned out to be as terrible as the disease. Brutality and oppression pervaded Ortega's regime and they were in most ways worse than what they had replaced.

Free elections in 1990, 1996, and 2001 ousted Ortega from power, but economic and political recovery proved difficult, and he returned to preside over the country again. The cycle repeated itself and after a somewhat brief flirtation with democracy, the Nicaraguans faced yet another despot in Sergio Zamora.

Zamora's intelligence apparatus remained as it was in the period before his assuming his position as head of government. Domestic intelligence was still the domain of the *Dirección de Asuntos de Inteligencia.* The Directorate of Intelligence Affairs engaged in internal political espionage and that contributed to the corruption that had reared its head again.

On the other side of such matters, the Directorate of Military Intelligence was responsible for military and foreign intelligence operations, though it, too, performed internal intelligence. That included surveillance of paramilitary and opposition groups that were operating within the country.

Therefore, the lines between the DAI and DMI were indistinct. Both agencies did anything and everything ordered by *el Presidente* Zamora. When word of Edmundo's claims that he had knowledge of foreign interference by the Zamora regime reached the intelligence organizations, they immediately notified the dictator.

The most troubling aspect of the blogger's assertions was that he had received the information from someone high in the despot's circle of advisors. The social media stories posted by the man who had fled Nicaragua and now lived in the United States were short on facts, but the possibility that someone had betrayed Zamora had thrown him into a rage. He dispatched the two men he knew he could trust with loyalty and results.

The investigators were the sons of his late sister, who had died along with their father when they were just children. Sergio Zamora had taken his nephews in and raised them as his own. Their true identities were unknown to the populace of Nicaragua, but their reputations as ruthless and cruel puppets of Zamora who administered his soulless violence was widespread. Relatives of their victims who disappeared or had been killed had given them the unflattering moniker of *los crótalos*, which could mean "the rattlesnakes." But more specifically, among the people who used the term, it referred to a Bothrops asper. The Bothrops was the most venomous snake in Nicaragua; a pit viper feared widely because of its lethal potential and large size.

Despite that they knew the moniker was intended as an insult – or perhaps, because of that very thing – the brothers had taken to the nickname. Santos wore a gold earring in his right ear in the shape of a partially coiled snake. Luis had taken the even bolder step of having a similar image tattooed on his upper right chest that continued onto his right arm down to his biceps.

The dictator's cold-blooded nephews used their adopted surname most of the time within Nicaragua to capitalize on their uncle's reputation. But to shield their identities and separate themselves from their widely despised uncle, when operating abroad at the behest of their uncle, the Zamora brothers went by their birthnames, Luis and Santos Gutierrez.

Luis was the younger of the pair by a little over a year, but he was the dominant personality, generally taking the lead in most matters. However, in terms of cruelty and the ability to perform unconscionable acts without remorse, there was no distinction between the two.

While Luis slept, Santos sat behind the wheel of the SUV watching the entrance to The Wharf, where they mistakenly believed Maggie Loughlin and Josh Morgan still lived together. The old information had been reinforced by the fact that the brothers had seen both Morgan and Loughlin at the complex in the last day.

The tap on his arm and the sound of his name stirred Luis from his slumber.

"Luis. The man is here."

The brothers had parked some distance away and used binoculars for their surveillance. Across the parking lot, they saw the young man they had abandoned tailing earlier in the day because his destination was so close to the White House.

Morgan still carried his backpack and nothing else, other than a to-go cup of coffee. The Nicaraguans noticed that he lingered momentarily until a man and woman leaving the building had put some distance between them and the door, as though avoiding them.

Finally, Morgan disappeared into the complex.

"Should we take him, Luis?"

The younger brother shook his head. "We have no real use of him. He is just a teacher and wouldn't have knowledge of Solis' activities."

"Unless his girlfriend told him of the information he gave her," Santos said.

Luis lowered his binoculars and considered that possibility.

"No. We can only *think* he knows something. We *know* the woman does. We will wait for her, but if getting her proves too *difícil*, we will return to him."

Los crótalos switched positions so that Santos could get some sleep.

♦

While Maggie Loughlin and Macarthur Marchman were inside the bar enjoying their drinks, Maggie's night shift bodyguard arrived for his shift. He caught up with her and her daytime protector, Special Agent Maddox, just as they were leaving.

"Maddox."

"Oakley. Bluebird wants to go back to her former apartment."

"Copy that," Special Agent Oakley said as, over his counterpart's shoulder, he saw another Secret Service Agent leave the bar some distance behind the Secretary but turn to go another direction.

As Maggie took a seat in the back of Oakley's Agency car and was out of their sight, the two men charged with watching over the Press Secretary exchanged a glance. Oakley nodded toward the departing Agent Mac Marchman. Maddox turned to see what his fellow agent was visually pointing toward. When he saw Maggie's date moving away down the sidewalk, he turned his eyes back to his night shift relief.

He shook his head, raised his eyebrows, and shrugged. Then he mouthed the words, "Who knows?"

Oakley and Maddox both smiled, as Oakley took his seat behind the wheel, buckled in, and moved the gearshift to "D."

As the vehicle pulled away, Maggie looked at Mac on the sidewalk. She felt terrible at how her "apology" date with him had turned out, but this was important.

♦

Edmundo Solis was facing another night of imprisonment. It was all he could do to keep from panicking. He wouldn't permit himself to eat any of the bread, for fear that he wouldn't have the willpower to resist taking more than he felt was a reasonable ration. The water was another matter because he knew he had to remain hydrated.

What sounded like an occasional single tap turned into a repeated pinging on the roof and outer wall of the dilapidated old warehouse the Gutierrez brothers had left him in. Eddie had been trying to sleep, as much for attempting to take his mind off of his predicament as for need of rest. And he was groggy from weakness and his injuries. But while full consciousness was still eluding him, what ultimately brought him to complete awareness was the impact of a single drop of water splatting on the floor from a leak in the ceiling.

"Rain," he said.

Soon the drop from a leak in the ceiling turned into another and then another, until becoming almost a steady stream. The darkness outside made his cell completely devoid of light, so he had to do his work blindly.

He took the metal bucket that he had used to protect his food from the rats. Next, he fumbled around for his UPS work shirt. He tore away a strip of material, beginning at a rip in the shirt that had been put there courtesy of his fellow countrymen as they beat him. He ripped off another section of the UPS garment and wiped the interior of the bucket. He poured a small amount from his water bottle onto it, hoping he would be able to replace it in short order. Then he repeated his effort to clean the metal bucket as much as possible. He felt inside the interior that he couldn't see for the darkness and wiped away further grime that he felt.

Once Eddie had satisfied himself that the container was as clean as it was going to get, he stretched the remainder of the shirt over the bucket and used the strip he had just torn away to wrap around the rim of the bucket, overlapping his shirt. Finally, he placed the pail with the makeshift filter directly under the steady drip of water from the ceiling.

"At least it will be a bit cleaner," he hoped.

Eddie knew that without the protection of the bucket, his bread would be like a buffet to the rodents that would appear shortly. But water was more important than the bread.

Still, he wasn't going to leave the loaf for the rats. So, he began to eat it. Eddie had trouble controlling his feeding frenzy. After a few voracious bites, the prisoner stopped.

"Have to try to keep some," he determined.

While he puzzled how he would protect the loaf of bread, the rain stopped. The steady drip turned into drops, which turned into droplets. Finally, the leak from the ceiling ceased altogether.

Edmundo's scream bounced around the metal walls of his room and the roof of the building.

"*Te maldigo, Dios!*" He followed the curse toward his Creator with, "*Por que? Por que?*"

Solis began to shake uncontrollably, as he fully succumbed to the rage and feeling of abandonment. But suddenly a flash of light appeared briefly in the gash on the exterior wall of the warehouse. Then it shone again, sustaining itself a short time and flickering as it did. The crash of thunder that followed the lightning rang on the metal exterior of his prison. Another flash of lightning shone through the wall, followed by another deafening clap of thunder.

Immediately after that boom, the room echoed with a deluge from the heavens. This time the rain pounded above him, without a buildup. There were no teases of a few drops at a time. It was as if the entirety of the clouds dropped all at once and washed away Eddie's anger. He could hear the steady splatter of water as it pummeled the cotton stretched atop the bucket. It might have been only a small stream, but it sounded like a torrent to Edmundo. Another bolt of lightning sparked through the tear in the wall and, though dim, lit up the water of life that was falling toward the small reservoir.

"*O, Dios… Dios! Gracias! Gracias!*"

♦

Secret Service Agent Spence Oakley stopped outside the door of The Wharf. He rushed to open his sedan's door for his protectee, surveying the surroundings as he did.

White House Press Secretary Margaret Loughlin exited the back seat, gave a cursory smile and "thank you" to the agent and headed rapidly for the apartment complex's door. Oakley fell in behind her.

"Ma'am, wait!"

Maggie stopped abruptly as she stared without emotion at the man who was slowing her down.

"Secretary Loughlin… please let me do my job."

"Sorry," she blurted out impatiently. Then Maggie followed it with a more heartfelt recognition of the agent's position.

"I'm sorry, Agent Oakley. I really am." She smiled and paused to let her Secret Service guardian take the lead.

"Thank you, Madam Secretary."

Oakley's pace was significantly slower than his charge's. He was deliberate, controlled. He looked forward and back and peered around each corner before proceeding. He led Maggie onto the elevator and pushed the button.

Oakley looked at Maggie, who he could tell wanted to sigh.

In short order, the elevator stopped. The Agent prepared for whatever danger might appear as the doors parted, but there was none. He escorted the woman to the door and turned the knob. The unlocked door necessitated another layer of security.

Morgan looked up with a frown at seeing Oakley enter first. Maggie followed. The agent searched the apartment as a precaution.

Once she thought the agent was out of earshot, Maggie gave her former fiancé a very serious look. Her eyebrows slanted downward, and her head tilted.

"Sir, are you a bad guy?" she asked earnestly.

"Sometimes, ma'am," replied Josh just as seriously.

Agent Oakley had heard the exchange and didn't think the question or answer to be very funny. But nobody would've known from his expression.

"I'll be in the car, ma'am. Call when you're ready to leave and I'll meet you here."

"Yes, Agent Oakley. And thank you. Really." She followed him to the door and locked it behind him.

♦

The rain lasted for about forty minutes and remained steady and hard for the entire time. When it quit, it did so as abruptly as it had started.

Eddie waited until he could no longer hear drops hitting what had collected in the bucket in order to wait for every possible drop. He removed the cloth filter he had created from his work shirt from the pail and lowered his hand into the water that had seeped through it into the receptacle.

"About a half inch," he guessed. It wasn't much but he felt it would fully replenish his bottle, so he allowed himself a relatively generous drink. He knew that what remained in the plastic container would be the last sterile liquid he would have for an unknown amount of time.

CHAPTER 14

"Those are the things that disturb me, Maggie," Josh said once he had concluded a summary of his thoughts about the missing – *possibly* missing Edmundo Solis. "Any one thing doesn't amount to much, but…"

"… But together, it's pretty compelling," his ex-girlfriend finished.

"I don't think I'd go as far as 'compelling,' but, yeah… it's something to wonder about. It's suspicious. Have you checked where he works? Asked about him, or tried to talk to him there?"

Maggie's eyes widened. She turned her head and pushed her hand through her auburn tresses.

"I'm an absolute idiot," she uttered. "Shit, Josh. I feel so stupid."

"Don't worry, Maggie. You can check in the morning."

Josh Morgan and Maggie Loughlin sat in silence until Morgan ended the pause.

"You know, Maggie. This is still probably nothing. Probably going to be a logical explanation for his not getting in touch with you."

"But it is compelling," Maggie said, blue eyes twinkling at the tease.

"Suspicious," Morgan corrected.

They smiled.

♦

"*Si. Gracias. Adios, Tio.*" With that, Luis concluded the call. When other people were present Sergio Zamora was *el Presidente*. But in private, he was still Uncle Sergio.

The older brother stirred from his nap just as the call ended.

"What did he say, *mano*?"

"He isn't pleased with the lack of a resolution, Santos." Luis scowled at his disclosure. "He believes the lunatic Solis still has information to divulge. He blames us for not getting it."

"What does he want us to do, Luis?"

The younger of *los crótalos* sneered.

"He said we should go to him and either get the information or kill him."

"Did you tell him about the woman?"

"No. Until we have something to show for our efforts, we should keep it secret."

"So, we are going back to Norfolk?"

"Not yet, brother."

♦

"Hey, Tom."

"Hi, Josh. Miss me already?" former Special Forces Master Sergeant asked his co-CIA contractor.

"Yeah, something like that. Anything on your plate right now?"

"Oh, the remaining crumbs of a burger and some fries," he quipped, looking down at his dinner. "But it's not really a plate. It's one of those little Styrofoam takeout boxes."

"Smartass. You know what I mean."

Josh's expression as he looked at her told Maggie that Lechler was being a smart aleck. He shook his head and rolled his eyes.

"Hi, Sergeant Lechler," Maggie said loudly enough that he could hear her over Josh's phone.

Maggie had met the ex-Green Beret along with the surviving members of his A-Team when they visited Josh in Landstuhl Regional Medical Center near Ramstein Air Base in Germany. Her then-fiancé had met the Army warrior in Russia and had been seriously wounded there. She knew from her boss, President Hendrickson, that Josh and Lechler were now working together on an *ad hoc* basis for Betsy Parnell at CIA.

Lechler needed a moment to put things together in his mind and make an assumption of the woman's identity. Finally, he responded.

"Is that Maggie? Wow!"

"Tom, I need your help on…," Josh Morgan said. Lechler had told Josh repeatedly over the last few months what a fool he was for breaking up with her; so much so that Josh was tired of hearing it. He was trying to move quickly past the awkward occurrence and the disclosure that he was with his former fiancée. Tom Lechler wouldn't have it.

"Tell her 'hi' for me. Better yet, put her on the phone."

The next attempt at moving on was more successful.

"Tom, can you go to Norfolk for a day or two? I need you to track someone down."

When MSG Lechler retired a few months earlier, he had convinced his wife Ava to move with him back to Fort Bragg, North Carolina, where he had trained in the U.S. Army Special Forces. Lechler had hoped that they could renew friendships with other couples they had met during his time at the John F. Kennedy Special Warfare Center and School. However, while the former Sergeant had picked up with some of his Army buddies, his wife's attempts at female companionship didn't work out. Not long after they moved in, his wife left him and returned to their previous home in Kentucky. The divorce was in process.

Lechler sat up and set his fast-food containers on the coffee table.

"What's up?"

"Yes, I'm with Maggie. I'm trying to help her find someone."

"Family? A friend?"

"Actually, she's never met the guy."

Josh filled Lechler in on the entire story. His friend had the same initial reaction as Josh.

"You know this is kind of crazy… right?"

"Yeah, I think so. So, does Mag. But it's weird enough that she – *we* want to follow up on it. You're less than four hours from Norfolk; about the same distance as I am. If you can, I'd like you to head up there for me. I need to check on some things here."

Tom Lechler's immediate thought was to wonder why Josh couldn't – or wouldn't go. Maybe he just wanted to stay around Maggie. He hoped so.

"Whatever you need, buddy. I'll drive up there tonight."

"Thanks, Tom, but tomorrow's fine. It's late."

"Okay, Josh. Send me all you've got on this Solis guy."

The men ended their call.

"What things do you need to do here?" Maggie inquired. She received a somewhat embarrassed expression in return.

"Things," Morgan stammered. "Just things."

Changing the subject quickly, he said, "Are you hungry? We could go somewhere."

"I can't, Josh. I have some work to do."

Josh appeared disappointed, but it was the truth.

"That's fine. I…"

"You could go get us some takeout… If you don't mind, that is."

"Love to," the former fiancé said to his ex.

♦

Luis and Santos Gutierrez, aka Zamora, aka los *crótalos*, watched the man they knew as a temporary Georgetown University professor walk to his car from the exit of The Wharf. He gave a curt wave to his girlfriend's bodyguard sitting alone in his sedan. It appeared the agent didn't return the gesture.

The Nicaraguan thugs looked at each other. Never ones to give much thought to strategic planning, they instead relied on reckless immediacy and boldness in their violence. Luis exited the vehicle and walked ahead toward the door of the complex while his older brother waited.

As his younger brother passed the Press Secretary's protector, Santos saw that the man immediately went on alert. Santos had exited his SUV quietly and moved along the same path his fellow *crótalo* had taken. As Luis neared the doorway, Santos was only a dozen feet from the bodyguard's vehicle, remaining careful to approach from his blind spot.

The doorman who manned the entrance each night greeted the younger Gutierrez with his iPad on which he had a list of expected guests to The Wharf. But before he could inquire as to the visitor's name, Luis pulled a suppressed Israel Weapons Industries Jericho 941 and fired into the man's chest. The doorman dropped to the pavement.

Secret Service Agent Spencer Oakley swung the car door open and stepped out, drawing his handgun. However, his distraction by the scene unfolding in front of him left him vulnerable to Santos who was now only steps behind. The Nicaraguan fired his gun at the same time that Oakley was firing his. The agent fell forward from the jolt of a .45 caliber slug hitting the back of his body armor. The force of the gunshot threw his aim off and the 9mm round from his Glock 19 grazed Luis Gutierrez in his left biceps.

The younger brother put his right hand, still holding his gun, to the wound and turned to see Santos fire a round directly into Oakley's head.

While the older brother dragged the agent's body into his car, the younger continued his walk into the building, pausing as he likewise put a fatal shot into the doorman's forehead.

Santos hurriedly shut the door of the deceased agent's sedan and rushed to drag the dead Wharf employee into the building and behind his desk.

Only then did it occur to the assassins to look about for any bystanders. There were none.

"Your arm…"

"It's fine."

The men returned their handguns to their waistbands and marched to the elevator and pressed the button for their destination.

♦

"What'd you forget?" Maggie asked as she opened the door.

Her smile quickly disappeared as a Latin man of about her height rushed in and pushed her roughly. She stumbled awkwardly backward and to her left, crashing into the end table by the sofa.

Santos Gutierrez looked down both directions of the hallway, then hurriedly closed the door.

Maggie dared not get up. The numbers were decidedly against her. The man who had attacked her stepped forward and straddled her. Though she tried to cover her head with her arms, the back of his hand burst through her attempted defense and struck the right side of her face.

Luis grabbed her left wrist and yanked her upward, but before Maggie reached her feet, he slung her onto her sofa.

"Don't fight!" the Nicaraguan said in a low voice to avoid attracting attention from elsewhere in the apartment building. However, to Maggie the intensity of the whisper sounded like a scream.

"I wasn't fighting," Maggie retorted, trying to demonstrate some resolve and courage. She desperately wanted to rub her bruised face but wouldn't give the men the satisfaction. She glared at them.

"Where is your boyfriend?"

"He's not my boyfriend. And I guess he went home."

"Lying *puta*" preceded another backhanded blow. "We know you both live here."

Luis drew back his hand again. This time Maggie refused to cover up.

"We haven't lived here for months," she said defiantly. "You've got some bad information."

The intruders looked at each other, not knowing whether to believe her or not. They spoke in Spanish and a very obvious characteristic suddenly took on significance. These were Latin males. They were not Middle Eastern, Russian, or, presumably, U.S. citizens, as she might've expected from the things in Morgan's past that she had been caught up in.

"Eddie," she thought.

The next words from her attacker confirmed her suspicion.

"You will tell us everything you know about Nicaragua and your source, Edmundo Solis."

♦

Mac Marchman felt like a stalker. He was more confused than jealous. So far there was nothing serious between him and Maggie, but he felt like a fool.

"If she still has feelings for Morgan, she should tell me. And if she doesn't, what's the deal? Dammit!" he said. He often spoke aloud to himself when he was trying to sort something out. At least, he did when nobody was around.

He knew Oakley was her night detail, and he knew where he was keeping watch at the moment.

Taking his keys from the small table by his apartment door, Mac determined that, foolish or not, he was going to perform a little overwatch on Ms. Loughlin himself.

♦

Luis and Santos Gutierrez were less impulsive leaving the townhouse building than going in. After all, they had left a pair of bodies behind them, and they couldn't be sure whether anyone had discovered them. So, Santos went first. He checked the hallways and texted Luis, who followed him that far. Then he checked outside. Remarkably, there was no law enforcement activity. He alerted his brother.

When the younger Gutierrez got word that things were clear, he rushed out the door with his captive. He hated that she was bruised. It would be apparent to anyone who saw them that she was injured and in distress. Furthermore, Luis knew that the bodyguard's associates could appear at any time. He assumed the man was Secret Service because of Loughlin's position in the White House. And that would mean that he reported in regularly and that the absence of a word from him would bring investigators rushing to his last location.

"Nobody saw you?" a somewhat flustered Santos asked Luis when he shoved his prisoner into the back seat and joined her there.

"No. And why are you acting like such a *mamaberga*. We've taken *jañas* before."

"*Si*, but none of those women worked for *la Presidenta de los Estados Unidos*. And don't call me a cocksucker. *Andate a la mierdad*, Luis."

"Ha! *You* go to hell, Santos." The younger brother laughed, but he was just as nervous as Santos. Not only had they never operated in the U.S., let alone dealt with a person of this importance, their Uncle Sergio's patience was waning.

♦

U.S. Secret Service Agent Mac Marchman was on his way to join the protection detail watching over the President's Press Secretary, though he really wasn't going there in an official capacity. He was going to spy on the protectee as a semi-jealous, boyfriend wannabe.

Mac was mildly concerned. He had called his fellow agent, who didn't pick up.

As he approached his destination, two federal cars roared past him with lights flashing. While he couldn't be sure which agency's cars they were, he felt a knot in his stomach. He flipped the switch that activated his own lights and fell in behind them. Agent Marchman called his office and got the scoop: possible agent down.

♦

Josh Morgan assumed Maggie still liked Chinese and the same type of Chinese dishes. He couldn't imagine that her tastes had changed that much since their breakup. The distinct aroma from the oriental dishes on the seat beside him was making him increasingly hungry.

His phone chimed an incoming call. Josh expected that Maggie was calling with another errand to run for her. Or perhaps she wondered what was taking so long. However, the caller was someone else.

"Hey, Tom. What's up?"

The conversation was brief. Lechler had called to say that he was on his way to Norfolk. He couldn't sleep and decided he might as well make use of the time to get in some or all of the three-and-a-half-hour drive to Virginia.

After the discussion, the retired soldier got to the real topic he wanted to cover.

"You still with Maggie?" Lechler whispered, in case she was indeed around.

"No. Sorry to disappoint you, pal."

"Aw, shit. I was hoping…"

"I know what you were hoping, Tom."

After a brief gap, Morgan elaborated on his half-truth.

"Okay. To tell you the truth, man, I went out for Chinese and I'm on my way back there now. Satisfied?"

Josh Morgan could hear the smile in the dead air.

♦

Mac Marchman's was the third car in the procession that pulled into the parking lot of The Wharf. He fell in behind the other agents streaming from the cars and rushing toward the sedan.

At first, none had their guns drawn, but Mac observed that the first Agent to reach Oakley's car recoiled as soon as he looked inside. Immediately he drew his service weapon and spun around, head rotating rapidly in all directions.

As if brought to attention by their conductor, the rest of the orchestra likewise retrieved their Glocks. If they hadn't been on full alert upon arriving, they certainly were now. Agent Marchman joined the others, brandishing his own handgun. Some took cover behind parked vehicles or whatever other protection they could find. Others fanned out to more distant locations.

Two Agents of the U.S. Secret Service bolted for the door to the building and took positions on each side. Only when they were situated there with guns at the ready did one of the men look back in the dim light of the parking area to see a pool of thick red liquid on the asphalt. It wasn't much of a surprise since there was an agent down, but it was disturbing just the same.

The federal officer on the hinge side of the building's glass door stooped to put his head at a lower-than-normal distance from the ground in the event someone inside was ready to fire at the agent's next move. He thrust his head around the edge of the door for a quick glimpse into the foyer, then snapped back into his concealed location. In the process, he saw a streak of blood across the tiled floor.

The Agent's expression, unreadable to most people, conveyed to his party that something was amiss inside. From his vehicle in which he had just arrived, Special Agent Andre Maddox peered through binoculars into the foyer. Seeing nobody there, he signaled to his two counterparts beside the door that all appeared okay. Still, the two agents breached with vigilance. The one on the door's handle side flung it open powerfully. Then while his partner seized the edge of the opening door, he stepped into the opening with his gun leveled.

The second Agent at the door mimicked the man in the lead and followed him in.

A quick, though thorough sweep of the interior revealed no danger, but the body of the doorman/security guard sat nearly upright, leaned against the wall behind the counter.

Special Agent Maddox entered the room, followed closely by Mac Marchman, who, ignoring proper Agency procedure, rushed to the door to the stairwell. With handgun prepared for action, he swung the heavy door open, looked in, and, seeing nobody, scrambled up the flights to Maggie's floor.

To Mac's horror, the door to the townhouse was partially open. With the same caution every other Agent exercised in a breach, he assessed first and then bolted through the entryway.

An end table was turned over, but nothing else seemed out of place. An examination of the entire apartment turned up nothing, so he holstered his Glock 19 and looked about for any clue as to where Maggie was and what kind of danger – if any – she was in.

Special Agent Maddox appeared at the doorway.

"Bluebird?"

"She's gone," Agent and prospective suitor Macarthur Marchman replied.

♦

A few miles away from The Wharf, a black SUV had crossed the Potomac River into Virginia from the District of Columbia.

Santos Gutierrez was behind the wheel as the vehicle cruised down I-395. His brother sat in the back with the White House Press Secretary.

Maggie knew her outlook was bleak. She had no blindfold or head covering preventing her from seeing the faces of her kidnappers or where they traveled.

For their part, the Nicaraguan kidnappers knew they had acted with a recklessness that could have botched the whole episode. But each feared their uncle's wrath, which was often powerful despite his affection for his nephews. The Latinos were glad to be out of Washington.

♦

Before former Wharf resident Josh Morgan turned the corner onto the street that led to the townhouses, he saw reflections of blue and red lights dancing on the buildings before him. Behind him, another set of flashing lights approached. He watched in his exterior rearview mirror as the emergency vehicle caught up with and passed him when he stopped to yield to it.

Oddly, despite the fact that the ambulance's lights flashed, its siren wasn't on, and the driver didn't seem to be in much of a hurry.

Morgan had no reason to suspect that anything had happened to Maggie, but the EMT truck turned the corner ahead of him in the direction of The Wharf.

Josh Morgan raced to the intersection and when he turned, he saw a mix of six or seven sedans and SUVs in the parking lot of his former home. The fleet of vehicles included D.C. Police cars. Unmarked conveyances were spread throughout and none of the officials scattered about moved with any apparent urgency.

He touched Maggie's name on his phone, but the call went straight to voicemail.

"Shit!" Morgan shouted loudly.

♦

Edmundo Solis had drunk too liberally from the rainwater that he had collected in the bucket below the leak in the roof of the warehouse where he remained trapped. His good fortune at the downpour had given him unwarranted confidence that things looked better. His body had cried for hydration, and he had yielded to it.

Eddie had eaten much of the bread that his captors had left for him. He had placed the remnants on a metal crossbeam of the wall facing the outside of the warehouse in an effort to keep them from the disgusting rodents in the room with him. Some presented themselves occasionally throughout the day. At night their numbers multiplied.

As he knew from his experience as a child in Managua, Nicaragua, very little prevented rats from going wherever they wanted. So, the final morsels of bread fell victim to the creatures' relentless attempts. The few crumbs that remained were scattered on the floor beneath where the Nicaraguan had placed the remainder of the only food he had.

With little water left, Eddie knew his time was running out. Short of another deluge to add to his almost depleted supply of water, it would be exhausted in less than a day. And even though Solis craved to be free to continue his investigation into the crimes of Nicaraguan Dictator Zamora, he wasn't going to endure the agony of death by starvation and water deprivation. He would find another way.

But that time had not yet come.

♦

Josh stopped short of where a District of Columbia Metropolitan Police Officer was positioned to prevent any traffic from entering the lot. He slammed on the brakes, scattering a bagful of Kung Pao Chicken, fried rice, and spring rolls onto the passenger side floorboard. He bolted from his car, leaving its door open, and walked briskly toward the officer.

The policeman put his left hand up, palm facing the approaching man. His right hand moved to rest on his holstered handgun.

Josh slowed his pace and raised his hands to show they were empty. The police officer lowered his left hand, but his right remained on his service weapon.

"I need to get inside. I live here."

Josh hoped the disclosure might make a difference in gaining access to his and Maggie's former home. He would deal with any fallout from his white lie later if it developed.

"Sorry, sir. Nobody is allowed inside just yet." The officer's demeanor eased somewhat but his gun hand remained in place.

"Can you tell me what's happened, Officer?" Josh strained to look over the Metro Policeman's shoulder. Through the open driver-side door to a sedan, he saw a body slumped across the seat with a dress jacket covering its head and torso. A man with a waistband-holstered handgun and without his coat stood nearby. Ahead of him, an ambulance that had obviously arrived prior to the one Josh followed in blocked his view into the apartment building.

While Josh surveyed the scene before him, he sensed another emergency vehicle's strobing lights behind him. The SUV slowed enough for the driver to show his credentials before moving to the crime scene.

Out of the truck stepped Keith Cortland, the man Morgan knew to be Director of the United States Secret Service.

"This isn't good," he realized. Rather than out of his understanding of the seriousness of a slain agent, his worry came mostly from the fact that Maggie was under Secret Service protection.

Josh Morgan nodded to the officer who had blocked him from The Wharf and walked away to employ the device that would bypass the human barriers to the complex. He hoped he would have better luck this time. But as before, he immediately heard Maggie's voicemail greeting. He pressed the pound key icon to bypass it.

"Maggie, please call me!"

The former fiancé waited a moment and then called his ex-fiancée again to leave a more extended message.

CHAPTER 15

Inside the townhouse Maggie and Josh had once shared, Secret Service Agent Mac Marchman heard a musical tone. It was Maggie's phone. Hoping it might be her, he grabbed the evidence bag that contained it and looked through the plastic at the display.

Mac read "Josh" before it disappeared.

"Dammit!"

In only a matter of seconds, the phone rang again.

The Secret Service Agent holding the evidence bag saw the caller's ID and opened the clear plastic container and pressed the green circle.

♦

At the edge of the parking lot of his former home, Josh Morgan breathed an immediate sigh of relief at the recognition that Maggie was answering. But the feeling evaporated when a man's voice greeted him.

"Mr. Morgan, this is Special Agent Marchman with the U.S. Secret Service."

A wave of nausea swept over Josh.

"Is Magg… Is Secretary Loughlin with you?" the Agent asked.

"What!? No! I mean…What's happened to Maggie?"

"Where are you, Mr. Morgan?"

"Answer me!" Josh paced frantically and pushed his left hand through his hair. His eyes scanned the area, looking for some way past the security personnel to the apartment.

"Where are you?" It was more a demand this time.

Morgan's breath was escaping in irregular bursts. His mind was racing to understand what was happening.

"I'm outside," he finally answered. "What is…," he began before the connection fell silent.

Josh looked at the phone. His face flushed as he whispered, "Fuck."

He resumed pacing, trying to determine some way, *any* way, to get into the building. None was obvious. As he looked over the area again, Morgan saw a man walking past the emergency vehicle that blocked the foyer. His brisk pace and direct eye contact with Josh, even across the considerable distance, made it apparent that he was heading toward the former CIA Officer.

Morgan typed in a quick text message and placed his phone in his shirt pocket.

Josh hadn't recognized the name, which was uncharacteristic for him, but upon seeing Agent Marchman's face, he remembered him from their few encounters during the time when Former President Weston was ill with what was at first believed to be a naturally caused stroke.

"Agent Marchman, please, can you tell me what's going on?"

"Were you with Secretary Loughlin tonight?"

Morgan understood the serious demeanor of the federal agent. They were always like that. Plus, they had apparently just lost one of their own. But this man's tone seemed to convey some personal animosity, which Josh didn't understand.

♦

Retired Master Sergeant Tom Lechler settled into his room in the Days Inn on West Atlantic Street in Emporia, Virginia. He had driven just over two hours and had grown sleepy during his drive northward from Fort Bragg. Besides, he didn't know what he was supposed to do when he got to Norfolk. So, he decided he would crash for the night and then hop onto U.S. Highway 58 East for the remaining seventy-five miles or so to Norfolk.

Lechler touched his pants pocket and then looked at his go bag on the bed. He checked the exterior pockets.

"Crap," the ex-soldier mumbled to himself and left his room to retrieve his phone that he had apparently left in his truck.

When he got his phone, out of habit, Lechler touched the display, which came alive with a notification of a text from his buddy.

"Maybe I'll finally find out something about what I'm supposed to be doing," he hoped.

As a highly trained veteran of countless special operations, Lechler was skilled at managing his emotions when hearing unfortunate news. But as he read this message, even if his expression didn't betray his worry, he felt a pang in his stomach.

maggie's missing

♦

As Morgan continued pressing Agent Marchman for information and the federal officer posed his own questions, both heard the former CIA spook's phone chime that a message had arrived. Morgan retrieved it from his pocket immediately and looked at the announcement.

Agent Marchman asked, "Is it Maggie?" and even took Morgan's hand and turned it toward himself in an attempt to also read the message.

Morgan forcefully twisted the device away from Marchman and read it. Then he turned it back toward the agent to show that it was from Tom Lechler. He used his thumb to hide the message he had sent Lechler about Maggie being missing, though he didn't figure it would matter. He just didn't like the idea of disclosing things to this federal agent.

And in addition to the man's aggressive presumption with regard to the text, another thing bothered Morgan.

Why had Marchman called Maggie by her first name?

The former federal officer stared at the current one before him. Morgan's eyes furrowed and he felt a slight sneer manifest itself. He didn't exactly know why, but his annoyance with the man had turned to dislike.

♦

The abducted Press Secretary stared out the window of the Chevy SUV. A light drizzle had begun, which she felt was perfectly suited to her circumstances. She wondered how things would end.

Maggie didn't know of the killing of the door attendant at the Wharf or of her Secret Service watchman, though she had wondered how her captors had managed to get past Oakley on their way into the apartment building and again, on their way out with her.

She knew that once the Secret Service learned she was missing, they would be all over it. But the other person she knew would move heaven and earth looking for her was Josh.

She smiled a bit at the realization that his stated motive for breaking up with her was to protect her from the violence that had continually invaded his life and affected her. Yet here she was again in the midst of a personal horror and this time it had nothing to do with Josh.

As the tires sizzled atop the wet pavement, Maggie's smile faded, and her eyes misted.

♦

Special Agent Marchman continued to press Morgan for any information he might have with regard to his former fiancée's whereabouts. The two men had moved to Marchman's sedan to escape the drizzle that had appeared.

Josh didn't know if Maggie had disclosed her concerns about the possible disappearance of Edmundo Solis. He decided that, if she hadn't, the Secret Service could uncover that on its own. And he knew they would, if only because Maggie had requested and received a background check on her Nicaraguan correspondent.

"When did you get in town, Mr. Morgan?"

"Yesterday."

Marchman waited for Morgan to add to his reply, but the former spy never offered information beyond an answer to what was asked.

The Secret Service Agent snorted slightly in objection to his subject not being more forthcoming.

"And how did you come to visit with Secretary Loughlin?"

"We're old friends."

"You were engaged, weren't you?"

"Yes."

"But not anymore?"

"Correct."

The Special Agent pursed his lips. Morgan thought it showed a growing impatience with him.

"Any possibility of getting back together?"

Morgan thought that to be an odd and completely irrelevant query, but he maintained a perfect poker face. Still, he thought he'd play with the opportunity a bit.

"You know, I never say never. We'd been together a long while. And in the last day since we've talked… Well, I wouldn't have thought we'd be together again, but some feelings have…" Morgan stopped there and shrugged, realizing his words were very true.

The questioner paused and bit at his lower lip. Morgan noticed.

"When did you last see Secretary Loughlin?"

"About an hour-and-a-half ago." This time Morgan elaborated on the amount of time he had been with Maggie that evening and the decision to get takeout. He left out the part about their working together because of Maggie's concern for Eddie Solis. Then a worrisome realization struck Morgan like a bolt of lightning.

Spread across the dining room table in the apartment where he and Maggie had worked earlier in the evening were his laptop and all the documents related to Edmundo Solis. Undoubtedly, the Secret Service had the collection of information in hand. So, why had Marchman asked him. Perhaps he was waiting to see what Josh would say. And that made Morgan think he should divulge what he knew.

But before the questioned could reveal the new information to the questioner, the latter got the distant look of a man obviously listening to a voice in his earpiece.

Marchman's eyes settled directly on his person of interest again, but his words were slow in coming.

"Director Cortland wants me to bring you to the apartment."

Morgan only nodded and opened the car door. He waited on the federal agent, who was looking away and who was noticeably less enthusiastic about ending the interview. Finally, Marchman emerged from his Agency car and followed Morgan toward the building.

♦

Eddie Solis heard the light tapping of raindrops on the roof. Earlier he had stretched the shirt onto the metal bucket again to filter the water in case of another rain shower.

He listened in the darkness for the sound of water splattering on the cotton shirt. Hearing nothing, he felt for the bucket as a reference point and moved his other hand above it. He held it there. It took a few seconds for a drop to hit his palm. A longer interval preceded the next drip of water to arrive.

The Nicaraguan blogger knew that the rain would have to increase dramatically to provide an amount of any consequence.

He slid on his butt back to a point where he could rest his back against the wall, hearing the sound of scurrying feet as he did. He even had to brush away one of the rats as he moved. Considering the relatively short time the rodents had shared occupancy of the room with him, they were already growing accustomed to him and therefore, less wary.

Solis felt an overwhelming sense of dread at what seemed to be the inevitable conclusion to his ordeal. He seemed to remember reading that a person might live up to two months on water alone. But he was going to run out of water in the morning without some miracle. And his recollection was that without food or water, one might live as long as three weeks, but the likelihood was around seven or eight days.

Eddie wondered what his remaining days would be like. Would he be in such a state of suffering that he wouldn't want to push on? However, the longer he held out, the more opportunity there would be for rain and additional water to let him live longer.

No sooner had that glimmer of hope occurred to him than Solis' thoughts returned to wondering why he would want to extend his life. If there was no promise of rescue or escape, why would he want to stretch out his agony?

So, for every notion that gave the blogger hope and a firm sense of determination, another scenario invaded his consciousness that shattered them.

Edmundo Solis determined he would try to rest and deal with the range of possible outcomes the next morning. He shifted to try to gain a more comfortable sitting position. He lay his head against the wall, let out a huge sigh, and brushed away a rat that was crawling up his leg.

♦

"Director," Morgan said.

"Morgan. I should've known," answered Secret Service Chief Keith Cortland. The Director extended his hand, much to the chagrin of Mac Marchman.

"I'd forgotten you and Secretary Loughlin were an item at one time."

"Yes, sir. Mind if I take a look around?" the former spy asked, cutting right to the chase.

"Not at all. In fact, we're hoping you might see something that can shed some light on things. Just don't move anything."

"Of course not, Director."

"If you do see anything that might help with the investigation, please tell the Police Detective in charge. The murders and break-in are technically Metro's jurisdiction. We're just a cooperating party at this time. Here comes the lead detective now."

Josh turned to greet the man. The look of disbelief on D.C. Detective Dillon Howard's face was as unequivocal as Morgan's.

"Damn," both men said simultaneously.

Detective Howard put his hand out.

"No hard feelings?"

Morgan resisted taking Howard's hand.

"Not if they would get in the way of finding Maggie."

Dillon Howard had been the lead in questioning Morgan when he was arrested for murder and treason. Jurisdictional authority had been cloudy at the time. The murder – rather alleged murder – of NSA Deputy Director Everson Blake had occurred in Texas; a fact that ultimately led to dismissal of that charge. The Federal Prosecutor in the District, who had the additional duty of prosecuting some aspects of criminal activity in Washington had tried to make the case that he had the authority to bring the charges from both a federal and local standpoint. The prosecutor was part of a conspiracy to take Morgan down for the crime, of which he was actually guilty, and moving the case out of Texas was imperative.

A pardon by President Hendrickson voided the treason charge.

"Just doing my job, Morgan," Howard insisted. "And I ultimately came to believe that you were being set up, just as you said all along."

Morgan folded his arms and continued to stare at the detective.

"As a member of the Department, I can't apologize on its behalf, but as a private citizen I can say that I regret the whole thing ever happened and offer you my personal apology."

Detective Howard held his hand out again, which his former murder suspect took.

"Accepted. Thanks." Morgan still held some animosity toward the man but believed his gesture to be sincere.

Howard swiveled his head around and made a sweeping wave of his hand around the room.

"Anything stick out?"

Morgan only had one thing on his mind.

"What have you found so far?"

"Not much. Secretary Loughlin's purse and phone. The room was just as you see. A couple of pieces of furniture turned over, suggesting a struggle – but not much of one."

"Find any notes? Anything she might've been working on?"

Morgan held his breath while anticipating the police detective's answer, simultaneously looking at the dining table where he and Maggie had looked over her information about Edmundo Solis.

"Not onc damned thing."

Morgan hoped his relief wasn't obvious.

"That does bring me to a question I have. What were you and the Secretary doing here?"

The ex-boyfriend of the head of the White House Press Department had thought through his answer to this question. It was the same one he had given to Agent Marchman when he had asked outside.

"You know that Maggie – the Secretary – and I were engaged a while back. We were mostly catching up."

"But why here? Kinda odd to come back to the place you lived to talk."

"I left Washington shortly after our breakup and haven't been back. I wasn't sure if I'd left anything of mine here."

"And Secretary Loughlin wouldn't have collected it for you? She wouldn't have let you know if you'd left anything important behind?"

Morgan saw that, unlike Marchman who seemed to be personally invested in the answers Morgan provided, Detective Howard was all business – and sharp as a tack.

The detective persisted with his more direct manner.

"Why did checking for things you might've left take so long? You decided to get takeout?"

"Like I said, we got to talking. Just catching up."

Morgan thought the man's smile a little suggestive. And when he lifted his chin and raised his eyebrows, Morgan resented it.

Silence extended into seconds until the detective waved his hand around again.

"Please. Look the place over."

Morgan knew he had to appear as though he was conducting a general inspection rather than looking for specific items. But documents and a thumb drive with information all related to Edmundo Solis were foremost in his mind. It occurred to him that the police already had them and were waiting to see what the former occupant of the apartment would disclose to them.

Nothing on the dining table off the kitchen, he saw. He tried to remember if he and Maggie had worked anywhere else. He assured himself they hadn't. With a measure of relief – albeit possibly temporary if the authorities were playing games with him – he continued his tour until he had made a complete sweep of the townhouse.

"Nothing stands out, Detective."

"See any of your old belongings?" Howard asked pointedly.

Josh Morgan hadn't really looked and said so.

"No, I was mainly looking for anything wrong or out of place."

"Oh," the police investigator answered. "Would you mind coming to the station and writing out a full report about the evening?"

Morgan desperately needed to get out of the building and start looking for his former girlfriend but didn't know how to gracefully decline. Fortunately, he got help.

"Is that necessary, Detective Howard?"

Arriving at Josh Morgan's side was Director Cortland. The question put the investigator in a predicament. If the Secret Service boss, who had just lost an agent, thought it could wait, Howard felt he couldn't insist.

"First thing in the morning then?" the detective continued.

"Of course." Morgan thought the suggestion had a bit of a snarl to it.

"But Mr. Morgan, if you think of anything before then," the D.C. investigator said, handing the missing woman's ex-fiancé a business card, "Please…"

"I'll let you know," Morgan completed his sentence.

♦

The Wharf's general manager sat in a room with a Metropolitan police officer and an FBI technical expert. It had become immediately evident to the federal authorities that the Federal Bureau of Investigation had joint jurisdiction with the local PD since the missing woman was a federal government official.

The manager was completely distraught, barely able to do more than give the investigators access to the video recordings of the property. She wept continually, making her utterly useless in providing relevant information. But none of the law enforcement personnel on site believed she knew anything helpful.

The footage was of surprisingly high quality, reflecting the upscale nature of the townhouse development. Four angles provided views of the things that had transpired. Three had pertinent images. The other less so.

Camera one showed a wide-angle view of the parking lot. On it, in gory detail, the viewers saw one man approach the apartment complex's employee and shoot him without warning. It appeared no words had been exchanged; no confrontation had taken place. It was just a ruthless, coldblooded murder.

And in the same recording, while Oakley had been distracted with the shooting in front of him, a second gunman shot him from behind. The first round struck the agent in the back on his body armor. The man coldheartedly fired a second shot into his head and callously moved his body into his automobile.

Near the building, the first unsub also made sure his target was dead with a headshot.

Those observations made it almost indisputable that there were two and apparently only two men who had acted. Another possibly important detail emerged from the first recording. It appeared that the first shooter had taken a round from Agent Oakley. The FBI video examiner relayed that fact to personnel outside who immediately assessed which of the blood might belong to the shooter.

The Bureau and local police analysts watched the replay until the unknown subjects disappeared into the building. Then the FBI technician fast-forwarded to the moment they reappeared, emerging from the door with Secretary Loughlin. One was roughly prodding the woman along. The second carried a briefcase and a backpack.

The second video recording was by way of a camera in the foyer. Hanging from the corner of the ceiling, it showed the second man dragging the first shooter's victim behind the counter. More importantly, the feed provided very good images of both men.

The Metro police technician observed, "Didn't make much of an effort to conceal their faces, did they?"

The Bureau counterpart nodded and grunted his agreement. He captured multiple still images of the two men, obviously Latin, and sent the files to FBI Headquarters.

The two analysts looked quickly at another parking lot recording that clearly showed the men and Secretary Loughlin getting into an SUV. There were no distinguishing features of the large truck and rows of cars blocked any view of the license plate.

Metro Police Detective Howard entered the room where the analysts were checking the videos. The local police and FBI technicians paused on the image of the SUV to confirm details. The FBI agent called out specifics to his local counterpart.

"Chevrolet Tahoe; likely this year's model; black. That's about it. We'll shoot off the limited details to our offices."

The FBI analyst was poised to resume the video when Howard almost shouted.

"Stop!"

The two men in charge of analyzing the video looked at the detective with bewilderment.

Howard pointed to the screen. "Can you enlarge that? Enhance it?"

"Not on this unit," FBI replied, still confused at what the investigator had seen.

"Can you capture an image and enlarge it on your laptop?"

"Sure." In a moment the man driving the analysis of the video had a still image. He pressed the "CTRL" and "+" keys, enlarging the shot significantly, but losing quality in the process.

"The HQ boys can do a lot better…"

He was cut off by the detective's finger pointing at the display.

"Look! There!"

"Holy shit!" exclaimed the local police technician.

"I'll be damned!" added the FBI agent.

Before them in the lower corner of the windshield as seen on the monitor was a small square sticker.

"It's a rental," FBI said at the recognition of what Howard had seen.

"Great catch, Dillon," exclaimed the Metro representative in the analysis.

"I'm afraid I can't make out anything on the sticker on my laptop," lamented the FBI tech. "But they can do a helluva job at HQ. Just means you'll have to wait a bit, but I'll upload it to their server now."

If they were honest, both of the technicians would have admitted to resenting the presumption of Detective Howard to intrude on their work, but they couldn't argue with his spotting the rental ID sticker. So, as he leaned in between them as they continued, they were hard-pressed to object.

However, the police detective had no additional observations. The second parking lot video had yielded just that one clue, so the techies and their backseat driver moved on to the final footage. The camera that was aimed down the hallway outside the Secretary's apartment showed the two Latinos clearly forcing their way into Loughlin's townhouse when she inexplicably opened the door. But Howard knew that resistance would've most likely only delayed their inevitable entry by moments.

The Wharf offered its tenants interior surveillance at an additional fee on their leases. And though Maggie and Josh had purchased the service when they lived there, Maggie thought it an unnecessary expense when Morgan, and then she moved out. It probably didn't matter because tenants mostly only activated the interior security cameras while they were away.

Detective Dillon Howard watched on the monitor as the two men virtually dragged the Secretary out of the apartment.

"Lying little shit!" the investigator shouted.

He immediately tapped in the number that he had gotten from Josh Morgan.

"Morgan. Leave a message," Howard heard. Then came the beep.

"Get your sorry ass back here right now!"

♦

Rapidly making his way from the District of Columbia into Northern Virginia, Josh Morgan played back the curt message from the Metro detective.

He brushed back his hair dampened from the light rain outside The Wharf and considered his options. He dreaded the thought of revealing the fact that items were indeed missing from the townhouse. It would lead to a line of questioning that would take time to answer. Furthermore, he knew the detective would demand that he return for an interview. And that he wasn't about to do.

Still, he knew that the more information the local and federal police had, the better the chances were that someone, even if it weren't him, would find Maggie before the unthinkable happened.

Morgan decided it was vanity – sheer personal pride – that made him reluctant to divulge what he knew. He felt like he was the best equipped to track her down. And more, he *wanted* to be the one to find her. His ace in the hole was that his not being a law enforcement official allowed him to be able to act under a different set of rules. And that was no rules at all.

"Shit… It doesn't matter who finds her," he resolved. He pressed the number of the detective to initiate a return call. But before he could say a word, a barrage of orders, curses, and threats exploded from the speaker of his phone.

"You listen to me, you fucking little bastard. I am going to hang you by your balls if you don't get your lying ass back here right now. I know the two Latinos took something from your apartment. What was it, fucker?"

"It was…"

"I've already got a BOLO out on you and will arrest your ass for obstruction and impeding a police investigation. I will have you back here so fast, you'll think it was magic!"

Detective Howard of the D.C. Metro Police continued his diatribe. His fury at everything about Josh Morgan, from his walking on murder and treason charges to the Secret Service Director interceding for him, to his withholding information that was material to a double murder and kidnapping to his thumbing his nose at Metro PD authority by taking off on his own – it spewed forth in a way that was more personal than professional.

While the detective voiced his rage, Morgan knew he had to make a decision. He had decided to let him in on everything he knew, but now the detective's next comment flipped the ex-CIA Officer's switch.

"What's more, I think you might be involved, Morgan!"

Morgan was out of his mind with anger. The detective had just made it clear that he intended to detain him and that would keep him on the sidelines and prevent him from searching for Maggie. He couldn't permit that.

"Screw you, you son of a bitch!" was punctuated with his ending the call.

The ex-CIA officer knew his phone would be used to triangulate his position. He turned it off and continued south into Virginia.

CHAPTER 16

Morgan was in a rental SUV, so he hoped it would take the authorities a while to track down when and where he had taken possession of it. As it was, he had no time to waste in explaining himself to the investigator. Morgan turned his phone back on and typed a quick message to Tom Lechler.

headed to you

Then he realized he didn't know where Lechler was. He fired off another message.

your 20?

He hated to do it, in case Maggie called. But he thought that unlikely since her phone was at the apartment. So, he slid the electronic bar that completed the power-down again and concentrated on his route.

His gut – along with Howard's inadvertent disclosure that the men who had taken Maggie were Latin – convinced him that this whole thing with her abduction was somehow connected to Eddie Solis.

After all, all the material he and Maggie had been poring over about the blogger was gone. Every last bit. Why would they want it unless it was important? And if they were involved in Eddie's possible disappearance, then it might make sense that they'd want to know what he and Maggie were up to. Morgan didn't know how the Latinos had come across Maggie unless they got the lead from Solis, directly or indirectly. Either way, Morgan figured the thugs would deal with Solis first.

The blogger lived in Norfolk, which is why he'd asked his partner Lechler to go there. He and Maggie had anticipated that she would have information from the Nicaraguan's employer or other information to give to the former Special Forces warrior the following morning. Norfolk was the only lead Morgan had. If this was all tied together then he felt like he should begin there.

♦

"And you…" Detective Howard's right index finger was inches from the face of the Director of the U.S. Secret Service, "…you told me to let him leave."

"So, let me get this straight," Director Cortland summarized. "The unsubs walked into the Secretary's apartment empty-handed and walked out with a backpack and a briefcase, and that convinces you that Morgan is withholding vital information."

"I went back and watched the earlier part of the security video I had missed and saw Morgan entering the complex with a backpack. Then Loughlin carried a briefcase in. Why wouldn't the fucker tell us they were missing, Cortland?"

"Maybe they just weren't important. Maybe it slipped his mind."

"Slipped his mind?! Oh, I know from previous experience that the SOB is one crafty little asshole. He's connected and he thinks strategically. Slipped his mind?"

Howard spun around and clutched a wad of his hair with each hand. He abruptly turned back to Director Cortland and pointed his finger at the man again. He tried to speak, but nothing came out. Finally, he grumbled something profane and took his phone out to call his office.

♦

"Honestly, this is the first I've heard of it," the Director of the CIA told the Director of the Secret Service. "But thanks for running a little interference for the man."

On the other end of the call, Cortland said, "After all he's done, I figured he deserved some consideration. If he wants to play it this way, okay. But this is about to blow up in his face – and maybe mine. He's in the wind, Betsy, and how this ends could jeopardize my career."

"I know. And I'm sorry. But you have my word. Josh Morgan is one of the good guys. He's not involved in whatever is going on with Maggie. My God, Keith, he still loves her. He might not know it, but he does. It'll all work out. But I'll see what I can dig up. I'll try to contact him and get back to you when I know something."

CIA Director Elizabeth Parnell knew it was pointless. Josh had certainly thought to turn off his phone. But still, she called it first. As expected, the connection went straight to voicemail.

"Morgan. Leave a message."

"Josh, I love you… but what the hell am I going to do with you? Call me."

Director Parnell was about to disconnect when she added, "ASAP!"

♦

"Fuck!" Tom Lechler had no idea what was going on but wasn't sure how he would convince Parnell of that. He considered not answering the call but knew that if Maggie – and even Josh – was in trouble, or if he was on some fool mission, then Betsy Parnell was someone Morgan could trust. And so could he. He took a deep breath out of character with his operator persona and tapped the screen to connect.

"Director."

"Oh, hell, Tom. Call me Betsy. Your pal Morgan is going to be the death of all of us. So, we might as well be on a first name basis when we go down."

"Fair enough. Do you know what's up?"

The United States' top spy filled in her contractor with all that she knew. And given her close friendship with both the FBI and Secret Service Directors, what she knew was practically everything they did.

"Honest to God, Director… Betsy… all I know is that Josh asked me to come to Norfolk to check into some things for him. He didn't say what. Then a little while ago, I get this message from him that Maggie's missing. The last thing I got was a text asking where I was. I texted back that I was at the Days Inn in Emporia but didn't get a reply confirming he got it."

"You know he's turned his phone off."

"Yes, ma'am. I know."

The former Master Sergeant could hear the Director's sigh through the phone.

"What do you want me to do, Betsy?"

"When you hear from him, tell him to call me! Pronto!"

"Copy that. What are you going to do?"

"I'm going to have a drink."

"Sounds like a plan, ma'am. Goodnight."

CHAPTER 17

DAY 4 – THURSDAY

It was around two in the morning and Eddie Solis was sleeping more restfully than he'd been able to up to that point. His near sleep ended with the sound of the metal door sliding back on the far wall of the building. He rose – slowly – praying to God that he was being rescued. Instead, lights flickered on and he saw Luis Gutierrez, dragging an auburn-haired woman with him. Santos followed, carrying two plastic bags.

Neither of the brothers spoke as they opened the door to the interior cage that had held Solis since they left him. Luis shoved the woman in roughly. Santos set the bags just inside the makeshift cell.

Eddie saw that the woman had bruises on the right side of her face and her right eye was swollen, though not closed.

The woman and Eddie watched the men walk back to the exit. Just before they slammed the sliding door to, they turned off the lights.

In the darkness, the battered blogger heard, "Eddie Solis, I presume."

♦

From the direction he came from, it was out of the way to Norfolk, but it was where Tom Lechler was, so Morgan was nearing Emporia, Virginia. He pulled into the parking lot of a gas station and turned his phone on just long enough to get Lechler's location. He also quickly jotted down phone numbers for Lechler, Betsy Parnell, Detective Howard, and, of course, Maggie.

He also replied to Tom's earlier note. His response read only "*25*." Then he turned the device off again and resumed his drive.

Twenty-plus minutes later, Morgan turned onto the premises of the

Days Inn Motel where he saw Tom Lechler leaning against his truck.

"I wondered if you'd get my meaning of '*25*.'"

"Being twenty-five minutes out was the only thing I could think of," Lechler replied. "Here. There's a Walmart here."

Josh looked into the white and blue bag at the half dozen prepaid mobile phones.

"Good thinking. Thanks. Why don't you take half?"

"No need. Got several of my own."

"By the way. Betsy said to call her."

"That can wait."

Lechler shrugged. And with no further words, the two men walked up the stairs to Lechler's room, where Josh filled him in on the whole story, from Maggie's concern about Eddie Solis to her disappearance.

"I think you're right. Taking her has to be linked to Solis. Latin males. Taking all your documentation about him. Why'd the cops let you leave? I mean, under the circumstances, I'd have thought they'd want to talk to you some more."

"That's odd, isn't it? The detective who was in on my arrest for murder… He wanted to take me straight to the police station…"

"Rubber hoses and bright lights?" Lechler quipped with a grin.

"Probably. Anyhow, he's smart. He knows I know more than I let on. But the Secret Service Director…"

"Cortland?"

"Right. He talked him into letting me go and meeting him at the station in the morning."

"He's in for a long wait."

"Yes, he is, Tom. Yes, he is. Got anything to drink?"

♦

Edmundo Solis was shocked to learn that his new roommate was Maggie Loughlin.

"I'm so sorry to have dragged you into this, Secretary Loughlin. Those guys are from my home country."

"I guessed as much. Why are they here, Eddie?"

"They are trying to get me to tell them who my source is in the Zamora regime."

"Did you tell them?"

"I honestly don't know."

"Okay. Then what's the important information you said you would tell me about?"

"I don't know that either."

Solis' last words were soft, barely more than a whimper. Maggie's pen pal's voice was pitiful. She wanted to be furious but decided she would save that for later. There were far more critical considerations for her – and Eddie, who continued his explanation.

"I was supposed to get a phone call from my source on Tuesday. That was the day after the Gutierrez brothers took me. In the call, the man, or maybe a woman… I don't know. They were going to give me full details about something Zamora was doing in another country."

"That's what you've been blogging about?"

"Yes."

"And you posted all of that without any confirmation?"

In the dark, Maggie ran her fingers through her hair. As she rubbed at her bruised cheek and swollen eye, she felt her anger at her cellmate beginning to boil up. She sat in silence until she regained control of her emotion.

"So, you really don't have any hard facts?"

In the dark, Eddie hung his head and put his hand over his face.

"I… uh, I guess I exaggerated some – about my knowledge of Zamora's plans. And about my relationship… my connection to you."

The pause in Eddie's disclosure and Maggie's questions lasted a full minute.

"Why, Eddie?" Maggie's inquiry broke the cold silence.

"I believe in what I'm doing. I really do. There are things going on in Nicaragua that people should know about."

"But the lies?" Maggie realized that was too extreme a characterization. "The embellishments? The exaggerations?"

Eddie swallowed at the truth that he had to face up to.

"I guess I just wanted to feel important. Like I was somebody."

Solis began to sob quietly.

"I'm so sorry, Madam Secretary," her cellmate said through his tears.

"Heck, you might as well call me Maggie."

White House Press Secretary Loughlin pulled her knees up to her chest. She was angry. She was terrified. But one thing was crystal clear. Edmundo had stumbled onto something serious. Serious enough that Nicaraguan Dictator Sergio Zamora had noticed and had sent thugs to look into it. And that worried her.

Though she couldn't see, she heard some rustling in the room, particularly in the plastic bags the brothers had left inside the door.

"What is that?" she asked, though she was certain she knew.

"Rats." After a moment, Eddie followed with a question of his own. "What's in the bags?"

"The bastards who stuck me in here brought some food and water, too. I guess that means they might be holding on to us a while." She wanted to say, "keep us alive," but couldn't acknowledge that out loud.

It startled Maggie as Eddie clambered to his knees and felt his way to the grocery bags. As he picked one up, he felt a rodent drop off of it. He handled the items individually and decided there were packages of chips, maybe some crackers, bread, and some other snacks and food. Most importantly. There were about a dozen bottles that he assumed held water.

Eddie stumbled back to the woman who had just arrived and handed her the bags.

"Here, Madam Secretary. Eat."

"I don't feel like it. You go ahead. Have all you want."

As inviting as that sounded, Solis took only a small package of crackers.

"No, we have to conserve what we have." However, he did take a bottle of water. After several rapid, satisfying gulps, he slowed his pace down. And given his level of dehydration, he drank almost an entire bottle before thinking better of it and replacing the screw-on cap.

Edmundo Solis took the bags of food and placed them under the bucket to protect them from the vermin. To his surprise, there was enough that the entirety barely fit. He didn't know whether to think that Luis and Santos Gutierrez planned to keep them alive longer than Eddie expected, or if they just grabbed a little of this and that while they bought the supplies. Regardless, if rationed wisely, the provisions should last several days. Maybe more.

♦

Josh marveled at his roommate's ability to sleep, but he was soundly in slumber. He thought at first that the man simply didn't have the personal involvement in this crisis that he did. But he realized, that as a former operator, Lechler had developed the necessary ability to turn sleep on and off, practically at will.

For his part, Josh wanted to sleep. He needed to sleep. But rest eluded him. The only lead he had about Edmundo Solis was that he worked for United Parcel Service. And he hoped desperately that finding the man would lead him to Maggie.

One problem that Morgan knew faced him was that all the law enforcement agencies involved in this had no doubt connected the plot to Solis. They would have the same clues as Morgan and far better resources. He was certain that they were already looking for the Nicaraguan blogger. In fact, they had likely already awakened managers or other UPS representatives in Norfolk to inquire about the man. Originally the ex-CIA Officer feared that he would cross paths with law enforcement officials during his search for Maggie. Now the hard truth was that he was going to be hours behind them. They, in fact, might stake out places after they left them, lying in wait for Morgan.

It even occurred to Josh that the FBI might find Maggie first. He didn't care. In fact, he hoped so. But he couldn't sit around doing nothing, answering their lame-ass questions, and explaining over and over his recent visits and conversations with her. In retrospect, he regretted heading out on his own. He might've got them going on the right track more quickly if he'd told them what this thing was about. But that was water under the bridge now. They would have already uncovered any leads he could have provided to them.

The ex-photojournalist/spy stretched and yawned and felt his eyelids drooping.

Josh Morgan awoke with a start. He hadn't awakened once and was shocked that he had slept at all.

"Morning, sleepy head." Tom Lechler handed him a cup of coffee.

"You've been out."

"Yep, and got this coffee. Donut shop around the corner. Don't thank me though. It ain't that great. But it does beat the shit they give you in a motel room."

Josh looked at his watch and was at once relieved and mildly appalled. It was five o'clock and he hated that he was getting up at this time of the morning. But he was mostly relieved because there was much to do and he knew there wasn't time to waste.

"Moved your Expedition around back. Even managed to switch license plates with another car. Could buy us some time, but it might not be much. Depends on how long it takes the driver of the car I stole 'em from to realize his are wrong. Like yours, it's a rental so he might not ever notice. The rental agency will, of course, but hopefully that'll be days."

"On the other hand," Morgan said, taking a sip of his coffee, "it might be quicker. The automatic license plate readers that cops are using could catch the number, regardless of the type of vehicle. They'll get an alert immediately that it's a car of interest because they're my plates."

"Only if they've got a BOLO out on you."

"They do."

"Yeah, you're probably right."

Josh drank again from his Styrofoam cup.

"And whether it's at the rental return or because the guy's been pulled over because of the plates, they'll find out where he's been."

"Well," the former operator said, "let's hope he's been a lot of places and won't be able to tell the cops when or where the plates were swapped."

"Oh, hell, Tom, it won't matter. By now, they've uncovered Maggie's background check request on Solis. They've even accessed her email and seen his messages to her."

"But you said they didn't say much."

"They didn't. I read copies in the files Maggie had given me. She didn't even read any beyond the first couple. Just took them for granted until they quit coming. But even without them, the feds will have tracked down everything about the guy. We know Solis works for UPS. We just don't know where. They'll already have nailed that down. They've got a huge head start on us, Tom."

"Maybe not," the ex-sergeant corrected, handing his friend a scribbled note.

"What is it?" Morgan asked, beginning to read.

"It's a lot of details about one Edmundo Solis: his home address, his social media project's P.O. Box, his phone numbers, his work address – tons of stuff."

Morgan read for a few seconds. Then his head popped up and eyes opened wide at Lechler.

"But, what? How?"

"Betsy. Oh, and she said she could've given it to you last night if only you'd called like she asked. She was pretty pissed when she called me this morning while I was on my coffee run. She said that if you ever want her help again, you'd better do as she asks."

"She called you?"

"Yeah, I turned on my phone for a sec to check messages and it rang. Nearly dropped the damned thing. Anyhow, I gave her the numbers for all of our burn phones. Gave her a specific order that we'd use them. It's on the note."

The ex-Green Beret sat on his bed and looked around, drinking his own coffee.

"You know, I'm glad Days Inn only had a room with two beds. Otherwise, I'd have gone for a single queen since I didn't know you were coming. It would've been pretty cozy in one bed." The retired soldier shuddered.

Lechler drank more coffee. Morgan smiled at him.

"So, Josh, I'm sure she's called you. The thing won't do you much good if it's not turned on."

The former CIA Officer turned independent contractor fired up the first phone on his list, which immediately signaled a message. He played it on speaker.

"It's Betsy. Guess you needed sleep more than help. Call me."

Morgan deleted the communication. Lechler smiled at the snarky comment as he finished his coffee.

The former Case Officer sighed and typed in the Director's private number while his CIA partner gathered his sparse belongings to prepare to leave.

"So, you decided to call, Morgan?"

"Sorry, Betsy. I'm pretty rattled by all of this. Seems I'm always looking for someone or someone's looking for me."

There was silence.

"I understand. But Josh, you have to know I'm always on your side. I have complete confidence in you. But I've been very patient while you handled some personal matters. I don't intend to get demanding now, but if I call, you pick up or call back. Understood?"

"You're right, Betsy. You've been more than understanding… And supportive."

"Okay, tell me more about the guy you think is related to Maggie's disappearance."

Her contractor didn't tell the CIA boss any details about Solis himself. She already had those. But his information about the man's passion for his homeland and the disclosure about his latest posts suggesting that Nicaraguan Dictator Zamora was about to launch some sort of operation in another country caught Parnell's attention.

"You're thinking Solis might actually be right about that; that Zamora might seriously be worried about this blogger mucking up some clandestine op?"

"I don't know about Solis jeopardizing the op. Zamora might just be concerned with the alleged leak in his inner circle."

"To the point that he dispatched some thugs to find out what Solis knew and who his source was?" Parnell asked.

"Maybe."

"Hmm. You know that the surveillance video at your old apartment showed the two men who murdered Oakley and the complex employee and took Maggie…"

"And…?" Morgan followed.

"They're Latinos."

"I know. Detective Howard let it slip."

"Of course, at this point there's no way of knowing if they're from Nicaragua."

"No, but their race sure seems to support my theory."

"The Bureau and the local police know you lied about nothing being missing from the apartment. The video clearly shows them with a briefcase and a backpack when they left. What was it, Josh?"

"It was all the research and other information that Maggie had collected about Eddie Solis. She and I were going over it."

"Well, that's another reason to think this is about Solis. But you're saying you have no clue what this Nicaraguan op is? Because where I sit, I have no knowledge of anything being initiated by the regime."

"Solis' emails were vague," the ex-spy clarified. "He said in his last email to Maggie that he would send details the next day. So, he was expecting to receive something from his source, or…"

"Or the man was bullshitting. Maybe some sort of conspiracy nut?"

"You know the old line from Joseph Heller: 'Just because you're paranoid doesn't mean they aren't after you.' Well, just because most of the people spouting conspiracy theories are full of shit doesn't mean there aren't some real plots out there."

"Yeah," the CIA boss agreed. "Guess you've seen a few over the last couple of years. Tell you what, Josh. I'll reach out to Gabe Austin over at the Bureau and Paul McClintock at NSA. I'll tell them I've heard a rumor – nothing official – about something going on by Zamora; that I'm just passing it along to them. But if they know something, they'll say so. However, if their resources have picked up chatter about something, I think they would've already read me in. Okay?"

"Okay. One more thing, Betsy. How'd Maggie look? Did the video show anything about her condition?"

The practiced liar behind the desk in the CIA Director's chair didn't miss a beat.

"She looked fine, Josh."

The truth was that an enlarged screen grab showed that Maggie had been roughed up some and was in obvious emotional distress. But it didn't appear bad, so Parnell figured there was no need to get Morgan worked up.

However, on the other end of the phone conversation was a trained former spy who had excelled at the requisite skill of reading people. The quickness of Betsy's reply and the lack of elaboration on her part made him suspect she hadn't been entirely forthcoming.

But Josh also believed that if she knew of anything serious about his ex, she would've told him.

Morgan ended the call. He joined Lechler at the door.

"I need more coffee, Tom."

It was 5:20 when the two men got in their respective vehicles. The first order of business was to ditch Morgan's rental. They didn't drive far. He just parked in the lot of another nearby hotel, where he hoped the SUV with its changed license plates would get lost amidst the dozens of other vehicles in the lot. He figured that if anyone tracked him to the Days Inn and didn't find his car there, they would figure he'd left town. Still, they probably knew he was headed for Norfolk.

Josh Morgan joined Tom Lechler in his pickup. It was a black Ford F150 and fairly nondescript. It was typical of all others of that make and model, with the exception of its lifted body and the oversized tires.

Next, Lechler drove to the same donut shop near their motel where he'd bought coffee earlier.

"Want some, Tom?"

"I'm good," the retired soldier said with a wave of his hand.

Momentarily Morgan reappeared from the shop with a coffee and a small bag of donuts. Once he was back in the truck, Maggie Loughlin's former boyfriend buckled up and said, "Let's go see if UPS has anything for us."

♦

Maggie hadn't slept. She noticed that her cellmate had managed to, albeit fitfully. It wasn't bright enough outside for light to stream through the slit in the outside wall that she had noticed. But she could see that the sky was definitely a paler hue. She never wore a watch anymore. She relied on her smartphone for the time and just about everything else in her life. So, without it she had no idea of the hour.

During the night, Maggie had retrieved one of the bottles of water near the upside-down pail. She was thoroughly undone by the rats she heard scurrying about. While she shared Eddie Solis' view that they should ration their food and water, she was unscrewing the cap for another drink when she heard the metal door on the far side of the warehouse sliding open.

It was a bit later than she had thought, as evidenced by the lighter sky that she saw through the open door. And silhouetted against the overcast sky were the Gutierrez brothers. She had heard them refer to each other by their first names, but Eddie had told her their surnames. It was another worrisome sign to her that things weren't intended to end well for her and her Nicaraguan pen pal. The pair had made no effort to hide their faces, identities, or other details.

The men walked to the door of the former storage room holding their prisoners. Maggie noticed that neither brandished a gun. She supposed they had enough confidence in their physical brutality that they didn't feel a need for a weapon.

"Stay back," demanded the older brother to the captives as he opened the mesh door to where they were held.

Luis strode in, shoulders back and chin lifted.

"Arrogant bastard," Maggie thought.

Aloud she made a plea for release by way of offering a bargain.

"So far you haven't done anything serious. But you must know I work in the White House for the President of the United States. Anything happens to me, you're in serious shit. Let us go now and just go back to Nicaragua."

At the mention of his homeland, Luis spun his head around and glared at their prisoner with the auburn tresses.

"So… Solis *has* been in communication with you about the spy who has provided him information about our *presidente*!"

"Shit," the Press Secretary thought. "Smart move, Loughlin."

She pressed on.

"Solis really doesn't know anything about any plot or anything else there. He just types out his little blog each day, making up things to appear important. And he has been pestering me for months. I guess he thinks he can brag about knowing someone in the White House. But we've never met. We've never spoken. And his emails to me are silly little rants that I immediately delete."

The editor/publisher/head blogger for *El poder salvador de la verdad* hung his head. He wondered if that's how the President's Press Secretary really thought of him. But he also felt some shame in that it was largely true. He knew Secretary Loughlin was making a case to turn them loose, but it still stung.

"If you let us go, we won't contact anybody for four hours," she offered. It was the same deal that never worked in movies or novels, she knew, and it was unlikely to work now.

Luis Gutierrez stepped toward the woman.

"You are a lying whore!" Then the younger brother stepped even more closely to Maggie with a raised fist. She recoiled and raised both arms to shield her face for his strike. But it never came. Instead, he collected himself and stepped back. He ended further attempts at negotiations with a loud, "Now shut up, bitch!" He strutted about the enclosure.

"Where is the *comida* and *agua,* we left?" he asked abruptly. Looking around the small mesh enclosure, he spied the upturned bucket. He snatched it up and the piled-up snacks and bottles tumbled free.

"*Inteligente*!" he offered in facetious praise, upon realizing the reason behind the precaution. Then he kicked some of the items through the open doorway, beside which Santos stood. He continued to kick until everything was scattered outside the little room.

"There! The *ratas* will be able to feed freely now!" Luis Gutierrez exclaimed with a laugh. Then he kicked the metal bucket at the two captives.

Maggie Loughlin and Edmundo Solis watched a smiling Santos Gutierrez exit the pen behind his brother and snap the lock on the chain back into place.

And when the two Nicaraguans left the warehouse and slid the door shut, the two prisoners' eyes turned toward the meager food and water that was now out of their reach.

They sighed in unison.

Outside the abandoned building, Santos asked, "Why are we leaving?"

"We are just going to let them – what do the Americanos say? - *stew* for a while."

♦

FBI Director Gabriel Austin had no knowledge of any suspicious activity inside the United States by the Sergio Zamora regime. Domestic matters were primarily areas of jurisdiction for the Bureau. He did ask why the CIA Head had inquired. She merely told him that a source had said that Zamora might be up to something. Though Parnell and Austin were longtime friends – in fact, precisely because they were friends – she didn't go further. She feared she would place him in a bad position.

However, on her next call, Paul McClintock, the head of the National Security Agency was another matter. And his delay in answering his CIA counterpart's inquiry made her take notice.

"Why do you ask, Betsy?"

She laughed, "Answer a question with a question, Paul? Okay, I'll go first. A source told my people…" By "source" and "people," Betsy meant Josh Morgan and herself. "…that this insignificant blogger Edmundo Solis…"

"The one who's missing and might be connected to Secretary Loughlin?"

"Right. My source told me that his rants might actually be based on real facts."

"Is Josh Morgan your 'source?'"

Director Parnell smiled. "You got me, Paul."

"Don't worry, Betsy. NSA isn't involved in this. At least, only to the extent that Gabe Austin asked me if we'd picked up any chatter about the Secretary. I told him that if we'd picked up anything beforehand, I'd have told him, of course. And I told him that we haven't heard anything since she went missing. Which, by the way, is true."

"You know that Josh and I talk. He's working for me on a contract basis now. He's just worried. That's all."

"C'mon. Betsy. He's also MIA. Gabe isn't too worried about it, but the Metropolitan Police detective is really worked up about Morgan disappearing. The way Gabe recounted it, the guy thinks Morgan lied to him about something material. It sounded personal."

"True. And true, Paul. Long story."

"And he thinks Morgan might even be mixed up in it somehow."

"And that is decidedly false."

"Well, don't worry. I won't volunteer your concern to them."

"Thanks, Paul."

"But Betsy…"

Parnell pulled her finger back from her intention to end the call.

"Where is Morgan? Is he out looking for the Secretary?"

"Goodbye, Director."

CIA Director Parnell would have liked to call Josh, but she really didn't have anything to give him. And it would simply burn another one of his phones.

♦

After he had hung up with the head of the Central Intelligence Agency, the Director of the Federal Bureau of Investigation sat silently at his desk. He folded his arms and leaned back in his chair, tapping his chin with a ballpoint pen.

"Why'd you really call, Betsy?"

He pondered her concern a minute longer. Then he dialed an internal number.

"Smitty. Austin."

On the other end of the call, Carl Smith stood, as he always did when speaking to one of the "suits," whether in person or by phone. Smith had recently been promoted to the position of supervisor in the Bureau's lab as a result of his stellar work investigating the attempted assassination of President Hendrickson and again on finding the murderers of Former President Trent Weston.

"Yes, Director Austin. How can I help you?"

"Smitty, I want you to take a closer look at the exchanges between Secretary Loughlin and the Nicaraguan who'd been emailing her."

"But sir, you just had me look them over."

"I know. But that was to see if there was anything that might lead us to Loughlin. This time I want you to look at it with an eye toward the things he wrote about on his blog. In fact, check his social media accounts, too. Specifically, I want your opinion as to whether Solis was a quack, or really onto something."

"Yes, sir.'

"And Smitty…"

"Yes, sir."

"Keep this on the QT. Just between you and me. Okay?"

"Director, can I bring Lane in on this? I'm great at the analytical assessment, but he's in a league all to himself when it comes to hacki… uh, accessing computers remotely." Like Smith, the Bureau lab's computer technician Alonso Lane had contributed immeasurably to uncovering files related to financial transactions of a D.C. District Attorney that eventually tied him to Weston's assassination.

"If you need to dig deeper, read Lane in. But only 'if.' Got it?"

"Got it… sir."

The FBI Head knew he hadn't given his lab supervisor very precise directions about what he was looking for or where to look. Austin didn't even know himself. But he knew if there was anything to be sniffed out, Smith would find it.

"Josh Morgan again." Austin shook his head and considered whether there should be an entire branch of the Bureau devoted entirely to the shit he got mixed up in. He was a pain in the ass, but Austin liked him. He also knew him to be one of the most resourceful young men he'd ever met. Furthermore, Betsy Parnell trusted Morgan implicitly. And she was the Head of the Central Intelligence Agency. She didn't trust *anybody*.

♦

At the same time the Bureau's boss asked his tech to look into Parnell's concerns, Paul McClintock, head of the NSA, was on his phone with Terry Henderson. Henderson was an analyst in his organization who was unwittingly caught up in former Deputy Director Everson Blake's treasonous acts against Former President Weston and Josh Morgan.

Despite Henderson's connection to Blake, he was very, very good at what he did. Few had the breadth of knowledge across the full scope of NSA's capabilities that he did. And the young man had incredible instincts to discern what mattered and what didn't in Agency collections. So, Henderson was kept on after Josh Morgan had exposed Blake and killed him, though publicly the Deputy Director died a hero in the line of duty. The analyst had received a demotion and a corresponding reduction in pay but was as conscientious about his job as ever.

"Director McClintock, what can I do for you?"

"Three things, Terry. First, I want you to quietly snoop around…"

Terry Henderson gulped at the phrase "quietly snoop." Sure, the National Security Agency was the king of quiet and snooping, but Deputy Director Blake had also asked him to keep his requests confidential. "And look where that got me," the analyst considered silently.

"…to see if there's any unusual traffic about Nicaraguan activities abroad, any kind of uptick about their military operations. Secondly, I want you to look for any chatter about any of their agents being on our soil."

"Yes, sir, Director. What else?"

"The last thing is to see what intercepts you can dig up about Edmundo Solis."

"Is that all, sir?"

"Yes. But be discrete and communicate only with me. Understood?"

"Yes, Director McClintock."

After his Agency's head hung up, Terry Henderson whispered aloud, "Is this where I say, 'Here I go again?'"

♦

Carl Smith wondered, in light of FBI Director Austin's request, if he should report what just came across his desk directly to him. He decided to stick with proper channels for now and called the Deputy Director instead.

"Deputy Director Drake, Carl Smith here. We just got facial recognition hits on both of the guys involved in the shootings at The Wharf. Well, really, we just got a hit on one of them but they're brothers, so it was easy to identify the other one. At first, it didn't occur to us to check family…"

"Smitty, get to the point."

"Right. Yes, sir. Their names are Luis and Santos Zamora. They're from Nicaragua and related to President Sergio Zamora. He's their uncle. Their real last name is Gutierrez. Their parents died and the dictator took them in. They do wet work and other rough business for their uncle."

"And they're here." It was a statement, not a question.

"Correct."

"Okay. I've turned this matter over to Supervisory Agent Liu. From now on you can contact her directly and she'll report to me as the investigation warrants. Thanks, Smitty."

Lab Supervisor Smith knew that Drake would call the Director, but when he had said "Nicaragua' in his report to Drake, he realized that it was something Austin had asked him to look into, so he should have called him first. He raced to connect with the Director before his Deputy did.

Austin answered and Smitty filled him in. When the two had completed their call, the Bureau Head rubbed his eyes and tried to make sense of what was going on. His desk phone rang, and he saw that it was his Deputy Director. Austin decided to play dumb for the moment and not tell Drake he had Smith reporting to him. He wanted to keep it private for now, no matter how much he trusted Tony Drake.

♦

Nicaraguan *presidente* Sergio Zamora wasn't outfitted naturally with much self-control. Therefore, when he became silent before speaking to a subordinate, it wasn't patience. It was the calm before the storm.

So, when Luis received no response from his uncle after his report, his eyes grew wide, and he looked at Santos. When his brother winced – he actually squeezed his eyes shut very hard, gritted his teeth, and dropped his head – the older brother knew that *Tio* Sergio had unloaded on Luis. He could overhear their uncle's shouts though several feet away from his brother's phone.

Luis Gutierrez winced again and separated the device from his ear by nearly a foot. Even with the phone moved away from his head, he leaned dramatically away from it and shut his eyes forcefully. Finally, he opened his left eye and turned to his brother, appearing to beg for some relief.

Nephew Santos had genuine sympathy for nephew Luis. Still, he looked away in an effort to distance himself from the verbal explosion.

"You did not! Tell me you did NOT!!"

"But *Tio"* didn't slow the onslaught.

"You took someone who works for *la Presidenta Americana*? You fool! You utter fool!"

Luis could tell that his uncle, the president, was pacing. Then he heard the bang that he knew was the man slamming his hand on his desk.

Neither uncle nor nephew spoke for some time. Luis waited. Sometimes Sergio Zamora calmed after his initial explosion. It wasn't the case this time. He erupted again.

"*Estúpido imbécil.* What made you do such a thing? *Maldito seas*, Luis! The entire *gobierno de los Estados Unidos* will be after you! AND ME! You have not only put yourself in danger, but ME as well! *Caramba*!"

Zamora paused as if reloading.

"You are on your own. I disown you – you and that *hermano idiota* of yours. This will jeopardize my entire plan and my arrangement, my reward. This matter begins this month."

Hearing Uncle Sergio begin to mutter to himself, Luis sensed that he might be able to get some words in. He would plead his case and, perhaps, his uncle would understand.

"But *Tio* Sergio, it is precisely because we are trying to save your operation that we did this thing. This woman, she is a confidant of the traitor blogger. We couldn't get information from him, so we have turned to her."

"*Sobrino*, nephew, as I ordered the other night, get your fucking information from the man. You do not lay a hand on her. If you are caught and she is unharmed, perhaps you can use her to bargain with the American authorities. But you WILL NOT admit to anything. Then when you get the identity of the man's source, the traitor in our midst, you will make the man and *Señora Secretaria* disappear."

"*Si, Tio* Sergio" was cut off by dead air.

CHAPTER 18

It was five minutes before seven o'clock. Josh Morgan sat with Tom Lechler in the ex-warrior's truck. On their way to Norfolk, the duo had decided to forego starting with the UPS facility where the CIA Director had said Edmundo Solis worked.

Instead, Morgan had binoculars trained on the entrance to the apartment building where Parnell had said the Nicaraguan lived.

"You know, some agency's investigators have most likely already been here."

"Yeah, you've said that before, Tom. But I've gotta start somewhere."

Morgan began to open the F150's door. Lechler reached over and grabbed his arm. Morgan glared at the man he assumed was trying to stop him from going in.

"Tom…"

"Let me go in instead," the man interrupted. "Hear me out. A lot of people are looking for you. Maybe they won't have any interest in me."

Morgan shut the door and considered the suggestion. He shook his head.

"I'm sure they know of our association."

"Maybe not. Why would they? And if they did, would they know what I look like? You know that I don't exist in most databases."

The former CIA Officer finally nodded. "Don't ransack the place, Tom."

The ex-sergeant smiled his "Who me?" smile and started for the building. He looked at info that Parnell had provided and headed for the second floor.

"208… 210… 212. This is it," he thought. Though he didn't expect an answer, Lechler knocked on the door. He knocked again. He was about to pick the door's lock, which didn't appear very formidable, when the door to apartment 210 creaked open. That surprised the ex-Green Beret, since it was so early in the morning.

"He's not home," said an elderly sounding voice through the cracked door.

"Well, darn," Lechler lamented. "I guess I missed him. I thought I'd catch Eddie before he left for work."

The door of the next apartment opened a little wider.

"You know Eddie? I've never seen you here before." The truth was that Mrs. Shoemaker had almost never seen any visitors to apartment 212. Not that she wasn't aware of everything that went on in her hallway. Eddie didn't have many friends or much of a social life.

Lechler turned to the door, which closed a little.

"He and I are sort of friends, I guess. He delivers my UPS packages. The other day I was expecting a package – a gift for my neighbor. She watches my cats anytime I'm away." Tom thought a cat would resonate with the old woman better than a dog since he could see a feline peeking through the partially opened door from her arms. He also figured she would think kindly of him if he was the sort who bought gifts for his fictitious pet sitter.

"Anyhow, somehow the company I bought the gift from got the address wrong. When I met Eddie at my door, the present was with the other things he delivered. You know, Eddie was delivering it to the wrong house, but he saw my name and knew it was wrong and made sure I got it. I mean, how many people would've done that? Most wouldn't have cared and just left it at the wrong place."

Mrs. Shoemaker opened the door a little wider.

"That sounds like Eddie."

"Well, it sure helped me out. I was leaving town that day."

Eddie's "customer" realized he was lucky that the neighbor hadn't wondered how he would know Eddie Solis' address.

Lechler had no idea where he was going with his story. He was just trying to explain why he was there and possibly ingratiate himself to the woman who had caught him about to break into her next-door neighbor's apartment. Then he hit on something.

"I wanted to come by and thank him and give him some money. But then I realized that Eddie wouldn't accept money."

"No, he wouldn't," agreed Mrs. Shoemaker said, opening the door fully and smiling.

"Oh, my, what a lovely cat. May I?"

When her new acquaintance reached to pet the cat, the woman stepped fully into the hallway.

"Reminds me of my Missy," the impostor said and smiled, scratching the woman's cat behind its ear. "You know, maybe I could give Eddie a gift card."

"That would be very nice of you, young man."

"Does Eddie have any places he shops regularly? Maybe a liquor store or restaurant?"

"My," exclaimed Mrs. Shoemaker, "I don't think that he even drinks."

"I don't either, ma'am," Lechler lied.

"There is this restaurant he goes to almost every day. I know because sometimes he brings me dinner. I'm a widow. The name of the place is something like Real Nicaragua… or something like that. He's from there, you know. Oh, wait."

The widow Shoemaker held up a finger and did an about face. Lechler was getting nervous about the amount of time she was taking.

In about a minute, just as Lechler was about to abandon the chitchat and get out of there, the friendly woman returned with a Styrofoam takeout container and a plastic bag. She held it up for her visitor to see.

"This was in my trash from a few nights ago. Silly me. It's the *Nicaragua Genuina*."

"This is wonderful," Lechler exclaimed and snapped a photo of the logo on the bag. It had the name, address, phone number, and website of the place.

"Thank you so much, ma'am, Eddie is blessed to have you for a neighbor." He took the woman's hand gently in both of his. "Goodbye, precious," he added, patting the cat on its head.

The liar walked slowly down the hallway until he heard Mrs. Shoemaker's door shut. Then he picked up the pace.

"That took a while," Morgan griped as his partner was getting back in the truck. "I assume you got in."

"Nope."

Morgan grimaced and sighed.

"Besides, I don't think it would've done any good. While I was talking to Solis' neighbor about Eddie, I noticed that the doorframe around the deadbolt and the knob were really messed up. I think someone had already gone through the place."

"What did the neighbor say?"

As the retired soldier started his pickup, he displayed his last photo on his phone and handed it to his friend in the passenger seat.

Morgan handed the device back to the driver and said, "What is this?"

"The old woman said Solis goes there – a lot."

Morgan smiled. "Well, that's something. Hope it pans out."

"Me, too. Oh, I patted her cat."

"But you hate cats."

"Yeah, tell me."

Lechler put the shifter in "D" and headed for the *Nicaragua Genuina.*

♦

Edmundo Solis was beside himself. The last he had seen of the Gutierrez brothers was when they had scattered all the food and water outside the mesh enclosure where the Nicaraguan and his Washington contact were being held.

Maggie, on the other hand, was trying to figure some way to escape. She turned the metal bucket over to stand on it to see if she could reach a point at the top of one of the former supply enclosure's walls. It was well out of her reach. Maggie was examining the barrier to see if she might scale it. It reached all the way to the ceiling of the warehouse, but the mesh sagged considerably at the top at one place. Before she began to climb, she heard the outer door opening again. She hopped off the pail and turned it over and moved away from the point where she had been standing on it. Then she hurriedly collapsed to the floor beside her cellmate.

Secretary Loughlin buried her face in her hands to demonstrate that she was as distraught as Eddie was.

Luis and Santos didn't enter the room where their prisoners sat. Instead, they stood outside and looked through the metal fabric that made up the wall. The two spoke about the next step in their plan, alternating stares between each other and their captives.

Then, inexplicably, Luis wheeled about and threw his hands up.

♦

Morgan and Lechler knew that *Nicaragua Genuina* wouldn't be open for business yet. The establishment's hours, as shown on the takeout bag that Mrs. Shoemaker had shown her "fellow cat owner," began at 11:00 AM. But the pair hoped someone would already be there as early as they were at 8:40. Most restaurants used the pre-opening time to prep for the day.

They parked short of the eatery and bar and scoped it out carefully through their binoculars to make sure that no federal authorities had uncovered Solis' hangout before they did and were presently there. The men were confident that no law enforcement officials were at the establishment. But though feds weren't on the scene, the place wasn't empty. Through the windows they could see a young woman moving tables and chairs about, then sweeping the floor where the dining furniture had covered it.

"Damned cleaning crew, Josh."

"Well, maybe they'll know what time the staff will start showing up.

Watch my back, Tom."

"Copy that." Lechler set the binoculars on the truck's console and watched his associate approach the Genuine Nicaragua.

When Morgan got there, he tapped on one of the pair of glass doors. The cleaning woman waved her hand side to side and shouted. Morgan couldn't hear her but understood that her lips had formed the words, "We're closed."

Since he knew the woman wouldn't hear him, Josh didn't actually say any words aloud. He simply mouthed, "Please. I need some information."

The lady with the broom waved her hands more emphatically than before and repeated, "CLOSED!"

Josh cupped his hands and leaned close to the slight gap between the two doors to the dining area. This time he not only said his words. He screamed them.

"WHEN WILL THE MANAGER GET HERE?"

The young lady shoved her broom against the bar and stomped to the door.

"WE'RE NOT OPEN YET!"

Her closer position to the door allowed Morgan to hear her voice and not just read her lips.

"Well, she should be able to hear me, too, then," he muttered. "When does the manager arrive?"

The woman stepped to about two feet from the glass that separated her from the annoying man. She folded her arms and locked her eyes on his.

"Please," Morgan mouthed, folding his hands together to plead.

The cleaner closed her distance by another foot and stared at the idiot a few seconds and decided that she wasn't getting through to him.

"I'm the owner," she disclosed.

Morgan's eyes widened and he held up his palm in the way that says, "Hold on." While he pulled up an image on his phone, he hollered, "I'm looking for a friend!"

No sooner had he held his phone against the glass door, showing an image of Eddie Solis that Parnell had sent, the girl grasped her keys out of her apron pocket and shakily attempted to put the right one into the lock. Her forehead wrinkled, her eyes spoke of worry, and her mouth quivered.

When she finally got the door open, she blurted, "Where is Eddie?"

CHAPTER 19

"Eddie was in here last Monday. He hasn't been back." The daughter of the owner of *Nicaragua Genuina* was near tears. Josh pulled at the cloth that covered some silverware by its corner, spilling the utensils, and handed her the napkin.

"Thank you." Ana dabbed at her eyes.

"And that's unusual?" asked the ex-spy.

A weak smile appeared on the young woman's face.

"Eddie likes me. He is here every night. We joke a little – a lot – but I… uh, I…"

"Don't like him like that?" finished Morgan.

Ana's head bobbed her answer. Ana's father entered through the restaurant's rear door and joined the meeting.

"He met two men – brothers – here. They were fans of his blog. I think that went to Eddie's head. Helped his ego. Eddie got very drunk. He never drinks more than one beer, but they kept the drinks coming. Rum, especially."

"Did Eddie leave alone?"

Ana shook her head.

"No, they helped him home."

"Are you sure they took him home?" asked the retired sergeant, who had joined Morgan inside.

The young woman's head raised suddenly. Her eyes widened and she felt even greater fear. "They took Eddie?!"

"Maybe," admitted Lechler.

"You don't have security cameras, do you?"

Ana shook her head.

"Which way did they go, Ana?" Morgan asked.

She gestured to the right of the doorway.

"West. I think to the lot where many of our customers park."

"Anything else you can tell us?" Morgan asked.

"No. Just please get Eddie back."

As Morgan and Lechler made their way to the parking lot, their eyes searched the immediate area for anybody else who might be arriving at the restaurant where they had left a sobbing Ana.

"You know, Tom, that girl likes Eddie more than she realizes."

"Nah, she's just worried."

"Where's your sense of romance, Tom?"

"My ex says I'm not interested in romance. Only sex."

Morgan smiled, but a look at Lechler revealed that he wasn't."

"This is Eddie's car, Josh," Lechler observed, as he compared it with the details they had gotten from Parnell.

Lifting the door handle, Morgan said, "It's open. And not broken into. But I guess that makes sense. They had Solis, so they had his keys."

The pair searched the interior of the sedan. It was a mess. Apparently, for Solis, cleanliness wasn't next to Godliness. Candy wrappers, empty water and soft drink bottles, and scribbled notes littered the floorboards and all the seats except the driver's.

"I'll almost need a shower after this," Morgan complained.

Lechler grunted and then asked, "What's this?"

Morgan took the handwritten note from his partner. "Looks like different handwriting than the others. Just an address."

He typed the address into his phone's navigation app. The map appeared with a red dot signaling the location but had no label identifying what was located there. Morgan selected "Satellite" view.

"Hmm." Morgan touched the display with his fingertips and moved the view around, zooming in and out. "Well, it's certainly out in the middle of nowhere."

"What do you think, Josh?"

"I don't know, Tom. I don't think we have any other leads to go on. Anything in Eddie's apartment has already been taken, I'm sure, by whoever was in before you got there. And I don't think we'll gain anything by going to the UPS distribution center where he worked."

"So…?" Lechler said.

"So, I think we check this place out. Could be Eddie was onto something there…"

"Or not."

"Yeah, which would mean it's a colossal waste of time."

♦

While the former spy and ex-Special Forces soldier were returning to

Lechler's pickup, two men in suits were asking Mrs. Shoemaker about Eddie Solis. They had knocked repeatedly on the missing man's door without a response. They didn't have a warrant to enter, though they had called in for one. So, in the meantime they were talking to his neighbors.

"No, I haven't seen Eddie for a few days," the man's neighbor said. "But that's not unusual," she added. Mrs. Shoemaker patted her cat on its head.

"Eddie goes to work very early. And many times, he doesn't get in until late. Sometimes I hear him opening his door, but not always."

The two FBI agents thanked the elderly woman for her time and walked to another of Solis' neighbors' doors.

As she shut her door behind her and began latching her three door locks, Mrs. Shoemaker wondered why everybody was so interested in Eddie today.

♦

The Nicaraguan dictator's henchmen made no effort to conceal their plans from their captives. They would both be dead soon. And what could knowing their destination empower them to do? So, they carried on their conversation just outside the mesh enclosure where Press Secretary Loughlin and Freedom Blogger Solis sat.

As they discussed the destination where they would move the pair, each listed concerns about the relocation. Finally, the older but subservient Gutierrez identified the most serious of the drawbacks.

"It is less remote; less private, Luis. It will be difficult getting them into the building from our truck."

"No, *hermano*. The door is large enough that we can drive inside."

"But this place… with other buildings so near, when they are left alone, they might make enough noise that someone will hear them."

"Perhaps. I don't intend to leave them alone. If we do, we will tie them up and gag them." Luis looked at the pitiful pair. "Besides, *mano*, I don't think they will live that long."

"Luis, I still believe the move is risky."

"*Si*, it is. But we agreed to move Solis around. It is not wise to stay too long in one place. The American Intelligence is impressive, and they might find us. I think that staying here any longer is even riskier than moving. We must stay with our plan, *mano. Estás de acuerdo*?"

"*Si*. I agree."

Next, the thugs' conversation turned to Uncle President's plans. They weren't privy to the details. Zamora had confided only what they might need to know to validate information they tortured out of Solis. They knew what he had planned, but not where.

Even as the smarter of the despot's two nephews, Luis knew no more than his brother.

The entire time that Luis and Santos Gutierrez discussed their plan and their uncle's, their fellow countryman watched in disgust as the pretty young woman next to him absentmindedly pushed rat pellets around. He worried that Secretary Loughlin might be losing it.

"Secretary… Maggie…" He tapped her shoulder. "I'm sure it will be alright."

The attempt at encouragement and reassurance was rebuffed with a quiet, "Shut up, Eddie."

When Santos opened the door of the former supply room, Maggie stood quickly and marched toward the door.

"Let's get this over with," she declared defiantly.

Edmundo Solis didn't share her resignation, but he stood with some effort and followed her out of their cell.

♦

It was nearly noon in the office of the Director of the National Security Agency. Terry Henderson tapped on the metal frame beside the open door of Paul McClintock. He held up a pad with handwritten notes on the yellow paper and raised his eyebrows.

The NSA boss waved his analyst in.

"Shut the door, Terry," McClintock said, figuring that the young man had some information about the subject he had asked him to look into.

Henderson started with a big sigh.

"Okay. Here's what I've got so far. It's not much but it's stuff that wouldn't have jumped out at anyone if you weren't specifically looking for it."

The analyst set the notepad on the Director's desk facing himself. But he also placed a sheet facing his superior that had lines of words obviously from a printer.

"First, I searched for anything that might suggest that the Nicaraguans have any ops going on anywhere that seemed unusual. I struck out. Then I looked at data to see if anything pointed to any of their agents being in the U.S. That resulted in zilch, too."

McClintock was becoming skeptical that his young analyst had anything at all. Henderson's next statement seemed to confirm that.

"So, I looked at Solis' phone calls. Nothing." And Henderson looked up from his notes at the Director.

"So, you found nothing relevant in his calls?"

"No, sir. I mean nothing at all. No calls of any kind since Monday; four days ago."

"Terry, you remember that the guy is missing – right?"

"Yes, sir. But I think I can tell you about when… And maybe from where. He last used his phone early in the evening on Monday. The call was very brief. You know, like he got no answer from whomever he was calling. Or maybe he was checking out something on the web through his phone and it didn't take long."

"How does this help me, Terry?"

"Well, I'm working on triangulating where Solis was when he made the call. Obviously, you'd expect he was in Norfolk. He lives there. And he was. So, hopefully I can get a more precise location for him. But here's the biggie."

Director McClintock saw that his analyst was smiling.

"As you know, Nicaragua is one of the countries that we capture all calls to and from, and there are a ton of them, mostly to California and Florida, and to a lesser degree, Texas and some other places. Those are the states where most Nicaraguan immigrants settle.

"But since Solis lives in Norfolk, I looked for any calls between there and Nicaragua. I only got a couple of hits, but one stood out."

He pointed with his pen to a line on the printed page before the NSA Head, who looked up with his mouth open and then immediately back at the paper. His right index finger pointed to the line that Henderson pointed out.

"Zamora's office? Are you shitting me? Damn, Terry!"

"It gets better, sir, I searched the text of the intercept for certain key words. Obviously, his name. Nothing. But then I said to myself, 'What does Solis do?' One of the words I chose was blogger and it was there. So, I pulled the entire transcript. Here's a printout of the translation."

NSA Analyst Terry Henderson retrieved another document from a folder he had brought with him. Streaks of yellow highlighted several words.

NSA Director McClintock put a hand to his forehead and pounded the other one on his desk. Then he rocked back in his chair and moved his hand from his forehead to cover his mouth. From beneath it, Henderson could barely hear the mumbled words.

"Holy shit!"

The Director scanned much of the transcript – it was relatively long – but stopped once more at the two words that had caused him such enthusiasm.

"*Señora Secretaria.* That's Spanish for Madam Secretary! You may have found Loughlin, Terry."

♦

Analyst Terry Henderson had barely gotten seated at his desk when his computer pinged him the results of his query. He copied the data onto his notepad and called the Director."

McClintock was just beginning to call his CIA counterpart when he noticed the name of his caller.

"What've you got, Terry?"

His analyst's voice gave him the news. For some reason the location for Solis' last call eluded his technical snooping, but he had pinpointed where the call to Zamora's office had originated.

"I just sent it to you, sir."

McClintock hung up without a word, leaving Henderson to remark aloud, "What is it with bosses around here? They're so rude."

♦

For the two weeks since he had come to be in the employ of the National Security Agency, Captain Michael Driessen, USN, Ret., had spent his time mostly meeting with his peers throughout his new organization, reading material, watching presentations, and otherwise familiarizing himself with the agency and learning his job. He'd had no real assignments of direct responsibility so far, but he was still on the distribution list for every intelligence briefing and report.

He leaned back in his chair and removed his eyeglasses. He rubbed his eyes and pushed his hand through his hair.

A cup of coffee put him back in the frame of mind to tackle some more of the orientation material he had before him. Before resuming a very dry technical report on surveillance capabilities in the Middle East, he opened the daily intelligence collections summary that appeared in his inbox each morning and afternoon.

Though he had spent much of his adult life in cyber warfare, the retired Naval Officer was continually amazed at the capabilities of his new employer. This summary wasn't very technical in nature. Instead, it contained bullets grouped by subject and location, and ordered from highest priority to lowest. About three quarters of the way through the report, well into the items of sufficiently low importance that each entry amounted to only a sentence or two, he saw a line that caught his attention.

"Anomalous signal detected again; single; four seconds."

Beside the succinct entry was a reference to an earlier report. Out of curiosity and a degree of boredom with his training regimen, Driessen opened the summary of two days before to which the current one referred.

- *Anomalous signal in District of Columbia*
- *Three short bursts: 5-7 seconds each*
- *95 minutes between signals one and two*
- *98 minutes between signals two and three"*

The NSA Deputy Director looked at other details, including one entry that indicated that the bursts were VHF in the area of 107 megahertz.

"That's weird."

♦

The NSA Chief called CIA Director Parnell.

"What's up, Paul?"

"Wanted to give you a heads-up. After your call, I had one of my analysts look into your concerns.'

"And?"

"Henderson found an intercept that was made to the Nicaraguan president's office. I can say with almost total certainty that the voice is Zamora himself. And the call originated in Norfolk."

Parnell sat up a little straighter. "That's where Solis lives."

"Exactly, Betsy. The call had to do with Solis. Zamora has his nephews – the two men IDed in the murder video from Loughlin's apartment – trying to extract from Solis what he knows about some op."

"So, something *is* going on."

"Appears so. Don't know what or where, but it's imminent. That's the part you need to know. It's directly in your playground. Now for the other part. Off the record now?"

"'Other part?' Of course, Paul."

"Zamora was in a rage at his nephew henchmen for taking the Secretary."

"We knew they had her," the CIA Director remarked.

"Yeah, but she's with Solis. In Norfolk."

"They grab her and head to Norfolk, where they had snatched Solis. Sure sounds like they're both alive," Parnell surmised.

"For now, at least."

The CIA Director didn't like the sound of McClintock's words. "What do you mean?"

"Zamora's uproar was because the Gutierrez brothers took someone who works for President Hendrickson. He ordered them to go easy on her for now and try to get what they need from Solis. But if they can't, the nephews can take off the gloves with respect to Loughlin. But either way, whether they get the information they need – no matter from which one –

or they don't, both Loughlin and Solis will disappear."

"Shit!" Director Parnell's mind was racing.

"Josh is in Norfolk, Paul."

"Hell, he's good. Always a step ahead. Pass this along to him." McClintock gave Parnell the address Terry Henderson had come up with.

"Thanks, Paul."

"You know I have to call Gabe Austin as soon as we hang up. This whole thing is the Bureau's case. I only told you because Josh Morgan – and you – have a personal interest in Loughlin. At least Morgan may have a bit of a head start."

Parnell expressed her thanks again.

"Oh… And Betsy, when you talk to Morgan, ask him, if he finds these guys before the Bureau does… See if he can find out anything about this possible op."

"I'll tell him to ask nicely and say please."

The two agencies' directors chuckled and hung up.

♦

Supervisory Special Agent Annchi Liu sat at Director Gabriel Austin's desk.

Austin had motioned Liu in while finishing up a phone call. She couldn't get the essence of the conversation, but assumed it was important.

"Sorry I'm late," apologized Anthony Drake as he also entered the office.

"That's fine, Tony. Close the door, will you?" his boss requested.

The FBI second-in-command did so and took a seat.

"Thanks," Austin continued. "Okay, Annie, what have you got?"

"Not much," SSA Liu regretted saying. "With the identities of the Gutierrez brothers, you'd think we'd have tracked them down. But no luck. And the rental decal on their SUV – the one the Metro detective caught – there's a huge glare over much of it that's preventing us from enhancing it to the point that it's readable. Lab is still working on it."

The Deputy Director began, "Agents have scoured the District for them. You'd think that…" before his boss held up his palm in the accepted gesture for "stop." Drake wasn't insulted but thought it peculiar.

"How's the effort in Norfolk going, Annie?" Austin asked with some urgency.

The SSA changed gears.

"Well, our agents have been investigating there since it's Edmundo Solis' home and, as you know, he apparently had some sort of ongoing email correspondence with Secretary Loughlin. We discovered him through her request for a background check. Of course, our focus has been on finding Loughlin, but we're doing what we can to find him and the Gutierrez brothers as persons of interest. They're all from Nicaragua, so we believe Solis might be involved in her disappearance. We've…"

"He's not," the Director announced. He hurriedly copied notes from his pad to another page, tore it off, and slid it to Liu.

"The brothers are in Norfolk. They have Loughlin there, along with Solis. They grabbed him, too."

Drake and Liu exchanged a look of astonishment.

"How…?" the SSA began.

"I just got off the phone with Director McClintock over at NSA. An analyst of his did some digging into their captures. Without going into a lot of detail, President Zamora has some operation about to start sometime soon at an unknown location. It seems that they snatched Solis before taking the Secretary. They might think he knows something about the op. Who knows? And we have no idea why they took Loughlin, but they've got them… right there!" Austin said, pointing emphatically at the address he'd scribbled down for Liu.

"You're sure?" Liu asked. It wasn't an insult, but rather a statement of complete surprise.

"Well, we know they *were* there. An intercepted call between Zamora and one of his nephews originated there. It seemed clear in the transcript of the call that Gutierrez was at the location where he had Solis. And the transcript mentioned a female captive a couple of times. He used the Spanish phrase for Madam Secretary and said she worked for President Hendrickson."

SSA Annie Liu was already making the call before Director Austin gave her the order.

"Get your agents there now, Annie!'

♦

"I don't think anybody's home, Josh," Lechler whispered as quietly as he could.

He had parked his Ford pickup on the dirt road that led to the warehouse at the address written on the slip of paper they had found in Eddie Solis' car. They had walked the remaining distance and crouched behind a pile of scrap metal. Each had his .45 caliber handgun at the ready.

The retired sergeant had the binoculars trained on the derelict structure.

"Maybe it's nothing," the ex-CIA Officer fretted, but Lechler shook his head.

Without removing the binoculars from his eyes, the man pointed in the direction of the building and generally at the ground.

"Fresh tire tracks. Lots of them."

Morgan stretched a little higher to peer over the pieces of scuttled iron and steel that hid him and Lechler. He saw a crisscross of tread marks in the dirt that, while not muddy, had been softened by a recent rain shower.

"Cover me."

The former warrior sprinted toward the warehouse. Even taking into account the soft soil, it amazed Morgan that Lechler was able to move so fast so quietly. While the man dashed to a position beside a wall, the ex-spy's head swiveled. He looked alternately to the building and behind himself in case anyone approached from the road.

Lechler stationed himself at a spot where there was a jagged gash in the building's exterior. Before he tried to look through the tear, he placed an ear near it and listened. He looked at Morgan and shook his head. Next, he placed an eye over the hole briefly and snapped it back. Nobody reacted, either with shots or movement to his position. Furthermore, no one had said anything. The interior was dark, and the retired Green Beret knew that the eclipsing of the glow of daylight through the opening would've been readily noticeable. Any bad guys would've reacted. And, he was sure, any captives would've cried for help.

Lechler wasn't hopeful that he and Morgan would find Maggie here. But before he entered the building, he wanted to exhaust his options for determining whether the building was truly empty.

He motioned his partner to join him. Both hands on his weapon, Morgan crouched and darted to the building while his associate watched his six.

Finally, Lechler took a very long look through the hole in the metal wall. It was difficult to make out much in the dim interior with his pupils closed down from the daylight outside.

Tom Lechler had noticed when he surveilled the structure that the sliding door was partially open. He moved stealthily around the corner of the place. He looked straight ahead while Josh Morgan followed him watching everywhere else.

The special ops veteran darted across the opening of the door, ready for any response. There was none. He raised a closed fist to his partner. Then he pointed his first and middle fingers to his eyes and then to where the door was partially agape. Obligingly, Morgan stayed put and looked where he'd been directed.

In one motion, Lechler snapped the bottom of his right foot against the edge of the door and dropped back to a ready position. The door was old and rusty, so his kick didn't propel it smoothly or rapidly. But it did open almost fully. And it made more than enough racket that it would've attracted the attention of anyone inside.

The retired soldier snapped his head into the opening and returned it immediately. As satisfied as anyone could be that the building was empty, he leaned in cautiously for a better look and then entered.

Morgan backed in after him.

"Close the door, Josh." Lechler wanted the benefit of the same warning by way of noise from the squeaky door that someone inside would've had when he and Josh had breached. Had there been anybody there, that is.

Lechler flipped a handle on a breaker box and very dim lights illuminated the building. Both men kept their weapons out as they began to look around.

Morgan's heart raced at the devastation he felt at not finding Maggie there. He had tried to keep his emotions and unwarranted hopefulness in check, but it had been impossible. If his ex-fiancée had been there, she wasn't now.

The two men took mini-mag flashlights from their pockets to improve on the very dim single light fixture of the warehouse and began to search every nook and cranny in the place in earnest. The structure was of but a single open interior, save for a small area that might've been a supply room when the building had been in use. It was in a corner of the structure, using adjoining outside walls to form part of the cage. Its remaining two walls were made of heavy steel mesh. They rose all the way to the twelve-foot ceiling.

Around the tops of the walls, a few mice and rats sat, scurrying only when disturbed by a direct beam from one of the Maglites.

Lechler turned to see Morgan's light fixed on some trash just outside the small room. He directed his beam at the same location on the floor. Two mice busily scarfed up morsels of chips and crackers from the packages they had gnawed through, unperturbed by the illumination.

"This is fresh, Tom."

"How do you know?"

Morgan waved his light around at some of the rodents perched on metal beams above them.

"Because it would be gone."

Maggie Loughlin's former fiancé entered the cage. Lechler followed.

Again, Lechler turned his attention to where Morgan was aiming his light as though it was a laser pointer in a business presentation.

Josh kneeled to look at something on the floor, but almost immediately rose. He had a better appreciation for it when standing. Lechler joined him.

"What the hell is that?"

Morgan adjusted the Maglite Mini's brightness to 25% to reduce the overpowering brilliance.

"That's my girl. That's what that is."

CHAPTER 20

Special Agent Phil Jeffries of the Federal Bureau of Investigation ended his phone call with his boss while his partner Miles Russell checked for messages on his.

Both men's devices chimed a received text simultaneously.

"That's an address from SSA Liu. It's where we might find Loughlin and Solis," Jeffries reported.

The agents darted for their agency car, with Russell trying to read the message as he did. The two Bureau investigators buckled up and sped from the parking lot of the apartment building where Solis lived and where they had executed a warrant, bashed in the expatriate Nicaraguan's door, and searched the place. The place had been ransacked, diminishing one working theory that Solis had been involved with the Press Secretary's abduction. He was possibly an abduction victim himself.

The agents had discovered no computer or other electronic devices. Nor had they found any useful notes or other information.

Now they had a real lead, it seemed.

"Where'd she get this?"

"I'll fill you in, Miles. But first, call the local police and have them send SWAT and some unis for backup.

Agent Russell called the Norfolk PD, provided his badge number and code, and made the request. Then he listened as Agent Jeffries gave him the entire details of how the Director had come into possession of the knowledge.

♦

The newly appointed NSA Deputy Director turned his attention to the afternoon intel briefing to see if it mentioned the anomalous signal again. To his surprise, Driessen saw a new entry about the signal manifesting again earlier in the day. He hoped for additional information, but it was practically a duplicate of the last one – one burst, five seconds, same frequency.

"C'mon, Mike. Let it go," he urged himself softly. Then silently, "The best analysts in the world are here and none of them appear to have raised a red flag about this anomaly."

Driessen tapped his pen on his work desk. Technically, the former Captain had an analyst assigned directly to him – Terry Henderson. But without any real work to be done by his new boss, who was busy with training, Henderson had been occupied working on something for the NSA Director.

"Still, he does report to me," Driessen assured himself. He picked up his desk phone and called his analyst.

"Henderson," said the voice on the other end of the call.

"Terry. Mike Driessen here."

"Yes, sir. What can I do for you?"

"You gotta minute?"

Terry Henderson really didn't have a minute, but the polite manner his boss had addressed him had made an impression.

"Sure, Captain Driessen. I'll be right there."

"Thanks. And call me Mike, Terry."

The pair hung up and Henderson felt like he was in uncharted waters with a superior treating him with such courtesy.

"Hope it doesn't wear off."

♦

Josh Morgan held his light so that the beam was at a more oblique angle to the floor. Lechler's eye widened.

"Shit! And I mean that literally. Isn't that rat shit?'

"Yep."

"And is that a word?"

Morgan nodded.

Both men cocked their heads and squinted, trying to make out the letters that had been formed from rat droppings. The patterns of the pellets of the excrement were irregular, so the message was hard to read.

"Maggie did this."

"How can you possibly know that?"

"When we lived in Jackson, she was always spelling out things with whatever she had. Pebbles. Peanuts at this bar we used to go to a lot. One day, not long after she moved in, I came home to find our pantry almost empty. Every can in the place was on the floor in the shape of a huge heart."

"Hell, man. Why didn't she just write something in the dust on the floor? It's sure thick enough. That would've worked… and been a *lot* less gross."

"Weren't you listening, Tom? This is how I would know it was from her. It's a signature. Besides, it's a lot less obvious to anyone else than letters in the dust would be."

"I hate to keep stating the obvious, but *shit*."

"Here. Keep your light at this angle," Morgan instructed, adjusting Lechler's miniature black flashlight to a direction approximating Morgan's. The flattened angle created longer shadows from the droppings, adding definition that made them easier to read.

Morgan turned off the flash to his phone's camera and snapped some photos. Next, he inspected the rest of the room. He found that an old rag he'd spotted was actually a torn-up UPS shirt. He held it up for his partner to see.

Lechler nodded at first and then shook his head.

"Whew."

"Let's get out of here, Tom."

The pair ran full speed to Tom's truck. The driver floored the accelerator and headed for the street.

"We don't know where we're going, Lechler."

"Sorry. It just felt like we should hurry." He slowed the pace and eventually came to a convenience store. He parked and went in alone to get some munchies and drinks while Morgan examined the images on his camera.

Ex-Master Sergeant Lechler returned, drinking from a bottle of Gatorade. He got in and handed his passenger a bottle, too.

"Got anything?"

He took the silence as a "no."

♦

NSA Analyst Terry Henderson knocked on the door frame.

"Sir."

"Come in, Terry." With his greeting, Deputy Director Driessen rose and extended his hand. "I know we met on my first day, but we really haven't had a chance to talk. First, if my door is open, please come on in. But please wait until I acknowledge you to start speaking in case I'm in the middle of something. And if my door is closed, but it's really urgent, knock. Almost every time, I'll make time for you."

"Yes, sir." Henderson liked what he was hearing.

"Great. Have you seen this?" Driessen handed him the report that first made mention of the signal that was popping up from time to time in the District. The specific note was highlighted.

"Lately I've been just browsing the daily report. So, not really. I'm sorry."

"That's okay. But does anything stand out?"

Henderson took a long look at the details of the signal. Finally, he spoke.

"Well, a couple of things. Just factual. Nothing that would explain the signal."

"Go on."

"First thing is it's VHF, so it's line of sight."

"Yeah, I got that, too," the Deputy Director said, disappointed that Henderson's initial observation wasn't anything he didn't already know.

"So, it's max range would be around two hundred miles based on the strength of the output. But with all the buildings, monuments, memorials – that sort of thing – that range would be drastically reduced here."

"Yeah, I agree. Unless it's positioned really high up, nothing has much of a chance of picking up the signal."

"Yes, sir, but that's the other thing I noticed. I have my private pilot's license and that frequency – 107 megahertz – is very close to what is used for VOR. A little lower, but very close."

The Deputy Director sat down on the edge of his desk and considered what that could mean.

Very high frequency omni-directional range, or VOR, was built as a short-range radio navigation system for aircraft. An airborne craft's receiving units picked up radio signals transmitted from a network of beacons on the ground to determine its position and stay on course. The system was designed essentially as a road map for aircraft.

"You think one of the VOR signals has shifted?"

"I'm pretty sure that isn't possible. All the frequencies used by VOR are reserved for the government for that purpose. I'm wondering if someone is trying to hide the signal by making it close to the real VORs. You know, so it wouldn't stand out."

"But, Terry, that suggests there's something deliberately criminal about the signal, doesn't it?"

"Sir… Mike, I guess it does. Maybe I'm just a little paranoid from working here. Especially with all the stuff that's going on right now."

"Then if that's a possibility, why isn't it being looked into? Too preoccupied with other stuff?"

"No. Trust me. The Agency has plenty of bandwidth to deal with everything that comes up. Besides, who says it's not being looked into? Just because it's not receiving lots of press in the briefings doesn't mean it's not on someone's radar."

"I suppose you're right. Well, it just struck me as odd."

The pair spent only a couple of additional minutes chatting about personal matters before the new Deputy Director suggested Henderson get back to his other projects.

♦

FBI Special Agents Jeffries and Russell were inside the warehouse where the Gutierrez brothers had held Loughlin and Solis. Norfolk SWAT Team members had breached and cleared the structure. Now they stood about, watchful for anything amiss. The trash in the empty building suggested that someone had been there. The tire tracks in the soft soil outside made it certain that it had been recently.

As the Bureau required at a crime scene, personnel were capturing images or imprints – plaster casts of tire marks, photos of the entire surroundings; everything. Even footprints were subject to forensic analysis.

The impressions in the dust floor of the warehouse weren't suitable for plaster molds because the layer of dust was too thin. Therefore, only high-resolution photos could be used. Other footprints on the outside of the structure were deep enough for casts. Some were around a heap of scrap metal. They led to and alongside the outer wall of the building. Tracking backward from the pile of iron and steel, Crime Scene Investigators came upon other tire marks that were large and of the off-road style.

Russell returned from examining the grounds surrounding the abandoned warehouse. Jeffries was standing with his arms folded, staring at the floor.

"Look at this, Miles."

Agent Russell stood beside his partner and examined the dusty concrete. He cocked his head, stooped for a lower perspective, and even walked around the pile of excrement that was the subject of Jeffries' scrutiny.

"I give up, Phil. What's so fascinating about rat poop?"

"The pellets don't appear scattered, random. They look like they've been arranged."

"From back here, those look like letters," a distant voice remarked.

The FBI agents turned to the man whose voice had correctly identified the pattern of poop. A tall, muscular man approached and introduced himself.

"Mac Marchman, Secret Service."

The Bureau agents introduced themselves.

"The Service's Director thought we should have a presence in the investigation since the new intel connects Solis with the men who killed our agent."

Marchman had practically begged his way onto the federal jet that had flown from Andrews Air Base in D.C. to Chambers Field at NAS Norfolk. He had insisted his motivation was the death of his fellow agent and friend, and that was true. But Marchman also wanted to help find Maggie Loughlin, and the news that the investigation into Solis' disappearance was connected had heightened his desire to be involved.

"Welcome aboard, Agent Marchman," Russell said.

"Call me Mac."

"I think you're right, Mac. Those do look like letters," Jeffries admitted. He shone his light in a shallower angle, in the same way Josh Morgan had earlier. And similarly to the ex-CIA officer who had found the warehouse before him, the FBI investigator snapped photos.

"I still can't make out what it says."

The newly arrived member of the Secret Service reached for his Bureau counterpart's phone.

"Do you mind?"

"Sure." Jeffries handed the device over. Marchman, with a tap here and another there, increased the contrast of the image.

"Hmm… The letters appear to say 'SPRDSTOR.' Any idea what that could mean?'

The FBI partners shook their heads.

♦

In the parking lot of the convenience store, Josh Morgan had enhanced the image on his phone in the same way that Marchman had, though he had no way of knowing someone else was also attempting to decipher the manure message. However, the former CIA Officer was an accomplished photographer.

Knowing a thing or two about how the play of light manifested on an image, he had taken the additional step of converting the photo from color to black and white. Morgan had much earlier made out the message that Maggie had left for him. But he was no closer to discovering exactly what her clue meant.

He leaned back in the passenger seat of Lechler's pickup and rubbed his eyes with the heels of his hands. Then he stretched and offered his phone to Lechler.

"Here. You take a look." Before the retired soldier could accept the device, the ex-spy pulled it back. He didn't look at it. All he did was hold it to his chest and tap his forehead with his fingers. Finally, he attended to the picture again, holding it so that his partner could see it, too.

"I might've been looking at this all wrong. I've been assuming that these letters are all one single string, Tom. The droppings are all spaced in a way that I assumed was irregular by accident. What if it's by design?"

Morgan stroked his chin briskly.

"I'm not tracking, Josh."

"I think this should be viewed in parts. You know – sections. The gap between the 'D' and the 'S' looks larger. Do you agree?"

"Maybe a little bit."

"I think the first part really says 'SPRD' and the 'STOR' is separate."

"Then it could stand for 'store.' Maybe she figured out or overheard that the brothers were going to move her to an abandoned store. But, hell, Josh, how can we figure out which store? The first letters must be a clue, but…"

"We need to buy a vowel, Tom."

♦

"I'll get right on it, Phil," Supervisory Special Agent Liu promised, and disconnected from her caller. She examined the text message Agent Jeffries had sent her.

"SPRDSTOR. What the hell does that mean?"

The SSA called her boss. Drake, in turn, told her to contact the Director.

Gabe Austin jotted down what Annie Liu read to him.

"I'll call McClintock over at Meade right now."

♦

At the headquarters of the National Security Agency at Fort Meade, Maryland, Director Paul McClintock checked his caller ID.

"Hey, Gabe, what's up?"

"I need you to get one of your whiz kids onto something, if you would."

Minutes later, McClintock was on the phone with his go-to analyst.

"Of course, Director. It's not something I can do myself, but I know who to call."

"I thought you might. Thanks. Oh, Terry…"

"Yes, sir?"

"It's urgent."

"Of course, it is," Henderson lamented after he had hung up.

♦

"S'up, Terry?"

"Need a favor, Zilla."

Like a number of the Agency's best techies, Eli Ownby had been brought in from the private sector. And also, like many of them, Ownby had been a criminal hacker; one of the best. In exchange for jail being taken off the table for his cybercrimes, he had agreed to work for "No Such Agency." As a matter of principle, the notion of working for "the man" disgusted him. But from a practical standpoint, the twenty-two-year-old man could do what he loved – break into other computers or solve technical mysteries – while using the highest tech tools in the world.

"Zilla" was short for Godzilla, his hacker *nom de guerre* among his criminal peers. He earned that nickname because he was a monster in plying his trade.

"Shoot, Terry."

"Write this down, pal. 'SPRDSTOR.'"

"Got it. 'Unravel?'"

"Yep."

"Context or filters?"

"Yes. Use Norfolk, Virginia. Nicaragua. Those are all we can think of, Zilla. Oh, and it might be in Spanish. And it's for McClintock."

"Interesting. Is he afraid his wife is stepping out on him? Find a cryptic love letter?"

Henderson couldn't help but let out an almost girlish giggle.

"Just hurry."

Zilla hung up and typed in the string of letters Terry Henderson had given him onto his keyboard, followed by a few keystroke commands.

Other agencies had tools similar to the NSA's, but the proprietary applications at Fort Meade used algorithms unlike any at any organization anywhere, domestic or foreign. "Unravel," unlike many of the codenames intelligence agencies used, spoke of an application that did exactly what it implied.

The program's user typed in any word, string of letters, combination of letters and numbers, and even symbols. Unravel would chew on the data. The app would consider synonyms. It would insert spaces or add characters to the user input. It anticipated misspellings. The algorithm rearranged the characters, deleted others, and searched foreign languages to come up with a list of possibilities for what a string of pure gibberish meant.

Lastly, the process would rank the likelihood of each potential solution. And if some context was provided, the precision of the output increased.

The capabilities of the relatively newly designed quantum computing system at the Agency were unmatched and it was believed that it could break any encryption, given enough time. The Artificial Intelligence algorithms that comprised the backbone of the active decision-making methodology were so intuitive that NSA engineers joked – everybody assumed they were kidding – that the machine could discover the meaning of life.

Right now, Zilla Ownby didn't need Unravel to find the meaning of life. He just needed the app to find the meaning of "SPRDSTOR."

♦

"Okay, Josh, let's say you're right. Let's assume the group of letters is actually two. Then the first half might mean 'spread.' 'Spread Store.'…"

"What if there are more than two parts."

"What?"

"Tom, if we decide there are multiple parts, who's to say there are just these two?"

"Is another separation obvious?"

"Not really. Let's break it down. Take the 'S' by itself. That could mean 'south.' But south what?"

The former sergeant pointed at the "S" and "T" together. What if that stands for 'street.' It would make sense that Maggie would try to leave a clue about where the bastards were taking her next. Although I'm not sure how she would know. Terrorists don't usually divulge their intentions."

"Okay. Then we've got 'SPRD' and street, leaving the 'O' and the 'R.' I've got an idea."

Maggie Loughlin's ex-boyfriend wrote the eight-letter message on a piece of scratch paper and switched his phone from the image to his browser. He touched the voice search icon and said, "Find a list of streets in Norfolk, Virginia."

Once the search ended, the ex-spook tapped one of the hits. It read, "City of Norfolk Street Name Index by Grid Number."

"Crap. I knew this would be the case. Do you know how many streets there must be that end in 'street?'"

"No."

Morgan shot an insulting look at his partner.

"It was rhetorical, Tom. This document is twenty pages long… and has two columns on each page. I can't search this."

The light bulb clicked on in Morgan's brain.

"Wait… If 'ST' means 'street,' then the name of the street might start with 'S' or 'SP.'"

Morgan scrolled to streets beginning with the letter "S." He looked at his friend.

"About two pages. Still a lot… but better." Morgan pointed at the screen as he counted. "Eleven streets start with 'SP.' We'll never be able to search all those streets."

He slammed his hand on the seat he was in.

"Dammit all to hell!"

"And I hate to say it, but if that 'S' stands for 'south,' then you've got to look for streets that are 'South' something or other – a second word that begins with a 'P,'" Lechler added.

Morgan swallowed hard. He looked out his window briefly and finally opened the power drink his friend had brought some time before. He knew it didn't matter because the resulting number of streets would be unmanageable, but the frustrated man began to count the additional streets that matched the latest assumption.

"I hate just sitting here, Tom."

"I hear you, pal."

♦

The room that was the new hiding place for Maggie Loughlin and Eddie Solis was wide enough for Santos Gutierrez to back the black vehicle into it, providing sufficient concealment to move his and his brother's prisoners out of the SUV without any possibility of being observed. But the area wasn't deep enough to move the black truck fully inside and still have room to move about.

The auburn-haired woman and the Latino man wore ropes and gags now. Luis shoved the pair down and took additional sections of nylon braid rope from his brother.

"Move the truck, *mano*."

The older Nicaraguan obliged and, once the SUV was clear of the overhead door, he got out and shut it from the inside.

Luis tied Solis' feet without anything in the way of resistance from him. But as he tried to bind his female captive's feet, she kicked the younger nephew of the Nicaraguan dictator in his balls so hard that he doubled over, falling into the woman's lap. The White House Press Secretary raised her tied hands over the groaning thug and began to pound furiously on the side and back of his head.

Luis Gutierrez rolled away and managed to rise to his knees. Since Maggie could no longer reach to strike with her hands, she flailed at the man with her legs. The blows proved ineffective as Luis easily blocked them. Kneeling, the enraged man punched his prisoner in the face once. Maggie raised her bound hands to protect herself. Her attacker yanked them away.

He was about to beat the woman more furiously, when Eddie Solis, inspired by the fight Maggie was putting up, delivered a kick of his own into Gutierrez's left ribs. That his ankles were tied together lessened the speed at which he was able to swing, but the combined weight of his legs generated enough force that Luis recoiled from the pain. He stood and delivered a brutal kick to Eddie's left temple. The blogger fell limp to the concrete floor.

The younger Nicaraguan turned to Maggie.

"*Puta desagradable*!!! Nasty, fucking whore!!! I am going to kill you." He was reaching for his gun when a hand stopped him. Luis' eyes grew wide, and he screamed. He turned and aimed the gun as his brother, completely out of his mind.

"Brother, *por favor*!" Santos backtracked with his palms chest-high, facing his brother.

Luis Gutierrez panted heavily. His nostrils flared with each outburst of air. Finally, he lowered his weapon. His crimson face began to return to its natural color. His breathing slowed.

"We will kill them, brother," Santos assured him. "But not yet."

Luis turned his attention to Maggie again and said calmly, "Soon. And before we do, I will make sure you will wish for death."

He placed his gun back in his waistband and walked away, leaving his brother to finishing applying the rope to a bruised, bleeding Maggie Loughlin.

♦

"There aren't any streets using the word 'street' that begin with 'south' and have a second word that begins with 'p.' And there are only two that begin with 'sp' – 'Springwood Street' and 'Spruce Street."

"And they both begin with 'spr.' Same as Maggie's clue, Josh."

"Right. If we assume the first three letters belong together, that leaves us with 'DSTOR' or 'D-blank-STOR.' I wish Maggie had been clearer."

"You know she did the best she could. She probably didn't have much time. And she sure had to do it when the bad guys weren't looking."

"Yeah, I know, Tom."

The former intelligence officer examined some of the other names on the index of streets. Then he looked at his scribbled version of his ex-lover's cryptic message.

"There are a lot of names ending with 'Road,' Tom. What if the 'RD' stands for 'Road?' There's only one in the list that begins with 'SP' and ends with 'Road.' That's Springhill Road."

"Okay, Josh, but that still leaves us with the last four letters – 'STOR.' What's that mean?"

"Let's try this, Tom."

Morgan returned to the search term field of his app and typed "norfolk va stor." The first of the suggested "hits" read "storage units norfolk va."

"What if she's pointing us to a storage unit, Tom?"

"That could sure make sense as a place to operate. But wouldn't that likely be less isolated than where they were at that warehouse? I mean, that place offered a lot of privacy."

"And yet, we found them, Tom. Maybe they're staying on the move."

Morgan touched the hit with his right index finger. His selection provided a list of self-storage places in the Virginia city. The former CIA officer scrolled down and saw four listings for such businesses. He looked at their street addresses. None seemed to connect with any of the letters in Maggie's hint. He touched "More Places" to display further matches.

None of the additional storage facilities' addresses corresponded with Maggie's letters either. That is, until Morgan looked at the eleventh item in the list. Without a word to himself or Lechler, Morgan changed his phone's screen back to the photo he had taken of Maggie's rat poop clue. He zoomed in to the extent the device allowed to examine the first part of the pellets.

Josh Morgan's growing smile told his partner that he was onto something.

"Look at this, Tom. After the 'S' and also the 'P' are single pellets of rat shit. You would've thought they were meaningless, but they're not. They're periods. The first two letters are initials."

He switched back to the list of storage units and pointed to number eleven.

"Store Space Self Storage on Sewells Point Rd. 'S-period-P-period-space-RD-space-STOR!' That's where Maggie is, Tom."

Seeing Morgan urgently buckling his safety belt, Retired Master Sergeant Lechler did the same, and turned the ignition key. As he put the shifter into "Drive," he felt he should warn his friend.

"*Could* be."

Morgan shook his head and looked directly into his partner's eyes.

"She's there, Tom. I'm sure. Now drive."

CHAPTER 21

"It's a long list. Two printer pages worth without context. There's a Strategic Policy Research Directorate, but it's in Canada. It had various suggestions for the 'STOR' part," Zilla Ownby reported to Analyst Terry Henderson, who was disappointed that the NSA's "Unravel" program hadn't narrowed the possible meanings of string of letters "SPRDSTOR" to fewer selections.

"What about after you add filters?"

"Unravel adds them one at a time; then, in combination. 'Norfolk' alone generated the fewest possibilities for a single contextual filter, which is good news, if you know for a fact that Norfolk is relevant. One was 'Special Purpose Rifle,' and Norfolk has a huge military presence, specifically Navy. And 'SPR' could stand for 'Specialist Recruiter' in the Navy."

"What else?"

"Well, 'Norfolk' *and* 'Nicaragua' resulted in fewer possible solutions, but only because the quantum computing didn't come up with any realistic ones."

"Okay. It was worth a shot…"

"Hold on, Terry. I have one more set of parameters I tried. You didn't suggest using the word 'location' as a filter, but since you're looking for someone, I tried it in combination with 'Norfolk.' It came up with twenty-something possibilities."

"What were at the top of the list?"

"Well, I just sent you that list, Terry, but none had more than a sixty-three percent likelihood of being correct. That's pretty low. The rankings included things like 'Super D Store,' which is the name of a business in Norfolk. It was the top-graded."

On his end of the conversation, Terry looked at the list.

Zilla continued his reveal. "There are results using the last part as 'store,' 'storm,' 'storage,' and more. Or using the last two as 'operating room,' and… Well, you get the drift."

"I thought Unravel was magical; bulletproof."

Zilla Ownby took the comment personally.

"Hey, asshole, you get me better search parameters, I'll give you a better product."

"Yeah, I know, Zilla. Sorry."

♦

The Gutierrez brothers weren't able to coerce anything in the way of new information from the editor/head correspondent/chief blogger of *El poder salvador de la verdad.* He was unconscious. The men were getting impatient, particularly Luis, who was suffering the same stress that was characteristic of many decision-makers.

Press Secretary Loughlin listened to the Nicaraguans' argument trying to determine what they were saying, but her limited knowledge of Spanish made comprehension impossible.

"Luis, calm down. You know *Tio* Sergio told us to leave the woman alone unless it becomes absolutely necessary to try to get information from her."

"And you do not think it has become necessary, Santos?"

"If you hadn't struck Solis so hard, he would be awake, and we could work on him some more."

Luis was nearly in a rage. "And what was I supposed to do? The man attacked me, *mano*!"

"He was gagged, and his hands were bound. You…"

Luis Gutierrez's hands flew around frantically. "The time to work on the woman has come, *idiota*!!! Fuck you, brother!"

"Fuck *you*, brother!"

Luis stalked some distance away from his brother. His mind was in such a frenzy that he had trouble finding a way to persuade his older sibling. The younger man had always been more willing to go against what Uncle *Presidente* ordered. Perhaps it was because he always seemed to be able to quiet their uncle's rage when they had displeased him. His brother was less so. Finally, he framed an argument that he felt would persuade Santos.

Luis walked back to the older Gutierrez, trying to display some modicum of calm. He placed a hand on Santos' shoulder. It was a ploy he often adopted when trying to influence him to his view of things. It was an act that, unknown to him, quietly infuriated his older *hermano*, who thought it to be condescending.

"Brother… Santos, hear me out."

Luis was confident that his tactic of appearing more rationale, more thoughtful would lead his brother to see things his way. And as with the pat on the shoulder, the change in demeanor incensed Santos. The older Gutierrez wasn't as pliable as the younger thought. Most of the time his acquiescence to Luis' demands was his own way of shutting the man up. He knew Luis was going to do what he was going to do, regardless of any disagreement from anyone, so why fight it when he was simply delaying the inevitable.

"I am listening, *hermano*."

Both brothers knew that Luis had won. However, Luis believed it was his masterful manipulation while Santos knew it was merely his own cowardly capitulation.

"Did not our uncle tell us to use the woman if we needed to? *Si*?"

In his mind, Santos Gutierrez considered that Zamora had also said to try again on Solis before going down that path, and that Luis had made that at least momentarily impossible. That reality was apparently lost on Luis. So, Santos said the only thing that would prevent a reescalation of his rage.

"*Si*. He did, *mano*."

"And *Tio* isn't a patient man. *Es eso correcto*?"

"*Es correcto*, Luis."

From a few feet away, Maggie saw the younger brother embrace the older, who seemed to grit his teeth and shake his head.

"Maggie," said the man who had been semi-conscious for a few minutes and listening to his abductors, "it does not look good for you."

Edmundo Solis kept perfectly still as he whispered to his co-captive.

"I'm sorry."

♦

"Geez, Josh, this place is huge! And it's gated."

"Well, we knew it was going to be, Tom."

"Gonna be a bitch to get into. We could wait until night, except that the feds might get to her first."

Lechler could feel the stare before he turned to look at his partner's dumbfounded look.

"What?"

"Goddammit, Tom. I don't care who gets there first. It's not a race. If it gets Maggie out safely, I…"

"Sorry, Josh. I get it. I didn't mean it to sound like that. Really… I'm sorry."

"The problem with waiting until nightfall is that Maggie might not have that long. Who knows what they have planned for her?"

"You really don't care if the feds get to her first?"

"Seriously, Tom? No."

"Then call them."

Former CIA Officer Josh Morgan didn't hesitate for a moment before he made the call.

"FBI?"

"No. I don't know where I stand with them. I think I'm good, but I'm not sure. But I know someone who'll call…"

Morgan stopped mid-sentence.

"Betsy, I need you to make a call for me."

♦

Luis Gutierrez had calmed considerably from his outburst to his brother. He nudged Eddie Solis with his shoe without response. The blogger had fallen unconscious again shortly after awaking long enough to overhear the brothers debating whether the time had come to take their efforts at getting information to the auburn-haired fellow captive.

Seeing that the male prisoner was motionless and unresponsive, the young Nicaraguan turned his gaze to the woman.

"It is almost time for us to have a conversation, *puta*."

Maggie's blue eyes shone with defiance and that served only to arouse the man.

"You would kill me if you could. Wouldn't you?" He knelt beside her bound ankles and pulled at the restraints. "Perhaps I will remove these later so that they will be less… shall we say, less restrictive to me."

Luis tapped the fly of his pants.

"You will give me what I want, and I am not only talking about information." He touched her breast with a single index finger, making circular motions with it. "I would like to have what your boyfriend enjoys. There is no use letting a good… What do your American bastards call it? Oh, yes. No use letting a good 'piece of ass' go to waste. Who knows, *Señora Secretaria*? Perhaps I will satisfy you so much, you will gladly give me your information. Then you will beg me for more. *Sí*?"

Maggie didn't look away or down. Instead, she kept her eyes fixed squarely on Gutierrez's, and that unnerved him. He ripped at her camisole violently, but the spandex material only stretched and failed to tear.

"*Pobre bebé*," she taunted with one of the few Spanish phrases she had picked up from Josh. "Poor, weak little baby."

Maggie reflexively recoiled and raised her hands in front of her face as the younger of *los crótalos* drew back his hand. Just as it began to move forward, another stepped in to stop his arm in the midst of its swing. Luis' head spun around to see Santos glaring at him. As the younger brother tried to pry his arm away, the older of the vipers tilted his head forward and to the side and squinted his eyes. The dare that it communicated ended the near violence.

"Enough!" Santos screamed and threw his brother's arm out of his hand. He stomped away muttering.

The older brother's momentary dominance and intervention embarrassed Luis. The interruption of his intentions stalled his assault. He stood meekly and walked to the SUV outside the storage unit. He threw things around in the interior, finally turning to Santos and throwing his hands in the air.

"Fuck! We have no more *cigarrillos*!" He pounded on the top of the SUV with his fist.

"Go get some me some fucking cigarettes."

Santos folded his arms and stared at his brother. Luis lowered his head, and his voice.

"*Por favor*! Would you go get some cigarettes?"

Santos uncrossed his arms and bit at his lower lip. He rubbed at his temples with his middle finger and thumb. Finally, he nodded his head and returned his eyes to Luis.

"And nothing will happen to the woman while I'm gone?"

"No. Nothing."

"*Lo juras*?"

"*Sí*. I swear."

Santos Gutierrez held out his hands and Luis handed him the keys to the black truck. As his brother headed for the driver side, the younger Nicaraguan hurried after him.

"*Gracias*, brother." And he patted him on the shoulder.

Santos Gutierrez stopped in his tracks and every muscle in his body seemed to stiffen. He gritted his teeth and took a deep breath, as if counting to three.

Finally, he took his seat behind the wheel.

"*De nada*."

♦

"So, let me get this straight. Josh Morgan has found Secretary Loughlin?" FBI Director Austin said. "And he wants us to go get her? Sounds a little out of character for him. Don't you think? I mean, he's always been a DIY guy."

"Perhaps so, Gabe. But he apparently doesn't think he could get to her in time," CIA Director Parnell replied. "Can I explain later? Because right now…"

"Right now, I need to get some agents there. I agree. What's the address,

Betsy?"

♦

Morgan snapped a photo with his Nikon of the driver of the black SUV leaving the storage facility. The man turned away from where he and Lechler sat in the former sergeant's truck, so he wasn't able to get a particularly good image. He zoomed in as tight as he could on the man's head in the best shot he had managed and the two of them compared it to images of the Gutierrez brothers that Betsy Parnell had provided. However, the post between the passenger-side front and back doors obscured much of his face.

"I don't know, Tom. I mean, it looks like him… I guess… a little."

"Yeah. Hard to say."

The pair searching for Maggie Loughlin stared at the display for several minutes, zooming in and then out.

"I've got an idea," Morgan said. The ex-soldier had come to understand his friend well enough to know that no explanation would be coming until he had finished doing whatever his "idea" meant.

He zoomed the Nikon D850's display in and out to examine different elements of the subject's face. With its remarkable resolution, the camera provided an exceptionally sharp image, so the difficulty with confirming the man's identity wasn't a matter of quality. It was the bad luck in not getting an angle that offered a good, unobstructed look at his face.

Morgan and Lechler resumed alternating their attention between their known images of Luis and Santos Gutierrez on Josh's phone and the ones on the camera.

"I think I'm willing to rule out this one," Morgan concluded, pointing to the image of the younger Nicaraguan. "His hair seems to be lighter than what the man in my photograph has."

"He could've dyed it."

Morgan bit at his lips and closed his eyes.

"You didn't have to say that, Tom."

"Sorry."

"Hold on." Morgan enlarged another image on his Nikon and turned it to Lechler.

"His face is turned away here because it seems he's checking for traffic to his left, but…"

"Yeah, I see where you're going with this. He's leaning forward enough that we can see the side of his head. It's clear of the post between the doors. And that's what you were looking for," Lechler exclaimed, pointing at the driver's right ear.

Ex-CIA Officer Josh Morgan slapped his hand onto the armrest of his door. He turned his attention back to the image from Parnell showing Santos Gutierrez.

"That's him! It's gotta be." Morgan pointed at the earring in Betsy's photo and then to the one in the image he had taken with his camera.

"Is it a snake, Josh?"

"I think so. I can't tell for sure. But whatever the hell it is, it's distinctive. And it's the same in both pictures!"

"You're right, Josh!"

"We've got our men. Well, one of 'em."

♦

FBI Special Agent Miles Russell put his phone away and filled his partner in on Supervisory Special Agent Lui's information.

"Josh Morgan, that resourceful son of a bitch. He's found the Secretary and the missing blogger."

"You're shitting me!" exclaimed an equally astonished Agent Phil Jeffries.

"Gather 'round, everybody!" Russell shouted.

"What's up?" asked Secret Service Agent Mac Marchman, who was standing nearby.

"You're not going to believe this, Mac…"

He related the news to his Secret Service counterpart, while all but a couple of personnel began running for their vehicles to hurry to the address the FBI SSA had given them.

Marchman felt intense guilt at his mixed emotions. He was genuinely thrilled to hear that a location for Maggie had been discovered, though there was no news of her condition. But Morgan!? Why did it have to be him? Marchman tried desperately to put the thought out of his mind and concentrate on the break in the case.

The few agents who stayed at the abandoned warehouse that had served as the first hideout for the Gutierrez kidnappers/murderers went about their business as if no new information had been uncovered. Their only concern was to investigate this crime scene.

But the remainder of the Bureau's agents, the Norfolk SWAT unit, and local police officers sped away in their respective vehicles. The lead of each federal or local enforcement organization radioed ahead to get their units on the scene of the suspected second hideout.

♦

"I can show you a sample unit, if you wish," the storage facility's employee offered.

"Oh, no, thank you," his prospect said with a wave of his hand. "My best friend knows someone who rents from you, and I'm going to meet him here. In fact, he's a little late already. Tell you what, if he doesn't arrive here soon, I'll take you up on your offer."

"Oh, what's his name?"

The question threw Lechler for a moment.

"Oh, gee…" He began to fumble around in his pockets. "I don't remember. But he's a Latino about this height…" Lechler raised his hand to a point a little below his own height.

"I do remember that he drives a pretty new Chevy Tahoe – black," Lechler continued with a smile.

The clerk stared blankly at his possible customer long enough that the former spec ops warrior was about to bail on the charade and leave. Finally, though, the storage employee nodded.

"Okay. Well, I'm here if you need me."

"Thank you so much."

Morgan and Lechler had decided that the retired soldier should play the role because, while Morgan was unknown to the storage business' on-site worker, he suspected that the Nicaraguan brothers had surveilled his and Maggie's former apartment and would know what he looked like. It didn't matter up until this point, but it was critical to what would come next.

Lechler moved to his right, away from the office door. He leaned against the wall at the corner of the small brick building, where he pretended to read the pamphlet and other literature he had acquired inside.

Josh Morgan watched the facility's employee through the window with binoculars. He saw that the man had lost all interest in Lechler.

"Probably decided he wasn't going to sell him anything today."

Lechler continued to hold the information, appearing to read although he was focused solely on the street. When he saw the black SUV approaching, he put the brochure in his pocket.

Morgan left the pickup and began to move quickly on the sidewalk that ran along the fenced perimeter of the storage lot.

Santos Gutierrez arrived at the keypad just as Morgan turned the corner of the chain link fence. The approaching figure drew the Nicaraguan's attention. And while he was occupied with one man approaching from his left, he was caught completely unaware of the other approaching from the passenger side.

The tap on the window to his right caused his head to spin immediately in that direction.

"*Hola, amigo,*" a cheerful voice said. "Glad you're here!"

Through the slightly tinted glass, Santos saw the unexpected man holding a suppressed semiautomatic handgun.

"Come on, Santos. The door's locked." Lechler maintained his smile and pleasant tone of voice, but he moved the end of the barrel slightly toward the driver.

As soon as he heard the sound of the door unlocking, he opened it and got in. Morgan got in the back seat from the other side. Keeping his weapon trained on the Nicaraguan, he turned to check the facility employee who was looking toward him from behind his desk through the side window.

Former MSG Tom Lechler smiled and waved to the man. He followed that with a thumbs-up. The employee nodded and smiled and returned to his work.

"Open the gate," ordered Lechler in a very quiet voice.

"No," answered Santos Gutierrez. He folded his arms and stared straight ahead.

"Can you drive with one foot?"

The man behind the wheel furrowed his brow and cut his eyes slightly toward his newly arrived passenger. He hesitated for a time before he felt compelled to respond.

"Why would I do that?" he asked, returning his stare to some point straight ahead.

In the quiet of the SUV's interior, even the suppressed, muffled report of the H&K MK23 reverberated loudly as the .45 caliber projectile left the barrel and passed through Santos Gutierrez's right foot.

The Nicaraguan jerked his right leg up and clutched at his knee. His scream was part gurgle and part gasp. He began to fall toward the man who had shot him. Lechler pushed him back to an upright position.

The elder of the viper brothers tried desperately to show no pain, but without success. He grasped his forehead with his left hand and bit down hard, grinding his upper teeth against his lower ones. His head fell backward against the headrest. He glared at the man who had just shot him.

"That's why, you Latin bastard. Sorry, I guess I should've been clearer. I should've asked if you could drive with just your left foot. Now if you don't enter the damned code, we'll find out if you can drive with no feet. And if you can't, you're of no use to us and I'll put the next round through your fucking skull. *Comprende, amigo?*"

Gutierrez hesitated and put his right index finger across his mouth and bit down on it.

Tom Lechler lowered the barrel of his handgun in the direction of Santos' left foot. Slowly, the injured man lowered his window and tapped numbers on the keypad. As the gate began to open, he moved his left foot to the accelerator and began to drive forward.

"Now, that's better. *Bueno*! Glad we understand each other."

The black truck eased forward. Once it was out of sight of the office, Lechler gave him his next directive.

"Get in the back seat!"

The senior *crótalo* stopped and opened his door slowly while Morgan did the same behind him. The ex-CIA spook looked about for any unwanted attention while aiming his own H&K .45 at the hobbling man.

Lechler moved to the passenger-side back seat and covered the Nicaraguan as he gingerly settled in the rear seat on the driver side. Morgan took his place behind the wheel.

"Phone," Lechler demanded.

When the Nicaraguan refused, the retired sergeant fumbled through his pockets until he found it. He also removed a gun, a second phone, and a knife after a more thorough search. He handed all of them to Morgan in the front, who set them in the passenger seat.

The man who was now in the driver seat glowered into the mirror at one of the men who had taken his Maggie.

"Where is your storage unit?"

Gutierrez turned his eyes away from Morgan and stared out his window. Immediately, a round from Lechler's weapon tore through his right knee.

"I can do this all day, *vendejo*. But I do much more… Well, I don't believe you'll have that long. Your call."

Lechler pressed his barrel hard into the bleeding man's inner thigh near his groin.

"Santos, I have my gun directed at a place in your leg called the femoral triangle. This triangle here…" Lechler traced on the man's quivering leg with his gun barrel as he explained. "It's a spot where the femoral nerve and the iliac artery meet…"

The retired sergeant stopped and fixed his gun in one spot and moved his gaze to his victim.

"You know? I think I'm just boring you. And really, all this information is unnecessary. I'm just showing off about how much I know about killing dickheads. Bottom line is that I pull this trigger, and you bleed out in a matter of minutes."

Lechler feigned a confused look and turned to Morgan.

"That is right, isn't it, pal?"

"Oh, I've heard that it can happen in as little time as ninety seconds. Of course, our friend here will likely pass out in under a minute."

"You don't say?"

"Yeah, I wonder what it would be like to feel your consciousness slipping away from you with the realization that you won't wake up."

Lechler shook his head and let out a muted whistle.

"That would have to be…"

"Six-eighteen. Six-eighteen. Our spot is six-eighteen. *Por favor*! *Por favor*! Please don't shoot. I beg you!"

Whether from pain or fear, the heavily accented voice had a whimpering quality to it. Tom Lechler leaned away from the viper.

CHAPTER 22

In storage unit number six-one-seven of the Store Space Self Storage on Sewells Point Rd. in Norfolk, Virginia, an impatient Nicaraguan man looked at the time on his phone. He knew that it hadn't been an unreasonably long time since his brother had left, but he was growing weary of the delay in getting what they needed so they could leave the devil country United States.

Luis Gutierrez stared at his two prisoners. The man had stirred from time to time but had never fully regained consciousness. And the American woman – he wanted his way with her and was as anxious to have her as he was to complete his mission.

Maggie avoided eye contact. She held Edmundo Solis' head in her lap and stroked his hair. Maggie's emotions toward Eddie ran the entire range from utter contempt for involving her in this mess to feeling compassion for someone who loved his homeland and was trying to make a difference for people who weren't as fortunate as he was in having escaped.

"It all got away from you. Didn't it, Eddie?" she whispered as quietly as possible.

"*Puta*! Whore! What did you say?"

Maggie Loughlin couldn't help herself.

"I asked Eddie if he thinks you're as big an asshole as I do."

The younger viper seized his weapon from his waistband and pointed it at the auburn-tressed woman. His hand quivered a few moments before he regained control.

"I will find out what I need from the traitor. Then I will rip your pants off and…" It was as though he couldn't get the words out for fear of losing control.

"And after I'm done, I will kill you. If I do not get what I need from him, then I will get the answers from you. I will take my time. I will enjoy it."

"Thought I was your bargaining chip."

The man holding the gun looked confused.

"I thought I was your insurance in case something goes wrong."

"Ah," Gutierrez said in recognition. "By then I will not need a bargaining chip."

He placed his gun in his waistband and walked to the closed door of the storage unit. He wanted to open it to see if Santos was approaching but dared not for fear that someone might happen to be passing by and see his prisoners.

"I wish Santos would hurry with my cigarettes."

♦

Santos Gutierrez had torn a strip from the bottom of his shirt to apply the material to his foot and knee. Lechler let him. His pain had increased dramatically, but, as with many victims of such wounds, he had become accustomed to it in a strange sort of way. His grimaces were constant, but he had ceased to moan as he had at the onset of each wound the American gunman had inflicted.

He motioned to his left as Morgan drove the vehicle toward the end of a lane between the drive-in units.

"That way. Not far around the corner." Suddenly a jolt of pure agony racked his body.

"Stay with him, Tom."

Morgan stopped and got out of the SUV and moved to the edge of the line of units that made up one side of the corridor between them and those on the other side. He leaned his head around the metal building for a quick glimpse in the direction of unit six-eighteen. Seeing no sign of anyone, he took a longer look.

The former CIA Officer gave his partner in the SUV a thumbs-up and motioned him to join him.

"Then what am I supposed to do with you?" the ex-army operator said as he faced Santos Gutierrez. As he debated with himself whether he should just kill the man now, he saw his friend returning to the black truck, first waving his hands like he was calling a runner safe in baseball. Then Morgan moved his fingers back and forth across his throat, signaling Lechler to forget the last instruction.

When Morgan reentered the vehicle, Tom Lechler smiled slightly, "I got it as soon as I saw you heading back here. Don't go up there, you were saying. I got it."

"Shut up, Tom. There's no way we're going to get inside without things going sideways."

"Okay, what's your plan?"

"He's going to get us in," Morgan stated, pointing at the man beside Lechler. "Get up here, mother fucker."

With little left in the way of resolve, the elder brother moved slowly out from the back seat to the one behind the wheel.

Lechler lowered into the rear floorboard, with his gun aimed at the back of the seat where Santos sat.

Morgan moved to the front passenger seat and pressed the button that moved it all the way to its rearmost position. Then he, too, crouched into the floorboard.

"Do you normally drive into the storage unit?" he demanded of the man beside him.

Santos shook his head. "It would give us no room to work."

"Then here's what you're going to do. You're going to park outside your unit so that your side of the car is nearest the unit's door. Then you're going to phone that fucking brother of yours and tell him to open the door. You're going to motion him to come to the car."

"Then what?" asked Gutierrez.

"That's all you need to know."

The older nephew of Nicaraguan dictator Sergio Zamora began to move the gearshift when his passenger spoke again.

"Understand this one thing. Anything goes wrong, anything... no matter whose fault it is, it won't matter – I'm gonna kill you. No matter what else happens, you die."

In the rear floorboard, Tom Lechler tilted his head, squinted, and thought for a second.

"Seriously, Josh? John Wayne?"

Being an avid fan of the Duke, Morgan had realized as soon as he finished spelling it out for his prisoner that his threats were very nearly identical to those that Wayne had spoken in one of his movies.

Lechler stifled a laugh. It seemed wildly inappropriate. Finally, the similarity got the better of him.

"Seen *Big Jake* one too many times, pal?"

Morgan didn't answer.

"Then you will ask him to come help you carry your bags. If all goes well, and your brother is reasonable, we'll trade you for the woman and man you have inside."

♦

"The word is that Morgan and his buddy were going to wait for us to get here before doing anything stupid," FBI Special Agent Miles Russell said to his partner and the Secret Service agent tagging along. "But I sure don't see him."

While SWAT Team personnel scrambled out of their vehicles, Russell, Jeffries, and Mac Marchman flashed their badges to the employee in the office of the Store Space Self Storage. They showed pictures of the Gutierrez brothers.

"Seen these men?" Russell asked.

The desk clerk looked at the photos and watched the men in black garb wearing masks began to fan out around the building.

"What is this about?"

"Have – you – seen – these – men?" Jeffries demanded, shoving the photos almost into the employee's face.

"Uh, yeah. I mean, they're customers. They rent a…"

"What unit?"

"I… I don't remember. I'll look it up."

The man grumbled a few unintelligible words while he typed his query on the computer keyboard. He looked up and tried to smile. He began to sweat. He retyped the command. He didn't look up this time.

"We've been having network problems. I'll have to reboot the system. It's like this…"

Jeffries wheeled around and threw his hands in the air. Russell put his hands on his hips and shot darts at the man from his eyes.

"I need that number," Russell insisted.

"I'm trying. Really." The storage employee was on the verge of tears.

"Open the gate," Russell commanded.

"What for? Don't you need a warrant?"

Jeffries repeated the demand. "It's coming! Open the damned gate! NOW!"

The employee's hands shook noticeably as he pressed the button to retract the chain link gate.

SWAT personnel stood at the ready to begin to enter the complex the moment the gate was even partially open.

The FBI and Secret Service agents were on their way to the door, when the employee yelled at them.

"Here it is. I've got it," he exclaimed somewhat gleefully. "Six-seventeen! It's unit six-seventeen."

All the federal agents returned to the counter.

"Show me!" the Secret Service agent ordered.

The employee pulled out a map of the storage area.

♦

Santos Gutierrez pulled the black truck alongside the door to unit six-eighteen and stopped.

"Here." Morgan gave the man his phone. "You call your brother. You tell him to open the door; that your hands are full. Any tricks, I WILL fucking kill you."

The older of the *crótalos* brothers nodded his understanding. Morgan raised to a position from which he would be able to see the door begin to open.

♦

The Command Truck for the Norfolk P.D. SWAT Team set up and established that all personnel were on comm. Members climbed to positions above adjacent buildings but found their lines of sight restricted by the compact proximity of the storage units to one another.

FBI Agents Russell and Jeffries and Secret Service Agent Marchman stood near the gate waiting for word that everyone was in position. It was all Mac could do to prevent himself from barging into the storage complex, but he knew that, more than ever, he needed to remain composed and trust the procedures established for this type of situation. And those procedures were developed largely by the FBI.

"Where are you going?" Russell asked of Jeffries. Russell and Marchman fell in behind him as he moved back toward the office. As he approached, a local officer opened the door.

The FBI Special Agent held up his phone and showed the storage facility employee an image of Josh Morgan.

"Have you seen him?"

The man shook his head.

"Look closely. You sure?"

The answer came again with his shaking his head and adding, "I haven't seen him."

"There was another guy who came in and asked about renting a unit, but it wasn't him. It wasn't that guy," he insisted, pointing at Morgan's face on the phone.

"The guy who came – was he Latino?" Russell asked.

Another shaking head.

"Where did he go?" asked Marchman.

"He said he was meeting a friend here. Well, friend of a friend. His friend rents from us and he was going to show this new guy his storage unit."

"Was he meeting the Latinos? Your customers?"

"Maybe. I couldn't tell who he got in the car with. But it was a black SUV."

"Phil," said Agent Russell to Agent Jeffries, "let everyone know, particularly SWAT that there may be three bad guys in there."

"Three Tangos," Russell repeated. "That can complicate things."

♦

"Luis, it's me. I have your cigarettes and food. My arms are full. Open the door, *mano*," Santos requested.

Josh Morgan became a little nervous upon hearing the man describe the results of his outing. What if he was warning his brother? But Lechler had checked the plastic bags and they indeed held those items. He watched to make sure that the man had disconnected from the call. While he did, he saw Gutierrez lower his window.

Then to Morgan's horror, the door of the next unit to the left of their position – unit six-seventeen – began to rise. It was only open about three feet when Santos Gutierrez began to scream to his brother.

"*HERMANO*, IT'S A TRAP! DON'T COME! CLOSE THE DOOR!"

As he finished his warning, the older of the two Latinos fell onto Morgan and grappled for the gun. Morgan's inferior position on the floor of the SUV left him with few options.

Tom Lechler raised himself from his hiding place to see the storage unit's overhead door slamming shut. He watched to see the outcome of the struggle in the front of the vehicle, not wanting to kill the Latino if he could avoid it. He grabbed at Santos and swung at him with his gun in an attempt to disable him.

Despite his wounds, the Nicaraguan's resistance was remarkable. He swung at Lechler with his right arm, while struggling with Morgan with his left. He slammed the former CIA Officer's hand downward and against the console, causing him to lose his grip on the gun. Morgan and Santos each grappled for it, with Gutierrez coming out the winner.

Seeing Lechler raise his gun, Gutierrez regarded him as the more immediate threat. The Latino twisted into an awkward pose to try to face Lechler and raised his gun. Morgan slapped Santos' left hand away from his neck and managed to get Santos' weapon from the passenger seat where he had put it earlier. He fired once. The round tore through the Nicaraguan's right armpit, causing him to fire wildly through the roof of the SUV.

Lechler desperately wanted to avoid killing the man, but when Gutierrez regained some control and raised his handgun, the ex-Green Beret knew he had no choice. He fired twice through the driver seat, hitting the man in the back.

At the same instant, Morgan fired bullets from Gutierrez's own handgun that entered his chest through his right ribs.

Santos Gutierrez's lifeless body slumped toward Morgan, who pushed him away and against the door of the truck, where it rested momentarily. Then his torso fell forward and wedged between the steering wheel and the door.

♦

"This is bullshit!" an exasperated Mac Marchman decried.

"If SWAT says they're not ready, then we're not ready either. Got it?" Bureau agent Jeffries was more than a little perturbed at his Secret Service counterpart and wondered what his hurry was. "Without any federal tactical personnel here, we defer to the locals. And they say they're not in place."

Senior Agent Russell, too, thought Marchman's behavior unprofessional. He'd inquired about the man shortly after his arrival in Norfolk and thought a former SEAL should be more composed. He stared at the man, who turned his eyes away and stepped a short distance from the Bureau men.

Russell shifted his gaze to Jeffries and both men rolled their eyes.

♦

"What do we do now, Josh? There went our trade bait."

Morgan remained silent, and simply shook his head and shrugged. A few moments of tense silence ensued before the younger man spoke.

"He doesn't know that, Tom."

Morgan grabbed the dead Nicaraguan's phone and tapped the icon to redial the last number.

"*Hermano*, are you okay?" a frantic younger brother yelled.

"He can't come to the phone right now, but he sends his love." Morgan waited for a response. There was none, so he proceeded.

"Okay, *amigo*, here's the way this is going to work. We get the man and woman; you get your brother. It's that simple."

There was still no reply.

"You have to know there's no way out of this for you, Luis. Your only…" Then Morgan saw on the phone's display that the trapped thug had hung up on him.

Almost a minute elapsed before the dead man's phone rang. Morgan tapped to connect.

"Don't you fucking try to play tough guy with me!" And this time he disconnected the call with a forceful tap on Santos' phone. It didn't have the same effect as it would to have the person on the other end of a landline hear it slammed down onto its cradle, but Morgan still felt better at having hung up on the man.

Retired Green Beret Lechler had learned to trust his partner's instincts but wondered if now was a good time to play hardball, with Maggie's life at stake. He arched his eyebrows and tilted his head toward Morgan.

Another minute went by without a call from Luis Gutierrez and Morgan wondered what was going on inside the storage unit, and if he'd overplayed his hand. Calling the younger Nicaraguan back now would be the negotiating equivalent of eating crow and would weaken Morgan's position. Still…

He was just about to touch "redial" again when the phone rang. He put his hand over his mouth and closed his eyes tight. Morgan looked at Lechler and took a deep breath. His relief was palpable as he connected to the call. He remained silent and listened.

The accented voice of the caller sounded less frantic this time. It was calmer, but harsh and direct.

"Let me talk to my brother."

"That's not going to happen."

"How do I know he's okay?"

"He's our only bargaining chip. Why would we hurt him?"

On the other end of the call, Luis knew the meaning of the phrase, hearing it for the second time in such a short time. He thought for a minute.

Finally, "How do I know you will let him go?"

"You don't, but it's the only option you have," Morgan said. "Police and federal officers are on the way. They will *not* let you go. I'm offering you a way out. You idiots killed one of their own. You'll be lucky if you make it out of this alive."

"You're not police?"

"No." Then Morgan had an idea.

"I'm just a friend of Eddie's. I help him on his internet page. He's told me everything about what your uncle has planned – who he's working with, where it's going to go down – *everything*. And I know who his source in your uncle's government is. I'll tell you."

Morgan looked to Lechler who didn't know whether he sought reassurance or approval. The former Master Sergeant nodded and gave his partner a thumbs-up.

"What do you say, Luis?"

The reply was long in coming.

"I need to speak with Santos. I do not think he would want me to hand over our hostages."

"That's not going to happen, you dumb fuck!" Morgan screamed in Spanish. "He already warned you that we were out here. I'm sure as hell not going to put him on the phone and let him say anything to discourage you from making this deal."

Morgan shut his eyes again and said a silent prayer. He followed up the offer with a threat, which he delivered in English.

"If we have to come in and get you… If we have to use our explosives to blow this door open, we will. If that happens, I will cut off your balls and stuff them in your mouth with the end of my gun barrel. Then I will blow your sorry brains out. But before we come in, I *will* kill your brother. And I will do it slowly and with you listening on the phone. *Comprende*?"

"I have to know Santos is alive. Put him on the phone."

Morgan finally felt stuck. He muted the phone and turned to his special operator friend.

"Said he has to see his brother."

"We could wait on hostage negotiators."

"I don't know, Tom. He's sounding like he's losing it. This could go south real fast."

Morgan got back on the phone.

"We're trying to come up with something that will satisfy you without letting your brother talk to you."

"Send me a picture from his phone."

Now Morgan was feeling panic setting in. He muted the phone again.

"He wants a picture."

"Try this," Lechler replied and laid out his thinking to Morgan.

♦

Inside storage unit six-seventeen, Maggie watched her captor with a mixture of hope and dread. She was sure it was Josh who was on the phone with Luis. And the man's starting to open the door and Maggie's hearing Santos shout a warning made it clear Josh was outside. But she also saw that the younger Gutierrez's composure seemed to be falling apart. His pacing was more frenzied. He continually ran his fingers through his hair. And occasionally, he walked toward her and Eddie and pointed his firearm at them.

Now Luis simply held the phone limply at his side. Maggie wondered if her former fiancé was no longer on the phone. And that probably didn't fare well for her and the semi-conscious man beside her. She let out a huge sigh when Gutierrez put the phone back to his ear.

"Are you there? Are you there, *gringo*?" he repeated many times.

Maggie wished she could talk to Morgan. She wanted to tell him that she still loved him; that she was sorry for her part in their breakup; sorry for ever doubting him in the first place. She was near tears when she heard the younger Nicaraguan speaking into his phone.

Finally, Luis got a reply.

♦

"*Si*, I'm here. But I'm locked out of your brother's phone's apps. I could take a photo, but I couldn't send it. I tried to get him to unlock it, but he refused. Sorry bastard doesn't realize we're trying to let him go. How about you getting a direct look at him?"

There was a delay before Luis said, "How do I do that?"

"Open the door. We'll have your brother stand outside the car. Once you see he's all right, you let the man and woman go. As soon as they are with us, we drive away, and you and your brother can leave."

"No. I will not open the door."

"Then we have no deal," Morgan assured him. He and Lechler knew the man holding Maggie and Solis wouldn't go for the plan, and already had an alternative offer.

"Then open the door a couple of feet and bend down for a quick look."

"And get shot? I don't think so."

"You could hold your phone down and take a picture in the direction of the SUV without ever having to show yourself. It'll show Santos."

Morgan pulled the phone away from his face and stared blankly at it.

"He hung up."

"Maybe he's thinking about it."

"I don't know, Tom. I don't think he's going to go for it. In fact, I think he might be ready to die. Maybe he's afraid of his uncle. I would be."

The phone rang and Negotiator Morgan answered quickly.

"I will open the door as you suggested but will have one of my hostages take the photo and show me. If anything goes wrong, I will kill the other hostage. Wait for my call."

Morgan sighed and set the phone down again.

"This isn't going to work, Tom. We can't stage a convincing photo of a living Santos when he's dead. And with Luis covering one of them, we try to rush him, we have a dead hostage. It just can't work."

♦

Inside, Edmundo was stirring. In spite of his tremendous pain, the blogger managed to sit up. Through his still half-closed eyes, he watched the younger of the two kidnappers pacing the entire ten-foot width of the storage unit. He would pound or kick each wall alternately before reversing course. He pulled at his brown hair with his left hand and hit his head lightly with his right hand that held the semiautomatic. He was talking to himself.

"What's he saying, Eddie?"

"Mostly he's saying 'think' over and over. A couple of times he said his uncle was going to kill him, or something like that. And once..." Eddie closed his eyes and shook his head, turning away from Maggie.

"What?" asked Maggie, eyes wide and lips quivering.

"Once he said it would be better to die here than answer to Zamora."

Maggie put her arm around Eddie's shoulder, as much to try to gain comfort from him as to give it. Her blue eyes moistened. She looked away from Eddie and rubbed at them. When she looked up again, she saw the younger *crótalo* walking briskly their way with his gun raised. Maggie clutched Eddie more tightly.

Gutierrez alternated his gun between his two prisoners. More than at any time in her life – more than during her ordeal in Jackson with the impostor Secret Service agent – Maggie Loughlin thought she was going to die as the gun settled in her direction.

"*Señora Secretaria*, stay here. You are the most important. You, Solis, stand."

Eddie had resigned himself that his fate and that of Madame Secretary were completely out of his hands, so he was no longer inclined to cooperate or even die willingly.

"How do you expect me to do that?" he said harshly, gesturing with his bound hands at his bound feet.

Luis retrieved a knife clipped to his pants pocket. Fearing the woman more than the almost completely incapacitated man, he grabbed the rope that connected his ankles and dragged Solis to what he thought was a safe distance from her. Eddie groaned and winced.

Gutierrez knelt and with a flick of his thumb the blade sprang open. A single cut sliced the bindings.

"Now get up."

Eddie rolled over and tried to push himself to his knees. He struggled mightily to show that he maintained some strength and resolve, but it appeared he was unable to accomplish it.

The younger *crótalo* grabbed the man he considered to be a traitor to his country under the armpits and jerked him upward to a point where he thought the man could stand. Suddenly, Solis summoned his remaining strength and pushed backward with both legs, sending his captor stumbling backward. Eddie lost his balance, too, and likewise fell backward, landing atop Luis.

"Eddie! No!" pleaded Maggie. "Stop it!"

Gutierrez shoved Solis aside and jumped to his feet. He leaned over and pointed the gun at Eddie's head. He held it there for a full five seconds before making his decision. He drew back the hand holding the weapon and prepared to slam it into the fallen man's head. But he stopped short of completing that action, too.

"I need you," he finally declared and started to walk away. But he turned back to the man on the ground and shook the handgun at him.

"But not for long."

♦

"Unbelievable!" the FBI Director barked into his phone.

"Sir, I believe they're just trying to get this right," Special Agent Russell assured. "There are only four of us here, plus Secret Service Agent Marchman. We need to let them fully deploy."

There was a long pause in the conversation. Supervisory Special Agent Liu had taken the call from Russell and passed it along to her boss, Deputy Director Drake. He in turn forwarded it to his boss. Liu and Drake walked into the Director's office shortly after the transfer. Austin put the call on speaker.

"I know, Miles. Right thing to do. In the meantime, we're getting a phone number to you that we're pretty confident belongs to one of the Nicaraguans. It was used to make a call to President Zamora's office. Try to establish contact with him.

"As you know, we had already dispatched a hostage negotiator when we thought they were at the warehouse. He'll be landing in fifteen and will take over the conversation at that point. Until then, try to get a status for Loughlin and Solis. Tell whoever answers that we want to get this resolved peacefully and that he'll soon get to talk to someone who can listen to his demands and agree to anything reasonable."

"Yes, sir."

Austin was in the process of hanging up when he heard Russell.

"There's one more thing, Director. You know one of Parnell's guys – Morgan – tipped us off to this location. He was supposed to meet us here, but so far, no sign of him."

The Bureau Director put his left hand over his face and bit the corner of his lip. He lowered his hand from his face, tapped on his desk, and shook his head at Drake and Liu.

"Shit," he murmured.

"Sir?"

"Miles, if I know him – and I do – he's probably already in there. You need to get Norfolk SWAT to pick things up a notch."

Director Austin hung up and leaned back in his chair. He tapped his desk with his glasses. The Deputy Director and SSA Liu waited for their boss to say something.

"Your thoughts?"

"Sir, I don't necessarily see that as a bad thing," suggested Drake.

"I agree, sir. If we learned anything about Morgan during the Russia thing and during the subsequent matter with President Weston's assassination, it's that he's resourceful," added Liu. "And he's not stupid."

Austin motioned for his subordinates to sit while Drake continued.

"He's very bold, but not reckless. Nothing in his past suggests he would put other people's lives at risk needlessly. Granted, he's put himself out there personally in foolish ways more than once. But others…? I can't picture it."

"I hope you're right, Tony."

♦

Luis Gutierrez reflexively looked at the caller ID when his phone chimed an incoming call. He expected to see his brother's name, indicating a call from the American bastard who was using Santos' phone. Instead, he saw "unknown." Being in uncertain waters, he answered.

"What?"

"This is Special Agent Russell with the FBI. Who am I speaking…?"

The younger *crótalo* hung up and almost immediately the phone sang its alert again.

"Leave me alone!"

"Sir, I believe it's in your best interest to speak with me. I can begin negotiations with you to try to…"

"Fuck you! I'm already negotiating."

♦

FBI Agent Russell slowly lowered his phone from his ear and reported the details of the brief encounter to his partner.

"Hung up on me. Twice. And get this – said he's already negotiating. Now who the hell would he be negotiating with?"

It was slight, but Secret Service Agent Marchman scowled.

"I bet I know."

The FBI Agents turned to Mac, whose lips were pinched tight and whose eyebrows were dipped inward.

"Josh Morgan."

"Why would you think that, Mac?" Jeffries asked. "The storage unit manager said he hasn't been here."

"No. He said he hadn't seen him. I know he beat a path out of D.C. as quickly as he could and refused to stick around and answer questions. Not only that, he withheld information that could've gotten all of us started in the right direction sooner. He was involved with Maggie – Secretary

Loughlin – and is hellbent on being the one who rescues her. I'm just afraid he's going to screw this up for the professionals. He's a loose cannon."

Both the Bureau agents folded their arms, but it was Jeffries who spoke.

"You do know that he's the one who tipped the Bureau off to this location. I'm certainly pissed that he wasn't here to meet us like he said he would, and he may very well be in there right now. But it sure doesn't seem like he's interfering with our investigation. If anything, he's trying to help."

"Yeah, well, he's a civilian," Mac groused.

"He's not your ordinary civilian, Marchman," Jeffries clarified with a smile.

"Right. I know all about that," the Secret Service Agent blurted. He folded his arms.

"And let's face it, buddy. Right now, if you're right, he's in there trying to do something while we're out here with our thumbs up our asses just trying to get organized." Russell's tone was tense, not just because he was rebuking Marchman, but because of his extreme frustration about things taking so long for law enforcement to move.

"I'd bet, since he called us, something changed to make him think he had to go in immediately. Now, if you'll excuse me."

Marchman held his tongue, but it was difficult. He made eye contact with Jeffries, who finally snorted and walked away with his partner.

♦

Even before calling Luis and suggesting the impromptu photo op, Josh Morgan and Tom Lechler were busy getting ready for it. They had found ropes and tape in the back of the Gutierrez's SUV. After all, the brothers had been driving it when they kidnapped Solis and then Maggie.

"If the guy takes snapshots, this might work. He takes a movie, we're toast."

"I know, Tom," Morgan answered. The pair stepped back to inspect their work. The corpse of Santos Gutierrez sat upright in the backseat on the driver side, held in place by tape and pieces of rope.

"I don't know," Lechler admitted.

Morgan moved away from the vehicle and snapped a photo with his own phone. He enlarged the image to the fullest extent possible.

"No, it's obviously bogus. His face looks like a dead guy. Crap!" he concluded. "Regardless, we've got to hurry. Luis could slide that door up anytime."

"Wait," the former sergeant said, and he ran back to the open hatch of the SUV. He tore two strips from a piece of cloth as he returned to the staged scene. He tied one around the body's mouth and the other around his eyes. Lastly, he began to apply tape to the blindfold and secured it to the

SUV's seat to prop the head up in a more natural way.

"That's better, Tom. Good thinking. It's the best we can do."

CHAPTER 23

Luis Gutierrez ordered Maggie to stand. She acted as if it was more difficult than it was, but in time realized she had no choice but to comply. She leaned against the wall to steady herself.

Turning back to Solis, he ordered, "You will take a photo." The Nicaraguan handed the blogger his phone. He promptly dropped it. Luis picked it up and handed it back.

"Don't drop it again!"

Edmundo Solis held his bound hands up. "Sorry," he said with a sneer. "But I can hardly hold this thing. How am I supposed to take a picture?"

Gutierrez realized he was right. He cut the tape away from his hands.

"Here's what I want you to do. When I say so – not a second before – I want you to slide the latch back and raise the door up about this high." The younger brother held his hand about three feet above the ground.

"Then I want you to bend down and use my phone to take a picture of my brother. The American said he would be near the truck. Take two or three. I assume you know how. After all, you believe yourself to be a journalist. Got it?"

Solis nodded.

"When you've done that, I want you to lower the door and slide the latch back into place. *Lo entiendes?*"

"*Si*, I understand." The answer was weak, barely audible, so much that Luis wondered if Solis could manage it.

The brother of the late Nicaraguan moved to Maggie. He pulled her away from the wall and slid in behind her. He grinded himself against her ass and held her in place by reaching his left arm across her chest and cupping his hand on her right breast.

Maggie squeezed her blue eyes shut and tears began to fill them. She would've fought back but she knew Josh was nearby. And that meant that this son of a bitch Nicaraguan molester would be dead soon. It was an odd thought, considering all that was going on, but for a brief moment she understood that there were evil people in the world who deserved to die. Josh had killed some of them.

The White House Press Secretary held back her sobs but couldn't prevent the tears from streaming down her face. Her closed eyes opened wide at the sensation of a gun barrel against her right temple.

"You send an injured man to do your work and hide behind a woman? What kind of a man are you?" she taunted.

He pressed the gun more forcefully against her head and himself more forcefully against her body.

"Solis is not a man. He is a pig and a traitor. And you? You are merely a whore." He leaned closer to her right ear. "And do not forget that we have unfinished business."

Luis Gutierrez pushed even more strongly against his hostage, and his arousal was even more evident to her.

Maggie's disgust didn't disappear, but along with the personal violation she felt, there was a growing sense of rage.

"You have no idea what unfinished business awaits *you*!" she thought.

Luis Gutierrez motioned toward the overhead door with his gun.

"Go. Now."

Edmundo Solis looked at Maggie and agonized over her suffering. Strangely, though, the Press Secretary smiled and winked at him through teary eyes. She mouthed, "It's okay."

Gutierrez knew she had tried to tell the blogger something but didn't care.

Eddie Solis hobbled to the overhead door and tried to lift it. It wouldn't budge.

"Slide the latch back, *idiota*!"

Eddie inspected the door and saw a sliding bolt mounted on the right side near the concrete floor that slid into the metal door frame. He took a deep breath, believing that he would die shortly. Hanging from a roller was a loop of substantial chain. He tested it and found that pulling down on the side closest to him raised the door.

His condition made the task nearly impossible, but he managed to raise the door to a height of approximately three feet.

Eddie dropped to his knees as slowly as he could, resting his hand on the concrete to steady himself. It took the full measure of the strength and control that he had left to lower himself to see beneath the partially open metal door. It occurred to him to try to escape, but he couldn't leave Maggie.

He lay completely on the floor and raised the phone to take photos.

Solis recoiled at the shock of the sight of a man lying just outside the overhead door along the wall. His left index finger was at his lips. His right hand held a gun.

"Shhh…, the man whispered. "Leave the door unlocked. Blink if you understand."

Eddie resisted the instinctive reaction of nodding and blinked his eyes very deliberately.

Morgan had taken a position beside the door, leaving Lechler to take a shot at Gutierrez if the opportunity presented itself. He had hoped he would send Maggie to raise the door and take the photos. He would've had no remorse at dragging her out to safety and leaving the Nicaraguan to deal with Eddie however he saw fit.

"Take the fucking pictures and shut the door!" came the shout from behind Solis.

Eddie pointed the phone's camera toward a black SUV in which Santos Gutierrez sat bound, gagged, and blindfolded. As he took a series of photos, he noticed that Santos never moved.

As the Nicaraguan patriot blogger backed away from the door, he took a furtive last look at the man lying nearby.

He blinked again.

"Good man," thought Josh Morgan.

Still lying on the concrete, Eddie pulled on the side of the looped chain furthest from him and the door crashed to the floor out of control with a noisy metallic clang. For show, he jiggled the metal latch noisily but without pushing it back into its slot. He raised himself to his knees. Then he pulled one leg forward so that his foot was on the floor. He steadied himself with his arm again and rose to stand on both feet.

Finally, he did an about-face.

Once the door closed, Maggie pulled herself away from Luis Gutierrez, who pushed her to the floor as he rushed to retrieve his phone. He put his handgun in his waistband and tapped the first image to inspect Solis' product.

It wasn't at all what he had expected. He had anticipated his brother standing nearby, facing toward the camera.

"Fuck, fuck, fuck!' he screamed. He swiped the image to the side and viewed the next. It looked exactly like the first. He thought it looked like Santos but couldn't be sure because of the blindfold and gag. He looked at the final image and prepared to call his brother's phone, which was in the hands of the American bastard.

Gutierrez's head spun around violently at the sound of the overhead door rising rapidly. He fumbled for his gun and looked desperately for a spot to shelter but the storage room was completely empty except for three folding chairs and an old metal shipping crate that had been left by a previous renter. A sturdy metal lid that appeared to fit tightly on the top edges served as a cover to the box.

The *crótalo* fired two rounds rapidly in the direction of the man kneeling at the outside edge of the doorway. He continued to fire in that general direction without aiming as he darted for his female hostage.

Ex-Green Beret Lechler had assumed the position by the door in place of Josh. He fired his handgun twice from his concealed position at the edge of the doorway, hitting his moving target both times but not dropping the man. The crease across Gutierrez's right ribcage turned crimson immediately. The dot on his right shoulder also reddened. Lechler fired two more shots in rapid succession but didn't connect with either.

Maggie was helpless because of the bindings still on her ankles and wrists. She tried frantically to crawl away but without success. Gutierrez grabbed her wrists by the tape and rope that held them and dragged her behind the crate with him.

As the Nicaraguan neared Maggie, the former sergeant stopped shooting. He yelled for Eddie to get out of the way. Flooded with adrenaline, the battered blogger managed to dart to the side of the unit. But when he reached the wall, the combined effects of the beatings, the stress, and the exertion caused his adrenaline to evaporate. He collapsed unconscious.

With the blogger out of the way, the sound of an accelerating engine crescendoed to a screaming roar as the brothers' SUV approached the gaping doorway to the storage room. Immediately the black truck slid into the building almost all the way to the front, its front left fender less than two feet away from the crate in the corner.

Josh Morgan flung the door open and jumped from the vehicle, using the open door for cover. Tom Lechler rushed from his position outside the overhead door and took cover at the rear of the truck. He crept around the passenger side, maintaining a protected position beside the vehicle, moving all the way to the front right fender.

El crótalo fired occasionally over the top of the box he was hiding behind to keep his attackers at bay. His cover was perfect, but he had no place to go. Morgan knew that there would come a time when something would have to give. He felt like it was time to let the feds take over. He and Lechler could wait until they showed up, he figured, until an accented voice changed his mind.

"My brother is dead, isn't he?"

Morgan knew he shouldn't confirm that.

"He's tied up in the back of your truck."

"Liar! I will kill the bitch American woman unless you allow me to drive out of here with her. I'll release her down the street." Luis Gutierrez tore a piece of duct tape from his prisoner's hand and slapped it across her mouth.

"Not gonna happen!" came out instantly, but Morgan was sorting through how that might work if the federal agents were on the premises. But what if they weren't. He couldn't understand the delay.

♦

The Norfolk SWAT Team commander approached FBI Agents Russell and Jeffries.

"Our guys are all in place. And your negotiator just arrived. Let me know what you need."

Each of the Bureau feds shook hands with the new arrival. Bill Antrim was a fourteen-year veteran of the Hostage Negotiation Team. He had lost a few, but very few.

"I understand the man holding the hostages refused to speak with you. I got word of that shortly after landing."

"You could say that. Hung up on me – twice," Russell reported.

"And what is this about him saying he was already in negotiations?"

Russell quickly told him the entire story and his speculation that Josh Morgan was in contact with the man. Mac Marchman folded his arms in the background.

"I see," Antrim said with an obviously disturbed look and tone. "You know how this complicates things, don't you?"

"Perhaps."

Without asking anyone's permission, Bill Antrim put through a call to Luis Gutierrez's phone. He waited until the call went to voicemail, disconnected, and tried again with the same outcome.

"What do your guys see?" the negotiator asked the SWAT commander.

"We have a shooter and a spotter on the roof of another unit with a direct view of six-seventeen. But the angle makes it impossible to see all the way into it. And their view is also obstructed by a black Chevy Tahoe parked pretty far into the unit. It's twenty feet deep and the SUV is almost all the way in so they can just see the rear. As we were setting up – before our shooter and his spotter got glass on the site, they believe they saw movement but nothing since.

"We have a man ready to get on top of the unit, but he doesn't think he can do so without being heard. The metal roof has a lot of slack in it; very wobbly. It'll make a lot of noise."

"What about the units to each side and the one in the back?" Antrim queried.

The SWAT leader began shaking his head. "With the door open, I don't think we can get into the adjacent rooms. But we've got a pair of our guys in the unit behind six-one-seven. They have to move some storage items out of the way and then they'll drill through the wall several feet off the floor to place a fiber-optic camera in to get a look. They've already put a microphone on the adjoining wall. Oddly, though, there is space between the unit our guys are in and the target one. We're trying to get past the cavity and through the rear of the actual target unit."

"Is your team set to go in?" Antrim asked.

"It'll be another seven to eight minutes to prepare a breach. The space between six-seventeen and the unit behind it makes blowing it out problematic. Setting a charge that will go through both walls makes the consequences highly unpredictable."

Jeffries spoke up. "So where would you breach?'

"Really, the only option is to enter through the open door. But there's a problem with that, too. If someone sticks their head out of the door and sees our guys approaching, the whole thing goes south. The best way will be to wait until the fiber camera is in place. Once we have eyes on the inside, we'll be able to assess the situation and make a better call."

Hostage Negotiator Bill Antrim spread his thumb and index finger across his bushy moustache several times.

"Okay. We wait. It should go pretty quickly – right?"

"Pretty much. It's slowed down a bit by…"

"…By the open space that separates the back-to-back units. Of course, it is."

Antrim tried two more times to get a call through to Luis Gutierrez. No answer.

CHAPTER 24

Things had settled into a stalemate. All three of the men who had weapons in storage unit six-seventeen had stopped firing almost immediately after the black vehicle came roaring in.

With his location behind the metal crate in the corner of the room, Gutierrez had superior cover. But he had no way to escape. Yet, since he had to remain crouched behind the metal container, he had no line of sight to his adversaries. That meant that Morgan and Lechler had the better angle for a shot if the younger Nicaraguan viper ever showed himself.

Morgan really wanted to turn things over to the FBI agents. He wished he had a number to call or text them. He didn't. Neither did he have his phone. It had fallen out of his pocket during his struggle with the now-dead Santos Gutierrez. If he could get it, he'd text CIA Director Parnell.

The former CIA Officer raised his head enough that his partner could see him. Morgan pointed at the special ops veteran, pointed to his own eyes with two fingers, and then tapped himself on the upper chest. Lechler acknowledged with a nod that he would cover his partner.

Morgan eased back into the Tahoe and reached across to the passenger floorboard and got his phone. Lying on his back in the driver seat, he held the device above his face and typed.

fbi phone in norfolk

Finished with his message to Parnell, he had a thought.

The vehicle was still running from when Morgan drove into the storage unit. He reached up from his half-in, half-out position of the car to turn off the key. The idling engine was distracting. Suddenly, he paused. He slid his legs all the way into the SUV and moved his butt up into the driver seat, keeping his head down. He pressed the brake pedal with his right foot.

Next, he moved the gearshift lever of the truck into "Drive" and eased his foot off the brake enough to allow the SUV to creep forward. He rotated the steering wheel as far to the right as he could to turn it away from the crate.

To his right, Tom Lechler raised slightly and pointed toward the crate in case Luis raised his head up. Surprisingly, the man never fired a shot.

"Low on ammo. Doesn't want to waste it," the ex-soldier speculated.

As the former spy allowed the SUV to ease ahead, he had the same thought. He wondered how the endgame would play out if that were the case. Would the younger nephew of Nicaraguan President Zamora choose to go out in a volley of bullets? Or would he take the cowardly way out and end his life? If he did, Morgan realized that he would probably take Maggie out, too. Morgan shook his head slightly, as if trying to fling the unthinkable out of his mind.

Morgan concentrated on allowing the black vehicle to inch forward as slowly as he could. To his right, Lechler moved in a crouch at a pace equal to the truck's to remain behind the rolling tire to prevent exposing his feet to gunfire from Luis Gutierrez.

In a matter of seconds, the Chevy made contact with the rear wall of the storage building. The driver didn't bother moving the lever to "Park." With the vehicle still in gear, the key wouldn't turn fully off, but it moved enough, and the engine died.

♦

In her office at CIA Headquarters in Langley, Virginia, the agency's chief stared at the message from her contract employee and turned her empty palm upward.

"What?" She put her hand to her face. "You want me to phone the FBI in Norfolk? What the hell am I supposed to say?"

Parnell typed her last few words into the text field and sent them to Josh Morgan.

♦

Morgan had eased back out of the vehicle and was squatting on the concrete floor of the storage room when his phone vibrated its announcement of a message. He snuck a quick peek at the message. He squinted and tried to understand its meaning.

"What do you mean – '*and say what?*'" Then he looked at his message to Betsy and understood it to be ambiguous. He was about to reply when the *crótalo* Luis yelled to him.

"Clever, *gringo.* You have boxed me in."

"So, why not just give yourself up and save me the trouble of having to kill you? You've got nowhere to go."

"If I am to die, it will not be by your hand. And your girlfriend, she will die by my hand."

Josh Morgan shut his eyes tightly. "That answers that question," he thought.

He wanted to scream but wouldn't allow himself the luxury of the release for the pleasure it would give his opponent.

"If you back the truck halfway out of the room, and then both of you exit far away, I'll take the woman and drive away."

Morgan considered complying in the hope that the FBI was on site, but the uncertainty and Luis' state of mind led him to reject the offer.

"You know, Luis, your brother wasn't much of a man. We shot him a couple of times just for fun. Then we finished him. He cried like a baby. *Pobre bebé!*"

Lechler knew what his friend was doing, but thought he was taking a huge chance in making the Nicaraguan angry. He feared he might just shoot Maggie.

♦

Just inside the gate to the storage unit area of Store Space, Agents Russell and Jeffries were growing increasingly impatient with the amount of time it was taking to get eyes on their targets. They knew the SWAT unit was following protocol, taking every precaution to ensure success in whatever tactic they were asked to take. But still…

"Damn!" exclaimed Jeffries. "I know it's only been a few minutes, but it seems like hours."

"Russell," answered the Special Agent in reply to his phone's alert.

On the other end, SSA Liu shared news.

"Deputy Director Drake just called me and asked you if you ever made contact with Josh Morgan. Director just got a strange call from CIA. Parnell said she got a cryptic text from her guy, and she didn't know what to make of it. She said he apparently wanted her to call the Bureau in Norfolk. Have you seen him?"

"No, ma'am. And haven't heard from him. But we think – that is, *I* think he might be engaged with the tangos right now. We have a couple of agents from the Chesapeake Field Office here and they would've said something, if they knew anything or had heard anything from him."

Supervisory Agent Liu cut her eyes and stared at the ceiling of her office. Russell heard the muted expletive over the phone.

"Annie, I was thinking of calling you anyhow. What's Morgan's number?"

♦

Josh Morgan felt his phone vibrate and stole a glance at the display. He didn't recognize the number and ordinarily wouldn't answer. But this was one of his burner phones and only two people had the number. And one of them was in the same storage unit with him involved with this standoff.

"Betsy?"

"Miles Russell. FBI. Are you engaged with the Gutierrez brothers?"

Morgan knew he didn't have time to talk but this man was part of the cavalry he'd been waiting on.

"The younger one. The older one is dead."

"What about the third man?"

"No third man. Just Luis."

"I heard that another man went in."

"My associate is with me. Listen, I'm really busy now. Are you guys coming in or not?"

"We're set up. The only thing is we're trying to get eyes on the tango. Five minutes; tops."

"We don't have five minutes."

"You need us to come in?"

"Well, that would be nice," Morgan answered dryly.

"On our way."

As he hung up, a thought occurred to the Agent-in-Charge.

"Where's Marchman?"

♦

The SWAT Commander passed along the "go" order to his men. Immediately, from around the corner and about one hundred yards from unit six-one-seven, six black-clad, masked officers began to trot toward the location of their tango and at least two friendlies.

The Commander received a report from the sniper positioned on the roof of a row of units across from where the action was taking place.

"Command, we have a man in a suit moving toward the storage unit. He's about to turn the corner of the row of units where ours is."

Hearing the report over the squawk box, Russel concluded, "Marchman! Damn it!"

CHAPTER 25

National Security Agency Director Paul McClintock had examined the results that Terry Henderson had brought him that Zilla had derived from Unravel. He didn't say a word during the entire time, so neither did analyst Terry Henderson, who sat patiently in a chair alongside the Director's desk along with Deputy Director Driessen, whom McClintock had finally involved in the matter.

The NSA chief saw the name of the caller on the display of his mobile phone lying on his desk. He touched "speaker" so Henderson and the former Navy Captain could hear the conversation. He figured it related to the issue the Agency analyst and Zilla Ownby had been working. McClintock spoke before the caller and without a greeting.

"Gabe. Glad you called. I've had a couple of guys working on the code. They haven't been able to break it. I've…"

"That's what I'm calling to tell you," interrupted the FBI Director. "We don't need it anymore. We got it. Sorry I didn't call sooner."

Terry Henderson slumped slightly, reflecting the embarrassment he felt on behalf of NSA that someone had beat them to the punch. McClintock sat upright and leaned back.

"What! How? Somebody 'fess up?"

"No. Josh Morgan figured it out."

Henderson sagged even more noticeably. McClintock picked up his phone and silenced the speaker.

"Figured it out?" he repeated.

"Yeah. It's a combination of an abbreviation for a street name and a storage rental business."

The NSA boss rested his left arm on his desk and shoved the papers away that had the results the Agency software program had churned out. He swiveled in his chair and looked through his window at nothing in particular.

"So, a quantum computer costing millions – hell, maybe a billion dollars couldn't come up with solutions with a high enough probability to act on, and Morgan does."

"Well, to be fair, he probably had more context since he's acting in real time on the ground. His work requires some gut instinct that computers don't have."

Director McClintock knew Gabe Austin didn't mean it as an insult. He also knew that he was right. But he still felt the observation to be a bit of a slap in the face. Finally, he smiled.

"The guy's good. No denying it. Okay, Gabe. Thanks for letting me know."

"Wait, Paul. I need you to do something else."

"Sure we can handle it? Why don't you ask Morgan?" McClintock said smugly.

There was a noticeable delay on the part of the Bureau's top man.

"It was a joke, Gabe," insisted McClintock, but it really wasn't. He swiveled his chair around and turned his phone's speaker back on.

"If you say so. We still desperately need the other piece of the puzzle you were working on. Your guy connected the disappearances of Solis and Loughlin. He also confirmed that Zamora has something planned and that it's pretty imminent."

McClintock nodded and winked at Henderson, who sat up a little straighter and smiled at the acknowledgement.

"Yes, he did, Gabe. You need us to keep digging?"

"Yes, we do, Paul."

"You got it."

The men hung up.

"Well, you heard the man, Terry."

♦

At the same moment that Morgan disconnected from Russell, from his place behind the metal container, Luis Gutierrez sat trembling at the confirmation that Santos was dead. His rage escalated further at the taunt by the American he assumed to be nothing more than a parttime university professor.

Morgan felt time slipping away for Maggie and therefore for him, too. He raised so that Lechler could see him and pointed at him. Then he showed him his left index and middle fingers spaced about an inch apart. Then he turned the same fingers into an upside down "V."

The retired Master Sergeant gave his partner a thumbs-up and prepared to stand up shortly. He knew Morgan was going to act if he felt he had to.

For his part, he peeked over the hood of the SUV that was his cover. All he could see were Maggie's and Luis' legs stretched toward him.

"Well, if I can't see him, he can't see me," the former operator knew.

The pain from the gunshot wounds in Nicaraguan *crótalo* Luis' ribcage and right shoulder was becoming unbearable. He knew he was about to die, but he was set on taking out his hostage's boyfriend. But that man would hear his girlfriend die first. He pulled the President's Press Secretary further up his body until her head lay on his upper chest, providing him maximum shielding for the assault that he knew his act was going to provoke.

Zamora's nephew believed that death was preferable to having to face his uncle. More importantly, he would not allow himself to be subjected to American interrogation, for fear he would divulge information. A peculiar realization struck him. He understood that the blogger Solis had maintained throughout the agony he endured that he had no real information to give him and Santos.

"Perhaps he was telling the truth," Luis said aloud in a whisper. The younger Gutierrez brother knew that, if taken alive, like Solis during his own torture, he would insist he really knew nothing of importance, and that he, too, would be telling the truth.

♦

Near the front gate of the storage facility, Washington Metro Police Detective Dillon Howard approached the federal agents.

"Looks like you're just in time, Detective," FBI Agent Jeffries quipped.

"Is Morgan here?" the DC police investigator demanded.

Agent Russell stepped toward the new arrival, hands on hip and practically nose to nose.

"Listen, Howard. I don't have time for your shit!" FBI poked a finger in the detective's chest. "You just don't get it. Morgan is a good guy. Sure, sometimes he mucks around where he shouldn't, but…"

The fed pushed his finger more forcefully on the man's chest and concluded to fellow agents, "Get him the hell out of here."

Agent Phil Jeffries tried to gently turn Howard's shoulder away. The detective pulled away from the gesture and moved briskly to a nearby sedan and leaned against the fender.

♦

Behind the cover of the large metal crate, Luis Gutierrez grabbed a handful of his shield's auburn hair, tilted her head up so that her face was near his.

"I would have enjoyed doing you. Perhaps, you would've enjoyed it, too. But now I am going to kill you. And I want you to scream to your fucking boyfriend and tell him what I'm about to do."

He set his weapon on his lap and yanked the tape away from Maggie's mouth. The hostage-taker and his hostage reached for the handgun simultaneously. The man got his hand on the grip first, but the woman was able to swing her bound hands sufficiently to break his grip. As she did, she screamed

"JOSH!!!"

The weapon slid only inches away. Gutierrez regained a grip on the gun instantly.

Tom Lechler didn't need a signal from Josh to know it was time to act. He stood up and stepped to his right. As he feared, he had no clear shot without risking Maggie's life.

Morgan bolted from his position, diving headfirst onto the metal container.

The former soldier saw first that Luis Gutierrez was raising his weapon toward him. But the man suddenly pulled it back and began to move it to Maggie's temple. Lechler was about to take a shot despite the danger to his friend's former fiancée when the Nicaraguan suddenly looked up.

The clatter of Morgan sliding across the metal lid alerted his target so that when his face slid past the edge of the top of the large box, he saw Luis Gutierrez looking straight up at him, face inches away, and gun moving to Maggie's head.

Morgan thrust his gun forward and pointed it at the Nicaraguan bastard's head. His bullet entered the man's head just above his right eyebrow, removing a substantial portion of the back of his skull. The force of the bullet into the metal wall behind Luis and the pressure of the remnants of his bone and flesh exploding into that wall threw his head forward.

Maggie pulled away from the dead man's grip and fell to the side. As she cleared Lechler's line of sight, the former Green Beret delivered two additional rounds into the man's chest for good measure as his torso began to slump forward and toward him.

From the doorway Morgan and Lechler heard a loud voice and turned to see a man in a suit by the left side of the doorway, yelling into his sleeve.

"Shots fired! Shots fired!"

Immediately, members of the Norfolk Police's SWAT unit spilled into the storage unit from the right, taking various offensive positions. Some surveyed the room for any additional unseen threats. One officer tended to a stirring Edmundo Solis and radioed for emergency personnel. But some aimed their weapons at the various individuals in the room.

Josh Morgan and Tom Lechler lay their handguns down and raised their hands. Morgan had rolled over and was lying on his back atop the metal crate. He hung his head backward over the edge and strained to his left to see a sobbing, smiling Maggie Loughlin looking back.

Tears filled Josh's eyes, too, as he realized how close he'd come to losing her.

"Clear!" came the cry from several voices, informing each other as well as their SWAT Commander.

Two members stood and approached Morgan and Lechler. Mac Marchman stepped forward with his gold badge with its blue accents and five-pointed star that identified his agency.

One of the SWAT Team told him, "Command said some Rambo was about to fuck up our op."

Marchman felt nothing at the verbal slap. He simply replaced his service Glock to its holster and said, "They're okay. They're the good guys."

A life of dangerous situations had taught former Special Forces sergeant Lechler to not take chances, so he kept his hands up, raised his brows, and leaned his head forward to the closest black-clothed team member, who nodded.

Ordinarily, Lechler's training would've demanded he clear the scene, but there was no uncertainty of the result of Morgan's handiwork. Gutierrez was dead and no other threats existed. Besides, his and Josh's relief was here.

Morgan's request was also unspoken. Eyes locked on the nearest SWAT officer, he tilted his head toward Maggie and pointed there with his still raised left hand. The man nodded and said, "Go."

Josh Morgan sat up and spun around so that his legs hung over the metal box. Then he dropped the four feet from his perch onto the floor. After he pushed Luis Gutierrez's lifeless body away from Maggie, he saw blood on the right side of her face and lifted her head to inspect it.

Maggie saw the horror in Josh's expression. Her hair bobbed back and forth with her shaking head.

"I'm okay. It's his."

Press Secretary Loughlin stared at the dead man slumped away from her.

Josh gently turned Maggie's head from the sight and pulled her head to his chest. Her weeping was quiet but uncontrollable.

Josh took his knife from a pocket and flipped the blade open. As he held Maggie closely, through his own tears he sliced through the tape and rope that held her feet. Then he released her hands, which she immediately thrust around Josh's neck.

"I love you, Maggie. I'll always love you."

"I love you, too, Josh. So much. I love you."

From the far side of the SUV Tom Lechler and Secret Service Agent Macarthur Marchman heard the exchange. Lechler turned away first.

Mac lingered for only a moment. Then he smiled with some genuine happiness for them, despite his own longing for Maggie. "Don't screw it up again, Morgan," he warned silently. Then he joined Lechler and introduced himself.

CHAPTER 26

Mac had left. It wasn't really his investigation anyhow. Plus, he had seen justice carried out for the murder of his friend and fellow agent, Spencer Oakley.

So, when Maggie scanned the numerous personnel who had arrived on the scene, her Secret Service suitor wasn't to be found.

She and Morgan had been inseparable since he rescued her. Neither would leave the other – not when EMTs tended to Maggie or when FBI Agents tried to debrief Josh. He insisted it would have to wait a few minutes. Agent-in-charge Russell told the investigating agents it could.

Seeing responders rolling a gurney to a waiting ambulance, Maggie moved to catch it, pulling Josh along with her.

As Maggie spoke with Eddie Solis, Josh inquired about his condition from one of the medics.

"He's in pretty bad shape. Took quite a beating. Extremely dehydrated. But he'll make it. The psychological side of it?" The medical technician ended his speculation with shrugged shoulders and a shaking head.

Maggie pulled Josh to her side and introduced Eddie to the man he had seen lying beside the overhead door when he opened it to take photos for Santos.

"Eddie, this is Josh. He's the one who found us."

"Well, a lot of people found you. I hear you're going to be fine, Eddie."

Solis weakly took Morgan's hand in his and began to weep softly.

The Nicaraguan blogger turned to Maggie. "I'm so sorry, Madam Secretary."

"I told you – Maggie."

Eddie's head barely moved as he nodded.

"Pain meds are really kicking in. He'll be out in a minute," informed the EMT. "Feds wanted him awake for a short time to ask him a few questions.

We finally cut them off so we could attend to him."

Solis' face was grimmer when he faced Morgan. "Thank you."

Josh smiled but said nothing.

Eddie turned to Maggie again. "You're lucky to have him."

And then Edmundo was asleep. But even without him awake to hear, Maggie answered.

"Yes, I am." She squeezed Morgan's hand tightly and lay her head on his shoulder.

Two EMTs rolled Solis to the waiting ambulance. When he was safely onboard and strapped in, the vehicle began its trip to the hospital.

Josh and Maggie felt someone move alongside them.

"Thank you, Tom." Maggie hugged him around his waist and pulled him close.

"Ah, think nothing of it. Was in the neighborhood anyhow."

After a few moments of silence, Tom had to ask.

"So… Do you write all your messages in rat shit?"

"Well, not *all* of them. Just the ones to Josh."

Morgan smiled as Lechler said, "You know, Maggie, that makes sense."

Agent-in-charge Russell joined the trio.

"Get anything from him?" Josh asked.

"Not really. His memory is spotty. Says he can't remember much right now."

"You believe him?" Lechler asked.

"Yeah, we do. Could be the trauma of his beatings – they worked him over pretty good – or maybe it's the drugs the medics gave him. Don't know. He doesn't even remember communicating with a source close to Zamora. Hell, he might never get his memory back entirely. We're going to need to talk to him some more with a shrink. For his sake as well as ours."

"Can I be there when you do?"

"Whew… I'll have to clear it, but yes. Probably, Madam Secretary. At least some of it."

A buzzing from a phone that Morgan had forgotten was in his pocket interrupted the conversation.

"Shit! I should've given this to you."

Morgan started to hand the phone to Agent Russell but pulled it back. He thought about it only briefly before touching the display to connect. Before he could say anything, which he wasn't going to do anyhow, an irate voice erupted in expletive-laden Spanish.

"Santos, you fucking fool. Where is your brother? I've called him many times and he hasn't answered. You shits better not have fucked anything up. *Comprende*? I will have your asses, nephew."

The former CIA Officer understood every word, learning Spanish as a child from the workers on his grandfather's farm.

The tirade continued until Morgan interrupted, speaking Spanish as well.

"This must be Uncle Sergio."

Upon hearing that, Russell reached for the phone. Morgan pushed his hand away and turned from him.

The prolonged silence confirmed to Morgan that he was not only correct but that it had seemingly touched a nerve.

"*Quien es*?" carried a defiant, superior tone.

"You don't need to know who this is. Your nephews are both dead. I killed them both."

Another extended silence.

"You fucking ass! You don't know who you're dealing with!"

"Fuck you, *el presidente.* Just know that you messed with the wrong person. I'm coming for you."

Then he ended the call and handed the phone to Agent Russell.

"Dammit, Morgan!"

"Wrong number."

♦

The three-way video call with the heads of the National Security Agency, Federal Bureau of Investigation, and Central Intelligence Agency also included NSA Deputy Director Michael Driessen and analyst Terry Henderson in his ultimate boss' office.

"So, Gabe, Betsy, this is Henderson's deal, so I'll let him explain. Terry… headline first. Okay? Don't bury the lead."

"Yes, sir." Terry Henderson cleared his throat, but it didn't help. He still sounded nervous.

"Madam Director and…" The analyst couldn't think of the equivalent greeting for a male. "And, uh… Sir Director…" He winced and silently told himself how ridiculous he sounded.

Three of the most powerful agency heads in the world all smiled in their respective offices at the same time.

"Hi, Mr. Henderson. Thank you for your time and the information you have," Elizabeth Parnell offered in an attempt to put the young man at ease.

"Yes, ma'am." Henderson took a deep breath and started again. "We're short on details but the headline is this. Not only have we confirmed that Zamora is planning an operation in a country foreign to his, but we've concluded with a high degree of certainty that it's going to be a chemical attack."

"You're saying you don't know where then?" asked FBI Director Austin.

"No, sir. I'm sorry."

"That's okay, Terry. This is something."

Betsy Parnell questioned him next.

"How did you arrive at this, Terry? Were there more intercepts from Zamora's office?"

"More intercepts? Yes. From Zamora's office? No. I suspected that the call between Zamora and his nephew could be on a burner phone. Of course, that means there's no name tied to an associated account. And any smart operator would purchase them in a way that he or she wouldn't be identifiable."

Henderson paused.

"Go on, Terry," McClintock requested.

"Well, even though we can't track down the phones' owners, we can often identify where they were purchased by the numbers. I thought it might be interesting to see if a number of phones were purchased along with the one Zamora's nephew used."

Henderson put a document up so that each Director could see it on their computer screens. It detailed a purchase many months before.

"A convenience store in Havana, Cuba, named *Galería Comercial Comodoro* sold eight phones at one time. You can see the date on my report. One of those wound up in the hands of Zamora's nephew."

"Cuba?" repeated Parnell.

"Yes, Director Parnell."

"You're suggesting that Cuba is involved in the chemical attack?"

"No, ma'am. Not at all. At least, not that we can tell. I'm simply saying that all these phones were bought in Cuba."

"And what evidence do you have that connects these phones to the presumed attack?" asked the FBI chief.

"The phones didn't have consecutive numbers but the final two digits of all eight were within a span of twenty. Since one made its way into the hands of a Nicaraguan agent, I wondered where the others went. We probably would've found any calls to or from any of these phones – well, *any* phones, at all – involving Zamora's office, simply because… well, simply because they involve him. They didn't. As I'm sure all of you know, NSA captures all calls going into and coming out of Nicaragua as standard practice."

"Right."

"Yes."

"I searched for these phone numbers in the catalog of Nicaragua intercepts. Two more were used in calls to and from the nation, for a total of three. I couldn't find records tied to the other five – anywhere. So, I'm assuming they haven't been used yet."

CIA Director Parnell asked, "Were any of them used more than once?"

"Yes. All of them. So, technically I was wrong about them being burn phones, even if it did lead me to them. More accurately, you would call them disposable phones."

"But you traced them," said Austin.

Henderson shook his head for the webcam. "I tied them to calls; not to specific individuals."

"And the content of the conversations?" inquired the FBI Director.

NSA Director McClintock took over the narrative.

"We all know that things are easier to find if you know what you're looking for. There were no keywords that would've been flagged by our filters; nothing that would've caused us to look at them suspiciously."

"Okay. Devil's advocate then, Paul," Parnell said. "Isn't there a danger of reading more into the intercepts precisely because you have a bias to look for something along a specific line of threat?"

"Fair question, Betsy. But no. We applied some proprietary algorithms to our analyses. The applications measure the likelihood of an interpretation based on comparisons of interpretations of other messages of known content and those of deliberately errant interpretations. Complicated, for sure. I don't understand the technology at all. But it's been proven time and again in the war on terror and in the battlefield."

McClintock waited for more questions before beginning again.

"What we've done…"

"Sorry, Paul. In summary – and I mean no disrespect, Terry – we are highly confident that there will be a chemical attack sometime next month. But we have no idea by whom or where? Exactly how does this help us?" Parnell questioned.

She might not have intended any disrespect, but even on her computer monitor, she could see McClintock's analyst shift in his seat, lower his eyebrows, and twist his lips.

McClintock sensed the resentment, too, and interceded.

"It's a fair question, Terry. Tell the Directors how you're using what you've learned."

The analyst's tone was icier for a moment until he got on a roll in his explanation.

"Director Parnell, we've taken the words and phrases from the calls that our algorithms suggest imply a threat. Then we add them as keywords and apply them to all intercepts. Is it a long process? Yes. Is there a chance that we won't turn anything up? Or might we find hits that have nothing to do with the current threat? The answer again is, yes. But we've limited the scope of our search to only calls made since the date the phones were purchased."

"And the more things we turn up, the more context we have for our search and, presumably, the more intuitive and accurate our analysis,"

McClintock assured his peers.

"And you're analyzing intercepts now?" Austin wanted to know.

"Our computers are churning their little butts off as we speak," NSA Director confirmed.

"I must say, I'm impressed," FBI Head Austin said.

"As am I. This is a huge step forward about a threat we didn't even know existed until the last day or two. Nice work, Terry," Parnell complimented.

"Yes. Outstanding, Terry."

Terry Henderson sat up a little straighter. Deputy Director Driessen patted him on the shoulder. Suddenly, Henderson thought the two Directors were pretty nice people again.

♦

On Sewells Point Road in Norfolk, Maggie Loughlin, Tom Lechler, and Josh Morgan were getting into a Bureau sedan when D.C. Metro Detective Howard approached. Maggie and Josh each recognized him; Josh, from his recent encounter at the scene of Maggie's abduction, and both of them from the time Morgan was arrested for murder and then treason.

The D.C. investigator's tone was especially friendly. It was almost as though he felt he needed to apologize, even if it held no sincerity. He extended his hand to Morgan.

"Looks like you've proved me wrong again. Just doing my job. No hard feel…"

Suddenly, a fist collided with the right side of his jaw, spinning his head to the left. Howard turned to see an angry, blue-eyed, auburn-haired Press Secretary staring him in the face.

"Go to hell!" Maggie said and pushed him in the chest with both hands. Josh took her by the shoulders and tried to lead her away.

Howard's head moved among the three as he worked his jaw back and forth with his left hand. The man he didn't know grinned broadly. Josh Morgan's countenance couldn't have held less expression.

Lechler said, "I didn't see anything."

Howard began to point a finger first at Maggie, then toward Morgan, who stepped directly in front, eyeballs to eyeballs.

"You bi…" Howard started, glaring at Maggie.

Lechler stepped between his friends and the D.C. Police Detective and tilted his head as he put his palm on the man's chest.

"Oh, I wouldn't," the former Special Forces soldier advised. His grin had vanished. "You got off lucky. I was thinking about just shooting you."

The two men and woman walked away and heard Detective Howard begin to talk.

Tom Lechler held an index finger up and waved it side to side above his shoulder.

Dillon Howard shut up.

In the automobile, Maggie was rubbing her left hand. Josh pulled it up to inspect it.

"I might've broken my hand, Josh."

Morgan kissed it gently.

"But it was worth it."

"You're a lucky man, Josh," the ex-Green Beret remarked.

"Don't I know it."

CHAPTER 27

Nicaraguan Dictator Sergio Zamora sat at his desk. His emotions were a mixture of rage and concern. He had ordered an aide to confirm his nephews' deaths. And he worried what ramifications there would be. The man who had answered Santos' phone – presumably American – knew of the brothers' relationship to him. What else did he know? How would this affect the attack and his compensation from the ones behind it?

The answer to his familial concern came quickly.

"*Sí?*" Zamora said in answer to the knock on his door.

His aide, *General* Geraldo Santana entered nervously, knowing that innocent messengers often received Zamora's wrath when delivering unwelcome news.

"*Presidente*, I'm afraid all things point to the deaths of Luis and Santos. There are reports all over American television about the deaths of two Latin terrorists. No names or photos were provided, but…" His words stalled.

The Nicaraguan despot motioned as though bidding someone to come. "*Diga me*, *General*."

"The killings were in Norfolk, Virginia, *Presidente*. And the American Secretary and Solis have been rescued. There seems no doubt." Santana braced himself for the expected outburst, but it didn't come.

"*Gracias*, Geraldo."

The presidential aide left and shut the door to his superior's office. He closed his eyes and sighed deeply.

Dictator Sergio Zamora swiveled in his sumptuous leather chair and stared out his window to the parade grounds beyond.

Despite his anguish at the loss of his nephews, the despot knew it was regrettably a fortuitous turn of events, in that their deaths put them beyond the reach of interrogation.

"Foolish children," he lamented.

♦

"Yes, Madam President. Thank you so much for your call."

Maggie sat inside the FBI sedan with Josh and Tom. The agent who had driven them to the Navy base in Norfolk had stepped out of the car to get details about the Presidential Plane's arrival to carry the trio back to Washington. His absence afforded them some privacy.

"She's going to address the nation about my safe rescue. She said that she has to attribute it to federal agents. She said the truth of a private citizen doing the job, even one who works for the CIA…"

"Especially one who works for CIA," Josh corrected.

"Probably, yeah. She said it sends the wrong message. You're not going to get any credit."

Josh pulled Maggie a little closer. "You know that doesn't matter."

"She insisted I go to Walter Reed Hospital."

"You going?" Josh asked.

"No. I'm fine. I just want to sleep in my own bed."

"I'll watch over you."

Maggie smiled and rested her head against Josh.

"The President also said to take all the time I needed before coming back to work."

Tom Lechler, who had felt left out of the conversation chimed in.

"Well, at least now you know how to get time off."

Morgan thought it was insensitive; that it was too soon. Until he heard Maggie laugh out loud. Soon all three laughed.

"Well, I need to stretch my legs. Might even call my ex," Tom said.

Once Retired Master Sergeant Lechler had shut the door, Maggie said what she had thought while the Gutierrez brothers had had her.

"In Wyoming, when the fake Secret Service Agent had me, I was completely undone when you…"

"Murdered him?"

"When you saved me. The way you did things. I got over it, but I still never really understood it."

"I don't want you to understand it, Maggie."

"Let me finish. Now I think I do understand how you are able to do the heroic things you do…"

Josh looked away at her characterization of him.

"When we first met, you were in this funk. You were depressed. You used to say that there were two Josh Morgans. I passed it off as some sort of self-psychoanalysis. You know, feeling sorry for yourself and trying to explain your depression."

"Oh, you did, did you?" Morgan turned to Maggie so she could see his smile.

"I did, but I think you were telling the truth; that you were onto something. It's like there really are two of you. There's the one who is the kindest, most caring man I know. And then there's this other you. He's the one that turns off his moral restraints to do what needs to be done for the people he loves and for his country. The common thing is that that guy is also kind and caring – enough to make personal sacrifices."

Josh's head was hanging, and he shook slightly at her words.

"I feel like I'm at war with myself, Maggie."

"Maybe you are. I don't know. I thought so. When you broke up with me, I thought the 'bad' Josh was winning. I thought *I* had to help ensure the *good you* won. But now I believe there is no winning or losing when it comes to Josh Morgan's soul. The separate *yous* can live together in peace. Let them each have their space and make sure the *real* you – the coach, I guess – keeps the right Josh in the game when he's needed."

Maggie tried to turn Josh's head to face her, but he wouldn't oblige. She settled for a tighter hug.

"I don't even know if that makes sense," she concluded.

"It does, Maggie."

The couple sat silently watching the sun dip onto the horizon.

♦

It was a quarter till 7:00 PM in FBI Headquarters. FBI Lab Supervisor Carl 'Smitty" Smith felt like he had wasted a lot of effort over the last day. Initially he'd done a deep dive into emails from Eddie Solis to Secretary Loughlin to try to uncover anything that might help find the woman. She was located without any help from him.

Then the Director had him shift gears to get a sense whether Solis was a nutjob or if there really was a Nicaraguan plot against another nation. According to SSA Liu, that matter had been cleared up, too. Turns out the blogger wasn't a fruitcake; that there really was some plot afoot.

So, without any further direction, Smith had set about to see if he could find anything that might shed light on the big reveal Solis had alluded to in his last email to Secretary Loughlin.

His lab coworker, Alonzo Lane, had made short work of hacking into the Nicaraguan social justice warrior's email account. Smitty felt he had done as much as he could in analyzing the email exchanges between Solis and Loughlin, though really, they were only from the man to the Secretary. So Smitty had shifted his focus and was poring over the emails between Solis and anyone else. But nothing appeared to be to or from his "high-placed source" in Zamora's regime.

The only conclusion Smith could arrive at was that Solis had communicated with the source by phone, either voice or text. And if that was true, he had done so via an as yet undiscovered device.

Carl Smith lay his arms on his desk and rested his forehead on them. Behind him, Alonzo Lane was having a similar crash of his physical and mental energy. He swiveled his chair around to face his friend and coworker.

"I think I'm heading out, Smitty." He rose and slipped on a hoodie. Smith only groaned. "Coming?"

"Uh-huh," the lab supervisor grunted. He sat up, stretched both arms, and yawned. Finally, he stood, grabbed his jacket, and fell in behind Alonzo, who was almost to the door. Alonzo was holding the door open for his friend, who was halfway out when they both heard the chime from Smitty's computer announcing that an email had arrived in Edmundo Solis' Inbox.

"Probably more spam," Lane said.

"Yeah, that's just about all he gets," Smitty agreed.

The two men exited the lab and closed the door behind them. Seconds later, the door reopened, and the pair of FBI techies returned and walked to the computer.

Smitty lay his index finger on the fingerprint reader. Instantly, the display lit up. Three new emails were at the top of the list of messages. Two were indeed spam, but the middle one…

"We'd better call SSA Liu, Alonzo."

"Yeah. We'd better."

♦

It wasn't "Air Force One" since that identifier applied only to flights when POTUS was aboard, but it was the same plane. This particular 747 was code named SAM 28000 when the Commander in Chief wasn't on it. Maggie had flown on the plane several times when it was under the Presidential call sign. Neither Josh nor Tom had. Compared to other such aircraft, it was luxurious, but none of the three felt like taking a look around. They sat on the runway mostly in silence, eating a light but wonderful meal that the President's own traveling chef had prepared. Hendrickson had sent her entire flight staff to escort the trio back to Washington and tend to their needs as they would for the President herself.

President Hendrickson's gracious act had transformed the two-hundred-mile trip from what would have been a car ride of nearly three-and-a-half hours to a mercifully short thirty-four minutes. They would barely have time to finish the meal.

As the huge blue and white aircraft began its roll down the runway to take off, the retired army sergeant said, "You know my truck's still back there."

"You could've driven," Morgan reminded.

"Ha! And miss this? Not on your life."

SAM 28000 rose in the twilight and headed toward Andrews Air Force Base.

◆

Director Austin, Deputy Drake, and Supervisory Special Agent Liu were all still at FBI HQ when the SSA got the call from the Bureau techies. And since the email was in Spanish, Liu had summoned Special Agent Juan Esquivel to join the group. Lab Supervisor Smith had turned the keyboard over to him for this matter. The three executives and two lab techs were packed together behind Esquivel, leaning in and staring over his shoulder at the monitor as he recited the contents of the mysterious email.

This isn't the best choice for either of us, but your situation prevented our call. Don't know if you have your computer in the hospital. Just wanted to say I'm sorry. Never thought this would happen.

Austin, Drake, and Liu straightened up. Esquivel spun around in his chair. Nobody commented at first. Finally, the Director broke the ice.

"Thoughts?"

"Annie?" yielded Deputy Director Drake.

"My guess is it's him – or her. But it's just vague enough that I'm not sure," the Supervisory Special Agent opined.

"Whoever it is, they're certainly aware of the recent events with Solis," Drake deduced. "Of course, his situation wasn't just a local story. It became world news the moment involvement with the Secretary's kidnapping was determined. So, anyone could've heard about it."

"Still," Liu offered, "there's something about the tone."

"I agree," said Austin, with Drake nodding. "We could…"

"Reply?" Esquivel completed the thought.

"Yes," Austin confirmed. "But as Solis. Juan, type this:

have computer, lost phone

"No, wait. Say he destroyed it," suggested the SSA.

Austin proceeded with the message 'from' Solis.

…but had to destroy phone. Ideas? Time is short.

"Is that it?" asked the typist.

"Yes. Don't want to get too wordy. First, we don't know for sure this is the source. Secondly, we have no idea what security precautions they might have cooked up – code words or something else."

The agent looked around at the three Bureau execs. All nodded their agreement.

"Okay. Here goes," Esquivel said and clicked "Send."

The six individuals around the computer were practically holding their collective breaths, hoping for an immediate response. When none came, Smitty provided a rationale.

"It's been nearly twenty minutes since we got the message. We called Annie immediately, but it took a few minutes for everyone to get here. Plus, we really don't know when it was sent. For all we know, it could've bounced around in cyberspace for a while."

"And it could've been scheduled to send at a later time," added Lane.

The possibility that a return message might not come as soon as they hoped prompted everyone to take a seat. They waited fifteen more minutes with no messages arriving other than a couple of spams and a phishing email.

"Let's all go home," Director Austin recommended. No one left their seats immediately, including the man who suggested it, but after five more minutes, he rose. Esquivel, Drake and Liu followed suit.

"I think I'll stay a while," Smitty said.

"Me, too," added Alonzo.

"I figured as much," the SSA said with a smile.

The Director patted the two lab workers on their shoulders and left, followed by the other two executives and the Special Agent.

Alonzo Lane took off his hoodie and Carl Smith removed his jacket. They settled in for an indefinite wait.

♦

SAM 28000 completed its rollout and moved to the tarmac. Air Base personnel pushed the stairs up to the 747 and the door opened. The entire staff, including the flight crew stood by to say a few words to their three passengers as they disembarked. Aside from the Press Secretary's abduction, none of the Presidential air crew knew of the circumstances in Norfolk. However, they knew that their boss, the President of the United States, had sent her plane to bring them home. And that meant there was something in their story that warranted their thanks and well wishes.

Several yards away from the aircraft sat a black armored SUV that served as one of POTUS' limousines. Nicknamed The Beast, it was formidable in its defensive and offensive capabilities.

Maggie, Josh, and Tom were informed inflight that Hendrickson was providing them transportation via her vehicle but to their surprise, as they neared The Beast, President Hendrickson stepped out.

"Hi, Maggie. I'm so happy you're safe." POTUS embraced her warmly.

And you must be Master Sergeant Lechler," she said, turning to the ex-service member. "I'm Sandra Hendrickson."

"Yes, ma'am, Madam President. It's an honor," he said, taking her outstretched hand. Army regulations didn't require a retired soldier to salute, but it still felt inappropriate to not do so. He did stand at something very near attention.

"First, thank you for your service. And thank you for your help in getting our Maggie back to us."

"Yes, ma'am. Happy to have been able to help."

"And you, Josh…"

"Yes, Madam President."

"I don't know what I'm going to do with you." POTUS pulled Josh into a hug as well.

"Let's get the three of you some place warm and comfortable."

The four entered The Beast. As soon as Secret Service Agents secured the door behind the passengers, it rolled away.

♦

Smitty Smith looked at his phone. 8:15. His chest expanded with his sigh.

"I hear you, brother," Alonzo Lane sympathized. "But you know, as soon as we leave, a damned email will show up."

"I know. I wish something would show up while we're here. I don't want to miss it and have the night techs get it."

Right on cue, the computer signaled a message's arrival. Having spent the entire evening hearing only the occasional alert – all of which were spam – neither of the FBI's techs were optimistic. Suddenly, Smitty jumped to his feet.

"It's him! Or her! Hell, I don't care. *Him*!" he decided, and sat down in his chair once more, with Alonzo hovering over his shoulder.

He dialed SSA Liu.

"We got a reply, Annie. Are you coming back?"

"I'm still here, Smitty. So are Juan, Tony, and Gabe. We'll be right there."

In short order, the entire group had reassembled, and Esquivel was back in the driver seat in front of the computer.

Don't you have the other phones?

"So, they have been communicating by phone," Smitty realized. "But what phones? Or more precisely, what *other* phones does he mean?"

♦

The Presidential limo stopped at a hotel the Secret Service often used for visitors. Tom Lechler thanked the President and stepped out.

Josh Morgan squeezed Maggie's hand and started to follow his partner. Maggie pulled him back.

"Where are you going?"

Lechler looked back and grinned and said, "Talk to you tomorrow, Josh. Night, Maggie."

"Goodnight, Tom," she answered. "Thank you again."

The retired soldier waved over his shoulder and a Secret Service Agent closed the door to The Beast.

Scant minutes later, the black vehicle arrived at the apartment Maggie had rented after Josh broke things off with her.

"Maggie, are you sure you want to do this?" President Hendrickson asked for the third time since they left Andrews. "We could put you in the hotel where Master Sergeant Lechler is staying, or any number of other places."

"Thank you, ma'am. I really just want to be someplace familiar… *With* someone familiar." She squeezed Josh's hand.

"I understand," the President said. "We'll have a more substantial detail for you this time, Maggie."

A brief drive later Maggie and Josh watched the black Presidential SUV drive away and within a short time, agents had safely escorted them into the modest apartment. The protectors had already checked and rechecked the place and declared it safe. Two agents would remain outside the door. An additional pair would stand watch in the parking lot.

"Nice place."

"Thanks." Maggie put her arms around Josh's chest and rested her head against it.

"Maggie, I'm sorry…"

"Tell me in the morning," she said and led him to her bedroom. They lay down on the unmade bed. Josh lay on his back and put his arms around her, and Maggie rested on her side with her head on his shoulder. Within two minutes, both were asleep.

CHAPTER 28

"They used phones and he has spares," summarized Special Agent Esquivel.

"Then where are they? Not in evidence. We searched Solis' apartment thoroughly. Of course, it had already been ransacked, presumably by the Gutierrez brothers. Maybe they have it," Deputy Director Drake stated.

"Well, we've been over every square inch of their SUV and found nothing of value there. But we still haven't found where they were staying," remarked the Supervisory Agent. "The phones could be there, I guess. But I don't know why they would leave them there. And we found Solis' car. Nothing in it either."

"Have you found a computer?" asked Austin.

"No. And that puzzles us," Liu replied. "We assume the brothers took it from Solis' apartment. But what would they have done with it?"

"Well, we need to reply to the email," the Director said.

"So, what do I say?" asked the Spanish-speaking agent.

The entire group pondered the question. Austin made the decision for his team. And spoke the words for Juan to type.

Can't get one until out of hospital. Keep on with email?

The response was almost instantaneous.

Who is this?

"Shit." Director Austin knew they'd been made but decided to press on.

The same person you've corresponded with for a while. Why?

The "new mail" icon appeared with the chime.

No. He only used full sentences and proper syntax. And he said that we would never use email under any circumstances. Adios.

Everyone was disappointed at the turn of events. However, they all put that aside and began to brainstorm about what to do next and about the last message from the emailer.

One topic of conversation was whether the Spanish speaker who was now believed to certainly be Solis' source was a Nicaraguan.

♦

Josh gently slipped his arm from beneath Maggie's head. He looked at his phone.

"10:20," he read. "Sheesh," he said at realizing he'd slept for less than ninety minutes. He pulled Maggie's comforter over her and slipped from the bed. He pulled the bedroom door to quietly.

In her fridge he found several bottles of Revolver Blood and Honey. Josh was surprised – and pleased – to find an ice-cold Texas beer. Revolver Brewing was located in Granbury, Texas, not far from where he was born and grew up. Josh opened a bottle and moved to Maggie's couch.

In the other room, the apartment's renter stirred. When Maggie realized that Josh wasn't there, she wondered if she'd dreamed it. But the aches and pains of her cuts and bruises validated that the last days had indeed been real. She walked quietly to the door and cracked it open. Through the narrow opening she saw Josh sitting on the sofa with a beer on the end table, looking at his phone.

She smiled because it seemed normal. It seemed… *right.*

Maggie closed the door quietly. She walked to her bathroom and, with some pain, undressed and showered to cleanse herself of the filth of her ordeal – both real and emotional. Then she pulled the over-sized T-shirt over her head and returned to bed.

As she snuggled in beneath the comforter, it occurred to her that if anybody had asked a few hours ago if she'd be thanking God for anything at the end of this day, she would've thought them insane. But…

"Thank you, God," she whispered. And was back asleep.

♦

In his office at the J. Edgar Hoover Building, FBI Special Agent Juan

Esquivel looked at the caller ID and answered, "What's up, Annie?"

He hung up the call from his boss and called his fellow agent, Miles Russell, who was at the Naval Medical Center at Sewells Point.

"What's up, Juan?"

"Hey, Miles. Still at JEH. You're at the hospital with Solis, right?"

"Yeah, but I'd sure rather be at home in bed. Why?"

"The lab guys somehow got connected with his source. It's in Spanish so I'm the lucky Latino who gets to interpret. Annie wants you to try to convince the doctors to let you ask Edmundo Solis some questions."

"That's why I've been hanging around here. The doc isn't having it."

"Wait ten minutes and ask again. Annie's getting Director Austin to call the doctor."

"I'll try," Russell agreed. The two agents hung up.

Russell looked at his watch to know when ten minutes had elapsed. However, in about six minutes, he saw the doctor approaching. He did not look pleased.

"Your director is pretty persuasive. Follow me."

The two men entered the Nicaraguan blogger's room.

The doctor explained what he was about to do.

"The patient isn't in an induced coma, although we're considering it. He's got a pretty substantial amount of pain killers, though. He's close to time for another dose, so the effects could be somewhat diminished. So, this might wake him up a bit."

The physician injected a liquid into the IV port in the tube that ran down into the back of Edmundo Solis' hand. Almost instantly, the patient groaned.

"There you go. If he becomes too distressed or in too much pain, I'm cutting you off. I told your director that. As long as you understand that, go ahead."

"Eddie?" The agent reached out to shake him. The doctor stopped him. Russell delivered a stern look and persisted.

"Eddie?" he repeated with a gentle nudge. "Eddie, can you hear me? This is FBI Special Agent Russell. It's very important that I ask you some questions."

Eddie grunted. His head barely moved, but the agent took it to be a nod.

"Eddie, do you remember that someone was giving you information?"

The patient's head moved back and forth, side to side.

"Do you remember where your phone is?"

Eddie had nodded off again.

"Eddie, this is important."

The doctor tried to pull Russell's left hand off his patient's arm. The agent pushed it away with his right.

"I'm ending this."

"No, you're not," the Special Agent countered without so much as a glance.

"Do you remember where you left your phone, Eddie?"

"No." It was barely a whisper.

"Eddie, do you have another phone?" The agent put his ear next to Solis' mouth.

"Uh-huh." Then he followed up with something incomprehensible.

"What, Eddie? Say that again."

The attending physician reached for Russell's hand and put his left hand on his shoulder to lead him away. This time the FBI Agent didn't resist.

♦

Josh sipped at his beer and tried to catch up on the news on his phone, He was astonished at how much Maggie's abduction had dominated the news cycle. It was a bigger story than the murder of Secret Service Agent Oakley and certainly more significant news than Edmundo Solis' kidnapping. Of course, nobody knew of the implications it carried in relation to a possible chemical terror attack. That was an ongoing investigation.

Josh watched a replay of President Hendrickson's news conference and as promised, she credited the rescue of Maggie and Solis entirely to the FBI and the Norfolk SWAT Team. And just as he had told Maggie, Josh didn't care. The woman he had loved for years was safe and sleeping in the next room.

A vibration from his phone preceded a window popping up. It was Tom Lechler.

Do you feel like we're not done yet?

Josh texted a three-letter reply.

Yep

He darkened his phone's display and polished off the last swallow of beer. Then he went back to Maggie's bedroom and, remaining clothed, slipped under the bedding alongside her. It felt at once both uncomfortable and natural at the same time.

♦

"I swear, Juan, it sounded like he said, 'Nicaraguan hen arena.' That can't be right… Can it?"

Juan Esquivel couldn't keep from laughing. "Seriously. You think he said that? 'Hen arena.' That's what you heard?"

Miles Russell was a little annoyed. It was late and it had been a long couple of days.

"Shut up, Juan."

The Latino Special Agent finally managed to stifle his laughter.

"Sorry, Miles. All right, let's think about this. To be fair, I doubt that you misheard 'Nicaragua,' so let's concentrate on the 'hen arena' part." He snickered a bit and to his surprise, Russell started laughing, too.

"I know they have cock fights in Latin America. They don't stage hen fights, do they?"

Both agents laughed again.

Getting back on track, Juan Esquivel suggested that he try to come up with words that sounded like "hen" or "arena." None of them sounded right.

"What if what you heard wasn't two words, but one?"

"I guess that's possible."

Esquivel began to say words that rhymed with "hen" and "arena" combined. They included Argentina, *disciplina*, *medicina*, *masculina*, and *feminina*. He suggested *cristalina* and *Antonina*.

"Hey, what about *encamina*. 'Hen arena.' '*Encamina*.' That's pretty close."

"I don't think so. What's it mean?"

"'Route.' 'Nicaragua Route.' Maybe? Miles, I'm running out of rhyming words."

Esquivel's silence between words grew longer as he struggled to come up with more. He said one here and another there.

"What did you say? What was that last one?"

"'*Genuina*." It means 'genuine."' He spelled it out for his counterpart at the Norfolk Navy hospital.

"So, that would be 'Genuine Nicaragua' then?"

"Hold on, Miles." Juan typed the phrase in the Google search field on his computer. "Holy shit! There's a restaurant named *Nicaragua Genuina* and…"

"And?"

"It's in Norfolk."

"Damn. What time do they close?"

"Eleven."

Special Agent Juan Esquivel didn't receive a "goodbye" or a "thank you" before his counterpart hung up. He looked at his phone and saw that the time was 10:52 and understood.

♦

There were no customers left at the *Nicaragua Genuina*, so the owner and his daughter were already closing up when the phone rang.

"Should I answer that, *Papi*?"

Carlos never looked up. He merely shook his head and continued counting the day's receipts.

The phone ceased to ring but started again momentarily. Ana looked to her father for direction. He was still engrossed in his accounting. The ringing continued until the restaurant owner, angry about the paucity of the day's business, stomped to the device, yanked up the handset and screamed into the mouthpiece, "CLOSED!"

Carlos hung up without hearing what the caller was trying to get in. Then he unplugged the phone from the wall. Almost immediately, the business phone's ringing resumed, audible on the extension in the office, but he could more easily ignore that one.

"Shit!" a very upset FBI Agent said to his mobile device.

Miles Russell had to take a chance. He figured he could leave Edmundo Solis. He was of no value for questioning in his condition. And local police had round-the-clock protection for him. So, the Agent scrambled down the two flights of stairs to the first floor and ran to his sedan.

♦

Director Austin of the Federal Bureau of Investigation called his lab supervisor on his cellphone.

"Smitty… Austin. Did I wake you?"

"No, sir. I'm still here in the Hoover Building."

"Yeah, me, too. I wanted to check. I know you were trying to track down the location the emails were sent from. Any luck?"

"I'm sorry. No. Alonzo just got word from a friend over at NSA that whatever application the source is using is pretty sophisticated. It's bouncing among servers all over the world. Zilla said he could probably get a solution, but it will most likely be tomorrow."

Director Austin didn't even ask about the reference to "Zilla." He just thanked Smitty and asked him to pass along the same words to Alonzo. Then he ordered them to both go home and get some rest. The FBI's top man intended to do the same and he sensed that neither man in the lab would give any pushback.

CHAPTER 29

DAY 5 – FRIDAY

FBI Special Agent Russell was pissed. The person at the *Nicaragua Genuina* wouldn't take his call, even though it was two or three minutes before closing. Now, at twenty minutes after midnight, he sat in his company sedan outside the restaurant. He had sped there, lights flashing, in the hopes of catching someone – *anyone* – before they left for the night. No luck.

He thought he'd caught a break when he saw a white piece of printer paper taped to the window, with the handwritten words, "In case of emergency," followed by a phone number. But when he dialed it, the fed got a message that it was not a working number. And that had ticked him off even more.

He had transposed a couple of digits twice and dialed the resulting numbers, first waking an elderly woman and then what sounded like some meth-head.

So, he sat in his vehicle waiting for help from the night shift at the Bureau lab. It was taking a while.

"Sometimes I hate this job."

Another fifteen minutes passed before Russell's phone rang. A quick exchange with a nightshift lab tech explained the delay. The owner of Nicaragua Genuina, Carlos Garcia, apparently had no phone outside the one for his business. He determined the name of his daughter but it took some time to track down the right "Ana Garcia." Garcia was the second most common Nicaraguan name, so, even in Norfolk, Virginia, there were several women who shared the daughter's name.

Miles Russell didn't really care about the background story and was about to say so when his caller gave him the phone number and the golden words.

"I spoke to her and she's expecting your call."

♦

It turned out that Ana had gone to the hospital after work. Since she wasn't family, the medical staff wouldn't allow her to see their patient. She appealed to the police officers outside Eddie's door. They did permit her to look into the room briefly.

Ana Garcia was horrified when she saw the frequent diner at the family restaurant. Bandages covered him, some of which were red from where he had bled through. Where he wasn't bandaged, his flesh was bruised from the beating. He was connected to all sorts of machines and a tube from intravenous fluid dangled on a stand beside his bed.

At the sight of his condition, Ana had put her hand to her mouth and had begun to cry. The female of the two officers guarding the hospital room put her arm around the Nicaraguan woman's shoulders and led her to a chair nearby while the male policeman closed the door quietly.

So, for nearly an hour, Ana had sat a few feet from Eddie Solis' room. When she wasn't dozing, she wept quietly. She wondered what had happened to her friend. Who could possibly have done it? And why? When her phone rang, she jumped at the alert. The man said he was from FBI Headquarters and asked if she was the daughter of the owner of the *Nicaragua Genuina*. When she affirmed that she was, the caller gave no further explanation, but said that an agent in Norfolk would be calling or coming to visit with her. When he asked for her address, she had informed him that she was at the hospital.

Moments after she had ended the call with the tech, her phone rang again.

"This is Ana. Are you the Agent?"

The caller said that he was and introduced himself as Special Agent Russell of the FBI.

"Is this about Eddie?" The young woman's voice quivered, and she was obviously crying softly.

"Yes, ma'am, it is. I desperately need to speak with your father. Can you tell me how to reach him?"

"He doesn't have a phone. We are together much of the time, so when he needs to make a call, he uses mine. And almost nobody calls him other than at the restaurant."

"Then I need his home address."

Russell texted the address to his partner, Agent Jeffries, and asked him to meet him there. Then he resumed his call with the daughter while he started for her father's apartment.

Ana Garcia had walked to her car while speaking with Russell and was preparing to drive to her father's apartment to be with him when the federal agents arrived there.

"Can you tell me what you know about Edmundo Solis?"

"Eddie – Edmundo – has been coming to our restaurant for a long time," she started. Then she proceeded to tell Russell all the same information she had told Morgan and Lechler when they had come to the restaurant.

"I was surprised that nobody else came to ask about him," she stated when she had finished her narrative.

"Else?"

"Yes. A man named Josh and his friend. Tom, I think."

Russell grunted, but also smiled.

Agent Russell and Ana Garcia arrived at Carlos Garcia's apartment at the same time. The fed was more than a little irritated when he realized that it was only three blocks from the restaurant where he had sat waiting for news from the Hoover Building. Russell and the *senorita* hadn't finished shaking hands when Phil Jeffries also arrived. As the three walked to the first-floor door, it opened. Seeing her father, Ana ran to him.

"*Papi*, Eddie looks so bad."

The agents gave the father and daughter a moment but then approached. Ana released her father from the embrace and dabbed at her eyes with a tissue.

"This is Agent Russell, and… I'm sorry…"

"Special Agent Jeffries, sir. Sorry to bother you at this hour."

Both of the federal officers noticed the unenthusiastic nature of the restaurateur's handshake and cool demeanor. Still, the man asked them in and offered tea. They declined.

"I told them, *Papi*, that I was surprised that nobody had visited us besides Eddie's friends."

"Agents came by, daughter."

"Wh… what?" Ana's face expressed her utter shock at the revelation, but neither agent was surprised. They knew that, upon finding Solis' car in the parking lot of the area near the restaurant, their fellow agents had walked to every business nearby. None had reported anything relevant to his disappearance.

"Why didn't you tell me?"

Carlos Garcia shrugged.

"Sir, why didn't you tell our agents that you knew Solis?"

Another shrug.

"I told Eddie's friends all I knew."

"Mr. Garcia, they *weren't* his friends."

"Well, they *weren't* police," he answered.

The daughter intervened. "My father loves America, but he doesn't trust police of any country. He lived much of his life during the Ortega days."

The federal officers were angry but decided to ignore it and move on.

"When we questioned Edmundo, he mentioned your restaurant."

Seeing his daughter's displeasure, the Garcia patriarch decided to open up a little.

"Eddie eats there almost every night. It is so regular that we worry when he doesn't."

"Mr. Garcia, we are looking for Eddie's phone. And we believe he may have more than one. Has he ever left anything with you?"

Ana answered for her father.

"No," she said with a shake of her head and a wave of her hand. "Eddie has never left anything with us."

Both FBI officers observed her father look up and away with his eyebrows arched.

"Sir?"

Señor Garcia looked at his daughter and scrunched his face. His squirming was obvious to her as well as Russell and Jeffries.

"That is not true, *hija.*" Then to the Agents, "*Sí.* Eddie has left a box with me."

Ana Garcia's mouth opened, and she leaned her head toward her father.

"Why, father? Why didn't you tell the police? Why didn't you tell *me*?"

"I forgot. *Esa es la verdad, hija.*" He redirected his gaze to his visitors. "It *is* the truth, sirs. Eddie gave me the box one night during dinner. He said it contained computer parts. It was taped shut. We were very busy. I was cooking, tending the bar, waiting tables. I was on my way to the kitchen and set the box on a shelf with some of our boxes of supplies."

"We need that box, Mr. Garcia," Jeffries insisted.

The fifty-plus year-old Nicaraguan native hung his head and nodded. He had embarrassed himself to the FBI Agents, and even worse, had embarrassed and disappointed Ana.

"We will walk."

Carlos Garcia put on a light coat and a fedora and led the party out the door.

♦

A forty-seven-year-old Nicaraguan sat in front of his laptop. He had been there for a half hour, sipping from his second *Macuá* since he returned home, and fifth of the evening. The cocktail was a concoction of white rum, guava juice, lemon juice, and sugar. The man preferred his homemade ones to those at the bar where he had been earlier in the evening. They tended to add too much sugar and too little rum. And it wasn't *Flor de Caña.*

He had sat in a booth at the back of the bar and used the Wi-Fi to connect to the Internet and the *Macuás* to bolster his courage. He and his contact in America, whom he considered to be naïve and little more than a useful idiot, had mutually agreed to never use email for their communication.

When he had heard of Solis' abduction, the man sipping *Macuás* had cut off all attempts at contacting him. But upon news of his rescue, he took the bold step of reaching out through his Gmail account after Solis had failed to answer his phone.

But when it became apparent that he was communicating with an impostor, he shut down and headed home. He was confident that it would take a very long time for anyone to track down his whereabouts. His precaution of sending his emails hopping around the world involved a level of technical sophistication on a par with that of any developed nations.

As he sat in his flat, he struggled with whether to reestablish communications with the one posing as Solis. Despite the very real possibility that the poser would turn out to be someone wishing to do him harm, he also considered that it could be someone in the American government. And that might well be a blessing.

The man had reached out anonymously to individuals in Hendrickson's administration but wasn't taken seriously. He had attempted to work with others with a social media presence and had actually pursued communications with a couple other than Solis. But Edmundo was the only one who appeared to have a contact in the White House. No matter how weak a link to the President it turned out to be, it was worth exploring. And now he was mulling over the possibility that it was someone in the U.S. government pretending to be Solis. And having an American act on the knowledge he had was, after all, his ultimate goal anyhow.

The barbarism of deploying a chemical weapon was such an act of inhumanity that he couldn't stand idly by. And so, he had undertaken to expose it. Yet, he was also overwhelmed occasionally by the fear of being discovered. He would be tortured and then killed. And the attack wasn't going to be in his country, after all, so should he really care?

The traitor to his leader and source to his fellow countryman in America, Eddie Solis, decided he would sleep on the matter.

Nicaraguan President Sergio Zamora's aide, General Geraldo Santana, swallowed his last sip of his country's national drink and went to bed.

♦

In the lonely quiet of his office at 1627 New Hampshire Ave NW in Washington, DC, a computer encryption specialist was ready to report to his superiors that he had found no way into the laptop. However, none of the leaders at the Embassy, up to and including the Ambassador of the Republic of Nicaragua to the United States of America, received such disappointing news with kindness. And the techie knew it was because that man's boss, *Presidente* Sergio Zamora also didn't tolerate failures well either.

So, it was with great relief that Jorge Rivas' latest effort resulted in seeing the laptop's contents some to life.

"*Gracias a Dios*!" he exclaimed. The outburst didn't bother anyone else. Nobody was there.

The cryptographer was talented but lacked the resources that his counterparts in more technologically advanced nations did. So, it was with a great deal of personal satisfaction that he began to explore the device's files. He had been astonished at how formidable the encryption of his country's traitor's computer was.

His first target would be the email program. He launched the program and looked at the most recent messages. Among the last several was what appeared to be a brief exchange between someone and Solis within the last several hours.

"How could that be?" the cryptographer wondered. He had been told that the traitor was in terrible condition in the hospital. He saw that the correspondent wondered the same thing and had cut off communication.

Rivas searched for other emails from the same Gmail account but found none. He copied the emails of interest onto his own computer and moved to a different line of inquiry.

He looked at the encryption program application next. His eyes widened. He leaned in toward the display.

"Shit!" he shouted in English.

♦

Carlos Garcia unlocked the glass front door to the *Nicaragua Genuina* and pushed it open. Ana and the two FBI Agents followed him in.

The owner shuffled to the back of the main room and through a swinging door on the right side of a small hallway. Shortly, he returned with a small box. He blew away a slight collection of dust and handed it to Russell.

Garcia received a stern look from his daughter when he drew himself a beer from the tap behind the bar, but he did it anyhow.

"Anyone?" he offered, holding the mug aloft. Each of the agents declined.

Miles Russell slit the tape along the seam where the two flaps of the small box met and pulled them back. His smile told his partner that he was pleased with the contents.

He held up two opened prepaid cellphones.

CHAPTER 30

Examining Edmundo Solis' prepaid mobile phones was something that needed to be done at the Hoover Building. Neither Miles Russell nor Phil Jeffries had even tried to turn on the devices for fear of using up the permitted number of failures before the phone locked them out. Such phones were rarely sophisticated, but the Bureau had learned in the past that such efforts required extreme caution because they would rarely get help from the devices' manufacturers or service providers.

So, Russell had remained in Norfolk in case Solis became able to answer questions, while Jeffries boarded a Bureau plane at Norfolk International Airport and had flown to Washington's Reagan National. At the time of night that he was traveling, no commercial flights were available. However, even with the time he waited for the craft to fly from the United States Marine Corps Base in Quantico, Virginia, and the completion of the round trip back to Reagan, it was faster than driving.

A driver met Jeffries. The travel time from Reagan National to JEH at 3:30 AM was brief – about ten minutes. Special agent Jeffries had spent more time aboard the Bureau's Gulfstream as it had taxied to the terminal.

A short walk and elevator ride later, the deliveryman entered the Bureau Lab. Both Carl Smith and Alonzo Lane had come back to the J. Edgar Hoover Building to examine the mobile phones. Liu and Drake were on their way. Director Austin had an early meeting on Capitol Hill, so that left his staff the task of dealing with Solis' secret phones without him.

Jeffries handed the phones to Smitty, who handed one to Alonzo. They each began to size up the devices.

"I suppose this could take a while, so I'm going to grab some coffee, if you don't…"

"I'm in," exclaimed Alonzo, with the look of a man who had just won a race.

"Me, too," echoed Smitty. He smiled but was disappointed at coming in second.

Phil Jeffries stopped in his tracks and turned around in disbelief.

"How'd you get in so fast?"

"I turned it on," reported Smitty.

"Yep. Same here," said the other lab tech.

"You… turned it on?" Jeffries said skeptically.

"Yeah. It appears they've never been used," Smitty stated. "I just entered the default code, and it woke right up. Battery's real weak, though."

Special Agent Phil Jeffries closed his eyes, put a hand on his face, and dropped his chin.

"So, after all that – waking Solis up, getting the location of the phones, figuring what it meant, finding the restaurant owner, and getting the phones – they're of no value at all?'

"I didn't say that," the Lab Supervisor contradicted.

"If you say so," Jeffries said snidely. He resumed his quest for coffee.

The lab personnel started their examination of the new evidence.

♦

Old habits died hard. It was 6:30 AM and Retired Master Sergeant Tom Lechler was awake and drinking his first cup of coffee in the hotel restaurant. He swiped through various photos on his phone of his kids and his soon-to-be ex-wife.

He considered what a lousy husband and father he'd been over the years. He was never around for his family for any length of time. And as with many operators, when he was there, he wasn't *really* there. He was always waiting for the next spin-up. Lechler had admitted to himself many times over the years that, while he loved Ava and his three children more than anything, it was heading back in the field that was his reason for getting up in the morning.

The retired warrior wanted desperately to call any one of his family. The early hour kept him from calling his kids. More than that, with his wife, it was that she didn't want to talk to him. He had left the Army Special Forces largely to spend time with Ava. But it had turned out that he was worse with her when he was out of the service than he was when he was still in.

In the relatively brief time he'd known him, Lechler had found a great friend in Josh Morgan. The man didn't have the extensive training as Lechler's former A-Team did, but his instincts were as sharp as any he had ever seen. And he was the most resourceful, cunning man he had served alongside. The operations with Josh were the only thing that made his life bearable. He was a true brother in arms. And because of the love and high regard Lechler had for Josh, he had decided he was going to do everything in his power to persuade him to leave CIA and stay home with Maggie.

♦

Josh was awake and had just finished gathering bacon, eggs, and biscuits to begin cooking breakfast when a sleepy, smiling Maggie Loughlin wandered into the kitchen, rubbing her eyes. Josh considered that, despite how demanding his search for her had been, she had gone through much worse. He wondered if she would ever recover emotionally.

"Morning."

Maggie's answer was another smile as she stretched both arms. Then she wrapped both of them around Josh and lay her head on him. He embraced Maggie with his left arm and ran the fingers of his right hand through her hair.

"Coffee's already brewed. Hungry?"

Still silent, Maggie took Morgan's hand in hers and led him back to the bedroom. She guided him onto the edge of the bed and slipped her oversized T-shirt over her head. Then she moved atop the seated man and kissed him passionately.

♦

Supervisory Special Agent Annie Liu and her direct boss, Deputy Director Tony Drake had arrived at JEH shortly after Solis' phones did. But with no texts or history of sent or received calls to look over, both had retreated to their offices.

As soon as Solis' secret prepaid phones were in his hands, Smitty had initiated a search on their numbers. He expected that the only thing it would reveal would be where they were bought, and he wasn't sure how much use knowing that would be.

And since they had never been used, he held no hope that the phones would be of value in trying to reengage Eddie's source in Zamora's inner circle. After all, the contact had abandoned the email exchange with them upon realizing that it wasn't Solis who was communicating with him.

Director Austin wanted another attempt at establishing communication. But he wanted to be present, and he wouldn't be at the J. Edgar Hoover Building until he finished his meeting at the Capitol.

So, Smitty poured another cup of coffee and decided he should look at the results of the search for the phone numbers' purchase location. He accessed the appropriate window on his computer and sat down. He stirred the java to thoroughly mix the cream and sweetener, took a drink that he desperately needed, and scanned the results of the query.

He nearly turned his mug over when he saw the data.

"Oh… my… God!"

♦

The tapping of the rain on the bedroom window added to the feeling that this would be a good place to remain for the entire day. Both Josh and Maggie thought that the world could get along without them for the foreseeable future.

"I've missed you, Maggie Loughlin."

"Mmm," was her reply.

The couple lay there for another ten minutes until Maggie finally spoke what she was wondering about.

"You're going after him, aren't you?"

"Who?" he asked, although he knew.

"The guy who sent the brothers after Eddie and then me. Zamora."

"How do you know it's him?"

"It is. And don't deflect. Aren't you?"

Josh propped himself up on one side on his elbow to face Maggie.

He wanted to tell her that he didn't even know where to start. Or that he would let others take care of that. He wanted to, but he didn't. He reclined again and put his arm back around the woman next to him. He took a deep breath.

"The thought had crossed my mind."

"I understand."

"Didn't expect that."

Now it was Maggie who raised up on her elbow.

"Josh, this is the kind of thing you're great at. It doesn't matter if a person is running or missing or sheltered under layers of protection, you find them. You found Trent when he was taken. You found an entire A-Team of Green Berets in Russia. You found Trevor in Terrador and Linus Schwartz in Qatar. And you found me."

Maggie lay across Josh's chest and continued.

"It just seems like you get to people, even when nobody else can. From what you've told me, there's a chemical weapon about to be unleashed somewhere. So, go find this dictator. Then come back to me and we'll talk about where we stand."

"Maggie, I…"

"We'll talk then, Josh."

"I'll talk to Betsy and try to get onboard. Tom, too, but he needs to go try to save his marriage."

The couple fell into a deep slumber.

♦

Bureau Director Gabriel Austin took just enough time to settle into his office and return three calls before he asked the group of people to join him there.

Deputy Director Drake, Supervisory Special Agent Liu, and Special Agent Esquivel were dumbfounded at the news Smitty reported.

"The two phones' numbers had nothing in common numerically. But they were both bought in the same place. One is from the group of eight devices we tied to the Gutierrez brothers that were purchased in Havana, Cuba. The other was bought at the same place, but two days earlier," the tech reported over the speakerphone.

"So, we have a group of phones connected to the Gutierrez brothers – bad guys – *and* Edmundo Solis, supposed good guy?" Austin summarized, trying to connect the dots.

"I think I get the common element, Gabe," Tony Drake volunteered. "Whether embellishing or not, Solis insisted in his blogs that he had a contact high in Zamora's regime. And the Gutierrez brothers were the dictator's nephews. I think Solis' source had access to the same pool of phones that the nephews did and provided some to our blogger. I don't know about the rest of you, but I think that confirms that he really is close to Zamora."

Heads nodded all around.

"So, is he legit, or is he playing Solis?" Esquivel questioned. "Although, as I think about it, what could be his rationale for tipping someone off if he's complicit in the terror attack?"

"I agree," Liu added. "And maybe his motive is that he's got a conscience."

Esquivel's thought was what all were thinking. "I say we call him. He sees this number pop up, he might answer." He looked around for agreement and, once again, got nods.

"We don't know his number, Juan," Deputy Director Drake pointed out.

Smitty spoke up next. "We could just go down the list and try all the phones one at a time."

"Risky," said Liu.

"I know. But checking activity on all the numbers of the original eight – well, nine phones – told my *compadre* over at NSA that all but five have been used. And of those five unused ones, we have two. Leaves three."

"Go on," Drake advised.

Smitty continued, "The one that was bought separately before the eight has been used several times to make calls to one of the ones we don't have. I say we start with that one – the one receiving the calls."

"Agreed. Except we don't call. We text," Austin suggested. "Two reasons. The unsub wouldn't recognize your voice, Juan. Plus, maybe they've texted all along."

"And if the guy's expecting a call, we can always attribute the text to Solis' – *my* – condition," added Esquivel.

"Exactly," agreed Austin. "But we need to imply a little familiarity. Here's what you send."

Esquivel typed in Spanish and sent the message.

I got one of the phones. Did my situation mess things up?

The group wanted an immediate reply. After twenty minutes, their expectations changed.

♦

General Geraldo Santana sat at his desk. He had decided that, with Solis out of the picture, he would try to contact someone in the White House directly. The blogger's contact, the Press Secretary, had herself been kidnapped and would almost certainly be out of action and not reply.

Santana was at a loss as to whom he should try to contact. He also wondered if he would be taken seriously or dismissed as some fool trying to capitalize on the recent events. He would have to demonstrate some intimate knowledge of the plot. But that would be extremely risky.

As *el presidente's* aide wondered about his options, his phone vibrated. The texter's number surprised him.

♦

Zilla Ownby had never been in the NSA head's office. He looked around at the shelves filled with books, the several TV monitors, and more. He wasn't impressed. It was about what he would have expected from every corporate bigwig's digs.

He and Terry Henderson waited for Director McClintock to end his phone call.

"This isn't why I called you here, but here's the latest from the Bureau. They have two phones that belong to Solis. One is from the group of eight purchased in Havana. The other was purchased separately but from the same store at roughly the same time. They are currently using one to try to communicate with the blogger's source. It was an oversight – they admitted to that – to not have us tracking the calls real time. We were going to develop an action plan, but I think we've just had one present itself."

"May I be excused, sir?"

"Of course, Ownby. I was going to ask if you'd get started on intercepts."

Zilla hurried away to his workstation. Henderson stayed put.

"This is a rather odd time to do this, Terry, but I believe you've proven your value to the Agency. I'm promoting you to your previous level, plus one. I'm convinced – and tell me if I'm wrong – that you understand the poor judgement you used when Deputy Director Blake had you do some things that crossed the line."

"Yes, sir, I do." Henderson tried to stifle his smile, but he could only manage to minimize it.

"A huge amount of our work is accomplished in very gray areas, Terry, and analysts like you have to be able to trust that the directions you receive from your managers is on the up and up."

"Yes, sir."

McClintock walked to where Terry Henderson sat. The young man stood and received the Director's handshake with a great deal of satisfaction.

"Sir, will I continue to be assigned to Captain Driessen?"

"I think that makes sense. Is that what you want?"

"Yes, sir."

The NSA chief sat on the edge of his desk.

"Done. Now, update me on the suspected terror attack."

After the good news he had just received, Henderson was going to have a difficult time with his report.

"We have nothing new, sir. The computers are still chewing on the past intercepts we flagged, but nothing obvious has been identified that relates to a chemical-attack."

Director McClintock took a deep breath. "I was afraid of that. Well, keep digging."

Josh had showered and dressed. Maggie was still in bed, but awake, with the comforter pulled up to her chin.

"Heading out?"

"Sorry, Maggie. Betsy wants a debrief. I'll be back."

"Sure you can't stay?" Maggie asked playfully.

"I wish, but…"

Maggie lowered the bed covers to her waist.

"Are you *positive* you can't stay?"

Josh leaned in and kissed her. Then he raised up and ran his fingers through her hair.

"I'll be back as soon as I can. I made fresh coffee."

Before he had made it out of the apartment, Morgan was calling Lechler.

"Ready to go?"

♦

General Santana was always careful. He never took or made calls or sent messages on his secret phones while in the presidential palace or other government offices. He would've never had the device with him except for the uncertainty of Edmundo Solis' circumstances. He decided to make one exception.

Despite his usual extreme caution, he typed one quick reply to the message he had received earlier that was ostensibly from his contact in America.

Do not contact me again. Should not have corresponded with you

And with that one sentence, General Santana ended his attempt at preventing a chemical attack. The aide to *Presidente* Zamora knew he had developed a case of what Americans called cold feet, but he had at that moment decided that the personal risk was too great. He had received no indication that his efforts were bearing fruit anyhow. Solis had made grand promises of his ability to get word of the plan to his contact in the American President's organization as soon as he received the details from Santana, but now that the blogger's source actually knew the details of the attack, he decided he couldn't go through with it.

He turned off the device and began to think of some way to dispose of it.

♦

The lengthy delay in receiving a return text from Solis' contact in Nicaragua had led everyone who was waiting in the Director's office to go about their work.

FBI Special Agent Juan Esquivel was at his desk with Edmundo Solis' phone lying atop it. The vibration and the chime got his immediate attention and raised his hopes. However, the content of the text dashed them instantly.

He typed a quick answer.

Must see this through

While he waited for a reply that would never come, he called Director Austin and delivered the unfortunate news.

♦

Inside the Republic of Nicaragua Embassy in Washington, D.C., a fatigued cryptographer sat with his manager in a group of people, including Ambassador Octavio Torrez. Jorge Rivas had decided during his overnighter that his country's representative to the United States hated being awakened in the middle of the night almost as much as hearing disturbing news.

So, the computer expert had worked on other things after his unsettling discovery. He was able to access the contents of the traitorous blogger's phone rather easily since it had no password but had found nothing useful. So, he took a nap that had lasted until others in his department had arrived for work.

Fabian Obando, the manager of his department had taken over for the man – after he rebuked him for being asleep at his desk. He berated him further once he learned what the subordinate had found. And once he had done his own analysis of Solis' laptop, he completely lost control and unleashed a barrage of expletives on the cryptographer.

The supervisor had immediately asked for a conference with the Head of Mission and his staff. The ambassador scheduled the meeting for an hour after the request, so now, in the middle of the morning, the supervisor and his cryptology expert were about to explain what they had found and why it was important.

Department Head Obando began the session by explaining how he had found his subordinate asleep when he arrived this morning and listed the appropriate disciplinary actions he planned to take.

Then Obando explained the discoveries that he had himself, he asserted, made. Rivas was accustomed to having others take credit for his work, but he wondered why he was even at the discussion.

"Rivas found nothing of consequence on the traitor's computer or phone. When I arrived this morning, I immediately recognized two things of immense importance."

Each of the men gathered exhibited great enthusiasm until they noticed the ambassador showing no such interest. Then they all adopted similarly passive expressions.

Ambassador Octavio Torrez waved his hand nonchalantly as an order for his worker to proceed.

"The first of my discoveries was that the traitor Solis used the same computer security software developed by our government and that only we use."

Instantly Ambassador Torrez lost his charade of indifference and sat upright.

"How can this be?" he shouted.

Obando flinched at the brief, but sudden outburst.

"The only way, *Señor Ambajador*, is for someone in our government to have given it to him."

Torrez spewed a string of epithets that seemed so personally directed at his computer security supervisor that Obando wished he had let his subordinate deliver the news. Finally, the Head of Station calmed enough that he gestured again for Obando to continue.

"The other thing is something I found in the mobile phone. I ran a query on all the numbers that had been dialed from the phone, that the phone had received calls from, and every number in its 'Contacts' file."

Obando handed a sheet of printer paper to the Ambassador and explained what it meant.

"There was a contact entry with the word 'Me' for the name. It had two numbers listed. My search revealed that each number was among prepaid phones bought in Havana."

Torrez exploded again. "So, this outlaw Solis was in contact with Mission personnel in Cuba?"

"Not necessarily, sir. It only means the phones were bought there. Perhaps it was our staff. It's possible, but unlikely, that they were stolen. We just don't know at this point."

♦

Eli "Godzilla" Ownby got the news to Terry Henderson, who practically ran to the Director's office to pass it on. He didn't knock.

"Sir, we got a hit on one of the numbers of the eight phones purchased in Cuba. A text."

"In Havana?"

"No, sir. Managua. It originated from the building where President Zamora's office is. It was brief. Sounds like the sender was cutting things off with the recipient." Henderson handed the transcript of the eleven-word text to McClintock, along with the response that the correspondents needed to "see this through."

"Whew!" whistled the NSA boss. "The other device's location?"

Henderson squinted and scratched his head. After a delay and a deep breath, he gave the information.

"That's the thing, Director. The other person was in FBI Headquarters. What could that mean?"

Director Paul McClintock knew exactly what it meant.

"Have a seat, Terry." Then he dialed FBI Head Austin. "Gabe, you know the prepaids you've been trying to use to establish Solis' contact?"

"Yes, a washout, I'm afraid. Guy wouldn't talk to us."

"Well, he talked to us, so to speak. We intercepted your communications with him."

"Go on."

He was in Zamora's office complex.

"I guess that answers our question whether Solis really had a contact high in the Nicaraguan regime, as he claimed."

The two heads of U.S. agencies sat in silence.

"It doesn't provide any good intel, Gabe, but it will add credibility to anything else we can come up with," McClintock finally said.

"You know, Paul, part of me wondered if there really was a plot. I hoped, actually, that someone was yanking poor Solis' chain; that Zamora's response in sending his nephews was out of an abundance of caution that he might have a leak in his regime. But now, I think that…"

"…the threat is real?" NSA asked.

"Yes."

♦

"You look happy."

Josh Morgan smiled, but said nothing, only taking a sip from the water Betsy Parnell had given him.

"He's been needing to do this for a while," Retired Master Sergeant Lechler told the CIA Director with a twinkle in his eyes. "Right, Josh?"

Morgan gulped and cast a sideways look at his friend with the bottle still to his mouth.

"You know, get a good night's rest," Lechler added, taking a drink of his own H2O.

Since she knew that Morgan had spent the night with Maggie, she was in on the insinuation.

"Yes, Josh definitely needed some… rest," she said in contribution to the tease.

"Okay, guys. Got it. You can shut up now," Morgan said, smiling behind his water bottle as he sipped.

Parnell had been in the loop about everything related to Solis, Nicaragua, the possible terror attack – everything – from the FBI and NSA. After all, she had really started the ball rolling with her inquiries to

McClintock and Austin. Before Morgan and Lechler had arrived, she had ended a call with her two peers in which the other agency directors had brought her up to date.

She passed the information on to her two contractors.

"Holy shit," stated the ex-soldier.

"So," Morgan summarized, "it appears that Solis was really onto something and that his contact really was someone high up in Zamora's circle. That certainly makes the chemical attack seem more real."

"But if the source won't talk," Lechler wondered, "what's next?"

"Fancy a trip to Managua?" the CIA boss asked.

"Sure." Lechler agreed instantly.

Morgan's reply was less immediate and not as enthusiastic.

"When do we leave?" the ex-CIA Officer finally uttered in agreement.

♦

El Presidente Sergio Zamora hung up from the call from his diplomatic representative in Washington. He sorted through all the known facts he had just heard. Combined with what he had learned a short time earlier from his cybersecurity team in Managua, the picture became all too clear.

The despot pressed a button on his phone summoning his aide. In only a few seconds, General Geraldo Santana opened the door.

"*Si, Presidente?*"

The Nicaraguan president walked to the sitting area at the side of his lavish office and motioned to a chair across from his.

Santana sat. Zamora called to a servant to bring him a glass of rum. The aide thought it odd that his president didn't offer him a drink. He never accepted but Zamora always offered.

When the servant arrived with the glass, Zamora also took a cigar from the tray. He turned expectantly and the server lit the cigar. Without any thanks or other acknowledgement for his waiter, Zamora drew from the cigar and blew the smoke upward. He crossed a leg and leaned forward to Santana.

The attendant took his usual position beside the door in the event his president needed anything further.

Finally, he held the cigar sideways inches from his face.

"Cuban, of course. These were a gift from *mi amigo*, *el presidente de Cuba.* He always gives me several boxes when I visit. I believe this one comes from my last visit there. Last January, wasn't it?"

"*Si, Presidente.*"

Zamora's countenance suddenly altered. His eyebrows inclined inward and his eyes narrowed; his nostrils flared; he clenched his teeth.

As the man closest to the president of the country, Santana often drew his ire, many times for things not of his doing. This seemed different, decidedly more intense.

Zamora walked to his desk and pressed the intercom button.

"*Coronel, por favor.*"

The door opened and a colonel of the Nicaraguan Army strode in. He saluted the president and stood silently at attention while his commander-in-chief returned to the plush chair in the sitting area.

Zamora drew from his cigar another two or three times. Finally, he propped both elbows on his knees. He dropped his head and shook it. Then he raised his face toward his aide. It held the same penetrating stare and piercing intensity it had held earlier. Without any hint of his action, Zamora thrust his right index finger toward Santana and shouted his accusation.

"Is that where you got the phones?"

The aide recoiled reflexively from the sudden movement.

"*Qué?*"

"The phones! The fucking phones! You got them in Cuba!" Zamora bolted upright and put his finger on Santana's chest and pushed. Then he moved it to only one inch from his face.

"Why have you betrayed me? *Por qué*"

"I… I…" The aide's words ended when he realized the pointlessness of continuing. Then his expression changed to match his superior's.

"*Sí!* I got them in Cuba. While you were with *Presidente* Lara, finalizing your assistance to this despicable act, I was planning a way to expose it. So, *sí!* That is where I got them!"

Nicaragua's dictator brought his fist into his aide's left jaw again and again and again. Zamora punched Santana in the stomach and chest, then more times to his head. Santana wanted to resist but the *Coronel* stood by, hand on pistol to react, so the aide endured it.

When the Latin American despot finally stopped pummeling the general, his wrath seemed to dissipate with his energy. He took ice cubes from his drink, wrapped them in his handkerchief, and placed them on his knuckles. He sat down and took a drink of rum.

"Once news came of the traitor Solis' claim that he had a source in my inner circle, we took precautions. Our security agency began following everyone in my regime. There were some things they reported about you that seemed unusual: sitting in a bar drinking and working on your computer; making and receiving phone calls from outside. I said, 'He doesn't want to go home to his wife.' 'A mistress,' I said. I defended you."

Zamora puffed his cigar again before waving it at General Santana.

"We never intercepted any suspicious phone calls or messages arriving to or coming from inside our offices. Until today, that is. Our processes aren't sophisticated enough to know who sent the texts, or exactly where they originated. But my Ambassador to the United States gave me two numbers linked to our traitor. One of them matched the number of our intercept from here today."

Zamora pointed to his glass. The waiter rushed to pour more rum. He relit Zamora's cigar and when the dictator held his bleeding hand toward his servant, the attendant tied the handkerchief in place.

"The final part came when one of the *Coronel's* men observed you throwing a mobile phone into a trash bin a few blocks from here. He retrieved it and found that the number matched the one that we intercepted."

The president removed the wet handkerchief and looked at his knuckles. They were raw and oozing blood. He repositioned his handkerchief on them. The servant started toward his president, but the despot motioned him away.

"We will find out what you have divulged – either directly from you or perhaps from the phone that you discarded. You should hope it is from the phone, so your end will be mercifully quick."

A signal with his hand was the order for the Colonel to escort Santana out of Zamora's sight.

CHAPTER 31

With fake passports in hand, Josh Morgan and Tom Lechler were in the boarding line at Washington Dulles Airport, about to take off for Managua, Nicaragua.

Josh had called Maggie to tell her he was going to be away for a few days. She only told him to come home safe and that she loved him. Once he left Langley, he had none of his own personal devices, so when his phone rang, he knew it wasn't the woman he loved.

"Yes," he answered, following his ex-warrior friend in line. Lechler was just about to hand his boarding pass to the attendant, when Morgan put a hand on his shoulder and steered him away.

"Betsy. Change of plans."

The two CIA contractors waited at Dulles for a driver to arrive, with no information other than that they wouldn't be going to Nicaragua. Lechler seemed disappointed. Morgan wasn't.

At 2:00 PM, the pair was back in the Director's office, getting the lowdown on what had precipitated the change.

"This is extremely sensitive information. We have a well-placed agent in Zamora's regime who just informed us that the dictator has arrested his top aide," Parnell reported.

"Geez! For…?" Morgan inquired.

"Apparently the man was Eddie Solis' source."

"Damn!" exclaimed Lechler.

"If you had an agent there, couldn't he figure out that the aide was in contact with Solis?" Lechler asked.

"No. We had no idea Solis was talking to anyone until he disappeared."

"Damn, Betsy. Eddie was posting it all over the Internet. A bit of an intelligence failure, don't you think?" Morgan opined.

The rebuke touched a nerve within the CIA boss.

"Do you know how many conspiracy nuts and theories are out there, Morgan? So, no. It wasn't a failure."

"Fair enough, Betsy."

"Anyhow, given that this was a recent development, we never asked our agent to look into it. We'd worry about burning him. Besides, if he had come across that, he'd have let us know."

"But he knows this Santana has been arrested? Who is he? What's his deal?"

"Sorry, Josh. You don't need to know."

"And this agent of yours doesn't know any details of the terror plot?"

"No, Tom. We had about four unknowns. Who is carrying out the chemical-attack; where it is going to occur; when it's going to take place; and who was Solis' source? We figured if we could root out the contact, we'd get the where and when. Unfortunately, Zamora got to Solis' source first."

"So, where do we stand, Betsy?" asked the ex-operator.

"Good question, Tom. I don't know. Sending you guys down there was a long shot. We didn't want to use our in-country officers for fear they'd get burned."

"Thanks, Director. Nice to know we're more expendable."

Parnell ignored Morgan's dig.

♦

With word from Elizabeth Parnell at CIA that Solis' source had been uncovered by Zamora, Paul McClintock and Gabe Austin decided to shut down all work at NSA and FBI, respectively, on who Solis' source was. It was a known fact now.

The only three remaining things that mattered anymore were who was carrying out the chemical attack, where it would happen, and when it would occur.

All that Parnell had disclosed was that Zamora's top aide had been communicating with the Nicaraguan blogger and that he had been arrested.

So, with respect to the three open questions, the CIA Director and her counterparts all agreed on a logical supposition for the "who." The NSA had determined that the cellphones had been bought in Cuba. Therefore, it *could* be reasonable that Cuban President Lara was involved, along with Zamora.

And that worried Parnell, McClintock, and Austin. *Numero uno* on Cuba's enemies list was the United States. If correct, while it wasn't specific, it narrowed down the "where" somewhat. Deducing that it would be an attack on the U.S. only provided some general direction.

However, if the phones' purchase location wasn't evidence that Cuba was behind the plot, the U.S. still didn't know who or where. The whole thing was stuck at square one. If it was only Nicaragua, then assumptions were difficult to arrive at.

One thing that was certain was the uncertainty surrounding the "when." Intel that existed on that was totally at odds with itself. Analyst Henderson had said NSA was reasonably confident that the attack would be "next month." That assumption had recently been arrived at from analyzing past intercepts. Within the last two days, however, Zamora said that his plan would happen "this month." People use the term "this" in different ways. Some meant the current month, week, or whatever. Others meant the one that is upcoming. Complicating matters even more was that the calendar had just turned the page into November. Were the references with respect to that?

The intelligence community was completely without a consensus concerning a definite timeframe.

♦

Maggie was delighted that Josh would be coming back "home" rather than leaving for wherever it was that Betsy Parnell had planned to send him. It was only 4:00 PM, but when Josh arrived at her door, she greeted him with a Glencairn style glass, a third full of Maker's Mark Bourbon Whisky. He gladly accepted it.

Josh was struck by how much the layout of Maggie's apartment was like the one they shared at The Wharf. And she had kept some of their furniture, too, so, when the couple sat on the couch, it was *their* old one. She had apparently bought an inexpensive new one for their old place and moved the one they had shared here.

There was no huge picture window here to look out at the D.C. skyline, but the sofa and the drinks and Maggie's head against him felt familiar.

"Can you tell me where you were going?"

"Doesn't matter now, Maggie." Josh took a very small sip of the amber liquid. "Oh, what the hell. You know everything that's going on. Nicaragua, Maggie. I was going to Managua."

"Why?"

"To embark on one of the wildest fishing expeditions I've ever been on. Supposed to find Eddie's source and get the details from him. But he got made by Zamora and was arrested."

Maggie sat up and squared herself toward Josh.

"Oh, no!"

"Yeah. Finding him would've been almost impossible, but now he's completely off the table as far as our getting intel from him."

Maggie pushed Josh gently forward and scooted behind him on the sofa. She began to rub his shoulders.

"That feels great," he admitted.

"So, do our guys have any clue about anything?"

"You haven't heard from the White House? Betsy just briefed the President. Well, you already know that it's supposed to be a chemical attack. Nobody is sure if or how Nicaragua is involved but the best guess is that Cuba is driving this thing and that likely means that…"

"…We're the target," Maggie understood.

"Yep. Any word on Eddie?"

"As a matter of fact, Agent Russell called to let me know that Eddie's awake and alert. Still in a lot of pain. Worse than it needs to be because Eddie insisted that the doctors reduce his medication. He wants to be more lucid to try to answer questions. Russell is going back down there in the morning."

"Want to drive down there?"

"To see Eddie? Why?"

"I think he knows more than he realizes." Morgan retrieved a laptop from his backpack.

"Your computer? Thought the Gutierrez brothers had it."

"Betsy got the Bureau to give it to me. It's not like the Nicaraguan bastards are going to trial." He looked at Maggie and grinned.

"Won't the feds want to examine it?"

"They already have. Besides, they cloned my hard drive."

The former CIA Officer was back in his element, examining information to track someone down or uncover some hidden truth. He set the laptop on the coffee table. Maggie leaned in with him, remembering when he deciphered a cryptic message from his late friend Ben Reid. Ben was a CIA analyst and had sent Josh information that put him on the trail to finding kidnapped Former President Trent Weston.

Shortly the laptop's display lit up. Josh navigated to the folders that contained all the documents that Maggie had given him that related to Eddie Solis. He opened a folder.

"These are all his blog posts. Look at this one."

Maggie peered in to examine the particular article that Josh had opened and read aloud.

"'My source in the Zamora regime has already given me information that he has said he will make clear very soon. He said he has a key that will open the doors to this plot, which he will provide in a matter of days.'"

Maggie's auburn locks swung with her shaking head.

"Don't you see, Maggie? Everyone who has looked at this – including me – dismissed it as bluster. We thought the 'already' was what I guess you'd call literary license. Eddie was implying more knowledge than he had to add mystery to his posts. And the 'key' reference – everyone has assumed that to be metaphorical. But what if he really has more information than he knows? Or he knows and is just waiting for the key to understanding it. His source, whom we now know to be Zamora's top aide, has been taking an awfully big chance. He probably wouldn't just spell everything out in plain English – well Spanish."

Maggie took Josh's glass, which still had bourbon in it and started for the kitchen.

"I wasn't through Maggie. Where are you going?"

"To get my jacket. It's chilly outside."

♦

General Geraldo Santana had resisted bravely. Finally, though, the torture had taken its toll and he spilled everything he had done. He admitted to selecting a man he considered to be a fool solely because of his professed connection with the White House Press Secretary. Reports from Luis and Santos Gutierrez to their uncle had led him to believe the claim was a fiction.

Santana disclosed that he had sent messages in other ways beyond texting. Some were encrypted in photographic images and the key was part of the functionality of the regime's privately developed software.

The aide had confessed that his computer held all the images, but that, after he had decided not to go through with his disclosure of the final piece of the plot, he had used the government's own cybersecurity facility to wipe the hard drive with a powerful electromagnet and then drove bolts through the device.

It was while agents of Zamora's security team were running to recover the hard drive that the intensity of the torture increased to a point that General Geraldo Santana had suffered a heart attack and died. When such brutal techniques were used to extract information, medical staff were on hand to prevent such an occurrence, but efforts to revive him failed.

El Presidente Sergio Zamora was furious. He sat alone in his office, drinking rum and smoking his Cuban cigars. He couldn't bear the thought of revealing to Cuban President Lara that parts of the plot had been compromised, but he called the man.

Zamora barely got the words out that a spy had uncovered parts of the plan and that he didn't know the full extent of the damage, before Lara simply said, "Fix it, fool!" and hung up.

The Nicaraguan President was at a loss. Without Santana's hard drive, he would not be able to discover the full scope of the information he had revealed to the traitor Solis.

Zamora pointed to his glass. His servant rushed immediately to the man and filled his glass from the bottle that was sitting right beside it.

A sudden realization struck the man that he might have the images containing the encrypted messages. He rarely initiated his own calls, but he pressed a button on the telephone on the small serving table at his side.

"Ambassador Torrez, I need you to copy the entire contents of Solis' computer and send it to me. Then I want the computer and his phone – everything you have – on a plane to me within the hour."

The dictator wasn't pleased with the reply the Head of Mission to the U.S. provided.

"You ignorant bastard! I don't care how difficult it will be or how long you think the transmission will take. You will send the data first, then send a courier with the computer."

Pleased with his solution, he was equally displeased with his representative in Washington, so the dictator slammed the handset down. Finally, he raised his hand to the height of his shoulder and snapped his fingers. His servant placed the call that *el Presidente* was ready for his dinner.

♦

The Secret Service wasn't happy and said so to their boss, President Hendrickson, but their orders were clear. The Press Secretary and Josh Morgan were not under anything remotely similar to house arrest. They could go wherever they wanted. And where they went, Secret Service went.

The one alteration to the couple's plans was that they would fly to Norfolk at taxpayers' expense. It had been raining all day and the Agency felt the air travel would be safer. And it would most definitely be quicker.

Consequently, at around 6:15 PM, Ms. Loughlin and Mr. Morgan were aboard a government jet bound for Norfolk.

♦

CIA Director Elizabeth Parnell hung up her phone and immediately called her NSA equal.

"Paul. Betsy. Our Station Chief in Managua just called. Here's what I need."

After the brief explanation, Paul McClintock confirmed his organization could accomplish the task and called Terry Henderson, who had in a very short time, become the Agency Head's go-to guy.

♦

Less than one hour after takeoff, Josh and Maggie were alongside hospital patient Eddie Solis. Upon seeing the Press Secretary, Eddie hung his head, embarrassed and ashamed of how he had brought such trauma into her life.

"I'm sorry, Madam Secretary, that I…"

"It's still 'Maggie,' and it's okay. The main thing is for you to get well."

Morgan smiled and nodded, but in his mind, he disagreed with Maggie. The main thing was to stop a terror attack and getting more information from Solis would help.

After some very brief small talk about how the blogger felt and other matters to help loosen him up for conversation, Maggie got to the point.

"Eddie, we do need to ask you some questions." She patted him on his arm.

"I know. I'm ready, but I'm afraid I don't know anything useful."

"I bet you do, Eddie," Morgan assured him. "We'll take it real slow and see what you come up with."

Edmundo Solis nodded and took a deep breath that hurt his bruised and broken ribs. Maggie took his hand.

"Eddie, you know that the Gutierrez brothers took your phone and computer – right?"

The patient looked confused at Josh's question. "I know they took my phone. How… how did they get my computer?"

"After they took you, they searched your apartment."

Eddie Solis groaned. "All my work! My backup will have most of it…" The patient paused to cough, resulting in much pain. "But it won't have all of it."

"Whoa! Backup?" Morgan seized on the comment. "What backup, Eddie?"

"I used to have Cloud backup but decided I didn't trust it. So, I backed up to an external hard drive."

Josh's voice raised in pitch but not volume.

"Where is the hard drive, Eddie?"

♦

Terry Henderson, on direct orders from NSA Director McClintock, had arranged with Zilla Ownby to capture any communications originating from the Nicaraguan Embassy in Washington in real time. The data header displayed the number of files and the percentage completion.

"It's going to take quite a while, Terry."

"I thought Agency capabilities were the fastest in the world."

"It's not our technology, bro. It's theirs. I don't know what they're using but it's very, very slow. Like Flintstones-era. This could take over an hour. Maybe two. What did you say it is?"

"McClintock didn't tell me. He just said get it," Henderson admitted.

"Well, get comfortable," Zilla advised.

♦

"Mrs. Shoemaker, I know it's late, but do you recognize me?" Maggie asked. "I'm a friend of Eddie's."

The blogger's next-door neighbor had her door cracked open just enough that her visitors could only see one eye staring at them.

"You look familiar, but… no, I can't place you." She started to close the door.

"Ma'am, please wait. Here's a picture of Eddie and me that my friend Josh took just a little while ago." Maggie held her phone up to the narrow space between the edge of the door and the frame. The image showed her and Eddie, and a nurse to add some credibility.

"First, Eddie wanted me to tell you that he is going to be okay… that he can't wait to see you again. He wanted me to ask how your precious kitty is doing?"

"What's her name?" challenged the elderly lady with a frown.

"Why, Charlie, of course."

Maggie realized she had another way to establish her trustworthiness.

"Agent Maddox, would you come here, please?"

The Secret Service Agent standing watch in the hallway looked chagrined as he walked toward his protectees.

"Yes, ma'am?"

"Would you please show Mrs. Shoemaker your credentials?"

The Agent displayed his badge and ID.

Josh thought Maggie's idea a stroke of genius. But both of them were disappointed when the door shut – until they heard the sliding of two chains on the other side. The door opened slowly.

"I should look around, Madam Secretary."

"We'll be fine, Agent Maddox."

"I remember now!" Mrs. Shoemaker said. "You're the young lady I see on TV from the White House. You're very pretty." Then, "She's very pretty" to Josh. "You look hurt. How did you get the bruises?"

"Yes, ma'am, she is very pretty," Josh answered. Both he and Maggie ignored the question about her injuries.

The pair followed Eddie's neighbor into her meager apartment. She had already made herself ready for bed, wearing robe and house shoes. She began to fuss with her hair, removing the net that she slept in.

"I'm so embarrassed. I never have company at this hour. Well, seldom at all, really. Would you like tea?"

"No, ma'am," Josh said, "and sorry for the hour."

The three sat on the sofa.

"Mrs. Shoemaker," Maggie started, putting her hand gently on the woman's arm, "Eddie told us that he keeps a hard drive with you."

Josh began to explain. "A hard drive is a box about this big that..."

"I know what a hard drive is, young man," Mrs. Shoemaker assured. "It's a computer thing."

"Yes, ma'am. Of course. We would like to get that."

The elderly woman's face showed a flash of renewed skepticism.

"It's for Eddie," Maggie added. "He said that he told you not to give it to anybody."

Mrs. Shoemaker's face softened at the reassurance by the pretty lady from the White House. She stood and walked to her kitchen, where she opened a very oversized cookie jar. She lifted a black plastic box out and brought it to Maggie.

"I hope I'm doing the right thing. I didn't tell the people who came here asking about him."

"Eddie's computer was taken during his unfortunate situation..." Josh began.

"The poor baby."

"Yes, ma'am. He got a new computer and wants to copy his data from this to it while he's in the hospital." Josh had just uttered the first real lie to the blogger's friend.

Having the device in hand made Josh impatient to leave, but Maggie thoughtfully continued a little longer with small talk.

"Mrs. Shoemaker, would you like to go see Eddie tomorrow? It would do him a world of good."

Josh was thinking that Maggie wasn't going to be here tomorrow. And neither was he.

"I'll arrange for a nice policeman or one of the Agents from the local FBI office to take you there."

♦

Dictator Sergio Zamora was beyond flustered. His impatience was manifesting itself through drinking more than he should and throwing things. How could it take this long to transmit information from Washington to Managua?

The despot didn't care that it was an incredibly large amount of data, nor that the technology the Nicaraguan government used lagged well behind what other nations had, as one of his computer technicians had informed him earlier.

He angrily demanded a snack from his evening shift servant.

♦

Seated on the Secret Service jet, Josh was booting his laptop.

True to her word, Maggie was on the phone immediately after boarding the plane, arranging for transportation for Mrs. Shoemaker to see Eddie. Once the ride was set up, she called Eddie's neighbor to give her the details.

"Now you be sure to check the officer's badge and ID carefully," she advised in closing.

"There."

Josh looked up from attaching a cable to the port on his laptop and delivered a smile that accurately reflected how proud and impressed Maggie always made him.

There was a slight whirring, almost inaudible, as the drive containing Eddie's backup files spun inside its case. He entered the password Eddie had provided and the drive spun some more. Once the copy was complete, Josh began to rapidly assess which folders and files seemed most important. He immediately seized on the folder titled "WordPress-Blog" and opened it.

Maggie sat in silence to allow Josh the time to look at Eddie's data without interruption.

CHAPTER 32

"Hmm. Look at this. I think it's odd that Eddie has these photos in the same folder with his notes about Nicaragua. So, I did a Google Photo Search on a couple of the images. They're both of scenery in Nicaragua."

"Interesting."

"Yeah, now watch this, Maggie." Josh double-clicked on one of the images. But rather than enlarging or launching some other type of photo-related process, the image sort of shook. Its pixels seemed to appear larger briefly before settling back into the image.

"So…?" Maggie wasn't getting it.

"During the whole thing with Russia, Ryan Crenshaw communicated with Pavel Orlov…"

"The head of the Russian Foreign Intelligence Service."

"Right. They hid messages in photo image files."

"And you're thinking that's what these are," Maggie guessed.

"I don't know, Maggie. Here's what I do know. I found these images on the Internet, so Eddie didn't take them. And neither did his source. Why does he have them?"

"Josh, he's from Nicaragua. Maybe he just collected them because he liked them."

"Then why are they in with his blog files? I looked through his posts and never found any scenic images; only pics of politicians, *et cetera*."

"So, what do you think?"

"The FBI has determined without a doubt that Eddie and Zamora's aide communicated through text. I think maybe Zamora's guy sent him these images by text and Eddie saved them on his computer."

"Wouldn't Eddie know they had messages in them?"

"You'd think so, but maybe not. Maybe his source was holding off for some big reveal. Or maybe Eddie missed something in one of the messages.

Or maybe he doesn't remember. I don't know."

Josh stared at Maggie and then double-clicked on three images in succession. Each "vibrated" in response.

"See. It just seems like something wants to happen. I just need the right decryption software."

Maggie let the possibility soak in for a while. Finally, she asked, "Why don't you tell the feds about this?"

"I will, but FBI and NSA are both going to catch this. At least, they will if these files are on his Cloud backup."

"And he said that he hasn't used Net-based backup for a while. These may be the only copies that exist," Maggie surmised.

♦

"End the transmission? President Zamora, that will corrupt the file."

The dictator insisted in a very loud voice that it would not. He had enough rum in him that he was even more belligerent than usual. And all his subordinates knew that when he was this way, there was no reasoning with him. And when the error in his logic appeared, as it always did in such matters as these, the staff always – *always* – got the blame. But there was no arguing with *el Presidente.*

So, Ambassador Octavio Torrez nodded to his computer technician, who shut down the file transfer.

The Head of the Nicaraguan delegation in Washington took a big drink of the Kentucky whiskey he had grown fond of while in the United States, wiped his brow with a tissue, and left for his office.

♦

Terry Henderson was on the phone with Director McClintock.

"Say that again. *What* happened?" the NSA boss asked in disbelief for a repeat.

"The transmission was cut off."

"Accidentally?"

"No," said Henderson. "Deliberately… from the sender. It doesn't make sense; not when you're eighty percent done."

McClintock put his desktop phone on speaker, stood, and paced about his office.

"Okay, Terry. Tell me you got that eighty percent." The lengthy pause before his analyst's reply made the Director uneasy. He even heard Henderson's sigh before his answer. That worried him even more.

"Depends, Director. According to Zilla, that is, Ownby – and he knows a lot more about this than I do – the communication was being sent as one big packet. That doesn't make sense; certainly not the way we'd do it. But we might be able to rip pieces of the data. I can't say for sure. Zilla's working on it now."

Paul McClintock wanted to rip his analyst, but knew it wasn't his fault.

"Okay, Terry. Nice work. Tell Ownby that, too. And tell him to stay on it. Bring in anyone he needs."

"Heading that way myself, sir."

Paul McClintock ran his fingers through his thinning hair. After he opened his drawer and poured himself the Bombay Sapphire that it contained, he took his seat and dialed the numbers of his CIA and FBI counterparts.

"Fuck…," he mumbled.

♦

It used to bother Maggie when Josh became so engrossed in something that he ignored her. Now, she was happy just to have him around. He had scrambled to collect his laptop, hard drive, and cables when the Secret Service's jet landed. He had barely gathered everything when the mobile stairway arrived at the jet and the aircraft's door opened.

Josh finished cramming everything into his backpack once he and Maggie were in the Agency car and headed back to Maggie's apartment. During the ride, Josh had spent most of the time resting his chin on his left fist and staring out the window. Maggie let him brainstorm without speaking a word.

"Are you hungry?" Maggie asked when they were in her apartment.

"We ate on the plane."

"Actually, just a snack. And I did. You didn't touch yours."

"Oh, yeah. Right. To tell you the truth, I am a little hungry."

The apartment's resident went to her kitchen and made a sandwich for Josh and gathered a few vegetables and some Ranch dressing for herself. She set them on the table where Morgan had set up shop. He fumbled around blindly until he had the ham and cheese sandwich in his hand and took a bite.

His intense attention to his work made Maggie smile. It wasn't a part of their relationship she would've ever thought she would enjoy experiencing again.

Josh powered through half his sandwich before setting it back on the plate. He moved his finger around his laptop's touchpad to explore more of the files that he had copied from Eddie's backup drive. When he finally looked up, Maggie had her head rested on one fist and was eating a baby carrot with her other hand.

Josh leaned over and kissed her, stealing a piece of broccoli as he did. He dipped it in Maggie's bowl of dressing and turned his attention back to his work.

"I don't know what this is," he remarked.

Maggie continued munching on a small bite of cauliflower while breaking apart another floret. She looked at Josh's laptop's display only to see that every word was in Spanish.

"Here," he said, pointing. "That's an application. I don't know what the word means. Probably a made-up word. Companies sometimes do that to have a unique brand name. It's Spanish but literally makes no sense."

"What does it do?" Maggie inquired.

"No idea. And I'm a little afraid to execute the app for fear of what it might do to my computer."

"I don't blame you."

"But here's the thing. I haven't seen one program that I feel confident will decrypt the photos. That is, if there is really anything to decrypt."

"So…?" Maggie held both hands palm up, while Josh's finger hovered over the touchpad with the pointer above the file name.

He looked at Maggie, eyebrows arched, and raised his shoulders. Maggie in turn, raised her shoulders and shook her head.

"I don't know what to tell you, sweetheart."

Josh laughed out loud and said, "Well, crap. Here goes nothing." He double-clicked over the file name. Instantly, a progress bar appeared, showing the rate at which the application was installing.

♦

Terry Henderson and Zilla Ownby were having little success recovering any part of the interrupted transmission from the Nicaraguan Embassy in Washington to Managua.

"Why would they do this, Zilla? Accident maybe? System failure?"

"No idea, Terry."

The outlaw hacker turned NSA technician leaned back in his chair. He'd been at his desk for more than twenty-two hours.

"Long shift, huh, Zilla?"

"Oh, hell, Terry, I've had gaming sessions that have lasted twice this long."

Suddenly the display on one of the two monitors changed. While the one on the left continued to show lines of automatically executing commands scrolling at a blistering pace, the rightmost began to list file names. After forty seconds, both displays ended their execution.

"That's it," the ex-hacker stated.

"Did we get it all?" Henderson's question was more a wish.

Zilla didn't answer. He scanned the final lines of computer languages. Then he turned to his NSA associate and shook his head.

"Only about sixty-five percent of the approximately eighty percent that we got before the transmission was cut off."

"Damn it." Henderson pounded his fist gently on the work surface several times.

"Can you re-run it?"

"I can. And I will. But it won't make any difference."

Henderson picked up Zilla's desk phone and called the Agency's boss.

♦

Josh Morgan breathed a huge sigh of relief when the installation to his computer of the unknown program ended.

"Looks like a cybersecurity program of some sort. Probably the one on Eddie's laptop." He looked at a list of filenames. "This has to be the main program," he said, highlighting a file name with his pointer. It read "PSIv12.2."

Maggie asked, "What does it mean?"

"Nothing – I think. 'PSI' is probably an abbreviation for the name of the application. The Spanish word for 'version' is the same as in English. I'll bet the 'v12.2' is the version number."

Ex-CIA Officer Morgan put his left hand on his chin. With his right, he moved the laptop's pointer back and forth across the file name. Finally, he highlighted it and copied the name. He pasted it in his Google search field. With "PSI" being an abbreviation for so many phrases, as well as a Greek letter, the query produced results ranging from "pounds per square inch" to the names of several fraternities and sororities.

He added the word "Nicaragua" to the search and tried again. Still a huge number of hits and nothing seemed relevant.

"Sure wish we'd asked Eddie what types of programs were on his computer," Josh lamented.

Maggie took out her phone and dialed the number of the hospital. When they refused to ring her through to Eddie's room, she called the local police department and introduced herself as the White House Press Secretary.

♦

Much to their dismay, only a matter of minutes after refusing to allow Secretary Loughlin to speak with Edmundo Solis, hospital staff watched the

Norfolk police officer guarding the room answer a call on his department mobile phone and then walk in and hand it to the patient.

♦

"Hi, Eddie. It's Maggie. How ya feeling? I'm so glad to hear that. Would you mind speaking with Josh a moment? Great. Thank you so much."

Maggie handed her phone to Josh.

"Hi, Eddie. I know it's late. Thanks for speaking with me."

After a brief conversation with the Nicaraguan blogger, Josh was back on his laptop again.

"Okay, Maggie. Here's what he told me," Josh said, without removing his eyes from the computer. "First, the program I installed to my computer is a cybersecurity program like I suspected. But get this, his source provided it to him. Texted him a link to download it. Eddie said his source said it's supposed to be extremely secure. I guess Zamora's aide wanted something pretty bulletproof on Eddie's machine if he was going to give him information."

Josh pulled up the menu of programs under the PSI heading. None had a name that indicated what it did.

"A lot of these are features of the security app, I guess. Eddie said he never did anything more than install and run the program and set up a layer of three passwords."

Maggie stood behind Josh and lay her arms on his shoulders and watched him work.

"Another thing; Eddie confirmed that his contact sent him the photos but said he didn't know why. I asked him if he ever looked at them. He said he tried but when he attempted to enlarge them, they just sort of shook and wouldn't open."

Josh bent his head back to look up at Maggie.

"I'm convinced that some feature of the software his source gave him will open encrypted photo files, but I can't figure out what any of them do."

Josh had a thought that perhaps now that he had installed Eddie's security app on his own computer, maybe it would automatically execute if any linked extension were detected. He double-clicked on one of the image files.

Nothing.

He looked at the various programs on his menu again. There were eight under the PSI heading. Josh started executing one after another. As soon as he decided an app had nothing to do with the photos, he would close it and go to the next.

When the fourth program opened, Josh saw a space that looked like what you would find on many software applications – a place where you could drag files to stage them for some operation. More encouraging was the presence of a "button" beneath the window that said, "*Descifrar*." *Descifrar* was the Spanish word for decipher – or decrypt.

"I may have it, Maggie," Josh exclaimed excitedly. He dragged one of the image files onto the open window, the oldest one in the folder.

"Here goes nothing." He clicked on the "Decrypt" button. Immediately the razor-sharp image of thatch-roofed buildings set on a beach alongside beautiful blue water began to dissolve into a highly pixelated version. Then pixels began to change or disappear completely as a document began to appear.

♦

In Managua, Dictator Sergio Zamora was on his phone with his ambassador to the United States. He was berating the man for discontinuing transmission of the data from Edmundo Solis' computer. The Nicaraguan representative knew better than to remind his president that he himself had ordered it.

"Well, start it again."

The Head of the Mission in Washington stammered and blubbered, not because he didn't know what to say, but because he didn't want to say it. Finally, the disclosure made it past his lips.

"*Señor Presidente*, the device is on a plane to you, as you ordered."

Zamora verbally ravaged Torrez again and then slammed the phone down.

♦

"Great job, Terry, getting what you did from that corrupt file," the NSA chief said. "You and Zilla saved our asses. Would you run it through a translator and send an English version to me, Parnell at Langley, and Austin over at FBI? Then you two dig into it. I'll do the same and ask my counterparts to get some people on it, too."

♦

By now, the plan to launch a nerve agent attack will be far along. I will send you messages in this manner, revealing what I know up to that time. Except for this one, each one will have a time stamp that will prevent you from opening it until October 28. This will allow me time to change my mind, if I choose. Each message will become impossible to decipher after you close the file, becoming only a photograph.

"That's it," said Josh when he had finished translating for Maggie.

"So, you get one shot at each message, and then it's gone," she concluded.

"I guess so."

Josh tried to copy the document, but a hidden subroutine prevented him.

"More than one way to do this." He turned on his phone's camera and snapped a photo. Then he closed the file. Just to satisfy himself, the former spook dragged the same image onto the PSI window and clicked on the "Decrypt" button. An error message appeared in Spanish saying that the "operation could not be completed."

"I'd sure like to skip to the end of the book, so to speak, and read the last message first. But what if Zamora's aide built in some more little surprises, like the one-view routine, and I wreck it by going out of order?"

Maggie counted the image files.

"There are only six. How long can it take?"

Josh started opening the files in order. There was one every other week, ending with one sent the night Eddie was taken. That would probably disclose what had Eddie so excited and that he had promised to tell Maggie about in his last email.

Decrypted messages one through three provided no information that the U.S. Intelligence Community hadn't already discovered: chemical terror attack and Cuban/Nicaraguan cooperation being the headlines.

Deciphered image/document number four was the one in which Santana, who had never identified himself to Eddie, laid out his motive for betraying his government. At what would've approximated a full page of typed text, it was a lengthy document, relative to the others.

"The bottom line is that Santana was profoundly disillusioned with the direction the dictator had taken, at one point referring to him as '*un demonio suelto en el mundo*' – a 'demon loose in the world.' And he had seen enough horror in his life as a revolutionary and soldier. He felt he couldn't stand by and let Zamora unleash this on the world."

"Pretty noble," Maggie said.

"Yeah."

Nothing more of importance appeared until the very last email. Josh's pulse actually ticked up at the knowledge that crucial details might be about to become known.

"What!? Dammit! What the…?"

"What is it, Josh?"

Josh stood up abruptly and grabbed his hair with both hands.

"Son of a bitch!"

"What?"

"Says he's having second thoughts. He identifies himself as being Geraldo Santana and that the United States is the target, but that's it, Maggie!"

"That's something, isn't it?"

"Not really. If Cuba's behind this, we knew that we're the target. Right?"

"Nothing else?"

The former CIA Officer put his hands on his hips and paced around nervously; uncharacteristically, Maggie thought.

"No. Nothing."

Maggie turned Josh to face her and looked him straight in his eyes.

"How about you have your pity party later and get back to work on this?"

Josh Morgan stared Maggie Loughlin in the eyes without expression until he burst out laughing.

"*Pity party*!" He laughed more. "Seriously, do people still say that? *Pity party*?"

Maggie blushed. "Well, I couldn't come up with anything else. I was trying to motivate you."

Josh tried to pull her close, but she pounded him in the chest and jerked away.

Josh put his hands on his knees, still laughing. He could see by the quivering hair that Maggie was laughing, too. He pulled her around and held her tight.

"Okay, Coach Loughlin. What do I do?"

CHAPTER 33

DAY 6 – SATURDAY

It was after midnight and things were at a standstill for everyone investigating the terror threat.

Josh Morgan had filled Betsy in on everything he knew. He wasn't surprised to hear of NSA's interception of the transmission from the Republic of Nicaragua Embassy. He *was* surprised that they didn't get any of the earlier encrypted images. Morgan learned that analysts at the National Security Agency had found the same computer security system that he had found on Eddie's backup hard drive. Turned out that "PSI" stood for *Primera Seguridad para las Instituciones.* First Security for Institutions was the name for a Nicaraguan government-sponsored enterprise that developed cyber security for the government and other related organizations.

The CIA Director told him that the U.S. Secretary of State, Gerard Lively, had summoned the Nicaraguan Ambassador to the White House to meet with the President. Everyone knew that Octavio Torrez would deny knowledge of any plot, but it would be an opportunity to lay out the evidence that the intelligence agencies had collected and to warn of the dire consequences to his country if an attack was carried out.

The meeting was scheduled for a few hours later. Parnell suggested Morgan get some sleep and promised to keep him informed.

Josh looked at Maggie lying on her – *their* – couch. She had been asleep for a short time.

He thought of all the things that had transpired in his life since he had met her. He wished for a different world. He wanted to magically step back in a way that meant he'd never been involved in any of the matters that had dominated his life.

Still, he realized, he and the people around him had done things – good things – that had prevented events that would've been catastrophic to people and the country he loved.

And here he was again!

♦

In Managua, cyber-experts had successfully accessed the mobile phone that General Geraldo Santana had tried to dispose of immediately before they had arrested him. What they found were texts to Edmundo Solis. The technicians discovered the same photos that Josh Morgan had and decrypted and read them. An aide to Zamora had informed them of the topic of concern to the president.

They would pass along their findings once President Zamora arrived at his office, but they felt that nothing of great consequence was divulged. One thing that concerned them was an unsent text that laid out details of a plot that were unknown to the analysts. It began, "If you're reading this…" Then it listed every detail of an attack of which the computer techs were unaware.

Apparently, Santana had elected to not transmit the message. And the computer analysts would pretend to have not read it.

The traitor blogger's computer had arrived via special courier on a private jet. It was an easy matter to access everything on it. But, as with the phone, there seemed to be nothing overly worrisome.

♦

Realizing that Josh must've carried her there, Maggie woke up in her bed. She looked at her phone. Six-fifteen was a quarter hour after her usual wake-up time for her workday.

Josh appeared from the bathroom, drying his hair. He hung the towel around his neck and sat on the edge of the bed. He gave Maggie a good morning kiss.

"I could get used to this," she admitted.

"Used to what; a good morning kiss from me?"

"Well, not necessarily from you," she teased. "No, I mean sleeping a little later every morning; not having to go in and deliver the President's take on things to the world."

"You mean, tell little white lies and avoid actually answering questions?"

"No, I mean telling the truth, but saying it so that it communicates the topic the way she wants me to, and… Well, yeah, mostly avoiding having to actually answer questions."

"Well, sleep a little while longer, Maggie. I'm going to check in with Betsy."

"You think she'll be in her office already?'

"If I know her, she slept there."

♦

Nicaraguan President Sergio Zamora was an early riser. Whether he went to his office or remained at home, he was always up by 6:30, regardless of his agenda for the day or, as in this case, no matter how much alcohol he had consumed the night before.

The dictator was surprisingly mellow as he stood in the computer security lab, listening to his subordinates' reports on the contents of traitor Solis' laptop and mobile phone. He was pleased that Santana hadn't communicated anything to the blogger that would jeopardize the planned assault against American interests. Zamora's relief was largely due to the fact that he knew, despite his protestations to the contrary, that he was the one who had caused the unnecessary delay in analyzing the data.

Like his technicians, the despot was concerned about the content of the final message. Though it remained unsent, it contained very specific details of his and his associates' plan. Where else, Zamora worried, might his former aide have passed the information?

"You did not read the final message, but you read the previous ones?"

The supervising cyber specialist didn't think of that apparent inconsistency in his narrative.

"That is correct, *Señor Presidente.* Once we saw the opening sentence, I determined that it would contain things I should not know and stopped reading."

Zamora was skeptical but didn't feel like inflicting the further pain to his already severe headache that yelling would produce.

"I have a question, *señor.*"

The tech gulped as he sensed that his nation's president was going to challenge him on some matter.

"If this message indicated to Solis that receiving it meant that something had happened to Santana, how would it have been delivered?" Zamora stared at the computer specialist with hands on his hips.

The security analyst knew he had to think fast.

"*Señor,* I believe that he had not gotten that far before his arrest."

Surprisingly, Zamora accepted the answer.

"I had come to the same conclusion," the ruler of Nicaragua said. "*Gracias.*"

Satisfied that the plan against American interests had not been compromised, Sergio Zamora left the lab for his office, where he would report his confidence to his Cuban counterpart, Felix Lara, and to the third partner.

♦

In a government factory near Havana, the island nation's *Presidente* Lara ended the call from President Zamora. He didn't share the same level of confidence as his Nicaraguan compatriot, but he was still optimistic that their jointly developed action would succeed, as would their other partner's. His attention turned back to the team waiting patiently before him.

"Continue, *por favor*."

The lead scientist resumed the briefing that Zamora's call had interrupted. Before Lara and his advisers were three missiles of about twenty feet in length each.

In 1962, American President Kennedy announced to the world that U.S reconnaissance had discovered Soviet-made nuclear missiles in Cuba, setting into motion a tense thirteen-day standoff. That stalemate had been almost exclusively between the two superpowers, with Cuba remaining largely on the sidelines. The crisis ended when Soviet Premier Nikita Khrushchev offered to remove the missiles in exchange for a guarantee from Kennedy that the United States would not invade Cuba. Kennedy had also secretly promised to remove missiles from Turkey.

However, this time Cuba wasn't solely a base of a larger country. At least with respect to these missiles, the nation was acting autonomously, although in partnership with Nicaragua and one other nation.

In 1962, the missiles were out in the open on launch rails mounted on trailers and were observed from U-2 spy planes. The current ones, however, had been assembled in the building where they remained and were currently being inspected by government officials at the highest levels. The structure kept them safely out of view from the prying "eyes" of the U.S. spy satellites that had largely taken over for aircraft.

The facility also housed the launch platform, making the operation totally self-contained, from manufacture to launch.

It was remarkable to Lara and his regime that the U.S. intelligence apparatus remained seemingly unaware of the missiles.

♦

CIA Director Parnell and her peers throughout U.S. intelligence and law enforcement communities were stumped at how a plot against the nation could get so far along and not be detected. More than that, none of the organizations had developed a clear assessment of the nature of the threat, despite everything pointing to its execution being imminent.

The briefing to the President had been tense. Hendrickson had been reasonable and even-keeled but she had demanded answers ahead of her meeting with the Nicaraguan Ambassador. She was about to accuse his country of conspiring to launch a terror attack against the U.S. with very little in the way of hard facts or intelligence.

None of the Commander-in-chief's advisers had been much help.

"And that's the scoop, Josh. You know as much as anyone else. In fact, you uncovered much of it."

"So, a *possible* terror attack. *Probably* chemical and *probably* against the United States, but the exact nature, timing, and specific targets all unknown," Morgan summarized.

"You got it."

"Then what's Hendrickson going to tell the Nicaraguan Ambassador, Betsy?"

"No idea, friend. What's worse, she doesn't even know yet."

"Wish I could help."

"You've done a lot, Josh. Say 'hi' to Maggie."

♦

The computer security specialists working in the regime of President Zamora knew their report would add nothing to what they had already told the man, but they had compiled all the information into written form. Satisfied that they had completed their examination of Edmundo Solis' computer and mobile phone, they powered both down.

They also turned off the laptop and cellphone that had been seized from the former aide to their president, Geraldo Santana. Not one of the techies noticed a significant change in the status of one file on the deceased general's email application.

After the cyber specialists had ended their investigation, a single email message had moved from "Drafts" to "Outbox," where it remained a few milliseconds before landing in the "Sent" folder.

♦

Carl Smith, Lab Supervisor for the Federal Bureau of Investigation, had turned his attention to matters other than Edmundo Solis and a suspected plot against the United States. He simply had no new avenues to explore. He had, however, left the blogger's email app running in the background of his computer. But the constant alerts at the arrival of all sorts of spam and other junk email had become so annoying that he unchecked the "Play a sound" option to announce new mail. So, in lieu of an audio signal, Smitty would check the inbox occasionally.

Smitty felt that it was pointless since Solis was in the hospital and his source was deceased. CIA's other asset close to Zamora had passed along that Santana had died during interrogation. Therefore, he was completely taken aback when he looked at the blogger's inbox to see a message from a dead man. Smitty didn't speak Spanish, but his attention seized upon two phrases that were almost exactly the same in that language as they were in English.

"'*Misiles nucleares*!' '*Arma química*.' Oh, shit! Not good! NOT good!"

While the lab tech was still staring at the email, his phone rang. Special Agent Juan Esquivel's voice was rushed.

"Smitty, Solis' phone just got a text!"

"From Santana?"

"How'd you…?"

"His account just got an email. I'll round up everyone."

♦

After a hurriedly arranged conference call with his internal staff, FBI Director Austin was on the phone with President Hendrickson, her senior staff, the Directors of CIA and NSA, and others.

Noah Chandler, the President's Chief of Staff, had caught his boss just as she was about to tell her secretary to bring the Nicaraguan Ambassador into the Oval Office.

Director Austin had transmitted a translated copy of the email to POTUS, so she was reading along with the Bureau Chief. Everyone else was hearing Austin without benefit of a copy.

> *If you're reading this, it most likely means something has happened to me. In recent days, I felt as though I have been discovered and for fear of reprisals against my family and, perhaps, fear for my own safety, I had decided not to follow through on my promise to provide details of the attack President Zamora has planned. But if this message reaches you, then all is lost for me personally, so I will provide what I know.*
>
> *In addition to President Zamora's planned attack, he has nuclear missiles…*

Gasps filled the audio from the various places where the participants sat.

> *…aimed at American targets. I am sorry that I do not know where in the world they are, nor do I know the nature or location of the targets. They might be cities in your country, or perhaps American interests elsewhere. There is also a chemical*

weapon that will be released on American soil. I have no further details on either. I do not know the nature of the toxin. I do not know the time of the missile launch. So, I have failed to do what I set out to do, and that is to stop the madman Zamora and others from committing an atrocity of infinite proportions.

I have word that agents of el Presidente have taken you, so perhaps you will not receive this. Still, I will continue to add details as I know them in the hope that someone else may read this in your place. At least at this point you, or another, will understand the existence of the plan. Perhaps that will help your President to at least know what to look for if I am unable to add to this.

"That's it, Madam President," her FBI Director concluded.

Murmuring, gasps, expletives, and many other expressions of outrage and fear dominated for several seconds until Chief Chandler pleaded for calm on the President's behalf.

"Please, everyone. Quiet."

POTUS had never been one to call out somebody in front of others, but the words leapt from her lips.

"McClintock, you said this was a chemical attack. You never said anything about nukes."

"Yes, ma'am. Everything pointed to that likelihood alone." However, the NSA Director couldn't wait to have a discussion of his own with his analysts after the call was over.

The continued whispers ceased as Hendrickson spoke again.

"Director Donleavy, Director Larson, and Director McClintock, I want you to be in the Cabinet Room in twenty minutes. We have stepped up our imagery over Nicaragua over the last few days without any results that seemed out of line. I want to go over that with you pixel by pixel. I'll be a few minutes late. Start without me."

A few other comments ended the call but as the participants were ending their connection, each heard POTUS mutter, maybe to herself or to others in the room with her.

"Nukes. Nerve agents. How did Nicaragua get either?"

CHAPTER 34

With all the other precautions Eddie Solis had taken, it seemed incongruous to Morgan that he'd kept a list of passwords on his computer. Yet, as the ex-spook examined the files backed up to the blogger's hard drive, there it was. The document's name was even "Password List."

Morgan had smiled and shaken his head when he had discovered the file. "Eddie, Eddie, Eddie," he had said. But with the list, it was a matter of launching the man's email application, connecting to the server, and typing in the password to receive Eddie's emails. It was the one thing about which he'd felt that he's crossed the line a bit. But that didn't stop him from doing so.

Therefore, at the same time that the FBI had received the posthumous message from General Santana, Morgan had read it right along with everyone else in the intelligence community.

"Oh, damn!"

Maggie was walking past him with her T-shirt pajamas on.

"What is it?"

"Eddie's source – you know, the dead one – set up a message to auto-send." Josh read the email, translating for Maggie as he did.

"How can that be?! That's far beyond what the interpretation of the intel has been."

"I honestly don't know, Maggie."

Morgan speed-dialed Parnell.

"I don't have time right now. I'm on my way to the White House."

"Then you've all seen Santana's message."

"What the hell! God damn it, Morgan! How'd you get that? Never mind. I don't want to know. Listen, you've done quite enough. Stay out of this now. I know I've read you in on a lot of things that I shouldn't have and given you a lot of latitude about… Shit! Just stay out of this. Really!"

When Morgan answered, it was to dead air. "Right."

"Maggie's right," he thought. "This is completely at odds with the analysis of the intercepts."

He studied the email – every word. Then he pulled up the snapshots he'd taken with his phone of the documents that had appeared when he had decrypted Eddie's photos. He read and reread each one several times. After twenty-five minutes, he leaned back in his chair.

"What am I missing?"

"What did you say, Josh?"

When the former CIA officer turned to Maggie, she was dressed and putting on earrings.

"Where are you going?"

"To work."

"But Hendrickson told you to take some time off."

"Josh, they haven't hired a replacement for my past job as Assistant Secretary. So, I don't know who's handling that position, let alone my new role. It's got to be a mad house, especially given that the Press will get wind of something going on and want answers. I need to be there."

Morgan didn't like it, but he understood.

"Don't worry. Once this is all over, I'll take some time off. If any of us is alive, that is," the Press Secretary remarked with a laugh. Josh didn't see the humor, despite the fact that it sounded like something he might've said.

Maggie left the apartment with one Secret Service Special Agent tagging along. When Morgan peeked out the doorway for a last goodbye, he saw another agent arriving to babysit him.

Mac Marchman said nothing. Neither did Morgan at first. The two men locked eyes briefly.

"Awkward," Marchman finally proclaimed.

"Yeah."

♦

When Maggie arrived at her office in the West Wing of the White House, she was surprised to see who was sitting at her desk. She shouldn't have been.

Former Press Secretary Marie Ginnetti stood and hugged her successor.

"Well, that has to be among the shortest retirements of all time."

"Oh, Maggie, dear, I was so worried about you."

The embrace lasted a short while until Ginnetti stepped back with her hands still on her protégé's shoulders.

"Why aren't you home taking a break?"

"I could ask you the same question, Marie. I thought they might need me here. I'm not going home."

"Neither am I."

The two laughed.

"Let's tackle it together, Marie."

"Sounds great, Maggie."

♦

President of the United States Sandra Hendrickson needed to change her tactic somewhat. The posthumous email and text from Zamora's aide had added nuclear-tipped missiles to the already known prospect of chemical weapons. POTUS wasn't going to make specific accusations anyhow, but the seeming contradiction between Santana's disclosure and U.S. intelligence agencies' assessment made the meeting more ticklish.

Still, she knew that all sides had absolute confidence that the Nicaraguan dictator's regime was up to something. So, she decided a frontal assault was still the correct approach, albeit less forceful than originally planned.

"Ambassador Torrez, we have intelligence indicating that President Zamora has planned some sort of action against the United States."

The Nicaraguan Head of Mission was shocked and a bit unnerved by the absence of cordiality. Given that, his "Good morning, Madam President" felt forced when he said it.

"I'm afraid I'm at a loss as to how to respond," he continued. "Our government has no such intentions."

The Chief Executive leaned forward, placing her elbows on her desk and folding her hands together.

"As you no doubt know, a U.S. citizen was kidnapped by your president's nephews, the Gutierrez brothers."

"I'm afraid I have no knowledge of their actions, nor of their purpose here."

"You have the computer they took from Mr. Solis."

Rarely would a U.S. President admit to such intel, even if nobody in the world would be surprised by the capability to collect it.

"I'm sorry, President Hendrickson, we have no such thing."

"You did late last night." POTUS smiled slightly and continued. "Tell me, Ambassador, why did you interrupt the transmission of the device's data?"

Torrez was trapped. On the one hand, he would like to protest the apparent surveillance on the embassy. On the other, doing so would be an admission to possession of the blogger's laptop. He decided to try to walk a tightrope.

"If that were true, I would protest in the strongest possible terms. Because it is not, I can only say that you are mistaken."

"We both know that I'm not," Hendrickson asserted. She felt she could press no further and only supposed that the meeting would serve its intended purpose.

"Ambassador Torrez, let me say – also in the strongest possible terms – that your country is on notice. If you lift so much as one metaphorical finger, if you undertake even the smallest operation against the United States of America, whether here or against our interests or allies abroad, the consequences to your nation and your leadership will be immediate and crippling. Tell President Zamora that he'd better consider the cost before he challenges us. I will hold him *personally* responsible."

The Nicaraguan Ambassador was about to respond when the American President stood suddenly.

"Now, if you'll excuse me, Ambassador Torrez, I have urgent matters to attend to."

The Latin American representative stood and extended his hand, but the U.S. Leader walked past him without acknowledgement. One Secret Service Agent escorted her out of the Oval Office, while a second arrived to show her visitor the way out.

♦

In the White House Cabinet Room, Director of National Intelligence Chris Donleavy, NSA Director Paul McClintock, and CIA Chief Betsy Parnell and their agencies' Defense Imaging specialists were going over the images created by satellites, drones, and aircraft for a second time when POTUS arrived.

Hendrickson walked to the giant screen on which the current image was displayed and folded her arms.

"Madam President, we have found no evidence of missiles of a type capable of carrying a nuclear payload in any of our images," said McClintock. "Furthermore, there's no intelligence to suggest that Zamora has purchased nuclear weapons. And they certainly have no ability to develop their own. They would be years, likely a decade away from that sort of technology."

"What about a chemical weapon delivered by missile? Perhaps Santana got some details mixed up," POTUS offered.

DNI Donleavy took over. "We don't believe they have anything that is capable of that either."

The CIA Director spoke up. "This information is very sensitive. The Agency has a source very close to Zamora. He and Santana were not aware of each other. We left it that way – a decision that has proven to be wise, given what happened to the general. We have tried to second source what the aide was communicating to Solis through our agent, but he could not support the information."

President Hendrickson concluded, "Then you think this is all a wild goose chase, Betsy."

"Not at all, ma'am. I trust Director McClintock's work completely. I believe something's going on. I'm simply saying that knowledge of a nuclear device would be pretty compartmentalized. So, General Santana would've likely known very few details, if any. It's not something Zamora would casually mention over dinner."

Everyone in the room knew when to be quiet while their Commander-in-chief was thinking.

"Okay, Betsy. Let's say there is no nuke – that Santana was completely wrong. Can we take that chance?"

"Of course not, Madam President. I'm simply saying that we need to avoid having tunnel vision. Let's continue to consider all levels of threat."

"Agreed," POTUS decided. "Thank you, everyone. Keep digging."

♦

"You're home earlier than I would've expected."

Maggie's face was flushed from having seen Mac outside her apartment door. She delivered her question to Josh with only the expression she had.

"Yeah… I saw him," Josh answered to the implied query.

Maggie thought of all the things that had happened to her personally and professionally in the last few days. She sat at her dining table and buried her face in her hands.

"Let's go on vacation somewhere – *any*where."

"Sounds good to me," Josh agreed. He set a glass of wine on the table beside Maggie. "I'm cooking."

"Mm-hmm."

Maggie seemed distracted the entire time Josh was preparing the meal and even into dinner.

"You know, I don't think he can look through the peephole in the door," Josh finally said as a joke. Maggie gave him an irritated look.

Halfway through their dinner, Josh answered a knock on the door. Mac Marchman said rather tersely that he was being relieved and would be leaving.

Morgan thought it a rather unnecessary pronouncement, and just said, "Okay. Uh… thanks."

From the moment her wannabe boyfriend left, Maggie's mood

brightened considerably. And that irritated Morgan. He set his fork down and moved his napkin from his lap to the table.

"So, what's with you and that guy? You like him?"

"We went out once, but it wasn't a date, exactly."

"'Exactly?' What does that mean? And it's not what I asked. Do you have a thing for this guy? If so, what am I doing here?"

"No, I don't have a thing for Mac!" Realizing she had said it somewhat angrily, Maggie repeated herself in a more mellow tone. "No, Josh, I don't have a thing for him. I've missed you and wanted you since the last day I saw you at our supposed-to-be make-up lunch. Finally, a guy asks me out and I go. Then suddenly, you're back and that's all I've wanted. So, it's awkward. Okay?"

"Then you don't want him?"

"No! Weren't you listening? I just think – know, I guess – that he wants me."

Josh smiled and reached out for Maggie's hand.

"You know who Taya Kyle is – right?" Maggie asked.

"Sure. Chris Kyle's widow. American Sniper. American Wife."

"Well, I read something she said on Facebook quite a while back," the fiancée continued. "She said somebody else came up with it. I don't know. I just know that's where I read it. Mrs. Kyle said to her husband once, 'If I want you, you don't have to worry about who wants me.'"

With some finality, Maggie reached for Josh's hand and said firmly, "Believe it."

After dinner, the couple was in their usual places on the sofa.

"So, are you looking into the last message from Zamora's aide?"

"Betsy threatened me. Told me to drop it, stay out of it, and so on."

"Yeah, but are you looking into it?"

"Of course." Josh sat up. "Here's what I don't get. How could our guys be so wrong about Nicaragua having nukes? I'm thinking that maybe they're not wrong."

"I'm not supposed to tell you this, but the President had a meeting this morning with Ambassador Torrez."

"And…?"

"She had to tell me about it because it was on her daily schedule. The White House Press Corps would ask. She told me what she really said so I could frame a plausible comment when a journalist brought it up."

"See, I told you that your job is to lie."

"POTUS said the focus has shifted from chemical weapons to nukes."

"Makes sense, Mag."

"Yes, it does. But our analysts can't find any evidence of a single missile in Nicaragua capable of nuclear payload. It just doesn't seem to be there."

"So, she's concerned that Nicaragua's not the one with the missiles and Zamora's aide was just wrong?"

"Obviously, she didn't say so, Morgan, but yeah… I think she's worried we're looking in the wrong place entirely."

"And while all eyes are on Zamora, we could get blindsided by another threat. That's awfully involved. It's hard enough to coordinate two threats, but the possibility that we're not even looking in the right place…? Extremely troubling," Josh worried.

The two silently considered the difficulty of such a plot until Morgan continued. "There's another possibility, Maggie. I keep coming back to our guys having it so wrong. What if they don't?"

"What do you mean?"

"The way you say Betsy sized it up was that NSA had to practically have the notion of an attack on us spelled out in capital letters before they would've uncovered anything – anything at all. If a planned chemical attack was just a red herring, Zamora would've made it less difficult to find. So, if it was hidden so well, then I think the analysis was probably correct. Only chemical, because the intel mentions nothing about nuclear. It's far easier to accept that Zamora could manage to have and to hide a nerve agent than to acquire and hide a nuke."

"I see your point, but it's risky to ignore it."

"Oh, our analysts are big boys and girls. They can walk and chew gum at the same time."

"And elsewhere?" Maggie injected. "NSA didn't find anything anywhere. With some concern that Cuba might be involved – initially chemical, we thought – our analysts have pored over every pixel of imagery there, too. And we have a lot.'

"And?"

"Not one thing," Maggie stated with a shake of her head.

CHAPTER 35

DAY 7 – SUNDAY

At 7:00 AM, with each man in his respective residence, President Sergio Zamora of Nicaragua called Cuban President Felix Lara. The call was brief.

"Are you doing it today, Felix."

"*Si*." And the called ended.

♦

Forty-five minutes after the two Latin American leaders had spoken, in a facility on the edge of Havana, almost the entire roof retracted on wheels that ran along beams. As it was opening the interior of the structure to the blue sky above, three missiles on their launch platforms began to point heavenward.

♦

Terry Henderson and Zilla Ownby had arrived at work very early.

The former hacker set his coffee down and began to look at reports that had come in overnight.

"See you, Zilla. Let me know if you get anything."

"Yep."

Zilla's concentration was interrupted by a chime.

"Terry, come here."

The pair looked at the computer monitor. NSA had taken the extra precaution of monitoring and scripting transmissions in real time that originated in any of the buildings where Sergio Zamora lived or worked. A special graphic and musical note were assigned to any hits.

The pair only had to wait three seconds until the transcript of a two-sentence exchange appeared, translated into English.

Immediately, Henderson was on his phone, calling the Director.

"Yes, sir. The caller asks the man on the other end if he is 'doing it today.' Doesn't say what. The intercept originated from the presidential residence in Managua. Of course, we can't be sure it's Zamora. But the call connects to Havana. We haven't determined precisely where yet. Outgoing calls are easier to pinpoint than incoming. But this is the interesting part. The originator calls the receiver by his name: *Felix*."

"Holy shit! He made a mistake!"

"Yes, sir. A big one."

♦

Within minutes of the intercept of the conversation between the Nicaraguan dictator – presumably – and the president of Cuba – presumably – news circulated throughout the various intelligence and law enforcement agencies.

"It definitely changes the way Cuba fits into the conversation," POTUS said to her Director of Central Intelligence.

Also on the call, the NSA Director updated his boss on his agency's efforts. "Madam President, we've dedicated another fifteen analysts to examine satellite imagery. We have aircraft overhead. We're doing everything we can to confirm whether it's Lara who has missiles pointed at us. Or anywhere else for that matter."

"You're not saying much, Director McClintock," observed the Commander-in-chief.

Parnell took over the commentary. "Zamora – and it's gotta be him – has to know we listen to everything he says on a line, even if it's secured. That just seems like a colossal lapse in judgement to call Lara by his name. It's almost as if he's telling us 'look at Cuba,' 'look at Felix Lara.'"

After a trying several days, POTUS had little patience in reserve. "For God's sake, Betsy, people do make mistakes. It was a brief slipup – a fortunate one for us. You are being very cynical."

Being a little on edge herself, the CIA Director snapped back, "Well, that's the nature of what I do."

Everyone on the call remained silent until the NSA boss practically yelled. "Shit! We've found missiles outside Havana. Three of them. They appear to be aimed north. I'm sending images to you now, Madam President."

"Send them to everyone, Paul."

The head of the NSA added the name of everybody on the call to the distribution list.

The Chief Executive of the United States rubbed her temples with her thumb and middle finger. "Are these all the images, Paul?"

"There are more, but they all look basically alike. They're from a satellite that we keep parked over Cuba. We've moved a high-altitude aircraft to a position away from the site to get some obliques. The shallower angle should provide us more detail. We'll be limited by the height of the walls, but we'll get them."

"Why haven't they launched?" asked the Director of Central Intelligence,

"DAMMIT, BETSY!!! Count your blessings."

"No, Madam President, she's right," said the Director of National Intelligence. Chris Donleavy was Betsy Parnell's boss at one time. He had always been the type to defer to his subordinates when they were carrying the ball successfully.

"We had no idea those missiles existed. Why would they expose them to our reconnaissance technology if they weren't going to fire them?" the DNI explained.

Parnell took back over the narrative, "They could've kept the roof closed forever and we'd have never known the difference. This can't be a slipup." Parnell used the President's earlier term.

POTUS lowered her tone and asked, "Is this some kind of bluff? Surely not."

"Maybe he wants something, ma'am. Remember Khrushchev got a promise not to invade Cuba, which was mostly something for him to save face about starting the whole crisis in the first place. And even though we were going to remove them anyhow, he got missiles out of Turkey."

"Then Lara might be showing his nukes as a threat to get us to the bargaining table?" Hendrickson asked.

"Maybe so," the CIA Chief speculated.

Unseen heads nodded among the participants of the conference call.

"Then how do we respond? And is there a connection to Nicaragua? If so, then what? And why?" POTUS said, mostly to herself.

♦

Being told to stay on the sidelines by Betsy didn't carry much weight. However, the reality was that Josh Morgan was out of the loop now. Maggie had gone to work again, so he was watching the morning show on cable news channel QNN.

> *The world is watching, waiting, and worrying once again as history is repeating itself with a failed Chinese rocket. It has been over a week since the latest rocket*

failed to reach orbit. It continues to tumble out of control in low orbit. It has made several unexplained erratic movements, presumably due to its instability, but the path hasn't degraded to the point where reentry into Earth's atmosphere is imminent or predictable as to a location. Unlike previous failures, this booster has a relatively steady orbital path lasting approximately 95 to 100 minutes each and taking it parallel to latitudinal lines. And unfortunately, the orbit takes it across large land masses. These include Europe, Asia, and the U.S. Until the orbit falls into full degradation, it will be nearly impossible to predict where the debris might fall.

Following the Chinese rocket story some feel-good piece was airing on the morning show when the network's Senior Anchor interrupted. Morgan always knew that when he saw Tracy Adams this early in the day, something important was about to be revealed.

Many times in the past few years, the former CIA Officer knew what the Primetime host was going to announce to the public, but this disclosure would be farther reaching than he expected. The newsman was engaged in the same ritual all of them used – looking down and shuffling papers, which Morgan thought a bit funny since all their notes were on monitors in front of them. Over the image blared the crescendo of synthesized music and the words, "Breaking News…"

QNN has learned of a significant threat to the United States. We learned of this a few minutes earlier from an anonymous source, but it is our policy to withhold reporting until confirmation. Other networks are reporting the news…

"And scooping you on the story. Huh, Tracy?" Morgan said aloud to the television while sipping his second cup of morning coffee.

…reporting the news that U.S. intelligence has discovered the presence of several nuclear-equipped missiles on the island of Cuba.

The former CIA spy leaned in toward the TV and turned up the sound as many people did, apparently in the belief that their understanding increased in proportion to the TV's volume.

"Nukes? Cuba?!"

Little is known about the seeming threat or exactly how the missiles were detected. To repeat…

And Adams did repeat, with a promise to add to the story as he – meaning QNN staff – learned additional details.

The same dramatic scale of notes that had introduced the news alert ended the report, but instead of returning to the fluff piece about a professional hockey player's charitable program for kids, Cameron Neal, another of the network's anchors, began to discuss the Cuban Missile Crisis of 1962.

"Wow! They're prepared for anything," Morgan observed silently. Then he reduced the volume, leaned back on the sofa, and placed the heels of his hands over his eyes.

A myriad of thoughts tumbled through Morgan's mind. Predominant among them was how wrong he had been the previous night in practically dismissing the notion that the impending threat to his country was nuclear.

Morgan touched Maggie's name on his phone to place the call.

"I'm a little busy, Josh."

"I know, Maggie, but wait. Try to find out when the media got wind of this."

"I have to go, Josh."

Next, Morgan dialed Betsy Parnell. Not expecting her to answer, he was prepared to leave a message.

"What is it? On my way to the White House."

"Sorry, Betsy. How'd the media find out about this? Wait! When did you find out about this?"

"Right before the first network ran the story. And we're not even sure they're nukes. But that they're in Cuba instead of Nicaragua certainly ups the stakes. Cuba is much more likely to have them than Zamora. Now stay out of this, Morgan. I mean it."

"Right. Gotta go, Betsy." He hung up rather than hear another warning to not get involved.

An update appeared on the television screen. The missiles were in a facility. They were covered by its roof until it retracted a short time ago. That was all.

Several thoughts began flooding Morgan's mind. His earlier supposition that he'd been wrong in discounting the possibility that some nation had missiles began to give way to a gut feeling that he'd actually been right. Or at least mostly right.

He turned over a piece of junk mail that Maggie had received and began to scribble notes on the envelope. He walked through what he knew, creating bullet points as he did.

"Eddie – warning from source in Nicaragua. Some op, some place, short on details. Nicaraguan agents – kidnap Eddie. NSA – uncovers possible chemical threat; unknown target. Eddie's source adds nuclear arms to the equation."

Morgan moved to the dining table with more coffee.

"Eddie's source – last email. No mention of Cuba. QNN says nuclear-tipped missiles. Missiles – located by satellite?"

Morgan studied his last note briefly and then added to his list.

"Missiles – Cuba: exposed deliberately???????" And finally, he added, "Networks know before much of the government." He ran his pen back and forth repeatedly beneath his last note, furiously underlining it to underscore for himself that it was a critical piece of the puzzle.

CIA contractor Morgan tapped out a text to the head of the Agency.

a ruse - won't launch

♦

As she was stepping from her car at the White House, Director of Central Intelligence Parnell saw the text from Josh. She would've replied if she'd had the time. She was furious with the man, but quietly, she agreed with him.

♦

Retired Army Master Sergeant Tom Lechler was back at his home in Fayetteville, North Carolina. President Hendrickson had arranged for a service to return his truck to his hometown from Norfolk. Lechler had flown home from Washington by commercial airline.

When he saw the news of the missile threat, he called his buddy.

When he heard, "Hi, Tom," his first word was, "Cuba?"

"Yeah," was the reply.

"I thought this was all about Nicaragua."

Since the pair hadn't spoken in a couple of days, Josh caught Tom up on all the developments.

"And they won't launch?"

"No. If they actually wanted to, why give up the element of surprise? And I'm not even sure they're really armed with nukes, Tom. Do you know how hard it is to hide the purchase or development of fissionable material?"

"Yeah, I suppose. Then what's really going on. Is Cuba just trying to scare the shit out of us? Or are they setting the table for some sort of *quid pro quo*?"

"I don't know. Either. Both. Maybe."

"Well, this has sure put Nicaragua on the back burner."

"Yeah, Tom. That's what I'm thinking, too. And that might be a mistake."

♦

Ambassador Rolando Matos, head of the Cuban Delegation to the United States, had very few details concerning the presence of nuclear weapons aimed at his host country. In fact, he'd only been made aware two days before their "unveiling." But it came as no surprise when President Hendrickson demanded his presence at the White House.

What was a surprise was that President Lara had provided no talking points. Often, Matos' home government would deliberately withhold information so that he could legitimately say that he had no knowledge of a matter. But this?! He was astonished that he'd received no direction about a development that could lead to nuclear war.

The ambassador's only guidance – deny that the weapons exist. Outlandish, he thought. As a student of his nation's history, he knew that President Kennedy had made a bold decision in 1962 to publicize reconnaissance photographs to substantiate his claims of missiles in Cuba. The world was astonished at the capabilities of super-secret U-2 aircrafts' top-secret reconnaissance missions as part of Operation Brass Knob.

However, that was decades ago. In the present-day world, everyone everywhere knew of spy satellites, drones, and far more sophisticated surveillance planes than in the sixties. And he was supposed to deny that the Americans had proof?

When Chief of Staff Chandler informed the Cuban Ambassador that he should enter the President's office, he stopped the diplomat's aide from going with him.

Matos had considered what his demeanor should be well ahead of entering the Oval Office, so when he did, it was well-decided. He walked toward the President's desk somberly without offering his hand and greeted the woman as seriously as he could.

"Madam President."

Hendrickson remained seated as he entered, no doubt to eliminate any expectation her visitor might have had about cordiality. In fact, it was her Secretary of State who greeted Matos.

"Have a seat, Ambassador," Gerard Lively said coldly.

The Cuban representative sat stiffly. The U.S. President was leaning forward on her desk with but a single folder before her. She stared without flinching, and silently. POTUS was a believer, as many powerful people were, that in a situation like this, the individual who spoke first lost. Matos lost.

"How can I help you, Madam President?"

The Most Powerful Person in the World never moved her eyes from her guest as she slid the folder toward him.

The Cuban ambassador looked at the blue folder with the U.S.

President's Seal and the words "Top Secret" And "Eyes Only" on it.

He opened the file and thought, "So much for denials." But he pressed on. He closed the folder and returned it to his host, whose eyes remained unwaveringly locked on him.

"What is this, President Hendrickson?" Even Matos knew he sounded unsteady as he spoke.

"Really? That's how you want to play this?"

Despite the forceful challenge of her voice, the Latin American diplomat was glad that she had finally spoken. He tried to refrain from answering, but willpower failed him.

"They appear to be missiles."

POTUS rose and looked out the window behind her desk, arms folded behind her. Matos looked at the several people in the room with him and the American Leader. Hendrickson let the silence extend to several seconds. When she faced the ambassador, she crossed her arms in front of her chest and moved to stand behind him.

"You know very well that those are nuclear missiles, resting on launch platforms in a facility just outside of Havana."

Matos shrugged as he reopened the folder to examine the photographs again.

"I assure you, Madam President, I have never seen those." It was technically true but everybody in the room knew he was avoiding giving a real answer.

POTUS returned to her chair and leaned forward with both elbows resting before her. After another pause for effect, she delivered what, in the rarified air of the diplomatic world, was considered to be a highly aggressive gesture.

Pointing her finger at the Cuban representative, she spoke in a measured tone.

"Do you know how close the world came to nuclear war in 1962? And that was between the United States and the Soviet Union – two adversaries equally capable of destroying one another. This time it is the U.S. and Cuba. Before you could blink, we can take out your missiles. Afterward, we will deal a crushing blow that your country may never recover from."

Hendrickson waited.

The exchange lasted only a short while longer and was largely one-sided. The President would threaten; the Cuban Ambassador would repeat his denials.

"This is a mistake – a colossal misunderstanding. What would you have me say?" insisted Rolando Matos. "Nevertheless, I will relay your words to President Lara, who I'm sure has a reasonable explanation."

After Matos left, SecState Gerard Lively grumbled, "That went well."

"Oh, hell, Jerry. It went how we all knew it would," his boss answered.

♦

The Dwight D. Eisenhower Carrier Strike Group, operating in the U.S. 6th Fleet was steaming toward Cuba from its deployment in the Eastern Atlantic. Other ships were nearer, based at Naval Station Mayport near Jacksonville, Florida. Guided-missile Cruisers USS Philippine Sea and USS Vicksburg and Guided-missile Destroyers USS Roosevelt and USS Farragut were preparing to make way to the waters around Cuba, along with frigates and support vessels.

Aircraft scrambled from Florida bases moments after the satellite photos were received and were already circling the island nation.

♦

The text Morgan received from Maggie didn't make sense at first.

> *don't jump to conclusions about TV. always think they know things before anyone else*

"Tell me something I don't know," he said facetiously. Then it occurred to him that she *was* telling him something he didn't know. He had asked her when the media began to report about the missiles. Maggie was saying that the media appeared to know about the missiles before U.S. intelligence discovered them.

"Then the 'anonymous source' of the existence of the missiles couldn't have been a leak from our people. It had to have come from someone who already knew about them. That doesn't make sense."

Josh got up to pace around Maggie's living room. As he often did, he tapped his forehead with the heel of his hand and talked to himself out loud.

"Think, Morgan. Think. If it was an asset of ours, they would tell their handlers, not a news outlet. Same if an ally was running an agent who developed this information. The ally would let us know."

The contract employee of CIA continued to tap his head until he stopped and put his hands on his hips.

"So, if it wasn't our asset and it wasn't an ally's, it was an adversary? An enemy? Now it *really* doesn't make sense."

Morgan sat before his computer at the dining table, although he'd been through all the information countless times. He checked Eddie's email account. Nothing.

Morgan had moved into his head-scratching stage, rubbing his thumbs and all his fingers vigorously through his shaggy brown hair.

"But the timing. Whoever leaked this to the media knew about it in advance and they wanted to make sure that the story was made public… that our intelligence couldn't sit on it. Why?"

The only conclusion Josh Morgan could come up with was that the source wanted to put U.S. citizens in a panic.

"That could probably cause Hendrickson to do something more quickly. Public pressure might put her every action under the spotlight rather than behind closed doors like JFK was doing. What does Cuba want? They've got to realize they don't have a big brother watching their back like Russia had done. They're still close allies, but Russia uncharacteristically hasn't made a sound about this."

Morgan made another call.

"Slava Larionovich. *Eto* Josh." Vladislav Larionovich Proskurkin was an agent of the Russian SVR, the Federation's Foreign Intelligence Service. Morgan had met him in Russia when he was working to try to prevent a war between that country and the United States. Despite the fact that Morgan had wound up shooting Slava, the two had become friends and spoke and texted on occasion.

Morgan made small talk in Russian and then explained the nature of his call.

"Slava, do you know if your country is connected in any way to this Cuban crisis?"

"To my knowledge, *nyet.* But you know President Tatarov. He plans to issue written remarks very soon assuring the world of the Russian Federation's solidarity with Cuba. He will warn against overzealous reaction with respect to our ally, and so on."

"Okay, Slava. *Spasibo.*"

"Do you want to hear the other item I could tell you?"

"*Da,*" said a surprised Josh Morgan.

"SVR has intelligence that tomorrow China and Nicaragua will announce a defense pact."

"Seriously, the People's Republic of China and Nicaragua."

"*Da.*"

"But it makes no sense. What does Nicaragua have to offer China?"

"Perhaps a presence nearer your country, Josh."

"They have to know we'd never stand for that."

♦

White House Press Secretary Loughlin and her boss were crafting a release to put the missile threat in the proper perspective when Chief of Staff Chandler entered the Oval Office. So, Maggie was hearing the news at the same time her boss was.

"Yes, Madam President, the NSA Director just informed me that Russian state-owned media of all formats jointly released a statement by President Tatarov. It was right along the lines we expected. Leave Cuba alone, and so on. But according to McClintock, his analysts believe the wording suggests that Russia isn't complicit with Cuba in this matter at all."

"Well, that's some good news. We sure don't need a confrontation with a superpower."

"Okay, Maggie, back to work. The Administration's position will be that we learned of the Cuban missiles during the night. We can't have our constituents believing that news outlets had the news before we did. We held the information until morning, then released it publicly."

While Maggie typed notes on her tablet, she realized to herself, "Josh is right. Part of my job is to lie." Maggie understood the need to time the release of information to control the narrative. She also knew that spin was a critical component of effective marketing communications. But this was an outright lie, she knew. Its only purpose was to save some embarrassment to the President and the White House.

♦

"Josh, I don't have time for you. For the last time, you aren't involved in this. You can't keep…"

"Betsy, did you know that China and Nicaragua are about to announce a mutual defense treaty?"

Morgan's interruption brought the Director's reprimand to a screeching halt, and it stayed there for a moment.

"Where did you get that information?"

"Did you know that?" Morgan insisted on knowing.

"Yes."

"Don't you find them to be an odd couple? What can the second poorest country in Latin America offer the ChiComs? Really? Defend them from what? This is a partnership between a housecat and a tiger."

"Where did you hear about this?"

"Proskurkin."

"The Russian spy?"

"I'm in the middle of a situation with Nicaraguan agents and you don't tell me this?"

"Not relevant to what you were doing, Morgan."

"It wasn't relevant?" her contract employee barked.

"Nobody in any of our agencies thinks so."

"Did it ever occur to you that the plot Solis was onto might involve the Chinese? Especially when the term 'chemical' came up?"

"Back off, Josh."

"How's this for backing off, Betsy?"

Morgan hung up.

CHAPTER 36

It had been a long day, but Maggie was still home earlier than she or Josh had anticipated. He was right where she had expected. She put her arms over his shoulders and looked to see what he was researching.

"Find anything new?"

"Did you know that Nicaragua and the Chinese were signing a treaty tomorrow?"

"What?"

"Betsy knows. So, POTUS has to know. But you know who *didn't* know? Pretty much every other person in the world! I can't find one thing on the internet about it. At least, nothing from a reputable source. Some nutjobs are sounding off about it. You know, conspiracy weirdos. But a little over a week ago, I would've considered Eddie one of those conspiracy nuts and he really was onto something."

"Come here." Maggie led Morgan to the couch and began to rub his neck and back. "So, are you saying that the Chinese are somehow involved with the plot Eddie was being fed information about?"

"I can't get my mind around it, but, yeah, I do."

Josh pulled Maggie around to sit beside him.

"China and Cuba already have a cooperative agreement to defend against aggression. It's always been thought to be mostly one-way. Big dog defends little dog with the only real return being little dog's proximity to the biggest dog – the U.S. China has been expanding its presence to the Atlantic for years and has established bases on the West coast of Africa. But they have to know we'd never permit them to set up shop ninety miles from us."

Maggie thought about the scenario a moment and said, "Okay, so the value of Cuba as a strategic partner makes sense. But Nicaragua? I can't see any value-add there. They're close to the United States but not as close as

Cuba."

"But as I said, since we would never allow China into Cuba, Nicaragua at least gives them a presence in the Western Hemisphere. Then, if we're ever compromised somehow… weakened in a way that we wouldn't be able to put up much resistance, it's a pretty easy thing to move assets from Nicaragua to Cuba."

"You're scaring me, Josh."

"It scares me, too, Maggie. And here's the thing. China knows we won't tolerate their presence in Cuba as long as we're strong enough to prevent it."

"But a nuclear strike against us would not only weaken us but could put into play a cascade of events where all bets are off about China's reluctance to do whatever it wants," the President's spokesperson said.

"Yeah, but I still think that Cuba's supposed nukes are a ploy. That leaves us with…"

"The chemical-attack," the woman deduced.

"Exactly, Maggie."

"So, while we're distracted by a phony nuclear threat, someone might have an easier time loosing some nerve agent on our soil," she speculated.

Morgan nodded.

"So, Josh, what if, as you suspect, Cuba's missiles aren't nuclear but carry some chemical agent?"

"I'm sure POTUS has everyone looking at that as a possibility. You can't dismiss it out of hand."

"But you don't think so? Do you, Josh?"

The former CIA Officer stood and paced as he explained. "No, I don't. There's still the confounding element of why Cuba showed us the missiles. I know the working theory is that they're setting the table to negotiate for something, but I think it's all just a big distraction."

♦

Terry Henderson was a master at making sense of intel that others gave him, but he had limited means to collect any on his own. He was analyzing and reanalyzing the images of the Cuban missiles and, like everyone else, wondering why Cuba had basically unzipped its fly. Had the roof on the missiles' enclosure shut immediately, you could make the case – a weak one – that exposing them was some sort of colossal mistake. But the roof had remained open for quite some time. It had to be deliberate.

"Terry, got a second?"

Henderson turned to see Deputy Director Driessen standing at his door.

"Of course," he said and started to rise.

Captain Driessen motioned for him to keep his seat.

"Terry, Havana is less than one hundred miles from the nearest point in the Florida Keys. As a target for a missile, the strategic value would be our Naval Air Station there."

"Agreed."

"Okay. And we certainly have other significant military bases throughout the state."

"Yes, sir."

"Three missiles could certainly deal a significant blow to us militarily. But let's assume, if these are nukes, that three are all Cuba has. We could obliterate the island in response to their launching those three. So, it would seem to me that they'd get wiped off the face of the planet and not benefit from their attack."

"Maybe some other country would, Mike."

"Perhaps. But no country is in a position geographically to take advantage of it. And again, Terry, why would Cuba sacrifice themselves?"

"Then what's their play?"

Captain Driessen finally took a seat and leaned toward his analyst.

"I know the current thinking is that this is some sort of ruse. And I agree. But we can't take that chance. So, what would make more sense strategically?"

"Well, I, uh…"

"Hit us politically. Hit our governmental structure. Terry, could the Cuban missiles reach Washington? It's significantly farther than our Florida bases but such a strike would do more damage to us in terms of our ability to respond – and to our national psyche. Could they get here?"

"Possibly. Depends on the sophistication of the guidance system. Cuba probably couldn't have built anything capable enough without help. And despite our intelligence failure with regard to these events, I still believe Havana couldn't have acquired such technology without our knowing."

"I agree," the retired Navy Captain said. "So, what if the help Cuba gets isn't about a guidance system? What if it's in the form of some type of homing device?"

"I'm not following, sir."

The retired Navy Captain spread a couple of pages in front of the analyst.

"The recurring signal around D.C. popped up again today. You said it was similar in frequency to those used in VOR. Right?"

"Ri…"

"What if that signal is indeed intended to operate along the lines of VOR?"

"And bring the missiles to D.C. more accurately?"

"Exactly."

Driessen waited for Henderson to put some thought to his theory.

"Mike, if that's the case, the perpetrators could use any line-of-sight signal over any frequency. I just made the comparison to VOR off the top of my head."

"Yes, but you also said they – whoever 'they' are – could've tried to slip the signal in because it's so close to the VOR range."

"You may be right. But it's around a thousand miles to Washington. They'd need some more help in the way of additional beacons along the way; every couple of hundred miles or so. And there aren't any others."

"Are you sure?"

"Yes, sir. We would've picked them up. We have so many military installations along our coast that we would've caught them."

"I see. I guess you're right, Terry. Okay, just a thought. I figured we'd be able to knock down missiles in-flight anyhow."

"Well, only one would have to get through, sir. I can double-check on the existence of other signals between here and Havana."

"No, that won't be necessary. You've got other things to work on. Thanks for your time."

Driessen left his analyst but now both of their brains were running a mile a minute about the anomalous signal.

♦

Secretary of State Gerard Lively hung up the phone after delivering his message to the head of the Cuban delegation to the United States. He had told Ambassador Matos that if any of our surveillance showed the now-closed roof to the missiles' location open so much as a crack, U.S. ships would launch cruise missiles immediately. They would be flying toward his country's capital at five hundred miles per hour and wouldn't be limited to just their missile installation.

"What did he say, Gerry?"

"Well, Madam President, he thanked me for my call and said he would pass the information along to President Lara. Of course, what else could he say?"

POTUS stood and moved to the sitting area in front of her desk. SecState Lively followed.

"Ma'am, one thing about this is the lack of logic in Lara's thinking."

"I know what you're going to say, Gerry. By allowing us to know of the missiles, he's given us the upper hand – in a way. He had to know that we have ships so close that we could have Tomahawks deliver their payloads before his birds get in the air."

"Yes, ma'am. There's got to be more to this."

♦

Despite the Deputy Director's suggestion that he not do so, Terry Henderson examined every report he could think of that might make mention of other anomalous signals between Havana and the District of Columbia, or anywhere else. There were none.

Still, the analyst couldn't totally dismiss the signal emitted in Washington, D.C., as unrelated to the current crisis. After all, it had first occurred almost exactly when the shit hit the fan concerning Nicaragua.

The problem with the transmission was that it never lasted long enough to triangulate the exact point of origin. But that didn't mean he wouldn't try.

In light of the recent developments, additional drones had been put in the air around Washington. In addition to the remotely flown crafts' use for real-time video and delivering powerful air-to-ground missiles, most had very sophisticated signals-gathering capabilities. The authority Henderson had gained with his recent promotion gave him a little more influence in how assets were used. So, the Unmanned Aerial Vehicles above the capital of the U.S. weren't just watching and protecting. The ones with the ability were tasked to "listen" for any transmissions of 107 MHz.

♦

It was after 11:00 PM and CIA Director Elizabeth Parnell was resigned to the fact that she would be sleeping in her office again. It was times like this that had her seriously considering retirement. At the end of each day, especially those like this one when it seemed the world was falling apart, she would drink and promise herself that she would begin making plans to step down.

Then morning would come, and she would be right back in her groove, dismissing any notion of leaving this life.

Parnell sat down on the small cot in the anteroom to her office and held her glass to her forehead. The CIA Boss' choice of nightly beverage varied. Tonight, it was bourbon on the rocks. She preferred her drinks neat but sometimes the contrast of the icy coolness to the sting of the alcohol appealed to her.

She checked the time and made her decision.

♦

Maggie had long since gone to bed. Josh was sitting on the couch. She was exhausted and needed the sleep, but he couldn't manage it.

He had forgotten to turn its ring tone down in the evening so when his phone sounded the arrival of a call, it startled him. He accepted the call without looking at the caller's name to try to keep it from ringing again and disturbing Maggie.

"Morgan," he whispered.

"Josh, it's Parnell."

"Yes, Betsy," he answered while moving to pull the bedroom door shut to avoid waking Maggie.

"I need to talk to someone – need to talk through some of this crap."

"Shoot."

For the next fifteen minutes, Betsy Parnell went through everything she knew and everything that bothered her about the current crisis. For his part, Josh hardly spoke. He listened to the slight slurring in her voice and though he knew she regularly had a nightcap, or two, he also knew she held her liquor well. Therefore, he knew her uneven speech was more from weariness than alcohol.

"So, what do you think, Josh?"

"I think…"

"You know what two things bother me?"

Josh smiled at the interruption. Maybe the slur *was* the alcohol.

"No. What?"

"Two things have pretty much fallen off the radar for everyone."

"Nicaragua and chemical weapons," Josh inserted.

"Nica.." Morgan's words sank in. "Zactly. Nicaragua and the chemical threat."

"Me, too, Betsy. Right or wrong, General Santana had counted both nukes and chemicals as threats. And NSA first tumbled onto a chemical attack as the looming threat. And Santana had implicated Zamora in the threat. Now we find ourselves largely ignoring…"

"Nicaragua and chemical weapons," Parnell said, her voice sounding a little steadier. "Are we sure Solis doesn't know anything more?" she continued.

"I don't think he does."

"Hmm. You know, there is one more thing that bothers me, Josh. Nobody has ever found where the Gutierrez assholes stayed. Could've been anywhere but my gut tells me it had to be near Norfolk."

"Mine, too, Betsy."

"Fancy a trip?"

"Norfolk?" Morgan figured.

"Yes." The Director's voice was crystal clear now. "You know, we're back to borderline illegal with you being in the employ of CIA and conducting an operation on domestic soil."

"I'm not operating. I'm going to visit Eddie. And while I'm there I might try to, as a friend, check around to make sure he's not in any more danger."

"And I'll make sure that you have access to anything the Bureau Field Office there has, as well as the local police."

"I'll drive down first thing in the morning, Betsy."

"Fly, Josh. The Agency is good for it."

Director Parnell had mixed emotions about reading Josh Morgan in on everything after threatening him to stay out of it. But this was such a crapshoot that she didn't want to involve other agencies. Plus, despite the man's bullheadedness, there was nobody she trusted more.

♦

Morgan slipped in beside Maggie.

"Betsy?" Maggie asked.

"Yeah. Sorry. Did I wake you up?"

"The ring did. I couldn't go back to sleep. Something up?"

"Going back to Norfolk tomorrow."

"I'd go, sweetheart, but this isn't a time I can take off."

"I know, Maggie. But I think this might be a time when you're better off sitting it out."

The warning unsettled Maggie.

The pair snuggled for a few minutes, and both fell off to sleep.

CHAPTER 37

DAY 8 – MONDAY

The American Airlines nonstop flight had been fifty-seven minutes. It was only barely longer than it took the ex-CIA Officer to get to his vehicle and out of the airport. CIA Director Parnell had instructed some of her administrative personnel to retrieve the SUV he had left in Norfolk when he, Maggie, and Tom had flown back to Washington on the President's 747. It had taken some doing, but the stolen license plates were replaced with the proper ones, too.

So, in short order, Josh Morgan was at the Norfolk PD precinct where Edmundo Solis' possessions were being held as evidence, along with everything else related to his and the White House Press Secretary's abduction by Luis and Santos Gutierrez. Morgan had insisted that he travel without a Secret Service chaperone. The Agency didn't like it but felt that they weren't in a position to demand it.

Morgan looked over everything in the evidence room. Nothing stood out until one thing caught Morgan's attention.

"Officer?"

The evidence clerk looked over at Morgan.

"This was in Solis' belongings. Any chance it was in there by mistake?"

The clerk hadn't been in on the investigation himself, but still took offense on behalf of the detectives who were.

"No."

"Hmm… Mind if I take a photo with my phone?"

"Knock yourself out," the officer said coolly.

Morgan got his photograph and finished examining the entire collection of evidence. Then he went to the squad room to find one of the investigating detectives.

"What's the story behind this, Detective?" Morgan asked, holding his phone to display the image he'd just taken.

"The matchbook? Was in Solis' car. He was out of it so we couldn't ask him about it. But we did go there and showed his photo around. Nobody recognized him. We figured he just got it somewhere. Or maybe he just didn't spend enough time at the place to make an impression."

"Okay. Thanks for your help."

♦

Eddie was much better but still several days away from getting out of the hospital. It was about 10:30 in the morning when Morgan arrived at his room. By the blogger's bedside was Ana Garcia.

"*Buenos días, señorita*," Josh said cheerfully.

The three chatted for a few minutes until Morgan decided he needed to get down to business.

"Eddie, can I speak to you – privately?"

"*Señor* Josh, you may speak freely in front of Ana."

"I think it would be better if just the two of us spoke."

"We have decided to start dating. It is okay."

Ana smiled as she took Eddie's hand.

"*Por favor*." Solis motioned toward his visitor to proceed.

Morgan hated to, but went ahead. He held up his phone to show the image of the matchbook that he had photographed in NPD's evidence room.

"Does this mean anything to you?" Morgan winced slightly.

"What is it?" Eddie asked before recognizing the logo as that of one of a local business. He tried to follow up with a "no" but didn't manage it before Josh answered.

"It's a matchbook from a strip … a gentlemen's club," Josh corrected to try to be more delicate. He winced more noticeably and saw that Ana pulled her hand away from her new boyfriend's.

Morgan wanted to resist as Ana reached to turn the display of the phone toward her. A silhouetted drawing of a nude woman was along the left edge of the book's cover. The neon green text on the black background read "Hello, Sailor" in large letters with "All nude men's club" in smaller letters below.

Both Josh and Eddie smiled awkwardly. Ana did not.

Eddie frantically blurted out, "That's not mine. I don't know… Where did you get it?"

"The… uh, the, uh, police got it out of your car."

"I've never seen that before in my life." This time Eddie was speaking to his new girlfriend, who had her arms folded across her chest. "And I've never been there," he added in Spanish.

Morgan had taken note of the matchbook in the first place because it seemed so out of character with what he knew about the Nicaraguan blogger. But despite his initial suspicion that the strip club matchbook wasn't his, he had to wonder if Eddie would've admitted to it in front of Ana. However, Morgan believed Eddie and decided to try to help.

"Eddie, everything I know about you told me this wasn't yours. You seem so decent and morally strong…" Morgan looked at Ana and smiled. She didn't smile back.

"…that I couldn't imagine you going to a place like this. I didn't ask if the matchbook was yours; only if it meant anything to you. I know I could've phrased my question more precisely and for that I apologize to you and Ana."

Ana's countenance softened, but only slightly. "Why do you ask?" she queried.

"Because it seemed so out of character that I had to wonder about it. Do you think a friend could've left it in your car?"

"No, Josh. *No!*" Solis repeated emphatically.

As he left the hospital room, Josh Morgan was pretty confident that Eddie had told him the truth. And that was in line with what he had believed in the first place. He thought about Ana's reaction.

"Well, that might be a short-lived romance," he worried.

♦

"I'll be darned!" Terry Henderson exclaimed. Two of the UAVs above D.C. had picked up the anomalous transmission and had logged the direction the signal had appeared from. Both drones had pointed to the same GPS coordinates as the point of origin. Terry moved to his computer to translate the location to a named place.

He typed in 38°54'45.27"N. Then 77°2'26.63"W. The name of the location appeared instantly.

Henderson put one hand to his mouth, another to his forehead, and gasped. He started to send the information directly to McClintock, then thought better of it and hit his speed dial button for a different recipient.

Only minutes after hearing the news from his analyst, Deputy Director Mike Driessen was on his way to the NSA Director's office. Terry Henderson joined him in the hallway.

A knock on the door resulted in the Agency Chief waving them in. Henderson waited on his direct boss to share what they had uncovered.

"Go ahead, Terry," Driessen insisted. "You're the one who came up with this."

"But only because you brought it to my attention."

"Oh, for God's sake! One of you tell me what's going on!" the impatient Director ordered.

"Paul, there's been an intermittent anomalous signal that our SIGINT has observed originating from here in the District off and on for a few days. Terry has determined the location of the source. It's coming from 1627 New Hampshire Ave NW. It's coming from the Nicaraguan Embassy, Paul."

"What?!"

Driessen looked to Terry for the explanation. He briefly explained how he'd added a command to Unmanned Aerial Vehicles circling over the capital.

"In a nutshell, Director, Zamora's diplomatic staff has been sending a signal out. It's line of sight so it has to be on the roof of the building."

McClintock said nothing for several seconds. He looked down and shook his head. Finally, he propped his chin on his left hand and looked to Driessen and Henderson.

"Any idea of the purpose of the transmission? I mean, with all the shit surrounding Nicaragua, it can't be just an innocent…" McClintock stopped abruptly and said, "What's your best guess, Henderson?"

"It was Mike's idea. We think there's a possibility that it's a homing device, sir. He brought up the idea. At first, I didn't think so, but I have no idea what else it could be."

"Homing device? For what?"

"We don't know, Paul," Driessen said with a shake of his head. "When we first discussed the signal, Terry said it was in a similar frequency range as VOR signals that help planes navigate. I wondered, only because of the presence of the missiles in Cuba, if the signal could help direct them to a target here. Terry said the maximum range for the signal would be two hundred miles. Perhaps a little more but not much."

Henderson picked up the narrative. "The only way to guide a missile from Havana to here with this type of beacon would be if there were others positioned along the way as waypoints. But there aren't. Trust me. I checked."

"Could the Nicaraguans or the Cubans have developed a receiver of heightened sensitivity that they could navigate with just the one transmitter?"

"I don't think so, Director. First, the curve of the earth would interfere with the line of sight," the NSA analyst assured.

"And besides, Paul," Driessen added, "if they could develop something that sophisticated, wouldn't they be able to just develop accurate enough guidance to program directly into a missile?"

"You're right, Mike. You'd sure think so. Well, we know that President

Zamora's aide was trying to warn us about a nuclear attack. And we know Cuba has missiles. Whatever this is, it can't be good."

"Shut the door, Terry, and you guys take a seat."

The Deputy Director and Analyst Terry Henderson spent the next half hour presenting the details of their discovery to every intelligence and law enforcement in the District, as well as President Hendrickson and her Chief of Staff. After significant brainstorming, not one person on the conference call could come up with a plausible explanation as to the purpose of the signal. But likewise, not one person on the call could honestly say they weren't unnerved by its presence.

"We need to figure this out," POTUS exclaimed, knowing it to be one of the most colossal understatements that she'd ever uttered.

♦

It was half past noon and there were only a handful of patrons at the Hello, Sailor strip club. Josh Morgan was among them. He knew the club's name was due to the huge Naval presence in Norfolk. The phrase was largely understood to be a sexual proposition by a woman to sailors who might be on the prowl after an extended time at sea.

It was terribly distracting asking questions that he hoped would provide a clue about the abduction of Maggie and Eddie when the person you were talking to was completely naked. Roxy was immediately suspicious of Morgan so he decided to stick to the truth as much as he could.

"Are you a cop?"

"No, no. This man…" and he showed her a picture of Eddie, "… is a good friend of mine. He's the guy who was kidnapped by the Nicaraguan terrorists."

Roxy pulled Morgan's phone closer. "Oh, yeah. That *is* him. I saw him on the news. And there was this White House woman, too."

"My fiancée," Morgan said, feeling a little funny about his characterization. It was the first time he'd used the term since before he and Maggie broke up.

"She's a lucky girl," Roxy said, apparently warming up to Josh. She sat down on a barstool beside him. She rested her right elbow on the bar, propped her head sideways on her hand, and leaned forward until her right breast rested on the bar. She continued to look straight at Josh.

The manager of Hello, Sailor walked up behind the bar.

"This guy bothering you, Rox?"

"No. He's just…"

Wes said, "Let me rephrase that. Is he spending money?"

"No, we're just…"

"Then he's bothering me," the manager declared.

"Aw, Wes," the exotic dancer began.

Morgan held up his hand and leaned his head forward.

"No. Wes is right." Morgan took a one-hundred-dollar bill out of his wallet and placed it on the bar. "Better?"

The manager reached for the bill, but Morgan slid it over to Roxy.

"I'll have a beer, please."

"Get this man a beer," grumbled the manager to another nude woman bartender. Then back to Morgan, "That'll be six-fifty. The c-note was for her time." Morgan laid a twenty on the bar.

"Stick around. Will you, Wes?"

He showed the club manager the photo of Edmundo Solis, whom he immediately recognized from television coverage.

"That's the kidnapped guy." Wes even loosened up a bit. "There was some government broad, too. Man, was she ever a hottie!"

"She's his fiancée, Wes," Roxy disclosed to her boss.

"Well, that doesn't make her any less hot," the club boss said directly to his customer, who bit his lip and swiped the display of his smart phone to the right a few times.

"Ever see these guys?" he asked, alternately showing images of the Gutierrez brothers.

"No, I haven't ev…," Roxy started before her boss interrupted.

"Yeah, I've seen them." The manager's remark was more growl than comment. "Couple of hotshot assholes. Really thought they were something. Kinda stirred up some shit with a couple of my girls. They were busy with other customers, and these guys try to run them off. I told them to get the hell out. They looked like they were about to fight me, when the other one of the three said…"

"Three?!" Morgan repeated. "There was another one?"

"Yeah. Not as willing to mix it up as these two, but yeah, there were three."

♦

President of the United States Sandra Hendrickson was as direct as ever.

"Ambassador Torrez, what is the purpose of the beacon transmitting intermittently from your Embassy's roof?"

The diplomat's face turned ashen. He tried to maintain eye contact with the woman behind the desk in front of him, but his eyes finally cast downward.

"I'm afraid I don't…," he began.

The American Leader stood and leaned on her desk toward him. Her stare was penetrating beneath her arched eyebrows. She tapped her right index finger lightly on the desk.

"What is it doing there? What is its purpose?"

"Madam President, it is part of a wireless communication…"

"Wrong technology. Wrong details."

"Beg your pardon?"

Hendrickson moved from behind her desk to the side of Torrez's chair.

"The VHF frequency wouldn't transmit a takeout order more than a short distance."

The Nicaraguan Ambassador looked down again.

"This signal has appeared only occasionally – not even every day. It transmits only in bursts of a few seconds and usually only once on the days we pick it up. On the couple of occasions where it has popped up more than once, the transmissions were something around ninety to ninety-five minutes apart. Now, Ambassador, what the hell is going on?"

"It is a wireless communication system. We are just now testing it, so we haven't been able to use it for great lengths of time."

The Nicaraguan diplomat summoned the courage to stand.

"Thank you for your time, Madam President. But I really must go."

♦

An additional UAV was now devoted solely to circling above the Nicaraguan Embassy, collecting high-resolution photos and picking up Signals Intelligence.

Terry Henderson wasn't an expert at image analysis, but Zilla Ownby was. Henderson looked over his peer's shoulder at the computer display where a crystal-clear image of a relatively small box sat on the roof of the Nicaraguan Embassy.

"I don't know from this. At least not yet. So far, it's just a metal box."

♦

"What did the third guy look like?" Morgan asked the manager of Hello, Sailor, who puffed up his chest and smirked as though it was the stupidest question his customer could've asked. "I don't know. They all look alike."

"You can't give me anything?"

"You should ask the girls that do the night shows. These guys were here a couple of times, always at night. Got real friendly with a couple of our ladies. Especially the two that were spending time with the other clients. Ask them tonight."

Morgan rose to leave.

"But the clock starts over, pal."

Morgan knew what he meant and pulled out another one-hundred-dollar bill.

"How's this?"

"Two girls. Two hundred," Wes demanded. He knew he had Morgan over a barrel.

Morgan set down the last Franklin he had but when Wes reached for it, he pulled it back.

"I'll bring it with me tonight. One bill up front. The other only if I get some useful information."

Wes sized up Morgan as he stood and smiled for the first time during the encounter.

"Fair enough."

Roxy put her arm through Morgan's and walked him to the door.

"I might stick around tonight myself."

♦

The White House Press Secretary was at her desk. Working weekends in the West Wing would be a fairly standard part of her job now as it had been as the Deputy Press Secretary. Maggie didn't mind as much this Sunday since Josh was away in Norfolk. She turned up the volume once she saw QNN senior anchor Tracy Adams shuffling his papers at the news desk and look up to the camera.

> *Earlier this morning the People's Republic of China and the Republic of Nicaragua announced that they had agreed in principle to a mutual defense treaty…*

The picture on the television changed to show a split screen with pictures of the leaders of each of the nations.

> *Though the formal signing will take place a month from now, the nations' foreign ministers endorsed the agreement at a signing ceremony in Havana, Cuba.*

The television images showed recorded images of the two diplomats shaking hands as the network anchor continued the report.

Maggie muted the TV and went back to work. Having sat in on a briefing by the U.S. SecState to POTUS, she'd heard the details and the official position that morning. Having sat next to Josh on their sofa last night, she had gotten the info even earlier. In the President's briefing, which included the Directors of the Intelligence arm of the nation and various members of the Department of State and several analysts, Maggie heard that they had come to the same conclusions as Josh had about the rationale for the nations' agreement. Furthermore, they had the same concerns about the People's Republic of China seeing the treaty as a means to gain a foothold in Central America.

But whereas the top government officials in the U.S. believed that the presence of any PRC military personnel in Nicaragua was in the distant future and indeed might never happen, Maggie knew that Josh thought the possibility might be more imminent. And so did the Director of the Central Intelligence Agency.

Maggie's phone rang.

"Hi, Josh. I was just thinking of you."

"Hi, Maggie."

"Any progress in uncovering any more leads?"

"Some. Maybe a biggie, but this is one time I probably should keep it to myself."

"I understand."

"I can say that my investigation took me to a strip club because the Norfolk PD thought Eddie had been there."

"Eddie? In a strip club? Wait… *You* went to a strip club?"

"Yeah. Dropped a couple hundred to dancers there." Morgan waited for some sort of reaction from his fiancée. To his annoyance, Maggie remained silent. But he started laughing.

"Sorry, Maggie. I thought I'd get more of a rise out of you."

"Well, I'm not exactly happy about it."

"Well, believe me, if I was the type of guy inclined to frequent such places, this wouldn't be one of them. But it turns out, Eddie wasn't the one who was there. It was the Gutierrez brothers. And…"

"Doesn't surprise me."

"I know. They must've dropped the matchbook in Eddie's car at the same time as their note with the warehouse address on it. And that's really where I should end my story to you. I am going back tonight though."

"Very funny, Josh."

"Sorry, Maggie, but I really am. The manager told me the Nicaraguan brothers talked to some dancers there and that I could catch them tonight."

"Oh, and I suppose the manager was topless, too."

"Actually, it's an all-nude place. And the manager's a man so, thank God, no." Morgan waited again for a reply.

Finally, Maggie said, "Is that so?" Then she started laughing. "Do what you've got to do, Josh."

The lovebirds spoke only a few minutes more, and only about personal things. They talked about getting away after the current mess was over and some other matters. Neither talked about living together again or marriage. But each knew they would talk about those things.

CHAPTER 38

The CIA Director was just arriving at the White House for the briefing to President Hendrickson about the agreement between China and Nicaragua and some new information from the National Security Agency when Morgan called.

"Sorry, Josh, but I don't have much time. Can we talk later?'

"It'll just take a second, Betsy." The CIA contractor quickly brought his boss up to date about his discovery of a possible third man linked to the action against Maggie and Eddie. The CIA boss and her employee came to a decision about how to proceed.

"So, you agree then, Josh?"

"I do, Betsy. I think we keep this between us until after I go back to Hello, Sailor tonight. As we discussed, this could just be someone they met here and might not be involved at all. Hopefully, tonight will clear it up."

"Right. But even if he's not an operative, finding him or at least learning who he is could help us figure out where the Gutierrez brothers were staying."

"And maybe more."

"Okay, Josh. Keep me posted."

♦

The analysts at the National Security and the Central Intelligence Agencies had come up with a new working theory about the signal that had been popping up from time to time from a transmitter atop the Nicaraguan Embassy in Washington.

"Admittedly it is pretty weak, Director Parnell and Director McClintock," said Captain Driessen. The NSA Head had decided to throw his new Deputy Director into the fray, partly because he was the one whose gut had told him there was something to the anomalous signal.

"We actually feel like we're grasping at straws."

CIA spoke first. "So, you think there's a possibility that the signal *is* akin to VOR, a homing beacon."

"Yes, ma'am," Driessen replied. "But it doesn't have the strength to reach missiles in Cuba – or anywhere else for that matter. Not without a series of the transponders."

"Then what would it be for?" asked NSA.

"We think it might be for a small aircraft."

"For the purpose of…?" Parnell shrugged her shoulders.

"A small craft could carry a dirty bomb," suggested NSA Director McClintock.

"Or a chemical agent," Parnell said.

"And that," said Analyst Henderson with a nod of his head, "is what our earliest intel about the threat from Nicaragua suggested."

"And one of the things Zamora's aide warned about," Driessen added.

Parnell continued, "But you don't have any further intel about the specific threat. Right? Whether it's imminent?"

"Correct," confirmed Henderson.

"So, we have missiles pointed at us that *might* be nuclear. And now this."

There was complete silence in the room. Managers and administrators enjoyed speculating and hypothesizing. Analysts preferred to stick to facts as a basis for predictions but avoided sticking their necks out by guessing without intel to support them. So, nobody spoke.

Finally, NSA Director McClintock changed the focus of the subject.

"This signal that has gained new prominence in our investigation – you don't believe it's related to the missiles in Cuba?"

Henderson deferred to the Deputy Director, but Driessen motioned his head toward the analyst to go ahead.

"No, sir, we don't. Technologically, it doesn't fit. And on a more basic level, any country capable of building a nuclear weapon could certainly put a sophisticated enough guidance system on its missile."

"And," Driessen added, "we have to realize that a nuke doesn't have to hit the intended target with great precision. Being close will do."

Everybody in the conference room and online hated hearing it, but they knew it was true.

♦

Josh Morgan felt ill at ease enough just being in Hello, Sailor again, so it was with a great deal of relief that he learned that at least Roxy wasn't there.

He had arrived at six o'clock, early enough that he hoped to catch the two strippers before things got really busy. But dancers were already filling the three stages, even without a significant number of patrons. Morgan figured that the show had a precise schedule to follow, and it wasn't dependent on the number of oglers.

Wes, the manager of the club had spotted the ex-CIA Officer as soon as he had walked through the door and was surprisingly cordial. Morgan was certain that his friendliness wouldn't translate into getting to speak with the two dancers free of charge. Even in a gentlemen's club, he figured, and maybe *especially* in a men's club, time was money.

"Katya and Desiree will hit the floor in about fifteen minutes," manager Wes informed Morgan, "They'll be on stage for about twenty minutes. As soon as they're done, they'll need to mingle with our guests and collect a few more bills.

Since Hello, Sailor was an all-nude club, Morgan wondered where they would put them.

"Then *I'll* call them over," Wes said. Morgan understood it to be a not-so-subtle hint that he wasn't to try to speak with them before he got permission.

"Want a beer? On the house."

"Sure," Morgan accepted.

The CIA contractor sat at the bar so that he could best avoid the dancers' routines. The two bartenders were nude, too, but at least they weren't writhing and thrusting and swinging around poles. He sipped at his beer mindlessly until he heard Wes.

"Morgan, this is Katya and Desiree."

Morgan turned to see one very young dancer and one a few years older. Katya was twenty. Desiree was probably in her late twenties. Both were attractive, though not beautiful, and were adorned with the heavy makeup and glitter typical of women in their profession. He thought each would have a natural beauty without all the extra paint.

Wes stood by expectantly.

"Oh," Morgan said, and took a one-hundred-dollar bill from his wallet and placed it on the bar to complete the payment he had provided half of at the end of his previous visit. Before he could slide the upfront money to the two girls, Wes reached for the bill and grinned.

All four – Katya, Desiree, Wes, and Morgan – moved to a table.

"Would you like something?" Morgan asked.

Each of the girls ordered an over-priced drink. They hardly touched them, and Morgan knew they were just doing so to add revenue to the club.

"Would *you* like something?" Katya asked after the drinks arrived, putting her hand on the inside of his knee.

The former CIA spy flushed. Had he been on an op, he would've played his part convincingly, but this was different, and Wes told his girls so.

"Morgan here isn't a customer. At least, not like that. He just wants to talk. Katya took her hand away and Morgan could see that in one respect, the two dancers were relieved that they weren't expected to "perform." At the same time, he could sense that they were on-guard, suspicious of anyone asking questions.

Normally Morgan would try to put people he was going to try to elicit information from at ease with a little small talk. He knew that would be completely uncomfortable here, but he was already uneasy, trying desperately to maintain eye contact with their *eyes*. He was about to open things up, but Wes, probably irritated with the slow pace of things, initiated the Q&A himself.

"Morgan wants to ask you about some guys that were here several nights ago." He turned to his guest. "Show 'em the pics."

The questioner selected a photo of Luis Gutierrez first and showed the girls. Then he swiped to an image of Santos.

"Wes tells me you spoke with these men."

Desiree took the phone from Morgan, looked at the pictures for a moment, and handed the device to Katya.

"Yes, we did," the older dancer acknowledged.

Katya handed Morgan his phone and added, "Real creeps."

Morgan wanted to ask if that wasn't generally the type of customer they met in this place, but merely proceeded.

"And Wes said there was a third man."

"Less of a jerk – slightly – but yeah," confirmed Desiree. "The two on your phone were brothers. Katya and I were talking to some other gentlemen and the younger one came up and took me by the wrist. The older one said, 'excuse me' to the men we had been talking to and they started to pull us away."

Morgan had heard this before from their manager but let them go ahead.

"Well, the first guys," Katya continued, "didn't take it too well and stood up to confront them. These guys in your pictures were ready to go at it. But the third guy tried to pull them away."

Desiree interrupted, "He was saying, like, 'We don't need this' and 'You're calling way too much attention to us.' It was intense."

"And that's when I showed up," the manager added.

Katya picked up the narrative. "Yeah. Wes settled things down and bought the first guys drinks for their trouble. But they were still pissed so Wes sorta escorted them away. The three Latin guys gave us each a fifty, so we hung out with them."

"After they acted the way they did?" Morgan couldn't help himself.

"Honey, we've both experienced much worse," the older dancer informed Morgan with a bittersweet smile. "It happens all the time. It's the nature of our profession."

Just to be thorough, the inquisitor showed Katya and Desiree a photo of Eddie Solis.

"Ever seen him?"

Both women shook their heads.

Finally, Katya asked the question Morgan had expected much earlier. "What's this about?"

"See this last guy," Wes turned the phone where he could see it, too. He tapped on the phone's display. "He's the one that got kidnapped. Some sort of terrorist thing. The first two pics – they're the guys who grabbed him. They're the ones on the news. They're both dead now."

Morgan noticed that Katya was horrified. Desiree showed no reaction at all.

"Can you tell me anything else about the last guy? What he looked like? His name? Anything?"

"Well, he was about the same age as the older one of the brothers. Not very good-looking but built. Muscular, you know. And he just had that look that he'd seen his share of shit. His name was Trini. Sorry. No last name," Katya said.

"Yeah, but that muscle bound guy… well I'll just say it wasn't that way under his clothes," Desiree continued without expression.

Morgan didn't want to know. Then he did.

"So, you were…" he struggled for a tactful way to say what he wanted to. "You were intimate…?"

Desiree rephrased it. "Had sex with them? Yeah, we screwed 'em."

Morgan held back what he wanted to say, but it was as though the older of the strippers could read his mind. He could see that the younger dancer hung her head while the more seasoned had a defiant look.

"You're probably wondering why we'd do it with slime like that. Katya is going to college and wants to be a doctor. And I got two kids at home to feed. Money is money, pal. So, don't get all judgy on me."

The interrogator started to deny thinking anything like that, but he knew they wouldn't believe him… because he was.

"I'm sorry," was all he could mutter. After a lengthy pause, he reached into his wallet for more money and was about to thank Desiree and Katya for their time when Katya spoke.

"Don't you want to know where they're staying? Or at least where they were staying before they died? I mean, the other one might still be there."

"You know where they were staying?" an astonished Morgan inquired.

"Sure, honey. Where do you think we… were intimate?" Desiree asked using Morgan's euphemism.

Morgan had figured it was in a car or some back room.

"We had a real party. They paid us good, too."

"Please tell me you know the address."

"Nope," Desiree told Morgan, whose disappointment was obvious. "But I can take you there."

With Wes' approval, the older dancer and the former spook arranged to meet when she had finished for the night.

Morgan pulled out two fifty-dollar bills to add to the payment he had agreed to with Wes. It wasn't just because he had gotten a very good lead. It was atonement for being judgmental. He handed one to each of the dancers.

♦

It was ten o'clock when Morgan finished dinner and returned to his motel room. His first call was to the CIA Director.

Morgan gave Parnell a recap of what appeared to be a very promising lead. The two agreed to continue to keep the newest development confidential until after Morgan had followed up on it.

Then Josh called Maggie, who had just gotten home from an extremely long day at work. He told her that he'd gotten a hopeful lead to pursue, but he didn't elaborate. And he *didn't* tell his fiancée that he had a "date" with a stripper after midnight.

CHAPTER 39

DAY 9 – TUESDAY

The sound of the alarm Morgan had set on his phone startled him. He realized as he often did after a short, fitful nap that he would've likely been better off without it. But he had left the strip club around 8:45 and had finished his calls to Maggie and Betsy by 10:20 and wasn't supposed to meet Desiree until after 12:00, so he had decided to try to get some rest.

Hello, Sailor didn't close until 2:00 AM, but Desiree was done at 12:30. So, Morgan was waiting by a back entrance where the exotic dancer had told him to meet her around 1:00 AM. He chatted only briefly with a security guard stationed there. The huge man had called Wes who confirmed that Morgan was permitted to be there.

At a few minutes before one o'clock, a voice turned Morgan around to see a very conservatively dressed woman with light makeup. If he hadn't been expecting the woman, he might not have recognized her.

"Desiree?"

"I'm not Desiree. Not once I walk through that door. Well, unless I'm still conducting business. My name is Kirsten."

Kirsten held out her hand. Her brown hair was entirely different than the black wig that "Desiree" wore. It appeared that she had taken a shower to rid herself of the glitter and heavy makeup that defined her alter-ego.

Morgan shook her hand and said, "I'm Josh." He held the door of his car open for the woman.

"I'm not used to that," Kirsten admitted with a sad sort of smile.

The ride to the location would be about twenty minutes, the transformed dancer told Morgan. The man followed Kirsten's directions. There were a couple of stretches in the route without turns so Morgan tried to make small talk. Finally, Kirsten asked about his involvement in the matter. Was he a policeman? Some other law enforcement? Morgan decided to stick with the story that Eddie was just a friend and that he believed there were still some loose ends.

"After you left, Wes said that your fiancée was kidnapped along with that guy."

"Yes, she was."

"Wes said she was very attractive. Well, that's not exactly how he put it. Do you have a picture?"

Josh was conflicted about sharing too much personal information but decided he trusted Kirsten, whose demeanor and speech were one hundred-eighty degrees from that of Desiree. He activated his phone's display and showed her a photo of Maggie and then one of the two of them together.

"She *is* beautiful, Josh."

Josh hesitated before finally asking, "Do you have time for a cup of coffee? I know you have your kids to get home to."

For a moment, Kirsten was on guard, but she said, "You want to see if I can remember anything else, don't you? As long as it's brief."

Josh pulled into a 24-hour diner.

Kirsten showed the man photos of her kids. "They are the reason I do what I do. I know you don't approve…"

"I'm sorry about earlier, Kirsten," he insisted with true regret as he looked at the photo of a boy and girl who appeared to be the same age.

"Twins?"

"Yes. They're eleven." She gazed lovingly at the image for another moment before putting it away. "Okay. Shoot. I think I've told you everything I know, but let's see what pops up."

After twenty minutes of back and forth, Morgan had only a few more details, none of which he believed to be significant. The pair resumed their drive to the small apartment where Kirsten said the three men had taken her and Katya, whose real name, Kirsten divulged, was Angeline.

Josh knew the likelihood of running into Trini was slim. First, the man probably was long gone. Secondly, it was two in the morning. Still, he wanted to get Kirsten out of the area so that if Trini were around, he wouldn't spot her. However, Morgan was sure that the man would never recognize her as Desiree.

Morgan drove Kirsten home. She asked him to let her out a few houses away from hers. Her kids, she said, often woke up in the middle of the night and she promised herself that she would never let them see a man drop her off. She started to exit the car but turned back.

"I'm not sure what you are. You're not just a concerned friend. But whatever you are, I hope you get all this straightened out and behind you,

Josh."

"Good luck, Kirsten." Josh knew that Kirsten was someone he and Maggie could be friends with and watched protectively as she walked to her home. While she let herself in, she glanced back at Josh and smiled. As he drove by the modest house in a quiet neighborhood he saw through the door, just before it closed, Kirsten hugging two young children.

♦

Chinese Leader Cheng Shun was satisfied with what he was hearing from his advisers.

"Then the target acquisition technology is in place?"

"*Shì de*," the missile expert affirmed.

"And the limits of its range will not present problems?"

"No, *Guojia Zhuxi* Cheng."

The State Chairman, what the leader was called at home rather than the title President, which is used by other countries, looked over the report for a few minutes of uninterrupted silence. He was pleased.

"And the second prong of the attack is ready, as well?"

The director of the Chinese Institute of Virology in Wuhan confirmed that the agent his organization had developed was ready to deploy as well.

"We have achieved the intended gain of function, sir."

"And we have agreed that the two acts do not need to be taken concurrently? Each can be executed independently?" the General secretary of the Communist Party of China Central Committee, another of Cheng's official positions, inquired.

"Yes, General Secretary Cheng."

The Chinese leader examined the written report again, as though he actually understood the highly technical language. He closed the folder containing the report.

"Then my order is that all may proceed at the earliest opportunity."

♦

It was an overcast morning about 8:20. Morgan had returned to his motel to try to get some sleep. It had been pointless. He had returned to the apartment Kirsten/Desiree had led him to around 5:30 AM. The Gutierrez brothers had stayed there along with a third man named Trini.

The ex-CIA Officer figured that Trini was long gone. He'd probably gotten the hell out of Dodge when his two *compadres* met their fate. Still, he would surveil the place for a while in case he was wrong. The only problem with the choice to stake out the place was that if he had to resort to his Plan

B – breaking in – he would be doing so in daylight. Either that or wait until night. And he wasn't going to wait.

Morgan hadn't decided just how long he would give Trini to show himself before initiating his backup plan, but it was worth a shot.

♦

"Yes, Madam President, a UAV observed them removing it at sun-up."

The NSA and the entire intelligence community had tasked the drones circling over Washington, D.C. with a number of missions. With the discovery that the source of the anomalous signal was atop the Nicaraguan Embassy, one of the unmanned aircraft had been assigned the sole responsibility of keeping watch on Zamora's diplomatic presence in the U.S.

Because of the difficulty that the closeness and height of surrounding buildings created for street-level surveillance by the UAVs, various agencies had undertaken other methods of observing the activity around the location, most notably the FBI. Agents sat in cars, perched on rooftops, and watched through adjacent buildings' windows.

"Any idea where they moved it?" asked POTUS.

"I'm afraid not, ma'am," Paul McClintock regretted.

President Sandra Hendrickson's stomach was churning at the loss of direct observation but was hopeful when she asked her next question.

"Any chance our little chat with them put the fear of God in them?"

"I'm sorry, ma'am. We don't know. At least not yet," the NSA Chief said. "There's a chance we'll get some human or signals intelligence, but as of yet…" His voice trailed off.

"Okay, Paul. Thanks."

The President suspected that her country hadn't heard the last from the Nicaraguans. But she realized that, until the signal was transmitted again and a UAV or some other device picked it up, the homing beacon could be anywhere.

♦

Shortly after ending her call with the NSA Director, POTUS called his counterpart at CIA.

"Betsy…"

"Yes, ma'am?" Parnell knew the nature of the call. She had received a heads-up from Paul McClintock. She didn't expect the first question, however.

"Where is Master Sergeant Lechler?"

"Uh, home, I think. Fort Bragg. I can contact him."

"Do that, Director. Get him to Washington ASAP. This is very important. Tell him he is being seconded to the Secret Service."

"Beg your pardon, ma'am?"

POTUS ignored the question and moved ahead with her instructions.

"I need you to prepare paperwork to the effect that he is being released from his contract with CIA."

"Madam President, may I ask…"

The line went dead.

CIA Director Parnell would have liked to have had more info. She would've liked to take some time to sit at her desk and speculate. Instead, she pressed Tom Lechler's name on her mobile phone's directory.

♦

MSG Tom Lechler, U.S. Army, Retired, had heard Josh Morgan speak about flyfishing often enough that he had decided to give it a try. He figured it couldn't be that hard. There were flyfishing shops and guides around the Fayetteville area, but the former operator had instead gone to an Academy Sports and bought an inexpensive package that came with rod, reel, line, leader, and an assortment of flies.

Lechler was standing on the bank of a small stream near his home with his new gear. A pile of line was at his feet from a cast gone very badly. He had already sorted through two such rat nests, had lost three of his ten flies from snagging on trees and brush in the water, and lost another one to a flycatching tree behind him.

"Yeah. How hard could it be?" Lechler reminded himself as having said. "Right."

When his phone rang, he barked, "Lechler," without checking the ID.

"Oh, yes, ma'am. Sorry. Frustrated with a little project I've got going on. What can I do for you, Betsy?"

The only direction he got from Parnell was to get to Bush CIA Headquarters pronto to get his orders and sign some papers.

On the way back to his truck, the ex-Green Beret stuffed the entirety of his new fishing gear in a trashcan at the trailhead parking lot.

♦

Morgan desperately wanted to call Maggie but knew he didn't need the distraction. He knew she would understand.

He had seen a number of people coming and going from the apartment building. There were uniformed sailors who were stationed at Naval Station Norfolk, men and women in casual attire, moms and dads pushing strollers. But only two were Latin and they were both women.

It was 9:15 when he saw a male Latino. He was entering the building instead of leaving.

"Been out on the town?" Morgan asked the man from his car. "Or maybe you just work a night shift."

As he surveilled the man through binoculars, he noted that he generally fit Desiree's and Katya's description, but that had been sufficiently vague that he wasn't sure it was of much help.

The Latino walked up the stairway and disappeared to the landing on the far side of the complex away from the target apartment.

"To heck with this," Morgan groused. He prepared to exit his SUV to break into the apartment when the man reappeared with a canned soft drink in his hand, apparently from a vending area.

Morgan removed his hand from the vehicle's door handle and grabbed his Nikon. He raised it and zoomed in to the maximum focal length and snapped a couple of photos. Then he watched the man as he unlocked the door to his apartment and walked in.

"Trini," Morgan said aloud. "Why are you still here, *amigo*?"

♦

"I know it's unorthodox," POTUS said to the Director of the Secret Service.

Keith Cortland knew it was pointless to argue with his ultimate boss, but also knew it was in his job description to advise the President on matters affecting her security and anything related to his department. It struck him as odd that Hendrickson had called, rather than having someone else do so.

"Honestly, ma'am, this doesn't concern protecting anyone. Nor does it involve investigating threats to U.S. financial infrastructure. So, how is this a fit for the Service?"

"Keith, it's just a practical matter. I need Lechler for something. It's domestic, so he can't be seen as working for Parnell."

"Sandy…," Cortland said, changing the tone of the conversation. He and President Hendrickson had been friends for a couple of decades. "So, it's just window dressing? Frankly, that isn't much better. He gets caught doing something, law enforcement isn't going to make much of a distinction where he's assigned on paper."

"Keith, if this goes sideways, I'll take the heat. I need someone who is used to operating as though he doesn't exist. And that person needs to be someone who can operate… Well, let's just say he needs to be capable of working a little outside the box."

"Then why does he need to 'work' for any agency at all?"

"Because he needs some sort of cover. He needs to know there is someone watching his back."

In his office, the Director of the Secret Service massaged his temples. The silence meant that his longtime friend was waiting on his agreement – whether he endorsed her plan or not.

"Okay, Madam President. I'll have someone prepare the employment paperwork."

"Now, please."

"Yes, ma'am. Now."

"Thank you, Director. You won't be able to access any personnel records on Lechler, so I'll have Parnell get something to you."

♦

Josh Morgan had been so sure that Trini was in the wind that he had no real plan. He had photos now but knew they wouldn't be much good. Even if facial recognition got a hit, it wouldn't provide any real intel on what he was up to. He then realized he had the same peephole reverser that he had used with Oskar Lammers in the backpack he had grabbed from Maggie's apartment when he headed to the airport to come to Norfolk.

It would be very risky, but he decided to try to use the device now while Trini was still in his apartment. If he got caught, he'd think of something. And besides, Betsy had arranged with the local FBI for one of their agents to meet him and deliver one of the Bureau's Glock Gen 5 semiautomatics. He stuffed the handgun in his waistband and exited his rental car.

The ex-CIA officer had barely made it to the other side of the street from his vehicle when the door to Trini's second-floor apartment opened and he walked out. Morgan flinched but dared not pause or change directions. Instead, he looked at his phone as though using the device hoping it would partially hide his face and kept walking. He turned right on the sidewalk since that was the direction he had first observed the Latino coming from.

Morgan paused at a bus stop sign, continuing to look at his phone. After a few moments of his quarry not showing up, the CIA contractor looked around to see if perhaps the man had turned the other way. He didn't see him at all. He had a dilemma. If he went to see if he could spot him, he might run face-to-face into him. But he couldn't lose him. Morgan put his phone away and moved to the opening between first floor apartments where the stairs were.

The stalker peeked around the corner and, across the interior courtyard beyond the pool, saw Trini leaving the complex. The man had such a head start that Morgan knew he wouldn't catch him. He bolted down the sidewalk to the corner of the building, hoping to spot a vehicle. None appeared, leaving Morgan with the conclusion that Trini had gone the other direction, on foot or in a car.

The ex-spook went back to his car. If he was lucky, Trini had gone a short distance and would return soon. In the meantime, he used his phone as a hotspot and connected his camera via Bluetooth. Once he had transmitted the best three photos to Director Parnell, he called her.

After he confirmed that she had received the files, he briefed Betsy on the situation and explained his planned next step.

♦

America's Top Spy only gave the photos from Morgan a cursory look before sending them to NSA and the FBI. She also sent them to her Agency's own analysts. She hoped at least one of the federal agencies would come up with something because she certainly hadn't learned anything from the images.

CHAPTER 40

Tom Lechler had caught a flight from Fort Bragg to Washington. After a call from Betsy Parnell at CIA, he headed directly to the Secret Service Headquarters on H Street NW. He was met in the lobby and escorted directly to Director Cortland's office. Inside with the Service Director was his boss, Director of Homeland Security Anson Larson.

After brief introductions, Cortland explained to Lechler that he was being assigned to the President's close protection detail, but that he wouldn't actually be providing security.

"You'll get your marching orders from POTUS," Cortland said.

"And I hope somewhere along the way, we'll get some details about what the hell is going on," added Larson. "You have to understand that neither of us likes this very much. The President isn't supposed to concern herself with operations. Nothing personal, Sergeant."

"Understood."

"A driver will take you to the Rowley Training Center, where you'll be issued a sidearm and, on orders from the President, anything else you want."

"Yes, sir."

Larson rose and said, "Good luck, Sergeant. I mean that. But don't fuck up. It'll surely come back to bite POTUS in the ass, and she doesn't deserve that."

"She's a fine person, sir," the retired operator agreed. "I'll never let her be hurt by my actions."

"See that you don't" Cortland warned.

The men shook hands and Lechler left with his escort.

♦

Josh Morgan was at the door to Trini's place. He had waited in his vehicle for ninety minutes after talking with Betsy. Once on the landing outside the apartment, he hung around for an additional couple of minutes, looking at his watch and pretending to be on the phone. He surveyed his surroundings and once he felt safe – or as safe as he was going to feel – he attached the reverser to the peephole. Morgan leaned against the doorframe with one leg bent underneath him in a show of faux nonchalance.

While he tried to appear that he was supposed to be there, perhaps waiting on the apartment's resident to arrive, he carefully examined the image on his phone. The rather poor quality generally only allowed him to pick up movement inside the flat. There was none. It was time to move in.

Having previously examined the door, Morgan had seen only one lock: the one on the knob. That was good because, even though he had lock picks, he wasn't very good with them.

He pulled out a credit card and pushed it into the gap between the doorframe and the knob, sliding it down until it was next to the doorknob. He pushed it in as far as he could, perpendicular to the frame. Then he moved the edge of the card up and down, pushing farther into the gap as he did. The intruder leaned against the door and wiggled it back and forth while flexing the credit card away from the frame. Finally, the improvised pick slid under the angled end of the latch, pushing it into the door. Morgan opened it quickly. He made a quick assessment of the area around him and was confident that nobody had seen him break in.

♦

In fairly short order, Tom Lechler was on his way from the Secret Service's training center to the White House with a virtual armory's worth of weaponry.

Arriving at the Visitor's Gate, the ex-sergeant met an escort, who instructed him to leave his weapons in the vehicle. "Secret Service" or not, he was an unknown entity to the real Special Agents and wasn't trusted. A good word on the part of the President of the United States notwithstanding, he hadn't been properly vetted.

A guard frisked Lechler so thoroughly that he felt the man should've bought him dinner. But he had been subjected to much worse. Electronic "sniffers" checked his body for chemicals or explosives. Once the guard was satisfied, he looked at a counterpart and said, "He's clean."

The second agent ordered Lechler, "Follow me," and led him into the West Wing where he was met by Chief of Staff Noah Chandler. Before leading him to his meeting, the Chief took his turn laying the law down to Lechler.

"My job is to advise the President, but ultimately follow her orders. Just so you'll know, I think this is a fool's errand – not the plan. It's the bringing you in that I don't like. Understood?"

"Loud and clear, sir."

Chandler stared at the guest to the White House for an extended number of seconds. He was impressed that the former Green Beret remained expressionless, never blinking or appearing ill at ease. But Lechler's file described a warrior from whom Chandler would expect nothing less.

"Having said that," Chandler finally continued, "thank you for your service. I believe you will do your best. It's nothing personal, Sergeant."

"I would understand if it was, sir. And perhaps it should be personal. I have found that personal investment is often a natural result of loyalty."

Some of Chandler's reservations disappeared, but not all of them. He led the President's hand-picked operator to her office.

♦

Josh Morgan's initial assessment of his surroundings was simply of a filthy apartment. The living area was trashed with takeout food containers, partially full and empty bottles of tequila and other liquor, and other trash. He moved around the den cautiously, alert for anything that might provide insight into what the Nicaraguans were carrying out in his country. But he found nothing of significance.

Moving to a bedroom, he saw nothing more than just a bedroom. The room had two twin-sized beds, a dresser, and not much more. Still, he looked at every scrap of paper, turned back the linens to see if anything was covered by them, and checked every item in the bathroom. Among the limited personal toiletries, he saw several condoms, some used. The intruder felt like he needed a shower.

When he turned around to move to the final bedroom, he found himself looking directly into the barrel of a semiautomatic handgun extended in front of a very formidable-looking Latino.

"Maybe you should've made sure the place was empty, *gringo*,"

♦

"So, that's the gist of it, Sergeant Lechler. We've been speaking all along as though you have no say in this. Forgive me for that. You don't have to do this, Master Sergeant. You've retired from military life so I can't really order you to do this. I can only ask," POTUS acknowledged.

"I will, ma'am. May I ask a question though?"

"Of course, Tom."

"Why did you select me?"

"Josh Morgan recommended you."

Tom Lechler had already sized up this plan as more or less a suicide mission.

"Well, Morgan never really liked me, ma'am." He was immediately embarrassed at his levity in front of the U.S. Commander-in-chief. But the President laughed.

"I only met you briefly when you came home from Norfolk with Josh and Secretary Loughlin – Maggie. You had done such a service to your country then and in your military career. I read your file and asked my military leaders about you."

POTUS lifted a file from her desk and took a seat beside Lechler on the small sofa in the sitting area of the Oval Office.

"You led the op in Russia when we – when I – acted on the belief that they were behind the attempt on my life and responsible for the deaths of the Vice-president and others. As a member of our Army SPIRIT Teams, you are familiar with scenarios in which, once deployed, you might be stuck with no hope of extraction."

Lechler had been part of an elite force of special operators in a unit called a SPecial Immediate Reaction Infiltration Team, or SPIRIT. It was a descendant of Green Light Teams of earlier days whose mission it was to parachute behind enemy lines and deploy a low-yield nuclear device. The current version not only employed nukes but also used drones equipped with non-nuclear Electromagnetic Pulse devices. But the things that both the Green Light Teams and the SPIRITs had in common were that they were stealthy, committed, and lethal. And both operated in the knowledge that their missions might very well cause them death at their own hands.

"Thank you, Tom. I made Josh promise not to discuss it with you until I'd had the opportunity to explain it you; to make my case for the importance of this operation. He considers you a trusted and valued friend. He was reluctant to throw your name out for this. But he believes you're the one most capable of succeeding. Who knows? You might never deploy."

"Just so I'm clear, Madam President. I basically sit and wait until put into the field?"

"Yes."

"And then my only job is to get the package as far away from D.C. in as short amount of time as possible?"

"Correct," POTUS confirmed.

"May I ask what the item is?"

♦

The former spy had been careless. Seeing Trini leave the apartment, he had assumed that all was clear. It never occurred to him that there might be a fourth player. The man with the gun wasn't Trini.

"Sorry. Trini told me to wait here," Morgan bluffed.

"*Mierda*."

"Yeah, that is bullshit," Morgan thought, but decided to play it out further.

"Seriously, I saw him on his way out. He told me to let myself in; that he'd be back soon."

"He isn't coming back," announced the Latin man who stepped slightly closer.

"That son of a bitch, I can't believe he…" Morgan's voice trailed off as he finally admitted to himself that it was pointless to continue.

"Who are you?" asked the man with the gun.

"I'm a friend of Eddie Solis," the former spy said. "Since he's out of action, a few of us guys he confided in about your operation have decided to take matters into our own hands." Morgan saw that this bluff touched a nerve in his present adversary. It would only work for a bit, but perhaps it could buy him some time if the Latino decided he had to find out who "us guys" were.

"We know exactly what your plan is and when you're going to carry it out."

The man's moustache lifted as he smiled from behind the gun. "If you truly knew anything about the timing, you would know that you arrived too late."

"Oh, shit!" was the immediate, although silent reaction. Morgan's heart leapt to his throat.

♦

"Why don't you explain the situation, Director McClintock?" POTUS directed.

"Master Sergeant, this target is a homing device. At least we believe it is. Something on the order of VOR – short range VHF. I'm sure you're aware of the missiles in Cuba. It could be related to them, but we don't think so."

"Yes, sir. Could only be received from two hundred to two fifty miles out."

"Exactly. Our current theory is that it will be turned on and serve as a beacon for a light aircraft at some point in the future. We have no idea of the timing. We picked up its transmission from the top of the Nicaraguan

Embassy."

"Them again," the ex-Army warrior thought.

"Here's our dilemma, Lechler. First, the Nicaraguans have moved it and we don't know where. If we find it and grab it, they could have another one."

"So, you're going after the aircraft instead of the transmitter?"

"Yes. It's risky but that's the plan," McClintock affirmed.

"And you try to locate the transmitter last minute and my job is to guide the craft away from its planned target. Then what?"

"Then, once the plane turns to follow the beacon, we'll have confirmed that it's the right aircraft." the NSA Director said.

"Any idea what the weapon is?" Lechler asked.

"Could be anything – chemical, biological, dirty bomb. We don't know."

"Obviously there are a few holes in our theory," POTUS remarked.

"More like a truckload," Lechler observed silently.

"If it's a light plane, we could blow it out of the sky and hope that the blast would vaporize anything dangerous on board. But that's a chance we can't take. And while it's not likely, the delivery system could be a car," POTUS added.

"Director McClintock, this is obviously way out of my area of expertise. I'm just one of the quiet professionals. But with GPS being what it is, why does anyone need a beacon?"

A tinge of ire appeared in the President's eyes. She'd had the same question, and nobody could answer it for her.

"We… uh, we don't know, Master Sergeant. We're just trying to prepare for any contingency. And one real possibility is that it will be unmanned – a drone of some sort."

"Well, Madam President, I'm at your service," the retired Green Beret reaffirmed.

♦

"Too late. What does that mean?" Morgan thought. He wondered if Trini was on his way at this very moment to do something. If so, then all the worry about Washington might have been misguided. The former spy decided to bluff a little longer.

"The authorities are waiting for Trini right now."

The gunman appeared skeptical, but Morgan saw a glimmer of concern.

"We thought you'd be with him."

Since the initial concern when NSA got wind of a possible plot by the Zamora regime was a chemical attack, the CIA contractor decided to go all in.

"He'll never get the nerve agent in play, *amigo*," Morgan told his adversary, watching for even the most subtle reaction. "Bingo," he said to himself as there was an obvious change to the man's countenance.

"You're bluffing," accused the gunman. "You know nothing. Otherwise, why would you come here?"

"Because we knew there were at least four of you," Morgan lied. "The Gutierrez brothers are dead. We're onto Trini. You're the last piece of the puzzle. I came here looking for you. I just got sloppy. We know everything."

The ex-spy could only hope his bluff would throw his adversary off enough for him to find an opportunity. He would prolong the ruse as long as he thought he could. So far, the man's distance kept Morgan at a disadvantage.

"You know you Americans are all alike – pompous, arrogant assholes. It is no surprise the world hates you. The Latino moved closer, but only slightly. "In a few hours, your national song will take on a whole new meaning."

Morgan realized immediately that an attack or attacks were imminent. But what did The Star-Spangled Banner have to do with anything.

The gunman sang a line from the U.S. National Anthem, off-pitch and shrill.

"*And the rockets' red glare.*" The Nicaraguan laughed and inched even closer.

Morgan had no idea as to the nature of the taunt.

"Tell me what you know!" the gunman demanded.

Morgan knew not to put a time frame to his alleged knowledge of the plot. If Trini was indeed in route to deliver some sort of chemical weapon, he could be going across town or he could be on his way to Washington. He didn't know.

"Why would I do that? Besides, he could be in custody already. Or dead."

"TELL ME WHAT YOU KNOW!" the Latin terrorist demanded again.

♦

Mid-afternoons were always the worst for Maggie at her job in the West Wing. She had put out fires in the morning and prepared press briefings, which she often delivered just after lunch. Then she returned to her desk only to find herself as far behind as when she had arrived in the morning. She took a bite of the veggie wrap the White House kitchen had brought her and turned the volume up on one of her TVs.

The QNN daytime anchor Cameron Neal was on-camera.

A breaking story just in. Scientists at NASA have announced that their calculations developed in conjunction with NORAD and the Department of Defense's global Space Surveillance Network show that the wayward Chinese rocket's orbit is decaying rapidly and has reached a point where reentry is close but not imminent. The booster's orbit has dropped to roughly 190 nautical miles. It appears that, if it continues to deteriorate at its current rate, it will fall somewhere in the North Atlantic. There appears to be little or no danger to populated areas.

"Well, at least there's some good news," Maggie thought.

♦

Tom Lechler was in a briefing about his responsibilities should the transmitter be found. The analyst speaking to him was an Army veteran herself, having worked in the Military Intelligence Corps.

"Should this device be related to the missiles in Cuba instead of a light craft…" – Former Lieutenant Beth Andrews rolled her eyes with the words so Lechler knew she was as skeptical about the scenario as everyone else was – "…and assuming we have it, then your job will be to fly it out to sea in a helicopter and just a few minutes before the missiles get to you…"

The last part sounded awfully personal to the former sergeant.

"…you will drop it overboard. Technicians will have attached a flotation device to the apparatus. If it submerges, the signal will be lost and who knows where the missiles will wind up. Once you drop the transmitter, you get out of there, Master Sergeant."

"Piece of cake," Lechler stated with unrestrained sarcasm.

"Master Sergeant, personally my thinking is that this will actually be a UAV of some sort. But the plan will work just the same."

Andrews' humanity finally overtook her technical explanation. She looked at the potential deliveryman sympathetically.

"I'm sorry, Master Sergeant."

"Like I said. Piece of cake." The pair exchanged minimal smiles.

"The military has abandoned the idea of Patriot Missile batteries trying to shoot the missiles or drones down. The explosion, if not nuclear, would likely be the equivalent of a dirty bomb. And there are a number of densely populated areas along the route," the former Army officer said.

"So, I fly a homing beacon, which, by the way, we don't have yet, out to sea so that missiles or a drone will follow me. The nukes are flying at five hundred miles per hour while poor little old Lechler's chopper is cruising at just north of one-fifty. We do it too soon and the Cubans call the whole thing off. Or worse, they bring out a backup at some point and do it all over at another time. In essence, we're setting D.C. up as the target…"

"It's already the target, Master Sergeant," Andrews corrected.

"…and then wait until the missiles or whatever are close to two hundred miles out and then I fly off with…" Lechler ended his assessment and sighed. "What could go wrong?"

♦

"I'M NOT GOING TO TELL YOU AGAIN! WHAT DO YOU KNOW!!!" shrieked the terrorist. While his prisoner held his hands at shoulder level, the gunman's right hand shoved the barrel of his semiautomatic to within a foot of Morgan's chest.

As soon as he did, the former Case Officer's own left hand flew palm-first onto the barrel and the slide of the sidearm, grabbing it forcefully. The continued momentum pushed the weapon to his opponent's left and Morgan's right. Simultaneously, the former spy leaned to his left and away from the end of the gun and brought his right hand right to his left and onto the man's wrist where it provided leverage against which Morgan continued pushing the weapon to his own right.

As the gun rotated around and out of the Latino's hand, the man winced in pain.

Morgan stepped backward, almost falling, and aimed the gun at his opponent. Undaunted by the turn of events and the pain in his finger, which had been broken and mangled by the trigger guard as the gun twisted around it, he flew toward Morgan. As Morgan fired the sound of the gun was powerful in the small hall between the apartment's two bedrooms. The attack had thrown Morgan's aim off from center mass. The man's left leg crumpled beneath him. He tried to sustain the attack but only managed to close in by another foot or so. Morgan had fallen to his butt and backpedaled himself away while still seated.

The Nicaraguan struggled but finally propped himself in a seated position against the wall. Morgan held the gun on him but wanted to avoid shooting him again. He had questions to ask. The ex-spy hadn't wanted to shoot him at all. He needed him alive. But a look at the carpeted floor told him that wasn't going to happen.

A pool of blood was expanding rapidly beneath his adversary's left leg, despite the man's attempt to quell the flow with pressure from both hands.

♦

The FBI's facial recognition was the first to come up with Trini's identity from the photos Morgan had taken. FBI Director Gabe Austin delivered the news to his counterparts in other agencies.

At CIA Headquarters in Langley, Virginia, Director Elizabeth Parnell didn't know if the information would make things easier or harder, but only

one word came to mind as a reaction.
"Shit…"

♦

"Femoral artery, pal. You've got less than five minutes. Tell me what you know."

The man's eyes dulled and turned glassy. He made an effort to smile but the agony of his wound rendered it impossible. At first his breathing increased, with air escaping through his mouth in exaggerated bursts.

The ex-CIA Officer lowered the gun, rose and sat on the sofa. The man was almost gone.

Shortly, the mortally wounded man's panting turned to small puffs, infrequent and irregular. Momentarily, he slumped to the side and breathed his last.

Morgan knew he had little time. He shoved the dead man's pistol into his waistband beside his own, which he'd never had the opportunity to draw. The CIA contractor had little use for the additional weapon, but it had his fingerprints on it.

Dashing into the other spare bedroom, Morgan discovered an entirely different environment than elsewhere in the small apartment. A laptop, piles of papers and maps, and a number of photographs lay scattered about on two folding tables. Morgan didn't have time to examine his discovery there. He knew the gunshot would result in the police arriving at any moment. He only hoped he could gather everything up before they entered the building. But even at the risk of officers appearing before he had collected all that he could carry, he wasn't leaving without it.

In less than three minutes, armed with the computer and arms full of other items, Josh Morgan was racing down the stairs outside the apartment. He wanted to hide his face from the few onlookers peering through cracked doors, but it wouldn't matter. As he reached the ground, he noticed several people standing in the open area of the building's courtyard, videoing him with their phones. He would've enjoyed waving his gun at them to show them what idiots they were. Instead, he continued his sprint to his car, threw his bounty in the backseat, and sped away.

♦

Norfolk PD issued a "be on the lookout" advisory for Trinidad Alvarez immediately upon receiving information from the local FBI Field Office, which had received it from the Hoover Building in D.C. Alvarez had his own apartment in Norfolk and local detectives and SWAT, along with federal agents, were already arriving there.

Not far away, a similar contingent, though much smaller in number, were answering reports of a gunshot in a small apartment complex. Callers had also described a man running across the street and leaving in an automobile.

♦

Josh Morgan was a few miles away from where he had killed his latest victim, albeit unintentionally, when his phone vibrated in his shirt pocket. He jumped at the startling action. He looked at the name of his caller. If it had been anyone else, he would've ignored it. He pressed an icon to connect and another to put on speaker.

"Hold on, Betsy."

The contract employee surveyed his surroundings and took a long look in all his vehicle's mirrors. Feeling safe – at least momentarily – he pulled into a shopping center parking lot and backed into a spot amidst other vehicles to hide his rental SUV's rear and only license plate.

"Okay, Betsy. I'm…"

Director Parnell interrupted and explained the news of Trini's identity.

Morgan listened and then exclaimed, "He's what?"

CHAPTER 41

At a diner near Norfolk Naval Station, Petty Officer 2nd Class Trinidad Alvarez sat drinking coffee and eating lemon merengue pie, trying desperately to calm his nerves.

PO2 Alvarez didn't need to report until eighteen hundred hours. He wanted to report early, but not too early. He had stopped at his apartment to change into his Navy Working Uniform and grab his sea bag. Looking about the small café, Trini saw other sailors in their N-Dubs but none that he recognized. He took another sip of coffee and looked at his watch.

♦

"A Navy Sailor?" Morgan exclaimed. "One of ours?"

"Yes. A Petty Officer Second Class. Twenty-two years old. Born here of Nicaraguan parents."

"What's his service record say?"

"Model sailor by all accounts. No criminal history. No record of involvement with any radical groups."

"Family?" Morgan inquired, hoping for a lead or a person he could coerce into providing meaningful information.

"None. Only child and both parents dead. And that's all we know about him personally. Except that he has his own apartment near the base. He's assigned to the USS George Washington in Norfolk. He's due to report at six o'clock. And the George Washington sets sail tomorrow."

"No idea what he's up to, Betsy?"

"None, Morgan. We already have BOLOs out, feds on the prowl, and MPs on and near the base looking for him. He hasn't reported yet, so at least we can keep him off the carrier."

"I don't have time to explain, Betsy, but there was a fourth guy at the apartment and…"

"Did you get anything from him?" the Director hoped.

"Well, he's dead. I had to shoot him."

"Damn, Josh, can't you just wound someone?" Parnell said, employing the line from any number of movies.

"I did. Shot him in the leg. Except it hit his femoral. Anyhow, the important thing is that for a moment he had the drop on me. I bluffed that we knew about Trini and the nerve agent attack. And this guy bit. Betsy, I'm sure Trini is going to spread some toxin, or virus or something."

"I'll spread the word."

"And Betsy, I got a laptop and a shitload of documents from the apartment. No time to get them to you. I'm going to look them over."

"No, Josh. Time for you to come in. Take it to the FBI Field Office."

"That'll take too much time. If I can't figure anything out quickly, I'll do that."

"*Very* quickly."

"Roger. And one more thing, Betsy."

CIA Boss Parnell always hated hearing Morgan say that.

"The police are looking for me."

Parnell rested her elbow on her desk and put her forehead in her hand. She complained, "Again?" But Morgan had already disconnected.

♦

Everyone in Washington from President Hendrickson on down knew about the development with Alvarez in very short order.

"Any chance that he's a threat to Washington, Paul?" POTUS asked her NSA Director.

"I think the threat here has to do with the transmitter. Being a sailor, Alvarez's part probably has something to do with the base in Norfolk. But Zamora's aide warned of a two-pronged attack. So, I suppose it's possible." McClintock accompanied his answer with a shrug.

"Well, let's keep our fingers crossed," the Chief Executive suggested, actually doing just that at her desk. "On another note, what's the latest on the Chinese rocket?"

"It's on its last orbit or two, it appears. West to east. It'll pass practically over our heads. But everyone says it'll come apart safely over the North Atlantic."

♦

A nondescript van was parked at a public garage on Pennsylvania Avenue NW in Washington, D.C. Even though a number of spots were open in the interior of the structure, the driver chose to park on the rooftop. He backed into a space on the western side, leaving just enough room to open the rear doors when the time came.

Moving from the driver seat into the cargo area, he examined his freight.

♦

Morgan knew that Betsy would call off the police. Until she did, he just hoped he could stay out of sight long enough to examine the intel he had collected. He knew that once he was in the hands of any law enforcement agency or department, they would take the computer and documents.

He had moved into the backseat for more room to work and was looking through the assorted papers. His fluency in Spanish paid off as he was able to speed through the written parts of the documents. He knew that what he read only alluded to a plot if the reader was looking for one. Everything was sufficiently vague and the things that seemed to be details meant nothing if you didn't know the context.

While he read pages and examined photos, Morgan booted up the laptop. He paused from his examination long enough to see that a prompt asked for a password. He wasn't surprised but knew he didn't have the time if Trini was indeed currently going into action.

Morgan opened his own laptop and put his finger on the print reader. He launched PSI, the Nicaraguan government's proprietary encryption software that Santana had given Eddie and which Morgan had copied from the blogger's computer. The CIA contractor had played around with the software some at Maggie's apartment, so he had developed some familiarity. He went straight to the menu.

He selected a menu option that he knew searched for other computers wirelessly. Morgan's tactic rewarded him with a short dialogue box indicating the presence of his newly acquired laptop. It asked if he wanted to connect. He clicked on the button that said, "*Sí*."

Morgan's hope vanished when the dialogue also asked for a password. He knew very few tricks when it came to hacking, so he looked at a few more of the paper documents while he pondered his next move with the computer.

"What the…?"

The ex-CIA Officer hadn't expected to see a document written in Chinese. It was translated into Spanish, which he easily read, but it offered no useful information. It did however change his approach to his examination, as he flew through pages looking only for any that were written in Chinese. Morgan found several.

Finally, he saw one with a Spanish translation that read, "Our part will require perfect execution at your location to ensure sufficient accuracy."

"Whose location?" Morgan asked aloud. When he looked at the recipient, he saw that it was sent to Luis Gutierrez.

"No help." Then the former spook realized there was a flaw in his thinking. He didn't need the "To" in the final translated version. He backed up one entry in the string of emails. The recipient's email address was to someone with a domain of *gob.ni.*

"*Gobierno.Nicaragua*," he correctly surmised.

"Damnation. The original recipient was someone at the Nicaraguan Embassy." Morgan's mind raced to interpret the meaning behind the message but realized that the "your location" in the email must mean the Embassy. Or maybe more generally, Washington, D.C.

♦

Cheng Shun sat before the State Council of the People's Republic of China.

"It is time, comrades. Our act of patriotism will cripple the American economy and spread chaos throughout its military. In one momentous act, we will solidify our position among the world as its mightiest superpower."

Approval was indicated unanimously around the table.

Cheng announced to his government's leaders, "Execute as planned."

♦

The driver and his associate opened the rear doors of their white van atop the Washington, D.C. parking garage. Though he couldn't see it, he knew that the American White House sat nearly due west of him. And when he arrived at his current location, he saw the dome of the American Capitol Building to the east.

Their bosses had given the Nicaraguan technicians strict orders not to activate their device until ordered.

But in the idle time between their arrival at the parking structure and the planned implementation, the two men had discussed the sternness of their superiors.

"Ambassador Torrez is a very unforgiving man."

"*El Presidente* Zamora is even more so," agreed his *compadre.*

"Arturo, what if this thing doesn't work? Wouldn't it be wise to know now while we would still have time to repair it?"

Arturo and Chico stared at one another, then looked away, then at each other again.

Finally reaching some sort of unspoken agreement, the two men nodded.

The Nicaraguan technicians removed the device from the cargo area of their van and set it on top of the vehicle.

With the press of a single button, the Nicaraguan technician activated the device. It sent a radio pulse that a meter that Chico held confirmed. The VHF transmission with a frequency of approximately 107 megahertz lasted about six seconds. He smiled and nodded to Arturo.

Confident that their apparatus was in good working order, the two men smiled again, and Arturo turned off the transmitter and moved it back inside the van.

♦

NSA Analyst Terry Henderson was poring over every piece of intel the Agency had about the anomalous signal his organization now believed to be a homing beacon. The intel was sorely lacking.

His eyes shot toward his computer at the sound of a chime, which loosely translated from computer lingo meant, "Hey! Look at me!"

Henderson picked up his phone and called his boss, Deputy Director Michael Driessen.

"Mike, we've got something."

Driessen only allowed his analyst to tell him the subject matter of his call before he stopped him. Driessen conferenced in his boss, Director Paul McClintock.

"Go ahead, Terry."

The same two UAVs that picked up the last VHF transmission before the beacon was removed from the roof of the Nicaraguan Embassy picked it up again. Only one signal."

"Tell me it was enough, Terry," McClintock begged.

"It was, sir."

♦

While he wasn't enthusiastic about his possible mission, the retired Master Sergeant was bored to tears. He mostly occupied his time watching TV or reading months-old magazines in a small room just inside a conference room of the United States Secret Service's James J. Rowley Training Center.

DoD's global Space Surveillance Network Analyst Beth Andrews burst into the room.

"We've got a fix, Master Sergeant."

Lechler tossed his reading material onto a table and grabbed his go bag. He rushed out of the building toward the aircraft that belonged to the FBI's Tactical Helicopter Unit that was uncharacteristically parked on the north lawn of the training center.

The ex-Green Beret took his place in the right-side pilot's seat, donned his headset, and began to spool up the rotors. A thumbs-up to Andrews and other personnel who had been hoping for this moment and Lechler opened the throttle completely.

While lifting the collective slowly, the chopper pilot depressed the left foot pedal, counteracting the main rotor's torque. As the helicopter began to slowly rise, the ex-operator nudged the aircraft forward with the cyclic.

"I love this," the pilot said.

"Come again, sir?" the support crew inquired, having heard the remark through his headset.

"Nothing," Lechler answered with a slight smile. But it was true. He loved flying helicopters.

As the pilot had made his way out of the Rowley Center, an NSA technician who had also been waiting for orders handed Lechler a small GPS unit. Lechler plugged it into the input port of the chopper's GPS and the transfer executed immediately. The Bell 407 banked right until it was pointing directly southwest.

"No time to waste. Let's see what you've got." The former MSG shot low and fast over suburban D.C., passing above Hyattsville. He got his orders on the way.

"Master Sergeant, we just got eyes on the location where we picked up the signal," said FBI Supervisory Special Agent Liu of the FBI. "Our UAVs and the spotters atop adjacent buildings haven't seen evidence that would suggest the presence of anything other than the transmitter, but we just don't know."

"Copy that."

"Your orders are to hover in the area of the Capitol until our SWAT Team has cleared the roof. Once you receive word that any human threat has been neutralized, you will land on the parking garage. A SWAT officer will bring the beacon to you."

"Any word on missiles or light aircraft inbound toward the target?" the chopper pilot asked.

"Negative," SSA Liu informed. "That suggests we have some time, but things could start happening pretty quickly."

"Roger."

♦

Josh Morgan tapped his forehead with his left palm.

"Think, Josh." The one email suggested Chinese involvement in whatever was going down. It further seemed to imply that D.C. was the target and that the Nicaraguan Embassy was the point of attack.

"But China and Nicaragua just signed the defense treaty, so what sense would that make?"

There were other emails originally written in Chinese that were translated into Spanish. But the content of every one of them was benign – at least so far as Morgan could determine without additional background.

He patted his forehead again. He knew he really couldn't spare the time, but he decided he would call Parnell.

Getting no answer from his boss, the CIA contractor decided to see what a quick internet search would turn up. First, he searched on "China" and "Nicaragua." He set a timeframe of "last 24 hours" and pressed the "enter" key. His screen lit up with articles from every news organization around the world discussing the Mutual Defense Treaty between the two nations.

He tried "Cuba" since missiles had been spotted there. Almost every search result had to do with their discovery. Morgan decided to go back to China. When he entered the name of the Communist country alone with the same parameter limiting results to postings of the last twenty-four hours, the search results included the same articles about the treaty. But interspersed with those were posts about the Chinese rocket that had failed to reach orbit and was tumbling uncontrolled back to earth. He made a phone call.

"Hi, Morgan. I have to fill you in." Maggie started before Morgan could stop her. They found the transmitter, Josh. Tom's on his way…"

"Stop, Maggie!" Josh practically shouted. In her office, his fiancée pulled back from the phone.

"Maggie, what's the latest on the missiles in Cuba? Briefly."

"Nothing is up down there. That's why…"

"What about the Chinese rocket?"

"It's coming down right now, but everything's good. It's apparently going to pass right over Washington before burning up over the Atlantic."

There was silence. Maggie said nothing knowing that Josh was in analysis mode.

Morgan mentally pulled up everything he knew about the Chinese booster. One fact that he recalled reading was that its orbit was around two hundred miles high. Rapidly he assessed what he knew about the missiles and the transmitter in Washington.

"Missiles are back in hiding," he mumbled. "Besides they wouldn't need a homing beacon."

Maggie knew Josh was just organizing his thoughts aloud, as he often did, so she let him speak uninterrupted as he moved on to another possible scenario tossed around by the analysts about the assumed homing beacon.

"A small plane would get blown out of the sky before it got anywhere near a high-value target."

The former spy came back to one thing and only one thing that involved China and the taunt from the man he'd just inadvertently killed with words from The Star-Spangled Banner.

"'*And the rockets' red glare…*' It's the rocket, Maggie. It's the damned Chinese booster. It's not out of control! It's doing exactly what it was intended to do. They're going to hit Washington with it!!!"

"Morgan, how do you…?"

"Maggie, I don't care what you have to do. Get in front of POTUS and tell her that the rocket is the weapon. Do it now!"

♦

Somewhere over the northern Pacific at an altitude of under two hundred miles, a panel blew away from the side of the Chinese rocket. A previously hidden outrigger emerged from the compartment. Secured by electronic clamps and receiving digital instructions via a wiring harness, a twelve-feet-long missile hung from the rocket.

From other hidden spaces on the booster's shell, four small thruster assemblies sprang into place and began to fire, slowing the rocket and nudging it into a lower orbit.

♦

Maggie tried to get to the President in the Cabinet Room, but armed security stopped her. She texted Chief of Staff Chandler, who she knew would be with Hendrickson.

Inside the Cabinet Room, Noah Chandler looked at the sender as displayed on his vibrating phone. He began to put his phone away with the message unread, thought better of it and touched the screen.

per josh china rocket is weapon aimed at dc

Maggie paced frantically a short distance from the armed guards while she waited for a reply from Hendrickson's Chief of Staff. The door to the conference room opened and President Sandra Hendrickson walked toward her with Chandler following. Director of National Intelligence Chris

Donleavy, CIA Director Parnell, NSA Director Paul McClintock, and FBI Director Gabriel Austin were also in tow.

Without regard to who else might hear, Maggie shouted, "The rocket failure is a ruse. The thing is going to come down right on top of us."

The President's face was a mixture of irritation at having been interrupted in the middle of a meeting to discuss the current threat to D.C. and worry that her Press Secretary might be right.

"Damn it, Maggie. Is Morgan sure?"

The head of CIA spoke respectfully but insistently to POTUS.

"Madam President, I would hope he's earned the benefit of our doubt."

Sandra Hendrickson pushed a hand through her hair. She paced only momentarily before turning back to Maggie.

"Tell Morgan we're looking into it."

Facing her advisers, POTUS followed with, "You heard her as well as I did. Go have your people put their thinking caps on. Is this even possible? GO!"

Everybody in the group of men and women hurried to get on their phones and rushed for the exit.

The President's hands were on her hips as she moved toward Maggie.

"This had better not be a wild goose chase. We don't have time for it." She turned abruptly and headed for the Oval Office. Chief of Staff Chandler shook his head and moved his hands up and down, palms down, signifying that he'd handle POTUS.

♦

The text from Maggie read:

they'll look into it

♦

In the van atop the parking garage on Pennsylvania Avenue NW, Arturo ended the call he had received from the Nicaraguan Ambassador's aide. He took a deep breath as he confirmed to his associate.

"It is time."

The two men placed the transmitter on top of the van once more.

Another deep breath and, "*Dios esté con nosotros*," Arturo prayed.

"*Sí*," Chico agreed. "God be with us."

Arturo pressed the red button, and the device began transmitting its beacon. Unlike in the Nicaraguans' earlier ill-advised test and unlike the tests from the roof of the Embassy, the device remained on and emitted its VHF signal continuously.

CHAPTER 42

When the beacon went live, receivers with the SWAT units positioned on the roofs of buildings adjacent to the parking garage began picking up the transmission at the same time as the Unmanned Aerial Vehicles circling above.

At NSA Headquarters, Analyst Henderson sat in a room with his boss and his boss' boss. McClintock had just arrived from the White House and had advised everyone about the possibility that the signal was going to direct the Chinese booster to its location about halfway between the White House and the Capitol.

Elsewhere in the building, analysts and technicians were investigating whether such technology was possible.

"Sirs, UAVs have picked up the signal again. It's transmitting continuously this time."

"I guess that rules out this being a test," Director McClintock concluded aloud.

Deputy Director Driessen nodded.

"Our SWAT Team had confirmed that they are receiving the signal at their locations," came the voice of FBI Director Austin through the speakerphone on the desk in front of Henderson. "And they confirm that the unit is on top of the van."

"That's to clear the signal from obstructions that would interfere with line of sight," Driessen stated, although he knew everyone else was aware.

Austin continued, "Our guys are all the way up the stairwell and prepared to take them down. And… Hold on… Shit! The door leading to the roof is wired. This is going to take a few minutes to assess and disable the IED."

At NSA heads shook. Others dropped. McClintock put one hand on his forehead and the other covered his mouth. He muttered an expletive that nobody could quite make out.

"Gabe, we need to get this thing in our hands immediately!" McClintock bellowed to his FBI counterpart.

"Dammit, Paul. I know, but I'm not going to get my guys blown up."

"Is there a way to breach from a distance?" Former Navy Captain Driessen asked. "Maybe blast the door and scramble through the debris."

"I'm checking on that very thing right now."

The room was quiet as the team at the National Security Agency waited on an update. A scientist/analyst entered and handed Deputy Director Driessen a report. The retired Captain looked at it only briefly and directed the woman to McClintock.

"The consensus is that, while it is possible to bring the rocket in with the signal, the few pieces of debris that survived burning up on reentry would hardly do damage that could be controlled in any way. The pieces would break up in the general area of the transponder, but we don't believe it is possible to direct the pieces to a specific target or targets."

"Chemical weapon?"

"It would almost certainly burn up as well," the scientist answered. "Unless it was somehow protected, that is. And then, it would still be uncontrollable."

"So, you're saying that the homing beacon may really not be related to the rocket at all?" the NSA Director inquired.

"Well, that's the other thing. The rocket's orbit is shallowing in what appears to be a controlled manner."

"SHIT! You couldn't have led with that!?"

McClintock turned his attention back to his FBI counterpart over the speaker.

"Gabe, we've got to hurry. It's happening."

"Understood," the head of the FBI said.

Driessen summed up what he and his boss had heard.

"It's probably too big a coincidence that the rocket is coming down at the same time the signal was activated. I'm not minimizing the damage any large surviving pieces could do, but the impacts would be so random that I can't imagine this transmitter could be serving any real purpose. Unless…" The Deputy Director paused.

"Go on, Mike."

"Unless there's more to this than just the rocket."

♦

As soon as he had seen Maggie's text, Morgan knew he had to move on to the matter of PO2 Trinidad Alvarez. Finding no information on the printed pages – except the one that led him to believe the Chinese rocket was a weapon – the CIA contractor returned to the computer he had taken from the conspirators' apartment.

Having successfully connected the device with his own, Morgan was still thwarted by his inability to get past the password prompt.

A thought occurred to him. He launched the PSI encryption app on his computer. One of the menu items was the same one almost all programs had: "Settings." He selected it, navigated his way to "Security Settings," and clicked on the "Password" tab. Morgan selected "*Cambiar la contraseña*" to try to change the password.

The wannabe hacker tried to display the current password but the only application he had access to was the one on his own computer.

"Crap!" he almost shouted.

♦

In the stairwell leading downward from the rooftop of the parking structure on Pennsylvania Avenue NW, some SWAT Team members were preparing to use their own explosives to blast the opening to the top level. They knew it would almost certainly set off the IED put in place by the men who had driven there with the homing beacon. But the size of the terrorists' device made them confident that the combined force of the blasts wouldn't jeopardize their ability to breach the roof. Positioned an additional floor down, the Team Leader felt certain that his men were out of harm's way.

"Three – two – one – fire in the hole!" a team member shouted.

The combined explosion of the terrorists' IED and the SWAT Team's charge blew apart the opening to the top level. The weakness of the structure caused more than the immediate area surrounding the door to collapse. But in a stroke of luck, the rubble formed a pile with the top portion of concrete rubble reaching to within eight feet of the deck above the SWAT unit. It was still too far to jump or climb but at least the path was clear.

Unfolding an assault ladder, one of the team's personnel climbed just high enough atop the debris to use a periscope to look at the van. It appeared clear. However, when he raised his head for a direct view, a bullet ricocheted off the concrete, narrowly missing him. He immediately retreated down a couple of rungs to safety.

♦

In the van, Arturo and Chico aimed their Chinese-made AK-47s at the huge hole where the door to the roof once sat. After his initial burst, Arturo held his fire. Chico changed to another weapon.

♦

On the top of an adjacent building to the west, SWAT sharpshooters desperately tried to find a clear shot. As the first shot hit Chico, only creasing his shoulder, he spun around toward the direction it had come from. SWAT knew that something more substantial than a rifle would take care of the terrorists – something on the order of a rocket launcher – but their orders were clear: maintain the integrity of the transmitter.

However, the Nicaraguans didn't share their restriction on using such a destructive weapon. Chico raised his rocket launcher and fired toward the sniper. The device's missile slammed into the side of the wall, failing to take out the sharpshooter. However, it collapsed a section of the façade on the top edge of the wall, forcing the sniper and spotter to scramble to new cover from their now-exposed position.

On the north side of the parking garage, an FBI helicopter belonging to their Critical Incident Response Group had moved from ground level to rise vertically along the wall to allow agents to drop onto the roof while their associates distracted the terrorists. The presence of a rocket launcher required a change.

The CIRG Agent-in-charge bellowed through the various headsets, "Helo 1, ABORT! ABORT! ABORT!"

The Sikorsky Blackhawk chopper pilot immediately halted his vertical ascent and moved a safe distance away.

♦

Staff members briefed Ambassador Torrez, who sat nervously drinking tequila.

"*Sí*, Ambassador. The plan appears to be falling apart."

"They only have to hold out a few minutes," the chief diplomat of President Zamora to the United States of America assured his advisers, although he didn't feel the level of confidence he tried to portray.

"But the Americans will attack our home country. There will be reprisals."

"Nonsense!" Torrez bellowed. "That is why we have the new treaty with China. We do this for them, they protect us. Besides, once the plan is completed, America will be so crippled – emotionally and in their government – that it will be in no position to retaliate."

"What if it fails?" a senior staff member worried.

The infuriated statesman slammed his fist on his desk. In doing so he toppled his drink and sent the ashtray with his lit Cuban cigar crashing to the floor, enraging him further.

"WE WILL NOT FAIL!" he thundered. In his mind, he wondered if that would be true.

♦

By the time the UAV had detected the signal going live on top of the Pennsylvania NW parking structure and was subsequently tasked to provide video reconnaissance, the terrorists had already made their preparations to fend off an assault. The rocket launcher had been the most dramatic surprise and had caused the FBI CIRG to rethink its tactics. The immediacy of the threat by whatever it was that was homing in on the transmitter had prevented the team from taking the usual care such situations required. And now that the threat was believed to be related to the Chinese rocket, there was no time to plan extensively.

Grenades or other remotely controlled explosives were out because of the danger to the device itself.

The SWAT agents were huddled on the floor beneath the top one. The Agent-in-charge had instructed them to make an all-out assault. They had placed an additional ladder alongside the first one. But with only two men able to breach the roof at a time, a second tactic was being prepared. Along the south wall of the next-to-top floor, agents were setting up to send a team member to the top level. Unit agents had raised a rigid aluminum assault ladder vertically until the hooks at the top of each rail were successfully secured to the concrete wall at the edge of the uppermost level. The bottom of the ladder was pulled tight and secured on the floor on which the team was staged.

An agent raised a handheld periscope for a look at their targets above them. Seeing nothing consequential, the observer pointed at another team member and shouted "GO!" The man swung over the concrete barrier onto the ladder. With its sling over his head, he rested his Colt M4 carbine in the crooks of his elbows and began to ascend the ladder. Feet on the highest rung on which his head wouldn't be visible over the barrier, the SWAT agent paused and raised a small mirror over the wall for a final visual check.

The sight caused near-panic as he saw one of the terrorists pointing his rocket launcher directly at his position. He had just begun to scramble back down when the impact of the explosive rocket hit the wall holding the ladder. Before the climber could jump onto the floor toward his teammates, his ladder fell over him. Additional SWAT agents joined the two who were already belaying the ladder with the rope. They were barely able to hold the assault ladder as it swung toward the ground. The climber's carbine fell, dangling from its sling as he hooked his right arm around the now upside-down aluminum frame. The desperate grab slowed his descent but as pieces of concrete tumbled on top of him, his grip failed, and he crashed the three stories to the concrete drive beneath him.

The slight break in his fall allowed him to land feet first, with only a broken ankle.

The leader of the planned assault team thought through what had just occurred. There was no way the Nicaraguan terrorist could have seen the agent climbing toward his perch. There was only one logical conclusion.

"Command, we have a problem. Those guys have a spotter somewhere."

♦

Retired Green Beret Tom Lechler listened to the operation through his headset. The assault was falling apart. Lechler had been hovering in his Bell 407 near the Capitol. He decided to creep forward. He eased nearly a half mile toward the parking garage. That put him within four hundred yards of the structure.

The ex-operator settled into an altitude of about three hundred feet and engaged the HOV function on his aircraft. Instantly the chopper's computer took control of the cyclic, collective, and pedals. The auto-hover function freed up Lechler to take a look around through binoculars. There were a number of people on roofs of a number of buildings whose attention had been drawn in the direction of the explosions.

The scene was so crowded with onlookers that the retired Master Sergeant might not have picked out the person of interest had he not been looking directly toward him and then alternately toward the parking structure. When Lechler pointed his glass back toward the roof of the garage, one of the men turned his attention directly toward the helicopter.

"That has to be the spotter," Lechler deduced. He radioed the location to the SWAT commander. "Problem is that it's gonna take some time to get a team there and they can't take the guy out without more of a rationale than I've provided."

The Blackhawk that had abandoned its plan to drop agents onto the parking structure had moved about a mile away in order to maintain what the commander thought was a safe distance from the rocket launcher. Upon hearing Lechler's information, the pilot of that chopper moved for a closer look at the presumed spotter. As he did, the man guarding the transmitter turned the launcher toward that helicopter and fired. The

Blackhawk took evasive action immediately and the projectile missed narrowly.

At the same time that he saw the terrorist turn his attention to the Critical Incident Response Group's helo, Lechler deactivated the auto-hover and assumed manual control of his craft. He raced at nearly full speed toward the roof of the parking structure.

On the rooftop, Arturo was desperately attempting to rearm his launcher while looking frantically toward the Bell helicopter speeding toward him. Just as he had inserted another rocket, the aircraft arrived. Using the collective, Lechler lowered to the corrected altitude. Left pedal turned the nose of his 407 to port, though the motion of the chopper continued toward the terrorist. The former Army Special Forces sergeant eased his throttle to slow his momentum as the craft slipped sideways toward the man raising the launcher. Just as the man aimed toward the chopper the right-side skid slammed into him. As he fell, the rocket screamed skyward from the shoulder-mounted tube.

As Arturo scrambled to his feet, Chico left the protection of the van for a better aim at the helicopter pilot. As soon as he did, he was dropped by a single shot by the sniper on the building to the parking garage's west.

Tom Lechler saw Arturo steal a momentary glance toward his dead partner. The ex-sergeant's position from his approach to knock the man down left him with a direct line of sight of him from the pilot-side seat on the right. He dropped the window and fired his Sig Sauer. The first shot hit the terrorist in the center of his chest. It hardly mattered where the second one hit.

♦

Josh Morgan had been on the phone with FBI Lab Technician Carl Smith for only a few minutes. He had simultaneously used his phone as a hotspot to connect to the Internet. Through that connection Smitty had gained access to Morgan's laptop. The ex-Case Officer was seriously angry at himself for not contacting the FBI earlier.

Morgan had accessed the dead Nicaraguan's laptop with his own a while earlier but had been unable to break through the encryption. A few keystrokes had given control of the former CIA operative's computer to Smitty remotely.

The Bureau had acquired the same encryption software from Eddie Solis' computer that the Nicaraguan government had developed for its internal use. It was the same one that was on the computer in Morgan's possession.

Smitty had established the initial remote setup with Morgan's laptop and therefore *de facto* access to the other computer. Then he had turned the task of hacking into the computer to his associate lab techie, Alonzo Lane. Lane had taken some time in the last couple of days to investigate the features of the encryption app while exploring the blogger's laptop. In no time, he was into the targeted computer.

Morgan didn't feel like he had the time, nor did he have the inclination to wait on the FBI techs to prowl around the laptop. He suggested they copy the files from it and then disconnect. He told them they had five minutes and that the clock was ticking.

♦

The records of the Norfolk Naval Base showed that Petty Officer Second Class Trinidad Alvarez hadn't yet passed through security prior to getting word to be on the lookout for him.

Alvarez had walked toward the entrance gate with his seabag and Camelbak Hydration Backpack. His heart had been racing since he awoke that morning. The coffee certainly didn't help. But he was committed to the plan. The U.S. Sailor born of Nicaraguan parents had no idea that he was being sought until he arrived at the entrance to the Naval base. Ahead of him, the place was teeming with MPs and civilian law enforcement.

One part of the plan had always been to "adopt" a new identity upon arriving inside. The Gutierrez brothers had killed one of Trini's shipmates. Alvarez had the man's credentials and uniform. The slain Petty Officer was third class, one rank junior to that of Alvarez. He was chosen because he was of similar size and appearance. The PO2 decided he would make the change of uniform and his identity to that of his shipmate early and try to gain entrance to the base as the dead PO3.

Alvarez retreated to the coffee shop where he had tried to calm his nerves. He felt that the change of his nametag and insignia rank would be so subtle that nobody would notice. After his change of uniform in the restroom, he took a seat in a booth at the diner again. He finally decided that he would never get onboard the carrier as an impostor; let alone himself.

Fortunately, he had been given a Plan B.

♦

Having dispatched one of the terrorists and seeing the FBI sniper take care of the second, Tom Lechler landed on the roof of the parking garage. By the time SWAT agents had scrambled up the debris from the collapse of the stairwell to the top of the structure from the floor below, the former sergeant had already retrieved the transmitter from the roof of the white van. He had attached a flotation device to it and tied the secured unit to a line that was in turn connected to the bottom of the Bell 407's fuselage.

As black-clad men trotted toward him, Lechler lifted off with a thumbs-up, which was returned by the entire SWAT Team.

The plan was for Tom Lechler to fly his helicopter over Maryland to the coast of Delaware, where he would hover while waiting for the Chinese rocket to come to him. Rather than keeping the homing beacon in the 407, he had been ordered to dangle it about fifteen feet from the bottom in an effort to maintain clear line of sight with the inbound booster. Analysts feared that if line of sight were lost, the rocket might fall into a densely populated area, causing the very catastrophe everyone was working to prevent. In addition, if its payload turned out to be nuclear, crashing anywhere on land would be cataclysmic.

Once the DoD's Space Surveillance Network determined that the falling booster was approaching the two-hundred-mile range of the beacon, Lechler would race eastward in the Bell helicopter. The disparity in the rocket's speed versus his own meant that the ex-ops warrior would never be able to outrun it. At some point, he would drop the device into the Atlantic and get the hell out of the area. Everyone hoped he would be able to fly clear of the blast zone – whatever "blast" meant.

The brainiacs who had come up with this plan had told the former Green Beret to use his "own judgement" about when to drop his package and run for it.

"If I was using my own judgement," Lechler had thought more than once, "I wouldn't even be here."

♦

Once the metaphorical door to the terrorists' computer had been opened, it wasn't difficult to find files related to the nature of the threat posed by Nicaragua. And it was obvious that they were acting as surrogates for Communist China. Morgan panicked as he thought of the rocket heading toward D.C., knowing that Maggie was in Washington. But he knew that the best analysts in the world were already working on that prong of the attack. And if they needed any more information, Morgan knew that back in the FBI lab Smith and Lane were seeing the same files he was.

The more immediate concern to the ex-spook was dealing with the other prong of the attack that was unfolding in Norfolk. It was the only part of the strike that he could impact.

Morgan called the CIA Director, who conferenced in FBI Director Austin, who subsequently added some of his staff at the Hoover Building and from the Bureau's Norfolk Field Office to the call.

Morgan knew he didn't have the time, but he had to ask. "Are you on top of the issue with the rocket?"

"Yes. You were right about it. Lechler is flying the transponder out to sea to try to guide the rocket there."

The ex-CIA spy had thought to himself several times what a stupid idea the plan with Lechler was. Only thing was, he couldn't come up with a better one. He moved on to the more urgent matter.

"Okay. The other part of the attack is chemical, all right. The plan is to board the George Washington for his deployment and release the agent aboard the ship."

National Security Adviser Edgar Templeton was also on the call from his office near that of the President.

"Any idea what kind of agent?" Templeton inquired.

"The data on the laptop suggests VX," Morgan said with a grimace.

Every face in Ed Templeton's office bespoke their alarm at the news.

"You there?" Morgan asked after several seconds of silence.

FBI Director Austin broke the silence. "Yeah, I think we're all still here, Morgan. Just taking a sec to come to terms with that."

"Yeah, I know," Morgan agreed.

The Special Agent in Charge of the FBI's Norfolk Field Office spoke next.

"But how do they handle that to release it? I thought that was particularly nasty stuff?"

Penny Severi, one of a number of FBI experts in various fields of concern related to chemical and bioterrorism who were in the Bureau head's office spoke up.

"I might have an answer to that."

"Is it as bad as in *The Rock*?" Morgan asked, referring to the Sean Connery/Nicholas Cage movie.

"In a word, yes," Dr. Severi lamented. "However, there are some differences. First, it's a thick, oily substance with a consistency like honey – not a gas. And your face doesn't explode. You'll suffocate inside your own body. Acetylcholine, a neurotransmitter, binds to receptors on the outside of muscle fibers, causing them to contract. Victims can't breathe because their muscles can't relax."

Silence overtook the group again.

"That's unbelievable. If you don't mind, then, I'm going to leave this with you and get back to work here," Morgan remarked, with a pained expression that nobody could see and left the call.

"So again, how can someone handle the stuff?" FBI Director Austin asked.

"They don't. At least not directly. VX is a binary agent, meaning it isn't stored in its active state. It requires two precursors that are less toxic than the activated VX. Even VX weapons have precursors that are separated and only allowed to come together when the weapon has been armed."

"You're saying that the precursors to the VX aren't harmful?" Director Austin asked.

"Often not. They're at least *less* harmful. For example, in 2017, two women assassinated Kim Jong-nam using VX. At one time he was thought to be the heir apparent to his dad, Korean dictator Kim Jong-il, but he embarrassed the regime and was pretty much shunned. Anyhow, one of the women grabbed Kim from behind and splashed a liquid on his face. The other covered his face with a cloth saturated with another liquid."

"And they were precursors. The combination of the two activated as VX," NSA Director McClintock deduced.

"Yes. Or at least that's what investigators have concluded about the assassination," Dr. Severi confirmed. "If the women had used it in its composite form as VX, even wearing gloves wouldn't have helped. The fumes would've killed the attackers. You see, you can produce VX by mixing an agent called Isopropyl aminoethylmethyl phosphonite, known as QL with dimethyl polysulfide, known as agent NM. It's a liquid sulfur compound. It is thought that the two women who assassinated Kim used those two chemicals."

"Oh, my God," CIA Boss Parnell exclaimed. "So, this sailor could transport the two parts safely…"

"Relatively so," corrected chemical weapons expert Severi.

"… and then mix the components… Oh, my God," Parnell repeated more forcefully.

"How deadly?" asked the FBI's Director.

"Five to ten milligrams will kill the average person."

Director Austin held up his palms and shrugged.

"That's thirty-five one hundredths of an ounce," Severi said in an attempt to clarify. Still seeing confusion on the Bureau chief's face, she said, "Imagine a few flakes of Mozzarella cheese. And that's if absorbed through the skin. Lethality is less if inhaled."

"How quick?" Parnell asked.

"Kim was able to report the attack but died on the way to the hospital."

♦

As soon as the pilot of the Blackhawk carrying the FBI's CIRG saw Lechler successfully retrieve the device from the parking garage's rooftop, he immediately flew to the location of the suspected spotter for the terrorists who had activated the beacon.

The man who had relayed information to his countrymen about possible threats to the plan had run to the metal door that led down a flight of steps and into the interior of the building upon which he had been situated. When the elevator was slow in arriving, he rushed to the stairwell and began his descent of the eight flights of stairs that covered the four floors to ground level.

When FBI agents on the helicopter saw the suspect abandon his lookout post, they were confident that he was indeed the person who had served as the sentry for the other men. The chopper hovered at about roof level and eight black-uniformed men fast-roped to the ground and deployed to positions guarding the exits.

The combination of his running and the poor reception his phone got inside the stairwell made placing and completing a call difficult. But as soon as he burst through the door into the lobby of the building, his reception improved, and the connection was made. He was about to report the failure of the device's deployment to his superiors from the Nicaraguan Embassy when he exited and found four armed FBI agents aiming their weapons at him. His first instinct was to run, but the shouting of the men convinced him of the futility of trying to escape.

His thumb inadvertently brushed the circular red icon and disconnected his call, and he dropped the phone. Instantly agents were on top of him, yanking his arms behind him and securing him with zip ties.

♦

Head of the Nicaraguan Mission to the United States Octavio Torrez heard the panic in the voice of his attaché.

"*Señor*, his call ended abruptly. And for a moment, we heard shouts."

Another of the envoy's aides added further bad news.

"We cannot reach our two men with the transmitter. I will send an update to *El Presidente*."

Ambassador Torrez's rage was surpassed only by his fear of reporting the news to President Zamora.

"No!"

"But Ambassador, we…"

"You will not! We know nothing for certain. We will not report until we do."

The diplomat and his senior staff sat in a safe house about two hours west-southwest of Washington, in Harrisburg, Virginia, to where they had fled secretly overnight. None of the staff they left behind at the Embassy knew of the plan to bring the payload of the supposedly wayward rocket booster down in the District of Columbia or the personal danger they faced in being left behind. Even the two men deploying the transmitter didn't understand the result of their efforts and that they would die.

♦

Master Sergeant Thomas Lechler, U.S. Army, Retired, hovered over the Atlantic coast of Delaware. All communications with government advisers had dealt only with the specifics of his mission – until now.

"Josh Morgan knows all about my family. He'll know who to notify in the event that… Well, if I'm not able to," Lechler said. Then he immediately turned the conversation back to the matter of the incoming Chinese rocket.

"How far out?" he asked of the DoD's Space Surveillance Network.

"Mid-U.S. Time to roll. It'll close sufficiently soon enough."

The ex-Green Beret nudged the cyclic pitch control forward. The main rotor of the Bell 407 tilted forward in response and the craft began to move slowly ahead in an easterly direction.

"Master Sergeant, the rocket is beginning to break up, I guess."

"You *guess*!?" the unforgiving pilot said. "What the hell does that mean – you guess?"

"A single piece has broken off. The bulk of the object is still intact. In fact, it appears to be on the course we originally predicted for it; the North Atlantic. We might be in the clear."

"What about the other piece?"

"It's moving considerably slower. Perhaps four-hundred-fifty MPH."

"Where's it headed?"

"Uh, lower trajectory. It's descending more rapidly. Due to the slower speed, we presume. Good news is that it's too small to do too much damage. And I think it'll miss D.C. Of course, that's not good news for the surrounding area. Wait a sec…"

The technician monitoring the space junk looked at his screens.

"This doesn't make a bit of sense. It's sort of wandering all over the place. And it's leveling."

Lechler immediately spun his chopper around and reversed course toward Washington.

"It's not wandering. It's searching! It's a damned missile!" he shouted to the Space Surveillance Network command.

♦

Over the Indiana-Ohio border at an altitude of about one hundred miles, a Chinese missile of about twelve feet in length and tipped with a low-yield nuclear bomb of ten kilotons sped along at two-hundred-fifty miles per hour.

Its airburst detonation would create a fireball of nearly five hundred feet and a radiation radius of two-thirds of a mile. Within that radius, the iodizing radiation dose would reach five hundred roentgen equivalent man. Five hundred REM would result in death by radiation poisoning within about one month for almost everyone who survived the fireball. Around fifteen percent of subsequent survivors would eventually die of cancer.

Third degree burns would be almost universal for any survivors of the blast within the thermal radiation radius of one mile. The results would be over eighty-four thousand fatalities and over one-hundred-seventy-five thousand injuries.

The fireball, if detonated over the parking garage where the homing beacon was intended to be, would annihilate the White House. The moderate damage radius would extend past the Capitol Building.

♦

Inside the White House, Secret Service agents were practically carrying POTUS. With no time to move Hendrickson to the bunker hidden away in Virginia's Blue Ridge Mountains, they were hustling her to the one built under the White House in the 1950s. Various staff rapidly followed.

♦

Tom Lechler had turned the Bell Helicopter Model 407 around and was pushing the chopper to its limits at full throttle. At its maximum airspeed of one-hundred-sixty miles per hour, it had covered the distance back to the Maryland border in just over fifteen minutes after departing from its position off of Rehoboth Beach. He figured that put him about seventy-five miles from Washington; and something farther than that distance from the missile. The helicopter's speed was sweeping the dangling transmitter aft and upward toward the fuselage.

"Dammit, command! Tell me what you're seeing. What's the fucking missile doing?"

"It's uh… Hold on, Master Sergeant." The voice carried a distinct tone of near panic.

"Don't 'uh, hold' me!" the pilot ordered. "I really need to turn this thing around!"

"It's leveling... Yeah, it's leveling! I think it's got you – I mean... the transmitter!" The disembodied voice had morphed into exuberance.

Lechler banked hard to port. His airspeed created a larger turn radius than he would've preferred.

The technician confirmed his report with additional information. "It's about two miles high. It's going to miss us."

"His '*us*' doesn't include me," the helicopter's pilot thought. "At least, not yet." The completion of his about-face put him on a course that would put him over the coast north of Bethany Beach, Delaware.

As most pilots do, the former special ops warrior had put a photo of his family on the aircraft's instrument panel. Center in the group in the dozen year-old image, he and his recently estranged wife smiled – not at the camera but at the joy of being with each other and their kids.

"Doesn't seem that long ago right now," Lechler realized and said so quietly.

"Say again, Master Sergeant?" the tech replied.

"Nothing. Just keep giving me updates, kid."

At various intervals, the technician at the Space Surveillance Network's command provided the chopper pilot with current data on the distance of the missile, its rate of closure, and the time to overtake him. Lechler was on the Atlantic coastline. At his craft's maximum speed, it had taken him fourteen minutes to get there from his turnaround point.

"Master Sergeant, it's time you drop the homing beacon. The missile is less than sixty-five miles behind you. And closing awfully fast, I might add."

"Negative. Too close to the coast. If that thing's a nuke – even a small one - an airburst will take out a lot of folks."

A different voice came through the pilot's headset. "Master Sergeant, this is Colonel Biggs. Your orders were to get that thing out of D.C. You've done that. Drop that package while you can still get the hell out of there."

"Negative, Colonel," Lechler said.

♦

Hearing the crackle of static over the speaker, Colonel Biggs demanded of his techie, "What the hell just happened?!"

"Sir, I believe he turned off his radio."

"Lechler!" the Army officer thundered into the microphone. There was more static. "Goddammed heroic bastard," he said somewhat quietly with equal parts admiration and anger.

♦

"That was going nowhere," the pilot said after flipping his comm switch off. "Now, how far out is good enough?"

He reached for his family photograph, brushed his fingertips lightly across it. He lifted it to his lips for only a moment before tucking it away in his jacket.

♦

At the command center, Colonel Biggs sat beside the techie. "What's he up to?"

The Army Sergeant First Class looked from his screen tracking the missile to a secondary screen of the type used by Air Traffic Control at major airports.

"He's losing altitude fast, sir."

"He's crashing?!"

"I don't think so, Colonel. I think he's just descending very rapidly."

"Could be he's going lower to drop the device. Maybe he's concerned that dropping it from too high would damage it."

"Could be, sir." The SFC paused. "We've lost him, Colonel. He's below radar coverage."

"I guess we can only wait."

♦

In the White House bunker, the Chairman of the Joint Chiefs of Staff received the update from Colonel Biggs and relayed the information to The President's Chief of Staff.

Chandler stood by as POTUS ended a call she was on. He passed the update on to his boss.

"When will we know?" Hendrickson asked her Chief.

"Satellites and other sensors will detect an explosion, if, as we expect, there is one. Then we'll know the nature of the payload, the extent of the blast, and damage, should there be any."

President Hendrickson said nothing. She was at a loss.

Though the immediate danger to the White House and central Washington appeared to have passed, none of the people in the bunker moved. All waited for information – confirmation of what occurred. In about fifteen minutes, they had their answer. This time the call came to the President's National Security Adviser Edgar Templeton.

"That was McClintock at NSA. They've received confirmation from their resources as well as from DoD of a low-yield nuclear explosion. It was about forty-five miles off the coast."

President Hendrickson stood. "Any word from the Master Sergeant?"

"No, ma'am. And there's one other thing," continued Templeton. "The detonation was an airburst. Low altitude but in the air."

"Not on the surface of the water?"

"No, ma'am."

"What else do we know?" she asked.

"We won't know for sure until we collect more data, but it appears the missile detonated at an altitude of four-hundred-seventy feet above sea level."

"Then that can only mean…"

"Yes, ma'am. The transmitter was still attached to the helicopter," Chief of Staff Chandler finished.

"Not necessarily," the National Security Adviser corrected. "The payload was probably set to go off when it reached a specific altitude above the beacon – say four hundred feet."

"But why would he fly so far out to sea, Ed?"

"The last word DoD got from him was that he needed to get farther away from populated areas. And he was right. Every minute he flew that chopper, the more time he bought before it detonated. That saved a lot of lives. Exploding that low also saved lives. It behaved more like a surface detonation because of the extremely low altitude. There'll be nuclear fallout, but even with surface detonation, it would've been catastrophic anywhere near the coast. And Master Sergeant Lechler saved many more lives by taking it so far offshore than had he merely led that thing some place away from Washington."

The President's National Security Adviser took another call. Everyone watched for any facial expression or other sign that would signal good news regarding their helicopter pilot.

Even before hanging up from the call, he looked at POTUS and shook his head.

"No word from the Master Sergeant. And nothing picked up from the helicopter's transponder or any sign of it on radar. I think it's safe to assume that Lechler is lost."

President Sandra Hendrickson only nodded. She sank into her chair and swiveled away from her staff. She placed her forearms on the conference table and sat quietly. Finally, she rested her forehead in her palm.

After nearly two minutes of silence, POTUS collected herself. Rising, she pulled at the bottom of her suit jacket, straightening it.

"General Richards," she said to the Joint Chiefs Chairman, "this constitutes an act of war. Please work with the National Security Adviser and everyone needed to plan a response. Chief Chandler, contact everyone else and inform them that the danger has passed. They can come out of their various bunkers and other shelters. And get Secretary of State Lively here now. We'll have to formulate our diplomatic approach… if there can even be one to such a despicable act."

Finally, POTUS turned to a woman who was in the White House bunker with her. She was in tears.

"Maggie, you should call Josh."

CHAPTER 43

In their safehouse in Harrisburg, Virginia, Nicaraguan Ambassador Torrez and his staff sat stunned at the report that the plot they had agreed to execute in participation with China had not succeeded. They knew that the failure left them in a weak position with respect to their intended victim, the United States. Intending to cripple the governmental structure, success would've weakened any response that might've come and allowed the Chinese to move on American interests abroad.

"But, Ambassador, the Americans know that the device was at our embassy. They'll know…"

"Shut up, you fucking little shit!" he roared in his native tongue. "Don't you think I understand the consequences. Every one of you who was involved in this disaster is a dead man."

The Head of the Nicaraguan delegation to the U.S. flung his drink at the nearest man. Then the ambassador sprang to his feet and began swinging his arms at everything within reach, breaking lamps, chairs, and more. He clutched his hair with both hands and unleashed a guttural scream.

His aide approached, whom he shoved to the floor. Almost whimpering, the man held a cell phone to his boss from his seated position.

"President Zamora," he said softly, continuing to lift the phone to Torrez.

The ambassador's face was pallid, and his eyes were wide. He knew the call would come, but it happened far sooner than he had anticipated. Droplets of sweat burst almost instantly from his forehead. He reached for the phone timidly.

"*Si, excelencia*," the diplomat finally managed to say.

♦

In Norfolk, efforts to locate sailor Trinidad Alvarez had been unsuccessful. The Military Police at the Naval Station were at their highest alert. FBI agents and local police were swarming the streets.

The Petty Officer's animosity toward the United States and her military hadn't begun to grow until well after the day he took his oath. When he was at sea, he actually enjoyed the camaraderie of his shipmates, even his job. But the deaths of his parents in an act of random violence had taken an emotional toll and afterward, each time he returned home, he socialized with Nicaraguan natives. They were not as enthusiastic about the American way of life as Alvarez had been when he enlisted. He had never known that the friends he had fallen in with were agents of the Zamora regime. And those agents were grooming him for some future operation. He was, in a sense, an American-born sleeper agent for Nicaragua.

But while his hostility toward his native country was firmly embedded in his psyche now, it was founded almost exclusively in his acrimony for the military and government. Plan B, for him, moved his emotions into another arena entirely. The backup plan was to introduce the precursor agents of the altered VX compound he carried into the nearest municipal water supply.

Even though VX never dissolved as easily as some other nerve agents, it could nevertheless disperse through the water. And citizens of the city wouldn't know they had been exposed for a few days due to the gain of function of the chemical introduced by virologists in China. Knowing that a great number of the citizenry was military helped assuage Alvarez's conscience somewhat. But thinking of the innocent people who would perish here – though he had few close friends among them – made execution of the plan a difficult matter. So, he was relieved when he received the telephone call ordering him to abandon the alternative plan altogether.

Trinidad Alvarez walked to catch a bus. He knew he could never come back to Norfolk, his apartment in particular.

♦

FBI Director Austin was sharing his meeting with his specialists in the area of nerve agents with other organizations by video.

Dr. Penny Severi delivered the briefing.

"NSA Director McClintock shared this first item with me. He said most of you have seen the information but probably don't remember it. It was in the President's intelligence briefings some time ago but it's not something you pay much attention to until it becomes relevant. Director McClintock said that NSA collections revealed that several months ago, China was working on ways to delay the onset of symptoms from chemical weapons. The goal was apparently to allow for more widespread transmission before the existence of the agent became known."

There was a noticeable hush among the participants on the conference call.

"We believe Beijing's scientists have succeeded in doing just that," Dr. Severi continued. "We think that they have introduced secondary agents that can prevent symptoms from being evident within a matter of minutes to possibly as late as ten days."

"But are the victims already infected with the agent, even though they're not symptomatic?" asked FBI Director Austin.

"That's a great question. Unfortunately, the answer is that they are."

The various directors' fear of the release of the VX was increasing at the same rate as their familiarity with it.

"But they can't spread it. Right?" Director Austin hoped.

Dr. Severi advanced her presentation to the next slide. It quoted directly from the CDC. It read, "A person's clothing can release VX after contact with VX vapor, which can lead to exposure of other people through contaminated clothing."

Austin's reaction was immediate.

"So, you're telling me that this means that this altered derivative of VX *can* be contagious, for lack of a better word?" He was aghast at the implication.

"I'm afraid so. Though unlikely, it could be possible. The delayed onset of symptoms from the modification could allow the agent to linger in the body and subsequently be absorbed by clothing from the inside by way of a person's perspiration. Then any other person coming into contact with the afflicted individual through an embrace or merely by brushing against it could absorb the nerve agent."

"Like the COVID pandemic then?"

"Not exactly, sir," the expert said, "in the sense that it would be far less communicable."

"But far deadlier," Austin added.

"Yes."

♦

"I'm sorry, Josh."

Maggie's fiancé was completely silent. Tom Lechler had become his closest friend outside of his adopted hometown of Jackson Hole.

"I can't believe he's gone. Any chance…?" The former CIA Officer wanted to believe some miracle was possible but knew what his fiancée's reply would be.

"Sweetheart, he flew the helicopter almost fifty miles out to sea. There's no sign of him or the aircraft. He saved lives. Lots of 'em."

"What about wreckage?" Morgan knew it was a silly question before Maggie had time to answer. "Wouldn't be anything left from a nuke, would there?"

"They have satellites searching the area. And some UAVs. It's too hot for manned aircraft. One of the drones is equipped to measure radioactivity and check levels of fallout. Maybe soon…"

"Has anybody notified his family?"

"The President called his wife but only said that he was missing."

There was another long delay.

"Josh, why don't you come home? You've done as much as you can there. Let the agents and police handle it."

Each of the couple could tell the other was crying.

Josh Morgan decided he would go home. More than anything, he wanted to hold Maggie and be held by her.

"I'm leaving now, Maggie."

♦

As a precaution against the Americans intercepting their calls, China and Nicaragua had ended all communications between them. The two nations even suspended communications with Cuba, whose role had been minimal, only creating a ruse intended to preoccupy the American President.

Nicaraguan Ambassador Torrez and his staff had returned to the Embassy in Washington. In retrospect, they felt they were now vulnerable to any actions the President ordered. In normal times, an attack on an embassy would never be contemplated. It was considered to be as sovereign a part of its country as though it were sitting on native soil.

"But we did attack the American capital with a nuclear bomb," Torrez thought.

The diplomat called his aide.

"Is our water system prepared?"

"*Si, Embajador.*"

♦

Petty Officer Second Class Trinidad Alvarez had retrieved a small sedan the Gutierrez brothers had loaned him for his use when in port. He never envisioned that he would be escaping in it. Nor was it ever considered that he would be driving it to an alternate target. He was supposed to die on the USS George Washington with his shipmates.

Perhaps he would die anyhow. His chances of survival, though better than had he deployed on the carrier, were slim regardless. If not killed through the exposure of the altered VX, he would almost certainly die at the hands of American law enforcement. He had decided that he would accept his death as a heroic sacrifice. After all, Washington, D.C., was the seat of American power. Killing a few innocents there was hardly as troubling as it would've been in Norfolk, if only because of the high percentage of targets in Washington who worked for the American *Presidenta.*

Alvarez didn't know and it would've hardly been of consequence to his way of thinking that the capital was once considered to be the primary target for the VX until the Chinese developed the idea of the nuclear missile attack. Nor did he know that a nuclear attack was even in play. The bombing would have been crippling. The release of the VX aboard one of America's mightiest warships would have been mostly for show.

There were a variety of means the Chinese could've employed to release the VX, but the scientists had developed this particular strain to be more soluble in water than unaltered VX. And it was the very deployment of the VX in a water solution that would also cause the delay of the onset of symptoms. Exposure to the reconstituted nerve agent before it was mixed with water would be as instantly deadly as in its original form.

The delay in developing symptoms was intended to ensure that the agent spread throughout the entire crew of the U.S. Navy ship before its detection. It had also offered the possibility that the VX would be spread to other ships via helicopters and airplanes. Therefore the transmission might've grown to tremendous proportions.

Those outcomes had disappeared, but the decision to release the nerve agent in the nation's heart would be fitting. And introducing it through the water supply would delay symptoms in the seat of American treachery just as it would have on the ship.

♦

With Morgan's disregard for the speed limits, he had covered the two hundred-and-one-mile distance from Norfolk to Washington in almost exactly three hours.

Being in Maggie's arms at the doorway of her apartment broke what little strength he had left. Maggie led Josh to the couch where they both succumbed to the crush of their emotions and the pair broke down in tears.

Other than the sound of their weeping, the couple sat in utter silence for forty-five minutes. Maggie had decided to hold off in delivering her additional information until much later, but Josh asked.

"What's the latest on Tom?"

She brushed auburn locks away from her forehead and dabbed at her blue eyes with a tissue.

"It's not good, Josh," Maggie started, before she began to sob again. Josh waited until she composed herself.

"We still can't send manned craft to the area – surface or by air. But additional data has come in from satellites. The information confirms that Tom flew the helicopter the entire distance to where the blast occurred. He dropped well below radar almost as soon as he reached the coast. Some think he was hedging against any damage to the beacon that might occur if he dropped it from a higher altitude. The other thought is that, if this missile was intended to only approach within a certain distance of the transmitter and not all the way to it – you know, an airburst detonation – then Tom's lower altitude would lead the missile lower before it exploded. That would minimize the dispersal of the radioactivity."

"And that's all they know?"

"That's all they know. Well, all they've told me. They still intend to send vessels to the area when they can, but…" Maggie' hung her head and her eyes filled with mist again.

"I know, sweetheart," Josh said.

♦

When China first began to consider an attack on Washington about two years earlier, the Communist nation's original plan had been to release VX into the city's water supply. Even before the Wuhan lab had successfully altered the VX, precautions had been taken in Beijing's Embassy there. Once they had conceived of the idea of a treaty with Nicaragua, they shared that information with their future defense partner.

Inside both embassies, special water systems existed that would mitigate the danger of VX-laced water. Without those safeguards already in place, Beijing would have never considered changing the alternate target from the aircraft carrier and Norfolk to D.C.

In each of their diplomatic headquarters, water contaminated with VX would be dealt with in a manner similar to how the United States and other countries destroyed their stockpiles of nerve agents in the early 2000s. Called chemical hydrolysis, huge water reservoirs would serve as holding points for water coming into the buildings from the District of Columbia's water supply.

Technicians would release a caustic compound into the giant container that served as a reactor. The next step would be to agitate the entire mixture while heating it to an extremely high temperature. Then they would biotreat the broken down base chemical agents' solution with organic waste, using living organisms such as bacteria, fungi, or protozoa.

Then the process would employ supercritical water oxidation (SCWO), heating the water again, this time to seven hundred degrees and pressurized to over 3,200 pounds per square inch. The density of the solution would be reduced by ninety percent, allowing the organic materials that had been introduced to more easily dissolve in the liquid. At that point, the process would add fuel to hasten destruction of the waste products through oxidation.

The final step of filtering the remaining mixture would create water suitable for any purpose, including drinking. It was an elaborate, expensive addition to the diplomatic houses, but at the time, the plan would've been to expose almost the entire population of Washington to the VX. So, it was an essential safeguard.

CHAPTER 44

DAY 10 – WEDNESDAY

Maggie had fallen asleep on the couch with Josh. When she awoke, Josh was awake and on a laptop.

"Josh, sweetheart, why don't you put that up and let's go to bed. It's one o'clock."

The fiancé pulled his fiancée close and gave her a light kiss on the top of her head.

"I can't. I feel guilty leaving Norfolk. I feel like I'm giving up on the damned thing. You go on and I'll come in shortly."

"No. If you're staying, I'm staying. You want me to make some coffee?"

"Trust me. I don't need caffeine to stay awake. I'd like nothing better than to fall asleep. And maybe not wake up for a few days."

Maggie lay her head on Josh's shoulder. "I'm warning you. I might be dozing again in just a minute or two."

"That's fine. Get some rest." Josh gave Maggie another soft peck.

The auburn-haired sleepyhead's eyelids were closing when she realized something.

"That's not your laptop, is it?"

"No. Belonged to the terrorists. Guess I forgot to hand it over to the feds."

"You *forgot*. Right." A soft "mmm" followed by a barely audible "I love you" and Maggie nodded off.

"Why haven't they found you, Trini? Everyone in Virginia is looking for you," Morgan wondered silently.

When Carl Smith and Alonzo Lane at the FBI lab had remotely hacked into the computer Morgan had acquired, they removed the password protection. The ex-CIA Officer had reread everything about the planned introduction of the VX nerve agent aboard the aircraft carrier USS George Washington. He likewise pored over every document relating to the backup plan. Morgan wondered if the traitorous sailor had already dumped the toxin into Norfolk's water supply. But he knew that the FBI had all the same information from the terrorists' laptop that he was reading, so they surely had cut off all access points to the supply.

And since they had the same files, it was also unlikely that Morgan would turn up anything before they would. But he would keep looking. And maybe, he decided, coffee wasn't such a bad idea. Morgan lay Maggie down on the couch and moved to the kitchen.

As the ex-spy leaned against the kitchen counter to wait for his cup of coffee to brew, he considered an offhanded remark he had made to himself only a few minutes earlier.

"Everyone *in Virginia* is looking for you," he remembered thinking. "What if you're not in Norfolk anymore? What if you got out of there because of all the heat? And you could drop your VX anywhere that would certainly be less intensively guarded than Norfolk is right now."

Morgan poured his java and thought about the possibility that Trini had lit out – either because he feared he was about to get caught, or because he had given up on his plan altogether.

The CIA contractor retrieved the laptop from the end table by the sofa and moved to the kitchen table. Nothing in the files on the computer had mentioned any individual by name, specifically Alvarez. But since he was by all accounts a native-born U.S. citizen, then he probably had been radicalized through some affiliation with an organization or friendships.

"So, could he have gotten cold feet? Would he abandon the plan?" Morgan's gut told him that the man would press on.

"He had a backup plan in case he couldn't disperse the VX on the ship. What if he has moved on to yet another target?" Morgan wondered silently. "But what would that be?"

The files about deploying the toxin were very detailed and well-organized on the laptop. They had provided a virtual step-by-step blueprint for the attack. So, nobody had devoted as much attention to other files that seemed less involved with the plan.

"It's going to be a long night," Morgan realized.

After another hour of reading files that seemed mostly irrelevant, the investigator's weariness was palpable. He stood to stretch and paced a few steps. By now, he'd consumed so much coffee that he was slightly jittery. Morgan scratched the back of his head. Then he rubbed his eyes. The yawn that came next told him that he'd had enough for the night. So, Morgan walked toward Maggie to take her to the bedroom.

As he neared the sofa, he stopped abruptly. The former spook put the fingertips of his left hand to his lips and got the same middle-distance stare that most people did when they'd had an epiphany.

Morgan thought about some of the crude sketches that he'd studied in some of the laptop's less suspicious files. Without some basis upon which to build a theory, they'd meant nothing. The suddenly energized man returned to the kitchen table and raised the laptop's lid.

Reopening a few sketches that had apparently been scanned as PDF files, the former journalist spy wondered what sort of framework he could apply to the crude drawings to add meaning. Fortunately, the textual parts were all in Spanish so Morgan had no trouble with them.

First, Morgan looked at the file dates and determined them to be generally two years old or more. Since the primary target for the VX agent was a Navy vessel by way of a military base, why would it have been selected above other military bases? Nothing in the drawings or the written parts seemed to concern such bases.

"Maybe," Morgan considered next, "the common element I should be considering in looking for clues isn't the target, but the means of delivery." The thought took him back to some of the older document files. Since some of the sketches resembled hand drawn maps, he started there.

After three or four failed to inspire any notions of what they could represent, let alone how they might apply to terrorism, Morgan moved on. One rough drawing, however, caught his attention. The scan was poor with the lines and letters very faint. The image consisted solely of two curved lines that were near one another at each end. In their middles, they diverged from one another, giving the appearance of parentheses. Between them at their widest point was a circle, or more accurately, an oval. There was also a straight line extending perpendicular to them at the point where the separation was greatest. There was a half-circle near the end of the line.

But it was the text that sparked the ex-CIA Officer's curiosity. The creator had written words in three locations. The Spanish words "*Grandes Cascadas*" was beside the curved lines near the straight one at a right angle to them. The phrase meant "large waterfalls." The word "*pequeña*" was scribbled along one edge of the sketch. That was Spanish for "small." "*Ro*" was between the irregular lines near the oval. Morgan assumed that to be Spanish, too, because the other words were. But unless it was an abbreviation for something, the word meant nothing in Spanish. Beside the "*ro*" was a short line with a half circle at the end closest to the edge of the "page."

All the former spy could come up with was that there was a place with a large waterfall, or rather waterfalls. *Cascadas* was plural. And that was it.

"If the person who drew this was suggesting large waterfalls, then perhaps '*pequeña*' is referring to small waterfalls," Morgan thought.

He looked at the time on the computer display.

"4:15. Sheesh. And I'm not even remotely sleepy anymore," he thought.

♦

Norfolk detectives and uniformed police were searching a small alley. A pedestrian had called 911 around two o'clock that morning and reported a body near a dumpster. The caller had stayed at a nearby bar until closing and was walking to his car when he found the dead man. The discoverer had desperately needed to piss and had stepped into the alley for more privacy, though there was little traffic on the street and even fewer people on the sidewalk at that hour.

"Yes, sir. Left him right where I saw him," the finder said.

"You didn't check for a pulse or anything?" the detective inquired.

"Well, his head was practically cut off. Didn't see any point."

The corpse was that of a Hispanic male. With the urgency surrounding the VX threat, everyone hoped he would turn out to be the sailor they were hunting. The Crime Scene Unit had fingerprinted the man, who had indeed turned out to be member of the U.S. Navy; just not the one they were looking for. The large number of sailors in Norfolk prevented them from assuming any connection to Trinidad Alvarez.

The dead Petty Officer Third Class' name was Julio Quevedo.

♦

Josh Morgan was beginning to lose interest in his investigation; not because he was any less motivated to try to help locate Trini Alvarez. It was just that, for all he knew, there was nothing in the files relevant to his quest. He had moved on to other files but had returned to the one that concerned the large waterfalls.

The map – if it was one – had obviously been drawn with a pencil. There were several smudges. When Morgan zoomed in on the scan, it became very pixelated, and the faintness of the marks became more pronounced, due to the low contrast.

Wondering if he could enhance it, the examiner copied the file onto a thumb drive and transferred it to his own computer, where he launched Photoshop. He increased the contrast and made other adjustments and zoomed in to study the details. The first thing that jumped out at him was that there was a small vertical line between the "r" and the "o" in "ro." It had appeared to be a continuation of the "r" in its original form.

"*Rio*," Morgan realized. He decided to Google "large+waterfalls+river." His search turned up a huge number of the great waterfalls of the world, so he added "united states." The revised results were indeed limited to the United States. Most were in the West, and none were in heavily populated locales.

"If this has anything to do with putting VX in a water supply source, the terrorists wouldn't get much bang for their buck," Morgan figured.

He returned to the words on the image and compared them to his search's hits. Nothing seemed to fit.

"What if '*grande*' means 'great,' and not 'large' in this case?" he considered. "Great waterfalls. Hmm. Great *falls*, maybe? Great Falls, Montana, perhaps?"

Morgan pulled up information about the Western city, but suddenly didn't feel like reading it. He scratched his head and stretched with a lengthy yawn. He laid his head on his arms on the kitchen table and fell asleep.

♦

The Special Agents from the FBI's Field Office and their local law enforcement counterparts were as frustrated in their search as Morgan was. All had concluded that there was no obvious connection between their terror suspect and the dead sailor that they had found. The city remained on high alert and authorities were considering locking it down.

♦

It was 5:40 AM and Josh stirred with the touch of a hand gentling shaking him.

"Josh… Josh," Maggie whispered to avoid waking him too abruptly.

He asked and heard the time. The two shared a "good morning" kiss.

"Any luck?"

"Not really. Read a few things and kept coming back to this one rough map. At least I think it's a map. The only thing I could relate it to was Great Falls." The groggy man touched the screen and brought his laptop to life. "But why would the Nicaraguans care anything at all about Great Falls?"

"Virginia?" Maggie asked.

"Montana," Josh corrected. "Wait… Why'd you say that?"

Maggie shrugged. "I don't know. But there's a Great Falls in Virginia. It's right across the Potomac from Maryland. I only know because right after you left… Well, after we, uh…"

"Just go on, Maggie."

"Well, I distracted myself with some sightseeing. There are some nice things in the Great Falls area. There's a neat old tavern…" Maggie stopped as soon as she saw Josh was no longer listening.

Her fiancé typed "great falls+virginia+little+potomac" into his browser's search field and pressed "enter."

The very first search result was "Little Falls (Potomac River) – Wikipedia" with a subordinate result of "Great Falls (Potomac River) – Wikipedia."

"There's also a Little Falls – *pequeña cascadas*," he mumbled.

He added "washington" to his search and came up with results that mostly had to do with outdoor activities – too many to browse through.

He lowered his head and muttered, "Come on. Think." Then he remembered what had occurred to him as the thing that might add some context to any plans the Nicaraguans might have.

"Water supply!" he blurted more loudly. Maggie could almost see the wheels turning in Josh's head as he added the two words to refine his search.

The second hit was a post titled "From the Potomac to your Pipes – DC Water." He hurriedly clicked on the link to the "DC Water" site and in short order learned that the U.S. Army Corps of Engineers had a water treatment plant called the Washington Aqueduct that collected water from the Potomac River at Great Falls and Little Falls. Drinking water for the District of Columbia came from the Potomac River through the Aqueduct, which treated it to make sure it was up to federal drinking water standards. Washington, D.C. purchased drinking water from the Washington Aqueduct to distribute to customers.

Morgan searched Google Maps for "Washington Aqueduct."

He turned his attention back to the hand-drawn map and compared it to one of the real thing. "*Río*" represented the Potomac near the Aqueduct. The "oval" represented Conn Island in a place where the river splits to go around it. The line leading away from there was an arrow with the half-circle being a haphazardly drawn arrow point. It likely pointed to the Aqueduct.

"Oh, shit!" he exclaimed.

He looked at Maggie and said, "They're going to poison the Washington water supply."

♦

PO2 Trinidad Alvarez was still wearing the uniform of his dead friend Petty Officer Third Class Julio Quevedo. He had no civilian clothes in his sea bag and all the apparel that was in there was his own and therefore carried his name. He wanted to purchase new clothes but felt like the exposure of his face – which was bound to be all over the news by now – was too great a risk. Instead, he ripped Quevedo's name patch off his blouse.

The handlers who had given him his package had been clear. The VX had to be delivered into a water supply after it had been treated. Preparing raw water for human consumption would scrub some of the toxin away – not much, but some. There was also the likelihood that, since the VX was by nature slow to disperse and blend with water, much would remain in the water treatment facility. The chemists in China had enhanced the VX Alvarez carried so that it would mix more efficiently than the original, unaltered VX agent would have. And water also activated the delayed symptoms component.

The traitor had arrived in Washington after dark and had tried to sleep in his car. But his fear of capture had made sleep impossible. The revised plan was disorganized. D.C. was the target but the means of introducing the nerve agent was up to Alvarez to determine. Almost two years before, when the capital had been considered as the primary target, the planning hadn't gotten that far before it was abandoned.

The Petty Officer had to scout for a location during the day since he wouldn't be able to in the dark. But he had to perform his act of terror – though he never regarded it as such – under the cover of night. So, the U.S. Navy Sailor would have to select a point in the water lines by day, hide for the remainder of daytime hours, then act as soon as it was completely dark.

His Camelbak Hydration backpack contained QL, or Isopropyl aminoethylmethyl phosphonite, the first of the two precursors that would combine to create the final VX agent. The second precursor was incorporated into a modified stainless-steel water bottle. The top three-fourths of the thirty-two-ounce container held agent NM, or dimethyl polysulfide. Beneath the solution was a disc filled with calcium hydride. The very bottom of the bottle had a small explosive charge.

The seaman of Nicaraguan descent would open the fill port of the backpack and hang it by its straps over an opening into whatever water main that he had found. Then he would pull the water bottle's lanyard forcefully to release a pin that served as a safety on the device. Once he had disengaged the pin, a simple full clockwise turn of the water bottle's lid would start a timer that would trigger the explosive thirty seconds later. Then PO2 Alvarez would attach the stainless-steel unit to the pack with its strap and drop the combined assembly into the flowing water of the city supply. The explosive charge would expel the calcium hydride disc and agent NM while the QL agent would be spilling through where the charge had ripped apart the Camelbak. Once the disc of calcium hydride came apart in the water, the chemical would begin to create gas bubbles that would serve to agitate the two agents as they began to bond. In addition to stirring the mixture to speed up the reaction, the bubbles would also speed the combined agents' dispersion into the water. It was a process based on what submarines used to create bubble curtains to act as countermeasures against torpedoes.

Alvarez's task was simple in concept, but the execution would be very difficult – locate a vulnerable spot in a water transmission pipe by day; cut a hole in it and introduce the two VX precursor agents under the cloak of darkness.

"No problem," the terrorist thought to himself.

♦

As she had for the past several nights, and many more times during her tenure as Director of the Central Intelligence Agency, Elizabeth Parnell had slept in her office. She had learned to sleep as well there as at her apartment, which was not very well at all. So, she was already half-awake when her phone rang.

"I'll spread the word, Morgan, but you've got to admit, it's thin."

"I disagree, Betsy. I think it was looked at as a target a couple of years ago, so maybe they've come back to it."

"Hold on. I did say I would pass it along. I've learned not to dismiss any of your hairbrained ideas out of hand. By the way, the FBI Director told me that they thought they had tumbled onto something in Norfolk. Came across a dead sailor in an alley."

"Any connection to Alvarez?"

"Not that they could find, but they're still looking into it. 'No stone unturned,' and all that."

"What's his name, Betsy?"

"Uh…" Parnell looked at some notes. "Julio Quevedo."

"Hispanic?"

"Yeah, but there are a lot of Latinos in Norfolk. And in the Navy."

"Okay. I might do some snooping around myself about the Washington Aqueduct."

"Thought you might. One more thing, Josh…"

"Yes?"

"Sorry about Tom. I know you two had become good friends."

"Yeah."

♦

The White House Press Secretary had long since gone to work. Her fiancé had studied more documents on the laptop but had come up empty with regard to more specific information about a starting point for a terrorist plot against Washington, D.C.

Instead, the ex-spy did an Internet search on Julio Quevedo. He partied quite a bit, as evidenced by his extensive presence on social media. And he was proud of where he'd been, whom he'd met, the people he'd hung with, and the women he'd dated. And all of the above, it seemed, made it into the pictures on his online accounts, all of which were "public."

Morgan realized he had never looked at Trinidad Alvarez's online footprint. He searched Facebook, Instagram, and all the other prominent sites. Alvarez's presence was very meager, especially when compared to the dead sailor's. Morgan clicked on the "Friends" tab on Facebook. Alvarez had forty-eight.

"Wow," the browser said to himself. "I thought mine was lame."

He rested his elbow on the kitchen table and his chin on his hand as he quickly clicked through each "friend." Quevedo's name wasn't there. Morgan went to the "Photos" tab. There were very few pictures there, as well, so the former CIA Officer decided to flip through them. He came to a series of three photographs that appeared to be taken at some Navy function. Trinidad Alvarez appeared in each with other sailors. He froze instantly at one of the shots.

The particular photo that drew his interest was of four sailors. Three of the men's names on their blouses were clearly visible. The fourth man was standing next to Alvarez and was leaning in such a way that his name was partly obscured. Morgan downloaded the photo from the site and opened it on his screen. He enlarged it as much as he could.

Despite the poor resolution, on the sailor's Navy Working Uniform he clearly read the last four letters of the last name.

"-VEDO"

Morgan returned to Quevedo's page and compared his face to the one of the sailors in Alvarez's photo.

"Close, but I'm not sure."

He had another thought. Morgan selected "Photos" on Quevedo's account and started digitally flipping through the dead sailor's images.

"I'll be damned," Morgan whispered as he looked at the same photo that he had seen on Alvarez's page. "They did know each other."

♦

The web of water mains that distributed water throughout Washington, D.C. all originated from the Washington Aqueduct and fanned out through the city. Most lay underground but there were a few places where the water had to be delivered across a creek. At these points, the large pipes crossed the waterway through the air. Sometimes they were attached to an automobile bridge or pedestrian walkway. Other times, when no other means was nearby to assist, they were suspended alone on their own supports.

Trinidad Alvarez had found one such structure. It was therefore more remote than it would have been were it attached to something else that was a means of carrying vehicles or people across the creek. A few feet before the pipe reached the point where it was above the water, it emerged from the ground.

The out-of-the-way location allowed for the privacy the Petty Officer would need, but the difficulty of penetrating the pipe was a formidable one. It was metal so a sledgehammer would be of little use. An acetylene torch would be most efficient but too cumbersome to get to the location.

Alvarez was at a loss, so the terrorist sailor decided he would check out the nearby area for any construction sites that might have tools he could steal and use.

♦

"Austin said he's having some of his agents look into it, Josh, but they still believe Norfolk is where the action is," the CIA Director said of her FBI counterpart.

"Even after my call earlier telling you that I established that Alvarez and Quevedo knew each other?"

"Maybe especially because of that. Quevedo's body was found in Norfolk. Alvarez was last seen in Norfolk."

"What was Quevedo's TOD, Betsy?"

"A couple of days ago, but…"

"So, if Alvarez killed him, that gives him plenty of time to get out of town. Right?"

"Josh, Austin said he'd have some guys check it out. But he's dispatched a lot of his Washington guys to Norfolk. Plus, you haven't given him any specific place to look. Do you know how large the water supply system is?"

"It's all I've been looking at," the exasperated former spy said.

"Well, Director Austin has had analysts looking at the same files you have been. First, they're not as convinced as you are that Washington is a current target. Secondly, the city is one of the most heavily secured metropolises in the world. And finally, if – and it's a big 'if' – if D.C. is now the primary target, the FBI techs and analysts have no better idea than you do where to look. So, agents and local police will check around. But it's an almost impossible undertaking, Josh."

"But Betsy, I…"

"Morgan, I've got to go," Parnell interrupted gruffly.

♦

Navy PO2 Trinidad Alvarez had walked the area near where he thought he would insert the VX into the city's water supply. He had found three construction sites close enough that, should he find anything useful to him, he might be able to spirit it away without much exposure.

The second closest of the work zones was a site where a multilevel office building was being built. He sat on a park bench, pretending to be on his phone, and surveyed the area. Alvarez saw a worker using one tool that he should've thought of since he had used one many times aboard the George Washington. The woman was cutting pieces of metal with a reciprocating saw of the Sawzall type. The terrorist realized instantly that the tool would be the best solution. It was battery-powered so an electrical outlet wouldn't be necessary.

However, this one, too, presented a problem: it was rather loud. Despite that, it was his best choice. Now if he could just get his hands on it.

♦

FBI Director Gabe Austin repeated what his caller had said to POTUS very recently.

"Didn't you just tell President Hendrickson that Morgan has earned a little benefit of the doubt, Betsy?"

The CIA Director normally didn't respond too well to having her words thrown back at her, but she knew her Bureau counterpart was right.

"Do you have the manpower, Gabe?"

"I can spare a couple of my agents, but I think the best approach would be to get Metro PD in on it. They can have their street officers be alert for anything suspicious."

"Aren't they anyhow?"

"Ha! Good point, Betsy. What should they be looking for now?"

Betsy Parnell thought for a moment and realized she couldn't come up with anything specific.

"Maybe someone with an 'I-heart-terrorism' t-shirt. Hell, Gabe, that's the thing. Nobody knows. We just think any attack will be against the water supply network. But like I already told Morgan, there's a lot of pipe and other facilities involved. I think the best thing would be to have the unis concentrate on the treatment facilities."

"Okay, Bets. I'll pass that along."

♦

Trinidad Alvarez, United States Sailor, had sat for a little over an hour and had decided he was on the verge of attracting too much attention by his lingering presence, if he hadn't already. He was about to leave when the construction workers broke for lunch. He sat back down.

Most of the workers left for various spots where, Alvarez assumed, they had lunchboxes. The woman who had been using the reciprocating saw off and on had set it down earlier and was carrying the products of her labor to another location several yards away. When the foreman had yelled "lunch break," she had been on one of such errands and didn't return. The thief-in-waiting decided this would be the best opportunity he would have. It was high-risk, stealing something with people around in broad daylight. But he knew that it was likely his only chance. He stood and moved toward the work area. If he got caught… Well, he figured his time was running out.

The site had a chain-link fence erected on its perimeter, but each side had a gate. And each one was open. Alvarez crossed the street and passed through the nearest opening. He tried to stay on a path such that equipment or other things would shield him from anyone's view. As he passed the location where the worker had been using the saw, the trespasser grabbed it by the handle without so much as slowing down. He let it dangle at his side that was furthest from where the laborers were congregated for lunch as he continued on a path almost directly through the fenced site.

♦

Josh Morgan was irritable and restless. He had conflicting feelings about the possible threat against Washington. On the one hand, when he had left Norfolk, he had pretty much reconciled himself to leaving the investigation and manhunt to law enforcement. On the other, he felt like he had come up with a plausible basis for reassignment of the terrorists' target to D.C. And either because they were unwilling, understaffed, or simply without a strategy to explore it, the ex-CIA Officer felt the professionals would do nothing.

With nothing better to do, Morgan had driven to a parking area near the Washington Aqueduct and walked around. The amount of security for the area was impressive, and rightfully so. Ever since the Twin Towers and the Pentagon had been attacked with almost three thousand lives lost, the nation's infrastructure had garnered a lot of attention because of its potential as targets.

The former spy and current CIA contractor even noticed that his presence was warranting a lot of interest from the facility's security. He moved on.

"No way a guy gets in there," he thought. "Besides, if Alvarez got in there, where would he introduce the VX? And if he found a way, the security measures would likely spot him, and the personnel would shut down the transmission system before the poison could get into the water supply."

Morgan continued walking but his conclusion remained the same.

"Alvarez won't act here."

Morgan got to the lot where he had parked his SUV and considered what to do next. He decided to simply use the Aqueduct as a starting point and begin to walk outward from it in the hopes that something would come to him.

He wasn't optimistic.

♦

"Hey! Get him!"

Trinidad Alvarez looked toward the voice. A man at the edge of the open second floor of the under-construction office building was pointing at him. He yelled again.

"Stop that SOB!"

As if from nowhere, two husky workers appeared behind him.

"Hey, soldier boy! You stop right there!"

The trespasser closed his eyes and stopped. A woman even huskier than the men emerged from behind a stack of wooden pallets upon which supplies had been shipped.

"You! Soldier boy! Turn your ass around!"

Alvarez faced the voice.

"What the hell do you think you're doing…?"

He was going to call him by name but saw that there was no name patch. But identifying the patch on the left breast, he corrected his previous ID.

"Okay, sailor boy. What are you doing here?"

PO2 Alvarez had already prepared his story with various details that depended on where somebody interrupted his hike across the property.

"I've been sitting over there…," he began in case he had been noticed loitering on the park bench. "…trying to get my girl to answer her damned phone. We had a big fight and… Well, she finally picked up and said if I'd come over, we'd try to work things out."

"And you decided to explore our site?" one burly spokesman challenged.

"I just decided it was a shortcut. I was… I am in a hurry."

The two men and the woman surrounded the sailor. They sized him up. The apparent leader of the trio circled his suspect completely. He saw nothing in the man's hands.

"And that's the truth, sailor?"

"Swear to God, sir."

The few moments it took for the worker to reply seemed like minutes.

"I served myself – Marine on the Nimitz – so I'm gonna cut you some slack. This is a dangerous place for a stroll. Even more dangerous if I catch your sorry ass in here again. Got it, squid?"

"I do. Thank you." The traitor turned around and walked past the woman who was the last in his path.

"Hey, squid!" the brusque voice called after him. The sailor stopped and squeezed his eyes shut tightly. Then he turned around and smiled.

"Yes?"

"Thanks for your service, Petty Officer."

Alvarez nodded his acknowledgement and left the work yard.

The man who had confronted the trespasser shouted up to the foreman who had called him out in the first place.

"Just some horny guy on his way to try to get some. Thought he'd get there quicker by cutting through here."

CHAPTER 45

Near the middle of the afternoon, former CIA Officer Josh Morgan had covered a lot of ground exploring the parts of the city's water supply that were visible. But without knowing what he was looking for, he had no way of knowing if he'd missed anything. And the occasional parts of the water main that he could see appeared far too formidable to penetrate. He decided he would only explore for another hour or two and then head home.

In the meantime, Morgan opted to return to his SUV and warm up. A cool front had passed through, and it was chilly for an early November afternoon. He figured he would use the time to drive to another parking area and establish a new point from which to investigate.

♦

Terrorist Alvarez had found another park bench to pass the time. He was a bit cool but had no jacket that didn't have his name on it. He needed to kill a few more hours before he could act.

♦

"Mick, you take my saw?" the woman shouted across the yard.

"Haven't see it, Norma."

Norma shifted her inquiry to the entire site.

"Hey, guys, where's my saw?"

She heard a few mumbled "I don't knows" but mostly got answers in the form of shrugs.

"Okay, you sorry shits. Who's got my saw?"

♦

Morgan had grabbed a cup of coffee and a sandwich. It was nearly four o'clock and he was heading home to Maggie's apartment. The ex-spook desperately prayed he was wrong about the whole thing; that there wasn't an attack planned on Washington. As he walked along the street toward where he had parked, he saw a group of police officers interviewing some construction workers.

The former CIA spy slowed his pace enough to eavesdrop.

"I only called it in because that thing cost nearly eight hundred bucks," the foreman told the officer. "We have kids run through here all the time and take whatever they can grab easily. It's just gotten outta hand."

The first officer scribbled notes. The second one asked, "And you can't shut the gates?"

"Do you realize what a hassle that would be? People come in and outta here all day long."

"Uh-huh," the uniformed policeman grunted with a headshake. "Anybody else in here that shouldn't have been?"

Not seeing from his vantage point on the second floor of the structure that the trespasser in uniform was a sailor, the foreman answered, "Just some Army guy in camouflage. He took a shortcut through here – people try to do that – but he didn't take nothing. Some of my guys checked him out. Clean as a whistle."

The huddle eventually broke up and Morgan kept walking.

It was overcast and getting colder. Morgan was in his rented truck and almost back to Maggie's apartment when his gut told him to pull over. He spotted a drugstore and pulled into a parking space. He stared out the window and tapped his fingers on the wheel.

"What if the guy at the construction site was a sailor and not a soldier?" he wondered. Then he scolded himself.

"That's nuts, Morgan. Don't try to make something fit just because you're desperate."

He tapped his fingers some more and blew short bursts of air through his lips.

"But what if it was Alvarez?" he added to his self-debate. "Still, they said he didn't take anything. So, what would he have been doing there anyhow? Nothing there has anything to do with the water system."

He lingered in the parking lot another twenty minutes, alternately running through what-ifs and chastising himself for obsessing about what was almost certainly nothing.

"Well, there's one way to find out," he concluded. Morgan backed out of his space and entered the flow of traffic back toward the construction site. He would see if anyone was still there and show them a photo of Alvarez on his phone. He looked at the time.

"Five o'clock. Nobody's gonna be there," he told himself, wanting to just turn around again. Then, "Oh, what the hell," and he continued on.

♦

The sun had just set, but the combination of clouds with the four- and five-story buildings made the street already dark. However, the workday was just ending for many. There was a steady flow of vehicles on the streets and even a number of pedestrians. Some were making their way to their autos or bus stops. There were joggers and walkers. Some had dogs.

Petty Officer and traitor Trini Alvarez would have to wait a while longer. He knew he would be warmer in a coffee shop or other store, but the fear of being recognized from some police bulletin kept him where he was.

He found a trash dumpster and tossed his seabag into it. He kept only his hydration backpack and water bottle.

Then he found a bench outside a closed café, sat, and folded his arms tightly to try to stave off the dropping temperatures.

♦

Morgan returned to the same parking lot where he had started the last of his treks in search of some unknown object or circumstance that would lead to a plot that was most likely a fiction.

"Stupid," he reprimanded himself.

He locked his vehicle and returned to the location where the office building was under construction and at which he had overheard the conversation about a missing tool.

As was common overnight, lights were on throughout the site, but no workers remained. Disappointed, but not surprised, he opted to wait to see if a security guard was present.

"But unless he was also here during the day, he's not going to have any idea what the soldier – or sailor – looked like," Morgan groused to himself. Still, he decided to wait. He took a seat on a nearby park bench and called Maggie.

"Hey, sweetheart, it's me," he announced to the greeting. I'm gonna be a while. Nothing's wrong. Just checking out something. It's almost certainly nothing, but… Hey, you know me."

He disconnected and pulled the collar up on the jacket he'd brought from his SUV. He needed to think.

♦

Two-and-a-half blocks on the other side of the construction site, PO2 Alvarez decided he would at least move closer to the area. The almost total darkness, even at just before six, made him less fearful of being recognized. But this was no time to get careless, he knew. He found a nearer bench on which to wait.

After waiting for a darker hour to act, the sailor decided he would circle the area to find the best place to break into the construction site.

Approaching the worksite from the direction in which he had left it earlier, the terrorist seaman began to move around it in a counterclockwise route. Staying near the chain link fence, he walked casually toward the corner. He turned left and southward toward the next corner of the lot.

♦

Ex-spy Morgan decided he was just being silly. He rose from his seat and began the return hike to his vehicle. He decided to cross the street to take one more look in the construction area in hopes of spotting a nightwatchman. Peering through the interlaced metal pieces of the fence, he saw none. So, he resigned himself to the fact that his effort had been futile and walked westward.

As he began his walk, he saw only one other person on his side of the street. He had just turned the corner ahead and was moving eastward toward Morgan. The light was dim on the sidewalk, much of it blocked by the new building undergoing construction. But it was clear by the silhouette that the figure wore loosely fitting clothing and a cap that was somewhat angular on the sides, widening as it rose from the bill.

"That's a cover," Morgan deduced, using the term that all members of the U.S. military used for their hats.

As the two grew nearer, neither slowed down. The service man kept his head down. Morgan did not and tried to determine whether the individual he now recognized to be wearing a Navy Working Uniform was Alvarez. Between the faint light and the sailor's downward gaze, the former CIA officer couldn't tell. But a couple of things stood out.

First, he had a Camelbak hydration pack on and he carried an oversized water bottle. Morgan thought it a little chilly to be concerned with so much water, although he admitted to himself that the bottle might have coffee, hot chocolate, or another warming drink.

But the main thing that Morgan noticed was that the sailor's uniform was in every way regulation but one. It had no name patch. The realization that no American serviceman would be so blatantly out of uniform in public caused the hair on Morgan's hair to stand up.

"Alvarez," he determined, and kept walking. When he turned right at the corner around which the sailor he presumed to be the terrorist had turned toward him, Morgan stopped. He leaned slightly back to look in the direction from which he had come. At the far end of the construction area, he saw his suspect going around the corner of the fence. As soon as the man was out of sight, Morgan began to sprint in pursuit of him. While on the move, he called Betsy Parnell. She might not be the right person in this situation, but as always, she was one person her contract employee felt would take his call.

"What is it now, Morgan?" the former spy heard as he reached the corner.

"I've found…"

Morgan's report to the CIA Director ended with a flash of light and a burning pain across his forehead. He heard the crack of the impact as if it had originated inside his head. He stumbled backward, trying desperately to keep his balance, but his right knee weakened, and his left buckled entirely. He fell leftward into the metal fabric of the fence. He clawed at it frantically in an effort to remain somewhat upright. But when his grip failed him, he fell sidelong onto his seat and then fully backward. His face raked across the linked chainwork of the fence.

Finally, his torso crumpled toward the rear, and the back of his head hit the concrete walkway. There was another crack, unbearable pain, a few flashes of light, and then nothing.

♦

In her office, the Director of the Central Intelligence Agency stared at her phone momentarily, bewildered and horrified at the interruption of her caller. She heard some scratching as if the phone was being shoved around. The only other sound was that of moaning.

"Morgan. Morgan! JOSH!"

She pressed the button to contact her secretary.

"Have someone locate Josh Morgan!" she ordered.

She called Director Paul McClintock at the National Security Agency.

"No time to explain, Paul. Just get someone looking for Josh Morgan's phone!"

♦

Traitor Trinidad Alvarez stood over the man who had recognized him, prepared to hit him a second time with his water bottle. But the man was unconscious. Seeing his phone and hearing the faint voice of someone screaming for the man, Alvarez crushed the device with a downward blow from his black government-issued boots. Another stomp. Then another, and the Petty Officer felt confident that the phone was out of working order. Still, for good measure, he picked it up and twisted the broken object until the pieces fell apart in his hands.

PO2 Alvarez surveyed the area. Seeing no one, he pulled the limp body behind a dumpster outside the construction site. He raised the unconscious man's torso enough to remove his jacket and then let him drop back to the sidewalk.

The American-born man of Nicaraguan descent had already determined where he would scale the fence. One place in particular was darkest and the three strands of barbed wire on the top sagged.

Alvarez jumped and caught the top of the eight-feet high fence with his left hand. The twisted points of wire at the top of the fabric tore into his palm before his fingers slid between them but he was able to grasp the galvanized rod that supported the steel mesh at its top. He leaned back against the security of his handhold and foot-walked up the fence slightly.

With his right hand, he flung the unconscious man's jacket over the three strings of wire to provide at least some protection from the barbs. Alvarez hung onto the rail at the fence's top and walked his feet up further at an angle to his body until they were at the top. Pressing all his weight against his hands, the sailor launched his feet to vault over the fence. But while his boots cleared, the ripstop material of his NWU did not. The nylon-cotton blend material of his right leg snagged several of the barbs. In his frantic attempt to maintain control of his flight, the sailor grabbed more securely with his hands. The act pulled his body back onto the top of the fence and the barbed wire that was stretched atop it.

The N-Dub's material didn't rip, but the points at the top of the linked chain and several barbs in the upper strands pierced into the cloth. Even though the blended material didn't tear, Alvarez's skin did. Several gashes inflicted immediate anguish to the man. Furthermore, he couldn't free his trousers. He hung as tightly as he could with his hands and flung his legs upward forcefully. Finally free of the entanglements, he dropped to the ground inside the site.

♦

Director Parnell of the CIA got word from her own people as well as from her counterpart at NSA that they couldn't find Josh Morgan's cell phone. NSA Director McClintock had assured Parnell that they could find his last call but that it would take time.

Parnell sensed that time was something her contract agent didn't have.

"Damn."

♦

Limping in pain, Trinidad Alvarez hurried toward the center of the work area. A huge construction dumpster the size of an eighteen-wheeler's trailer sat there. Trucks often delivered the containers to construction sites at the start of a project. During the job, the workers simply tossed all manner of waste and other materials to be discarded into the dumpster. At various times during the project, trucks switched out the containers as needed and at the end of the project, a final one returned to retrieve it and dispose of the contents.

PO2 Alvarez had known he would never make it out of the work site with the saw – he really didn't believe he would be able to pick it up it without being spotted – so he had planned to hide it. The dumpster was about fifteen feet from where the woman had been using the Sawzall. So, when he successfully took it, he simply tossed it into the refuse container. He had only made it three or four steps after that before being halted by the workers.

Now he looked around the protected area of the structure that would soon become an office building and found a ladder. The Petty Officer moved it to the dumpster and climbed the six feet to its top. Alvarez couldn't see the tool at first. Workers had tossed other waste material on top of it. But after a little time to uncover it, the thief was out of the trailer and back on solid ground.

However, his focus on finding the implement he needed had consequences. Just as his feet reached the ground outside the dumpster, a beam of light hit him from behind, casting a large shadow on the container.

"Stop! What are you doing?"

Reflexively, Alvarez spun about, swinging the reciprocating saw. It struck the unarmed security guard squarely in the jaw. As the man fell from the blow, the continuing motion of the tool raked the twelve-inch blade across his left eye and cheek. Out cold while still on his feet, the guard crumpled to the ground.

Trinidad Alvarez felt some remorse for the man. He was, after all, just an employee doing his job. But for the one who had confronted him on the sidewalk, he felt none.

Until that moment, the sailor/thief/terrorist had been completely hidden from the view of anyone on the street by the various objects scattered about the work yard. But once he moved only a few feet, he would be exposed. He started to drag his ladder toward the fence but had a better idea.

Alvarez proceeded to the nearest gate. The sailor's newly acquired tool made short work of the padlock securing the gate. Once outside the fenced area, he returned to where his assailant still lay unconscious and retrieved the backpack and water bottle that he had left there.

He started to use the saw to finish off the man but didn't have the stomach for it.

♦

"Josh, it's me. Please call. I'm worried." Maggie hung up. Her call had gone straight to voicemail. She hated to – Josh might walk in at any moment – but she called Betsy Parnell.

No answer.

♦

It was only a slight murmur, but it was the first sign of life in quite some time. Then Morgan muttered again. He rolled onto his back.

He put his hand to the bleeding side of his head. Then he reached for the equally excruciatingly painful back of his head. He felt the thick liquid in the mass of his hair that he knew was also blood.

Unaware of exactly where he was, he instinctively reached in his pocket for his phone. When he didn't find it, he looked around him. He spotted the shattered device a couple of feet away.

As the recollection of his encounter with Trinidad Alvarez began to take form, the urgency of the circumstances generated a rush of adrenaline. The "fight or flight" hormone produced a burst of energy and gave his memory a jolt, too, though it didn't mitigate the pain Morgan felt.

He stood – unsteadily at first – and walked to the corner of the fence where the terrorist had waylaid him and peeked around. At the far end of the fence, he saw Alvarez walking casually away. Without a phone, Morgan had no way to summon the cavalry. And if he tried to find help, he would lose the man. He had to follow him. With that realization came the thought that pursuing the man hadn't worked out too well a little earlier. But he knew he had no choice.

The ex-CIA Officer had worked hard over the last several months to become a more formidable warrior. He had wanted to ensure he was up to the task of taking care of Oskar Lammers. But he knew that his current battered shape left him in no condition to put up much of a fight. He would try to think of something while he followed his quarry.

One thing was certain though. Morgan wasn't going to walk around any more blind corners.

♦

"Betsy, my analysts have tried everything, and we can't come up with Morgan's whereabouts. Just as yours did, my agency discovered that his phone is offline. And we just haven't been able to find any data indicating where he might've called you from."

CIA's Boss blurted out, "Hang on, Paul." She put McClintock, who had called his analyst Terry Henderson to his office, on hold and selected another name from her contact list.

"Maggie…"

Maggie interrupted with, "Where's Josh?"

"Does Josh have a rental car, Maggie?" was her reply.

Now Maggie was really frightened, but she answered, "Yeah, an SUV. WHO…"

"Where did he rent it?"

"Uh, Reagan. Budget is where he normally rents. I…" She realized Parnell had hung up.

"Paul, check on this for me. Morgan rented an SUV at Reagan. Probably Budget."

"On it," ended the call.

♦

In his office at NSA, Director McClintock related the information to Henderson. It was a matter of only three minutes until the analyst was in the rental agency's network.

"Here it is, Director. And it has a tracker. I'll locate it."

Most car rental agencies, including Budget, installed GPS trackers in their automobiles that allowed them to locate them in real time. The system helped the companies find them if stolen or abandoned. They also helped ensure they weren't used for illegal activities.

"Got it, sir." Henderson gave McClintock the address.

"Map it, Terry."

The Head of NSA knew he needed to call Parnell but when he saw the location appear on Henderson's display, he decided to call his counterpart at the FBI first.

"Gabe. Paul. Josh Morgan's gone missing. He's completely off the grid. But we located his rental car. It's in a parking lot on the northwest side of the city. And it's in the general vicinity of the Washington Aqueduct. You don't suppose he really found something, do you?"

"It wouldn't surprise me one bit. I'll have SSA Liu get some agents on it. Send me the address."

♦

In short order the damage to his body was outweighing any benefits his adrenaline burst had provided. The barely alert former spy was finding it increasingly difficult to keep up with the terrorist. The only good news was that Alvarez apparently wasn't aware that he was trailing him. If he were, he would probably fall back and meet him. He would know, as Morgan did, that the pursuer's state would make him no match for the sailor.

Morgan pushed on in the hopes of being able to flag down an officer. The old joke was never really true, but it seemed to be accurate right now. A policeman was never around when you needed one.

The fatigued and battered man followed his subject into an area that was more wooded. It was at the edge of a park through which a fairly good-sized stream ran. He knew that the amount of natural cover might cause him to walk right up on Alvarez without knowing it. He slowed down and tried to muster additional energy and alertness. But it was pointless. He was done.

♦

Trinidad Alvarez hadn't made as precise mental notes as he thought he had. It took some time to return to the location of the water main where he had determined that he would introduce the VX agent into Washington's water supply. When he finally found the place, he paused to rest. His own adrenaline had created a heightened anxiety and the enormity of what he was about to do overtook him. He began to shake uncontrollably. Beads of sweat appeared on his forehead. In fact, he felt like his entire body was awash with perspiration, despite the cool temperature.

The terrorist knew he had to go through with his part in this plan. And he *wanted* to. But now that the time was at hand, it was proving to be more difficult than he had imagined.

"For God's sake, Trini. Get a grip," he chastised himself.

His mouth was completely dry. He found it ironic that he had carried a hydration backpack all this time that was capable of carrying three liters of water and yet he didn't have any to drink.

♦

Some distance away, Morgan had collapsed to the ground. He was sure that even if he saw Alvarez running toward him, he wouldn't have the strength or resolve to put up a fight. And the truth he had to face was that he had lost the man.

Struggling to his knees, the former spy begged God for the energy to at least find a policeman. He knew that Alvarez was nearby. He just had no clue where… or even where he was himself.

The area was relatively quiet. But in the distance, he could hear traffic. He would head that way.

♦

The sailor/terrorist was regaining some of the resolve he'd had when he first agreed to his role in the plot. He sincerely wished there was some way to limit the VX poison to individuals who were involved with the U.S. government. That would've been the case if his original target hadn't been compromised. The carrier USS George Washington would have nothing but U.S. Sailors and Marines on it. He'd had no qualms about that.

But now he had come around to thinking that collateral casualties were unavoidable. He had known little about the other part of the plan; the part that involved nuking Washington, D.C. And he wasn't aware that that part of the plot had failed. He only knew what his orders were.

Alvarez looked at the large pipe. It was one of the older thirty-inch cast iron transmission pipes that made up nearly eighty-five percent of D.C.'s distribution system. Then he examined the twelve-inch blade on the Sawzall. To lower his backpack into the pipe would require a substantial hole. He determined that he could cut at a forty-five-degree angle in one direction from each side of the pipe and then in the opposite direction at identical angles for a total of four cuts – two per side – that would create two wedged incisions. It would be similar to cutting a slice from an apple. He estimated that the result should be a hole large enough to drop in both containers holding the precursors. Despite the water main's large diameter, the interior space would be confined enough for the QL and NM precursor agents to mix efficiently once the small explosive charge initiated the bubbling.

The terrorist rested the carbide-tipped blade on the curved surface of the pipe and pulled the trigger. The blade walked sideways. Alvarez stopped and rethought his approach. He began again, this time cutting directly perpendicular to the pipe. Once he had a small cut in the water main, he stopped and repositioned the blade at an angle in the groove he had just created.

It took only scant seconds for the sailor to realize that the blade on the saw wasn't suited for this purpose. It was going to take longer than he thought and that meant the chances of his being discovered would increase dramatically. Alvarez's heart raced with the thought. He triggered the tool again and the blade began its back-and-forth motion but was only making slow progress, cutting from the center of the transmission pipe at its top toward him.

♦

Morgan stood only briefly before dropping to his knees again. The landscape was a swirling, spinning mishmash of unrecognizable shapes. The injured man dropped to his butt.

"C'mon, Josh. Pull yourself together," he urged. He squeezed his eyes shut to close out the distorted visions of the spinning landscape. He tried to force himself to concentrate on thoughts, mental images, sounds – anything that would help him focus.

The ex-spy tried to isolate anything his senses were registering to push away the spinning that seemed to continue in his mind even with his eyes closed.

Faintly, amid the congregation of distant sounds was one that was a fusion of rattling and jingling. Morgan picked up on a whirring noise accompanying the metallic audible shimmy. Though not very loud, it was obviously fairly close. It would stop; then start. Upon each resumption there was the jangle of a sound that was clearly metal on metal. Interspersed with the annoying vibrating clatter, there was occasionally a split second of reverberation that had an almost musical character. Then the noise stopped.

The ex-spy shifted and positioned himself on hands and knees. Morgan had seen nobody in the area save Alvarez, whom he had lost sight of many minutes before. He opened his eyes and tilted his head to look at the glow of a hazy streetlight that was barely visible through the leafless limbs in the wooded area. He forced himself to maintain a steady stare at the light. Finally, it began to come into sharper focus.

The dizziness was still intense, but he compelled himself to stand, hands resting on his knees. He managed to come to a fully erect position. Morgan maintained his visual fixation on the distant light.

In time, the dinging sound of metal objects resumed. Morgan forced a step and then another, pushing his body toward the odd sound.

♦

Petty Officer Alvarez found his work to be more difficult than he had supposed. He had believed – and hoped – that the reciprocating saw would make short work of the water pipe. Perhaps, he wondered, the blade was of the wrong type. Because after nearly twenty-five minutes of sawing, he had managed to complete only one of the cuts he needed.

The terrorist repositioned himself on the opposite side of the main and began work on the second of four cuts. Inserting the blade into the slice he had made from the other side, he began work again, cutting toward himself. After a great deal of effort, he finally completed the first side of what would become two adjoining forty-five-degree incisions into the pipe.

Alvarez transferred the saw's blade to begin the second cut of the final angled side that would converge with the first, creating the diamond-shaped wedge. Once done, he would be able to lift the entire section away and introduce the VX components into the city's drinking water. As he had found necessary on the first gash in the cast iron, he started with a small vertical cut. Then, as before, he angled the blade to roughly forty-five degrees with the teeth in the small cut. He pulled the Sawzall's trigger and the vibrating, jingling action resumed as he drew the tool toward him and sawed downward.

♦

Morgan realized he had passed out again. He didn't know for how long but the sound of the metal on metal was still audible. He forced his unwilling body to stand and pushed himself onward and could tell the sound was increasing in volume, though only marginally, as he neared it.

"If this is Alvarez," he thought, "he's still some distance away." He knew he had to pick up the pace. A wave of nausea overtook him, and he paused to recover from it. Then he resumed his effort, turning his slow walk into something more of a trot. The sound stopped, but he continued to move toward where it had come from.

♦

PO2 Alvarez ceased sawing to take a break. Not only was he worn out from the task, but it was becoming apparent that the saw's battery was weakening. Furthermore, the blade was dulling enough that the cut was harder to perform. But he had less than an inch to complete the first half of the second cut that would connect to the first one.

The sailor engaged the tool again. After several minutes of labor his current cut joined the first one in a "V" on the side of the iron transmission pipe nearest him.

The PO2's body and mind begged for relief, but the man pressed on. He returned to the side of the cast iron water main on which he had made the primary incision and began the cut that would complete his task.

Instead of moving steadily through the pipe, the dulling blade was struggling. Alvarez found himself pushing downward on the saw in an attempt to expedite the process, though it proved of little additional value. In time, he was within one-quarter inch of finishing. Suddenly the saw stalled. The battery wasn't dead but was weak enough that the diminished power wasn't enough to continue cutting the thick-walled pipe.

The traitor to his country looked about for something, anything he could use as a prybar. He found a small piece of metal, but it only bent as he tried to wedge the incomplete cuts open.

"DAMMIT!" he screamed with no regard for who might be nearby. "SHIT!"

♦

The half-moon among the sparse clouds of the clearing sky was bright enough to illuminate the area sufficiently for someone to see his surroundings. That is, unless that someone was addled from being clubbed on his head with a heavy water bottle. The ex-CIA Officer paused as the mechanical noise stopped. Then the eruption of two expletives told him that he was far closer to the person creating the racket than he'd imagined. Energized by the fact that the end of his hike seemed at hand, he stepped forward with more purpose. His mind cleared marginally. Even Morgan's vision sharpened somewhat.

♦

Alvarez realized that his only hope of completing his mission lay with the saw. He inserted the blade into the unfinished cut, praying that the battery had enough charge for one last cut. He stopped and held the cutting blade just short of where the cut had ended. The sailor took a deep breath and pulled the trigger to initiate the back-and-forth action of the blade. The reciprocating motion was less powerful than before but at least it was moving.

Alvarez dropped the blade onto where the cut had previously ended.

The immediacy of the contact stalled the sawblade entirely and it failed to finish the cut on the side of the pipe toward him. The pair of cuts connected on the far side, but not the one where he now worked.

Alvarez gave the saw a break from its task, hoping that some residual voltage would miraculously appear. But after several periods of waiting and retrying the saw, he knew the battery was hopelessly dead. A quarter inch of metal on the near side held the wedge in place. He pulled upward and toward himself against the nearly completed section of pipe and felt it wiggle. But the motion only held it in place. The pie-shaped piece he had been trying to separate from the water main needed to be lifted to remove it.

Realizing the saw was no longer of any use, the U.S. Sailor inserted the blade into a cut. He twisted and turned the metal saw. It only bent. He worked vigorously but the thin, flexible cutting blade was no match for the strength of the cast iron water main.

Alvarez yanked at the saw, but the bent blade wouldn't straighten enough to pull it from the cut. He slammed the tool against the incomplete wedge of pipe he had created, but as before, its shape prevented it from collapsing into the pipe. He tugged on the tool and twisted outward. Finally, the blade came out and the man fell backward, saw in hand.

Angered at his inability to complete his work, the traitor flung the saw down the slope of the creekbank. He lay fully back. His panting was as much from frustration as from exertion. Trinidad Alvarez stared at the moon as if hoping for inspiration from the lunar orb.

Finally, a possible solution came to Alvarez. He slid down the bank and recovered the lifeless saw. He bent the blade until it was nearly straight again. Once he had scrambled atop the bank, he inserted the mangled blade into the incomplete cut. He pulled the saw back and forth, using it as a several hundred-dollar handsaw. The progress was painfully slow, but eventually the dull blade cut through the last bit of metal.

With some difficulty, the sailor managed to lift the pie-shaped wedge of steel out of its place.

He sat to rest.

♦

The CIA contractor had moved to within a handful of yards from where he had heard the noise. In the moonlight, he could make out the camouflage-uniformed man struggling with a tool. At far less than full strength, Morgan tried to come up with some manner in which he could go for help. But the outline of a large pipe stretching over the creek made it clear he had no such time.

Morgan considered some type of bluff but couldn't arrive at one. And he had no weapon, or anything that could serve as one.

All his conjecture about what things were at his disposal, all his speculating about a possible plan, his trying to come up with a solution – they all ended as he saw Trinidad Alvarez lift a section of metal away from the water main. Time had run out. He had to act.

The former journalist spy called upon what little strength he had. Sheer willpower propelled him along toward the terrorist.

PO2 Alvarez heard footfalls and looked up to see the man he had left unconscious at the construction site rushing toward him. The traitor's first thought was to try to go ahead to combine the precursor agents that would activate as VX, but he knew he didn't have time. Wheeling about, he rushed toward his opponent.

Just as Alvarez neared Morgan, the former CIA Officer dropped down, flipping the onrushing man over him. The partial collision drained much of Morgan's adrenaline. Still, he managed to get to his feet and prepare to fight. But the terrorist knew his opponent was weak and flung himself toward him. Morgan sidestepped much of the impact, but the combination of his lateral motion and the brush of Alvarez knocked him toward the creekbank. His feet slipped over the edge, and he began to slide down the incline that was covered by alternating grass and mud.

Alvarez began to run toward Morgan but thought better of it. He changed course and headed toward his backpack and began to unscrew the cover of the fill port.

As he slid down the embankment, the ex-CIA Officer had managed to grab the concrete pad that supported the pier that held up the water transmission pipe. At first his feet slid out from underneath him as he tried to gain traction to climb back up the bank. Grabbing the base with his second hand, he managed to make some headway.

The terrorist struggled with the cap on the Camelbak. He had overtightened it to prevent any of the fluid from leaking. The sight of his adversary climbing over the edge of the bank of the stream shifted his attention back to him. He lunged to kick him back down the slope, but he lost his footing and fell. Morgan grabbed the Petty Officer, and both skidded down the slope into the edge of the creek.

The ex-spy grappled with the sailor and knocked him further into the gently flowing water. Seizing the opportunity, he tried to climb the bank to escape a fight that he knew he had no chance of winning. Morgan desperately hung onto the edge of the opening in the pipe as the man who had cut it hung onto his legs. Morgan shook him loose and pulled himself upward and over the edge. However, Alvarez easily managed the climb and overtook him just as he reached the hydration backpack.

The U.S. sailor slammed Morgan facedown onto the grass and climbed onto his back. The former CIA Officer managed to flip the terrorist over, but the man wrestled the pack away from him. He bucked Morgan off his chest and unscrewed the cap of the fill port the rest of the way. He rose to his knees and lifted the container toward the gap he had sawed into the pipe.

Morgan made a final frantic lunge and though he slammed Alvarez's torso forward and into the side of the water main, the traitor managed to hang the hydration pack onto the edge of the slice in the metal pipe with a plastic hook. A small amount of the QL precursor splashed onto the terrorist's shirt, but he knew that each component chemical alone was virtually harmless.

Alvarez also knew that the precursors activated as VX the moment they combined. And since water was the final component that delayed results from the chemical, until the final product was introduced to water, symptoms – and death – could manifest almost instantly. He would have to exercise extreme caution.

Morgan believed Alvarez had dropped the backpack entirely into the pipe. Unaware that the VX existed as two separate components, he assumed he had been exposed to fumes of the poisonous nerve agent. He fell away in order to distance himself from the small amount of the chemical that had splashed from its container.

The man who had tried so hard to prevent a chemical attack on his country's capital was sure that he had failed. He panicked at the thought of the agent flowing through the city's water supply and killing a large number of citizens, possibly including Maggie. And he was certain that his own death was imminent from breathing in the fumes of the spilled toxin.

CHAPTER 46

FBI Special Agents Phil Jeffries and Miles Russell were airborne with one of the Bureau's pilots and a copilot in a Bell 407 helicopter identical to the one Tom Lechler had used to direct the nuclear missile away from D.C. They circled the area around Morgan's rental vehicle, which had been located by its GPS tracking device. With the aircraft's powerful floodlights pointed downward, the pilot concentrated on executing search patterns while the other three pairs of eyes on board scanned the ground for any sign of the missing former CIA Officer.

On the ground, other FBI Agents and members of the Washington Metro PD fanned out from the parking lot where they had found the SUV. None knew whether anything was truly amiss or if Morgan was merely out of touch. But as FBI Director Austin had said when he ordered his agents into the field, the man always seemed to wind up in the middle of everything. So, it wouldn't be unreasonable to assume he had again.

D.C. detectives were also arriving at the scene of a construction project. A security business had become concerned when one of its guards had failed to check in. A company supervisor had driven to the site and had found his employee unconscious and severely injured with jagged gashes to his left cheek and eye.

A search of the area turned up two curious finds.

The detective on the scene called his watch commander, who, upon hearing the report, patched him through to FBI Supervisory Special Agent Annchi Liu.

"That's right, Special Agent Liu. A crushed phone – we'll have no idea whose until we get someone to check its SIM card – and a duffle bag. That was in a dumpster nearby. The uniforms were all marked with the name 'Alvarez.' That's the terrorist we've been advised to keep an eye out for."

SSA Liu put the man on hold briefly to conference her boss and his boss on the call.

"Go ahead, Detective. I have Director Austin and Deputy Director Drake on with us."

"Okay. So, in addition to the injured guard and the phone and the bag, there was a report of a theft from this spot earlier today – a power tool. It was a… hmm, let's see," he said, looking at the details of the report. "Some sort of reciprocating saw, whatever the hell that is. Supposed to be pretty powerful."

None of the three of the FBI personnel on the other end of the line knew what the theft of the saw meant. But the seabag had to belong to Trinidad Alvarez. And the phone…? They could only guess.

SSA Liu radioed the new information to her agents in the field.

"That's right. It appears that we have an active terror situation in the city."

♦

Morgan figured Alvarez's fate was as sealed as his was. The man had even spilled a considerable amount on his shirt. But oddly, for a man who had seemingly completed his mission, he was still very active. He was frantically working on what appeared in the moonlight to be a thermos or water bottle. The ex-spy decided that if it was important to Alvarez, it should be important to him, too.

He shook off any remaining grogginess from his injuries and from the just concluded fight and stormed toward Alvarez. The sailor looked up just in time to see the persistent bastard running toward him, head lowered, and arms stretched out. The force of Morgan's collision with the terrorist slammed his back against the heavy water main.

Alvarez groaned in pain and dropped the water bottle. It rolled beneath the large pipe but lodged against the concrete pad of the support. The sailor pushed against his attacker, who resisted with far more strength than he should've had at this point. The man hardly budged. The Petty Officer grabbed Morgan by his shirt and attempted to fling him to the side. No success.

Morgan pushed his left palm against his opponent's chin. With his right fist, he delivered blow after blow into the traitor's stomach and rib cage.

Finally, Alvarez managed to push the man off of him. He swung his legs over the ridge of the creekbank and slid down the short distance to where the stainless-steel bottle rested against the block of concrete. He grasped it and then crawled beneath the water main to the other side to put the pipe between himself and the onrushing attacker.

Even with his feet slipping on the damp grass and mud, the terrorist finally scrambled over the rim of the stream's bank and turned his attention back to the water bottle. Morgan remained on the side of the water main where he was and, with slightly surer footing than Alvarez had had on his side, reached the top of the bank almost at the same time.

Morgan couldn't figure out what was so important about the container that his opponent continued to obsess with it. But he knew he could worry about that later, if he lived.

He lunged over the top of the pipe and landed on the terrorist. Alvarez slammed his left fist in a hammer blow against the right side of Morgan's head. It was still oozing blood from the wound the terrorist had made at the construction site when he bashed him with the same water bottle that they were fighting over now. Morgan slumped to the side motionless.

Trinidad Alvarez stood and walked to the open hole he had sawed into the water main. Devoid of energy, he dropped to his knees. The traitor pulled the lanyard from the water bottle which released the barrier between the bottle's lid and the trigger. With the safety removed, the bloodied terrorist knew that after a clockwise turn of the container's cap, he needed to only attach the bottle to the Camelbak and drop both into the water main. The blast would release QL, the first precursor, to mix with NM, the second, which would be spilling into the water through the backpack's open fill port and opening from the explosion.

The traitorous sailor twisted the cap to the stainless-steel container. After a full turn, it began to make a ratcheting sound much like an auto's fuel tank cap did when it was fully closed.

As Petty Officer Second Class and traitor to his country Trinidad Alvarez lifted the water bottle to attach it to the backpack suspended inside the water main, an intense white light swept across him.

♦

Inside the FBI's Bell 407, Special Agent Jeffries screamed and pointed.

"There! What's that?!"

The copilot reversed the floodlight's beam to the man it had just illuminated. He was dressed in a camouflage uniform and appeared to be holding something over a break in a water main.

Special Agent Russell was already radioing the information to their colleagues on the ground.

♦

Trinidad Alvarez looked up and winced at the brightness of the floodlight. He instinctively looked away and raised his forearm to shield his eyes. Just as rapidly, he turned back to his task and reached to connect the water bottle's lanyard to the open hydration pack.

Suddenly a crushing blow to his left side knocked the sailor to the ground. The water bottle flew several feet away. He tried to crawl to retrieve it, but Morgan held both his ankles.

The traitor tried to kick his way out of the man's grip, but only managed to free one leg. He kicked at his other foot with his loose one, but the man's hand wouldn't come off. Alvarez looked again toward the stainless-steel container. It was hopelessly out of reach.

Alvarez knew the charge in the bottle would explode at any moment and spray him with the chemical it held. He threw up his forearms to cover his head.

Seeing the terrorist attempting to shield himself, Morgan let go of his ankle and scooted away toward the edge of the creek bank. Just as he slid over the incline and down the embankment toward the creek, he heard a small explosion.

A short distance from Alvarez, a disk spewed a bubbling solution, covering the terrorist with liquid.

A second floodlight lit up the area around Morgan while the first remained on Alvarez.

CHAPTER 47

As the helicopter hovered overhead, Josh Morgan initially put his thumb and forefinger together to indicate he was okay. But in truth, he wondered why he wasn't dead already. He was certain he had breathed the deadly vapor of the VX gas when Alvarez had put the backpack into the water main. He had seen that much of it had sloshed out.

Over the embankment, he heard the voices of people approaching. Suddenly, he began to wave his arms wildly back and forth over his head toward the chopper.

Over the bank, he heard someone shout, "Stop."

Morgan crawled up to the edge of the slope and rested on his knees. The peril he was in hit him like a hammer. His thoughts turned instantly to Maggie and tears formed in his eyes. He rose to his knees.

"There's VX poison over the area. I've been exposed."

The Bell 407's pilot set down in an opening near where Morgan and the terrorist were. Special Agents Jeffries and Russell ran to the scene. The ex-spy stood. Alvarez lay on his back, understanding the pointlessness of his predicament.

"The area's covered in VX. I breathed it," Morgan said. "You should stay away and get a team here. I breathed it," he repeated and sagged to his knees. "I breathed it."

"Did you breathe it after both parts were mixed?" Special Agent Jeffries said, having been briefed on the existence of the two precursors that had to be combined for the VX to become active.

"What do you mean? Both parts? Mixed?"

Special Agent Russell gave Morgan a brief explanation of the existence and need for both of the QL and NM precursor agents.

The former CIA Officer thought through the scenario in which he had just found himself. He concluded that the backpack held one part and the water bottle had held the second.

Josh Morgan smiled.

"I think I'm okay. But you should probably take whatever precautions you need to. Just in case. Him…" Morgan pointed to Trinidad Alvarez, "you should stay away from."

Long before Morgan had warned about the presence of VX in his area, the FBI and Center for Disease Control had bioterror/chemical attack response teams on their way. They arrived within minutes.

Law enforcement on the scene had been given orders to shoot Alvarez instantly if he tried to engage anyone. He did not. Specialists had tended to the terrorist based on Morgan's speculation that he had been exposed to both agents. And the former spy's conclusion had turned out to be correct. Some of the QL had spilled on him when he had opened the fill port of the Camelbak. Then the discharge of the water bottle had sprayed NM on him. Enough of the second precursor had mixed with the first that had soaked into his shirt that it had formed the active binary agent VX.

The response team had wrapped him in protected covers, but U.S. Navy Petty Officer Second Class Trinidad Alvarez died shortly after the ambulance left for the hospital.

The bioterror/chemical attack response team examined Josh Morgan and found no trace of the VX nerve agent. Nor were the precursor agents present. However, the responders insisted that he spend the night in a hospital for observation.

CHAPTER 48

DAY 11 – THURSDAY

It was six-thirty and Josh Morgan awoke to see Maggie smiling at him through the window of his hospital room. Almost immediately upon noticing her, he observed a doctor approach her. The MD also smiled at Josh and then at her as he spoke a few words.

With the all-clear, Maggie flew through the door and into Josh's room. She wanted to throw herself onto his chest and smother him with hugs and kisses, but knew he was in rough shape from his most recent ordeal. So, instead she kissed him lightly and brushed his hair on the top of his head, careful to keep her hand away from the huge bandage on the right side of her fiancé's face.

Josh had another such bandage on the back of his head where it had crashed to the sidewalk after Alvarez had battered him with the water bottle.

"I love you, Josh."

"I love you, too, Maggie."

"Are you okay?"

"Just another week at the office, Mag."

Morgan took his fiancée's hand. "This is really getting old."

"I know, sweetheart."

"You know, I thought Alvarez had dropped his backpack into the water main. And I thought it had the whole VX nerve agent in it."

"You don't know, Josh? The city had taken some precautions. After you called Betsy, she requested – actually, I think demanded is a better word – that Director Austin alert every agency in the city responsible for responding to a biological or chemical attack. Then when you went missing, she had them begin to take actions. She was sure you were onto something."

"No kidding? She basically told me my theory was bullshit."

Maggie laughed.

"Anyhow, the water department turned off valves anywhere remotely in the area where they found your rental. Just in case."

"So, nothing would've even happened?"

"There would've still been homes and businesses at risk – an enormous number. Any place located before where valves were turned off would've been affected. But the precaution would've spared anyone downstream. So, even if the VX had been released, you would've saved much of the city just because the delay you created allowed the valves to be turned off. But as it is, your actions kept the entire city from exposure."

Josh and Maggie visited longer than the doctors would have preferred. After a few minutes, another visitor arrived.

Preceded by her Secret Service detail, President of the United States Sandra Hendrickson entered the room.

As if reading his mind and the awkwardness he felt at not being able to stand, POTUS said, "Where are your manners, Josh?"

The President hugged Maggie and then took Josh's hand with one of hers and brushed his hair, much in the same way Maggie had. She started to speak but couldn't manage to get her words out. Her eyes misted and she dabbed at the tears with a tissue.

"Don't you dare tell anyone," she warned everyone with a laugh.

With her emotions finally in check, POTUS finally spoke.

"I was going to give you the usual line about how grateful the nation is and all that. You know, the same things I seem to have made a habit of telling you over the last couple of years. And while it's all true, I think the thing I really want to tell you is that I hope that my son grows up to be the kind of man you are."

POTUS teared up again. Josh didn't know what to say.

President Hendrickson stayed for more time than her Chief would've liked. And the visit was more personal than from any official obligation. But when she was about to leave, and the goodbyes had already been said, Morgan pulled at her hand.

"Can I ask a question? And if it's something you can't tell me, I understand."

"Go ahead, Josh."

"What China did… Nicaragua… I guess even Cuba, too… Those were acts of war. How will we respond?"

POTUS thought for some time about whether she would answer. Finally, she asked the doctor and nurse who had stayed in the room to leave. She figured they were only there because the President of the United

States was and not out of medical necessity.

President Hendrickson seated herself in a chair next to Josh's bed. She sighed and brushed her hair with one hand. She bit at her lip and stared across the room at nothing.

"You deserve to know. Yes, it was an act of war. Oddly, Cuba only exposed some missiles. So technically, we have no public position to act against them. However, privately we have told them to dispose of them and that we'll be keeping a very close eye on them. And Congress will reinstate all of the old sanctions against them."

Morgan shook his head.

"And Nicaragua is fairly easy, POTUS continued. "First of all, we're going to freeze their assets. We're going to blockade both their Atlantic and Pacific coasts. Carrier groups are on their way now to take up positions. We've already recalled our ambassador and expelled Ambassador Torrez."

Hendrickson took another deep breath.

"Then we're going to demand Zamora hand himself over to us."

"And if he doesn't?"

"We already have operators in-country to go get him."

"But they just signed the mutual defense treaty with China. What if they…?"

"Josh, this thing blew up on the Chinese in such a big way, that right now they're more worried about our response to them. They won't interfere with things in Nicaragua."

"And what will our response be to China, ma'am?"

"That's the tough one. Almost everyone in the world would understand if we blew the shit out of Beijing. Except that nobody knows of their complicity. The American people know a lot about Nicaragua's part because of all the news surrounding the kidnappings. And word got out, of course, about the VX attack." POTUS smiled at Morgan. "Well, the *attempted* attack."

"Of course, we have played the whole event down. But China…" The president shook her head. "Regarding the missile, all that people know is that another one of their rockets failed to reach orbit and came crashing to earth. I mean, how many is this? I've lost count. So, the public's reaction to that is a yawn and a 'ho-hum.' Nobody knows they fired a small nuke at the White House."

"That brings up another question. Why did they need the transponder? Couldn't the missile use its own guidance system?"

Hendrickson shook her head. "After the fact, our scientists told me that an active guidance program running on the nuke would've been obvious to our monitors. We would've been aware of the missile as soon as the guidance went active and would've had time for preemptive actions. A simple homing receiver was stealthier, believe it or not."

There was a lull in the conversation.

"So, after all that, because of the public's lack of awareness of how serious this was, you'll just ignore it? China walks?" The former spy couldn't believe it.

"Hell, no!" POTUS corrected with a scowl. "But bombing Beijing would start a war that neither of us could win. And it would kill a huge number of Chinese who probably don't like Cheng any more than we do."

The President paused as if reconsidering whether to continue her narrative to Morgan. She finally resumed.

"The Secretary of State and I met with the Chinese Ambassador last night. Our demand is fairly straightforward. Cheng and his top aides – his entire Central Committee – will admit to corruption in their country and will all resign immediately. They will state that they are going into exile after stepping down. Their plane will presumably crash but will actually land at one of our bases – South Korea or maybe Okinawa. The entire group will go to prison for war crimes. No international trial – no nothing. And nobody will be the wiser about their fate."

"Will they agree to it?" the patient asked the President.

"We'll see. If not, it will likely be war. We have the Theodore Roosevelt and Nimitz Carrier Strike Groups in the East China Sea already and are deploying more assets to the region. I have told Cheng that if we so much as get a blip on a radar of one of their ships or planes, we will blow them out of the water – or sky.

"Furthermore, Taiwan is off-limits to them in the future. No more blustering about its being a part of China. And the crackdowns in Hong Kong stop immediately."

"Wow!" a weary Morgan exclaimed. "Any room for negotiation?"

"None whatsoever. The way we positioned things with the Chinese ambassador is that we already consider ourselves to be in a state of war with his country. It's a war they started with an unprovoked attack on us. We will provide our evidence of the missile attack and Cheng's complicity in the VX attack."

President Hendrickson could see the doubt in Morgan's eyes.

"Josh, we have every right to attack them. But I believe – along with the Joint Chiefs – that they never really wanted a real war with us. They wanted the one quick strike to so weaken us, to so destabilize us that they could move in and take over our assets abroad. This might have appeared to be a military strike, but it was actually more of an economic and political one."

A few moments of silence underscored the seriousness of the tensions.

"They also anticipated that our leadership would be decimated to such a degree that they could establish bases near the U.S. virtually unchallenged."

"Madam President, how long do you think they've been planning this?"

"This specifically? I don't know. But NSA has reviewed some

collections from almost two years ago that have taken on more meaning in light of current events. It seems that the Chinese Embassy installed a system that would purify any water contaminated by a nerve agent. Pressurization, super-heating, filtering – things like that. We assumed it was out of an abundance of caution. But now it seems they have been contemplating a chemical attack on Washington for some time. And more recently, the Nicaraguan embassy installed the same system."

"So, the two countries appear to have been in bed together for a longer time."

"Yes."

"So, I guess we'll see."

"Yes. We'll see," the President agreed. She smiled but Morgan was sure there was little sincerity behind it.

As she stood to leave, Hendrickson paused. She looked directly at Morgan.

"Don't ever let anyone convince you to run for President, Josh. It's a lousy job."

"Mine hasn't exactly been a piece of cake, ma'am."

POTUS furrowed her brows briefly. Then she laughed softly.

"I suppose not, Josh." And then to Maggie, "You take care of that guy. He's a keeper."

"Yes, ma'am. He is."

An hour after the President had left, Josh was asleep. The painkillers in his IV drip were fairly mild – just enough to take the edge off the pain and let the patient get some rest.

Maggie hadn't left his side since the doctors had first allowed her into his room. She dozed as she leaned on Josh's bed. When her personal phone announced an incoming call, she stirred enough to look at the Caller ID. She never answered calls she didn't recognize. This one was from another hospital.

"Hello," she said, suddenly alert and puzzled.

Maggie Loughlin's eyes widened, and she put her hand to her mouth.

"Oh, God," she whispered.

She shook her sleeping fiancé lightly. It took a few tries to rouse him enough to speak.

"Josh, honey, I think you're gonna want to take this." She handed her phone to the patient, who looked mildly annoyed at being awakened. His eyes were only half open as he sighed deeply.

"What?" came the terse greeting.

"I hear your phone's out of order."

Morgan tried to sit up but couldn't do so. However, he was instantly fully alert.

"Yeah, it is."

"Mine, too."

The nature of his remark didn't betray the enormous smile and the joy he felt.

"Thought you were dead," Josh said.

"Thought I was, too," a hushed, tired voice replied. And then Tom Lechler laughed. It sounded labored, but it was a hearty laugh.

"So, how are you, Josh?"

"Oh, fractured skull. Pretty bad concussion. The usual. You, Tom?"

"Not much better. Cracked fibula. Broken ribs. I don't know, maybe sixty stitches. I don't have a cracked skull, but I do have a concussion. I've had worse."

Maggie watched Josh put his hand to his forehead and lower his chin. She knew he was fighting back tears. Josh couldn't speak for several seconds. She could tell that the retired Green Beret wasn't saying anything either.

"How hard silence must be for those two?" she joked silently. Her tears flowed freely now, and she lay her head on the edge of Josh's bed and merely looked at him. He finally lifted his head and raised his eyebrows. He shook his head gently and smiled at her.

"I, uh… I heard you flew a chopper into a nuclear blast."

"Who? Me? You think I'm stupid?"

"Well, you never have seemed too bright."

"Ouch," Lechler said with feigned hurt at the good-natured insult.

"So, what? I suppose the helicopter just flew itself until the missile caught up."

The two hospital patients were very tired. Neither felt like a conversation. Master Sergeant Lechler had much he wanted to say, but it could wait. The ex-SpecOps warrior had wanted to hear Morgan's voice. And he wanted to let him know he was alive. They agreed to talk in a few days.

"I don't think I can do this anymore, Maggie," the patient admitted after he had hung up.

Josh Morgan's eyes began to cloud up. Maggie began to cry, too, and she caressed his cheeks with both her hands. She brushed away his tears as he closed his eyes. Then she kissed the drops as they flowed down his cheek.

"I know, sweetheart. I know."

EPILOGUE

Seven days later

Josh Morgan had spent a total of three days in the hospital and four more recuperating at Maggie's apartment. Still in concussion protocol, he was supposed to remain in bed, in dim light, and stay completely quiet with little to no noise. He was supposed to avoid texting, working on his computer or other devices, and avoid television – anything that demanded focus, memory, and concentration.

So, when Maggie came out of the bedroom dressed for work, she found her fiancé sitting on the couch surfing the internet on his laptop with the TV on. She squeezed her eyes shut in frustration and shook her head. After days of dealing with this, she wanted to just let it go. But…

Josh looked up to see the exasperated look on her face.

"But Maggie, I'm not focusing. I'm not paying attention at all. Really."

Maggie's expression was unchanged.

"How about we split the difference? I'll turn the computer off and keep the TV on?" Morgan negotiated, shutting the lid to his laptop.

"There," he said with a thumbs-up.

Seeing the blue eyes still staring at him from beneath the auburn hair, Josh hung his head in surrender. He sighed, grunted "all right," and clicked the TV remote. With a brief, quiet crackle of electricity, the image disappeared.

"I'm only going to work a half day. Then I'll drive us over to Walter Reed to see Tom."

"I can drive," Josh suggested until he saw Maggie's "firm" look reappear. "Okay. You drive," he relented.

The impact of Maggie's silent scolding lasted only as long as it took

Morgan to become confident that she was safely out of the apartment complex's parking lot. He turned the television and laptop back on.

The former spy tired of the news rather quickly, if only because he knew firsthand that there were a lot of things going on behind the scenes that would never make the news. He flipped through channels, finally landing on the Comedy Channel. It happened to be replaying an old performance by comedian Mitch Hedberg. Josh knew his style of comedy wouldn't demand too much mental energy.

With the one-liners flying in the background, he called Scott Taggart, his friend in Jackson, to catch up on things and see how Biscuit, his Golden Retriever, was doing in Tag's care.

Finally, he called Betsy Parnell at CIA. He had only spoken with her a couple of times since his latest adventure landed him in the hospital. The pair spoke for almost thirty minutes.

The bored man smelled the coffee wafting from the kitchen and knew that to be a sign of improvement. For the first few days after getting his head whacked, Morgan had trouble smelling some things at all and almost every odor was diminished. His olfactory abilities seemed to be almost back to normal and his doctor had told him that such a development would be a good sign after a concussion. The former CIA Officer went to the kitchen to pour himself a cup.

He made other calls – to Alicia Weston, widow of his good friend and Former President Trent Weston and to a cousin back in Texas. His daughter was at Purdue University on a Naval ROTC Scholarship. Josh always enjoyed hearing about the young lady. He made promises to both the former First Lady and his cousin to visit soon.

Finally, Josh turned the TV back to QNN. Anchor Cameron Neal was in the middle of announcing another of the seemingly unending bits of "Breaking News."

> *There have been two astonishing developments on the world stage, both regarding presidents of separate nations. QNN has learned that Chinese President Cheng Shun and his entire Central Committee have resigned amidst allegations from within his own government of widespread corruption. Their resignations are said to be effective immediately. Though Cheng and his advisors have denied any wrongdoing, he has said he cannot live in a country that 'falsely accuses a national treasure' such as himself. He and the members of the Central Committee will go into self-imposed exile. They did not specify where.*

"I bet I know where," Morgan remarked, sipping from his cup and returning to the sofa.

And in another major story, Nicaraguan President Sergio Zamora is dead. He was found with an apparently self-inflicted gunshot wound in his official residence…

The ex-CIA spy would've preferred to take care of the dictator himself. The despot's agents had kidnapped Maggie. But taking down an old cancer-ridden private citizen like Oskar Lammers was one thing. Taking out a Head of State with immense security was another matter entirely and a job for professionals. He would remember to offer a more satisfactory toast later, but for now he lifted his cup of coffee.

"Well done, men. And well-deserved, you sorry son of a bitch."

♦

It was early afternoon and the first time Josh had been out of the apartment for almost four days.

"Hey, Tom. How ya doing?" Morgan took the retired Special Forces soldier's right hand.

The President had arranged to have Lechler transferred to Walter Reed National Military Medical Center in Bethesda, Maryland, from the Delaware hospital where he'd spent two days recovering from his injuries.

"Getting there, buddy. Hey, gorgeous."

Maggie hugged her fiancé's friend and, as of late, fellow warrior around his neck. When she released, she kissed him on the cheek and took his hand.

"I'm *much* better now, Morgan," he said and winked at Maggie.

"We thought you had been…," Maggie began before starting to choke up. "Well, it's just so good to see you, Tom."

"Hey, asshole, why haven't you called?" the former Army sergeant challenged his friend.

"Hey, you didn't call either."

"I called."

"Once," Morgan said holding his index finger up.

"That counts," Lechler rebutted, holding his middle finger up.

All three friends laughed.

"Honestly, I just wanted the next time we spoke to be face to face," Josh explained.

"I know, buddy. Me, too."

The men grasped hands again, more holding than shaking.

"Anyhow, first things first. Why aren't you dead?"

"You sound disappointed, Josh."

"Turd. Seriously. Word was you flew that chopper out until the missile reached you."

"I'm not that heroic, partner. I mean, nukes are interesting – as long as you're a long way off. Too close and… Well, let's just say they'll ruin your whole day."

"C'mon, Tom. Betsy told me the plan was for you to drop the homing beacon once you were over the Atlantic and get out of there."

"Yeah, well, I never was real good at following orders." He saw the impatience on both Josh's and Maggie's faces and decided to get serious.

"I decided I couldn't leave the transmitter so close to shore. Nobody knew at the time if the missile was nuclear-tipped, carried a dirty bomb, or what. But if that thing was set for airburst – which, I might add, it turned out to be – then radioactive particles or even the blast itself would take out a lot of people on land. I couldn't live with that. I know that in the minds of many, it would be a win if it didn't come down in Washington. But I decided that normal citizens were at least as important as politicians. It needed to go farther out to sea."

"But you still didn't drop it, Tom. Why?" Maggie asked, puzzled.

"By the time I would've gotten it as far out as I thought it needed to be, I wouldn't have had time to get away. The extra time would've let the missile gain too much ground on me. It was going twice as fast as I was."

"So, how'd you do it, Tom?" Morgan inquired.

"I compromised. Instead of dropping the transmitter offshore, I dropped me."

"How?" Maggie asked.

"Autopilot," Morgan surmised.

"Correct," Lechler confirmed with a nod of the head. "About ten miles off the coast, I dropped to about forty feet. Hell, I'd jumped out of choppers at that height before. I put the helicopter on auto-hover. I unbuckled my safety straps and prepared to get out. But I still needed to switch from auto-hover to autopilot. And I couldn't chance reaching from too far away from the console. If I fell out before I engaged it, it would continue to hover, and I'd be right below. And you know what I said about being too close to a nuclear blast."

"Then?" Maggie wanted to know.

"Well, I was still pretty much in the pilot's seat when the autopilot engaged. It's not like a rocket taking off or anything, but the nose does dip and the chopper surges forward pretty abruptly. So, I bailed. It wasn't the most elegant exit from an aircraft you've ever seen. Hit my head on the bottom edge of the hatch. That flipped me around and the skid caught me pretty good. Then I hit the water pretty flat. That hurt. But lying in the water I saw the beautiful sight of that Bell flying off to the horizon."

"And a boat picked you up?" Morgan guessed.

"Nope."

"Then how…?" Maggie wanted to know.

"I swam in. I couldn't find a handheld radio before I jumped. And I lost my phone when I hit the water. I wish I'd thought to get a flotation device from the chopper, but I didn't. The water is pretty cold in November, but I took my jacket off. There's a way you can flip it forward so that it catches air. That was my flotation device – my jacket with air trapped in it. I would swim until I was too tired. Then I would flip it forward, catch more air, and float and rest."

Josh and Maggie were stunned.

"I guess the adrenaline had run its course because someone found me passed out on the beach. I was unconscious for about a day."

"Why did it take so long for anyone to notify somebody, Tom?"

"Well, first Maggie, I didn't have an ID on me."

"What about fingerprints?" Maggie asked.

"I don't know if the hospital tried or not, but it probably wouldn't have mattered."

Maggie gave Josh a bewildered look.

"Our Master Sergeant doesn't exist. At least not in any of the databases that public agencies would have access to."

The patient nodded.

"And that's it," he said with some finality.

The three talked some more; mostly small talk, before Lechler turned serious again.

"Josh, I need to talk to you."

"Sure, Tom. Maggie, could you give…?"

"No. She needs to hear this, too."

"Okay, Tom." Josh put his arm around Maggie and held her close.

"Josh, most of my life has been a fucking mess, at least in a domestic sense. Excuse me, Maggie," he apologized.

She answered the gesture with a smile.

"Anyhow, friend, I've given my whole life to the Army; to my country. And I don't regret that at all. But it cost me all the things that matter most. I've lost my wife. Special Ops is a jealous mistress. Even more so than regular military service. And my daughters won't speak to me. I don't have a family to go home to."

Tears began to gather in the retired Master Sergeant's eyes.

"I swore to myself that I was going to tell you the truth about what you're doing. Tough love, I guess you'd call it." The former Green Beret smiled weakly as he continued. "Brother, you're not far from the same path I was on. I didn't know you very well then, but when you and Maggie broke things off, it broke my heart."

Maggie and Josh hugged more tightly.

"Hell, I didn't know whether you guys were going to wind up together forever or not. I had no idea. But I saw you breaking up with her for the same type of stupid shit that cost me everything. Josh, you need to get the hell out of CIA. There. I'm done."

The ex-Army soldier didn't receive a response until a few seconds had passed.

"You're right, Tom. In fact, I already have."

The former sergeant recoiled slightly at the news. "Have what?"

"Gotten out of CIA."

Maggie's head pivoted around to face her fiancé. Her mouth dropped open slightly and she leaned back.

"Morgan?" she said.

"No shit," Lechler remarked, astonished. "I'm one persuasive SOB."

"I talked to Betsy this morning. I told her that I needed to be there for Maggie. Ever since we've been together it seems like I always expected her to support me in whatever I was doing. I think it's time to flip that around."

"Josh, you've saved my life twice. And Trent's. And…," Maggie reminded.

The former Green Beret interrupted. "I know your guy here. And I know he'll always take care of you, Maggie. But the other shit…" He turned to Morgan. "It's time to let somebody else take care of it. You may think like I do about myself sometimes; that you're the only one who can do the job right. But you're wrong. Just like I'm wrong. Let it go, Josh."

The former spy hung his head and then looked at Maggie. There were a few moments of silence until Maggie spoke.

"How'd the Director take it?" she asked.

"Surprisingly, she was all for it. I offered to refund all the retainer money CIA had paid me. I really hadn't done anything in the way of a real assignment for the Agency anyhow."

"I think you've more that earned your keep," the former sergeant opined.

"That's what Betsy said. Well, actually she said it was worth letting me keep all the money just to get rid of me; that I was more trouble than I was worth. She was joking. At least I think she was."

"What about your job as a visiting professor at Georgetown?" the fiancée asked, alluding to the job Former President Weston had arranged for him when Maggie had taken her first job at the White House.

"I don't think I'm cut out for that."

Lechler laughed. "The way I hear it, you never even actually taught a class."

"Hey, I prepared class outlines once," the professor said with a smile.

Josh faced Maggie and took both of her hands in his.

"Sweetheart, I just want to be there for you. You're everything in the world to me. I'll do whatever you need from me to support you… to make you happy. I'll go anywhere with you."

"Even Wyoming, Josh?"

The fiancé pulled away slightly and put his hands on Maggie's shoulders. "What are you saying?"

"I'm not sure if I resigned or got fired but I leave the West Wing after Thanksgiving."

"Seriously, Maggie?" Morgan's mind was swirling. He had never expected this. "You don't have to do this, sweetheart."

Maggie shook her head. "No. It's what I want. I was going to offer to quit when we met for lunch those months ago, but then things all fell apart. So, I stayed on. But this morning, I went to speak with the President. Before I could tell her my intentions, she said that she thought I should go back to private life."

Josh was quietly thrilled, but he wanted to be sure that this is what his fiancée wanted. She continued.

"The President said that all successful careers in the government – especially at the federal level – are held by people for whom the job is their life. She said I wasn't a good fit because I had a real life. Press Secretary was just my job. President Hendrickson told me that it was her great honor to have had me work for her. She said I was the best person to ever serve on her staff, with one possible exception: Marie Ginnetti. And she's already talked to Marie and she's coming back. She said she'll stay as long as necessary. So, at the end of this month, Josh, we can go home."

An extended embrace with whispered words continued until a voice interrupted the moment.

"I'm still here, you know. Go get a room. They probably even have one here, but I wouldn't recommend it."

"What about you, Tom?" Morgan asked. "Staying with CIA?"

"No. Figure with you gone, I don't have to stick around to constantly save your ass."

"Save *my* ass? *I'm* always saving *your* ass, Lechler."

Maggie found a chair and listened to the two men argue about who the alpha male was in a way that only great friends could.

♦

It was after ten o'clock and the two lovebirds sat in their usual places on the sofa with Maggie's head on Josh's shoulder. Each had a glass of champagne to celebrate their decisions.

"So, Tom's going back to the Army. Are you surprised?"

Josh shook his head. "Not in the least. I thought he might try to reconcile with his wife, but he's said a number of times that he was a far better soldier than he was a husband or father. I know he believes that Ava deserves to have him fulltime."

"That's too bad, Josh."

Maggie snuggled even more closely to Josh.

"Are you going to miss working in the West Wing?" the now ex-CIA contractor asked.

"No. I'll miss the people, the President in particular. But the work and the hours…? Not at all. It nearly broke us apart."

"Yeah. A lot happened that I wish we'd never had to go through. That I wish we'd never been a part of," Josh agreed.

"If you hadn't been a part of all of it, who knows what the outcomes might've been? Don't underestimate what you did."

Josh simply shrugged. "Maybe. Regardless, I'm ready to get back to Wyoming."

"Back home," Maggie added.

The pair looked out the window at a bright, sunny day. Then they held each other tightly and sat in silence.

The end

AFTERWORD

In my second Josh Morgan Novel, *SPIRITs of Retribution*, I included a section explaining which of the book's details were made-up and which were real. I didn't include such an explanation in my subsequent novel, *Hell In the Meantime*. I really didn't think much of it until a number of my readers contacted me to say that they missed it. So, I'm bringing it back in *Binary Agent*.

The process of creating a novel can be agonizing in many ways. But part of the fun for me is the research that goes into each one. Research takes at least fifteen percent of the time involved to create a first draft. And it's an ongoing process as I endeavor to be as accurate as possible when referring to real people, places, history, technology, etc.

But as I said in *SPIRITs*, novels are by definition fiction. So, I sometimes make up what I need to suit the story. Sometimes the fiction is to distance the plot from facts and reactions from the real world that might get in the way of it. Still, it is always my goal to present the fiction in such a way that it is plausible; never outlandish or too convenient. I describe all the fictional elements as though they are real.

My goal with regard to my fictional creations is to craft them in such a way that, if they don't exist, they could, and the manner in which I present them is consistent with reality.

So, with that in mind, here are some examples of things from *Binary Agent* that you might wonder about.

FACT or FICTION?

FACT

- With the exception of Terrador, which is fictional and was created in my debut novel, *Half of Faith*, all countries and their respective locations, airports, etc. are real. The departure from this is only when a particular business I need doesn't exist as I need it to. Or I might choose not to use a real one for fear that I might offend or even slander someone. For example, Nicaragua Genuina and Hello, Sailor are entirely made-up.

- References to airports, cities, and histories of countries are accurate. However, I make up "history" when it represents events and people immediately prior to the beginning of the story's timeline. This is to bridge real events with the ones in the world of Josh Morgan.
- Josh Morgan's CIA cover was as a journalist. Normally, the U.S. has made it illegal for journalists to serve as intelligence officers. However, there are exceptions. This is explained in detail in *Half of Faith*. You can refer to that or you can research The Richardson Amendment to the 1997 Intelligence Authorization Bill that made it illegal and the subsequent Murtha Amendment that provided some exceptions.
- The descriptions of the various weapons, aircraft, and other materiel are accurate. The specifications are correct. The types of weapons I indicate various agencies use is accurate, as are types of aircraft used by specific agencies or other organizations, or foreign countries.
- To the best of my ability, all geographical descriptions are accurate. I could show you on a map where the private jet crashed (or landed, if you share Morgan's characterization) with Morgan and Lammers on board.
- The primary duties of the U.S. Secret Service are to protect federal officials and investigate crimes against our economy and financial institutions, just as described in the novel.
- The initiation of and continued presence of the U.S. Army in Colombia, specifically the 82nd Airborne, are historically accurate.
- Except for the gain of function of the variant of VX that is at the heart of this novel described in the "Fiction" section below, all facts about actual VX are accurate, including the assassination of Kim Jong-nam. The descriptions of the precursor agents used to yield VX are accurate. Here are a couple of interesting online sources.
    - https://sciencevshollywood.com/vx-nerve-agent-and-the-science-of-the-rock/
    - https://www.cdc.gov/nceh/demil/methods.htm
- The effects of a nuclear blast of the size of weapon I described are realistic as based on a simulator found online at the following link.
    - https://nuclearsecrecy.com/nukemap/
- Accounts of Chinese rockets failing to reach orbit are accurate.
- Can a small nuclear missile be launched from a rocket booster? I don't know, but it seems feasible.
- The layout of the White House is accurate to the extent that such

information is publicly available. For example, the existence of the bunkers is based on public information.

- The Green Light Teams that are described are factual as described. (The SPIRITs are fiction. See Fiction Section below.)
- The process of how nations destroyed their stockpiles of nerve agents in the early 2000s is factual as described in the book.

FICTION

- The change of Saudi Arabia from a Royal Kingdom to an Islamic one is fictional. It was a device to set the stage for my first novel, *Half of Faith*.
- There are many more layers to the direction and management of U.S. Agencies than as written. To be more accurate would've created an unwieldy cast of characters. Top level bureaucrats and agency directors wouldn't be as involved in mundane matters as in the book. The hierarchy is generally correct. However, much of the nuts-and-bolts duties you see done by upper management in the story wouldn't be handled by high-ranking executives. Upper management of bureaus and agencies don't get as involved in mundane day-to-day matters as they do in my books. The leaders of the various agencies and their duties are greatly broadened.
- Similarly, there would be far more layers of specialists in various agencies than as represented in the book. Many of the responsibilities and duties of the personnel have been synthesized into fewer individuals. The storyline that a few individuals would possess such a wide array of skills is made-up. There would be far more specialists involved in much of the work, particularly at CIA, NSA, and FBI. Real world personnel are more highly specialized than in the book. There are fewer generalists. But I created individuals in the story who are experts in multiple fields to keep the cast of characters somewhat smaller.
- I have some things happen by coincidence that are advantageous to the good guys and, in some case, even to the bad guys. That said, one of my main gripes in literary or cinematic entertainment is the overuse of coincidence and good luck to solve problematic plot "glitches." I try to limit fortunate happenstance to what might actually be plausible in real life.
- Lower tier personnel and operators wouldn't fly around as much in private US government jets, as I have them doing.

- The security software used by the Nicaraguan government – "PSI," *Primera Seguridad para las Instituciones*, or, in English, First Security for Institutions is entirely made-up.
- The variant of VX that is at the heart of this novel with its gain of function allowing for greater solubility in water and delayed onset of symptoms is made-up. (As far as I know.)
- As described in the book, "Unravel," the program that deciphers codewords, is made-up. However, such programs do exist.
- The SPIRITs (SPecial Immediate Reaction Infiltration Team) are fictional. These special operations units are based on actual Green Light Teams described in the book.
- The adaptation of one method of destroying stockpiles of nerve agents to a process to treat water is made-up.

ABBREVIATIONS USED IN THE BOOK

- SSA – Supervisory Special Agent in the FBI; oversees the activities of agents under their command
- SA – Special Agent
- AIC – Agent In Charge; equivalent to a Chief of Police at the department level, or the ranking Special Agent in the field at a crime scene
- Uni – a uniformed police officer
- BOLO – Be On the LookOut; an alert from one law enforcement organization to others in an area to watch for a particular person, vehicle, etc.
- APB – All-Points Bulletin; an alert from one law enforcement organization to all others in an area to apprehend a particular suspect or suspects

ABOUT THE COVER & TITLE

- The Chinese character on the cover is their symbol for death.
- The partially exposed molecular formula is for VX.
- Yes, I'm aware that the word "binary" has been adopted for sexual identity purposes. Unfortunately, some people will assume that the term has lost its generic definition as meaning two parts. I have made the conscious decision to use the word in its actual meaning.

ABOUT THE AUTHOR

After a career in the Financial Services industry, Rod Johnson retired to devote his time to his family and writing.

Binary Agent is the fourth novel in the *Josh Morgan* series that carries the protagonist's name. It follows Rod's debut work, *Half of Faith*, the sequel, *SPIRITs of Retribution,* and *Hell in the Meantime.*

Among the author's influences are great novelists in the thriller genre such as Clancy, Ludlum, le Carré, and others. Nelson DeMille's *Charm School* remains an all-time favorite novel, along with anything by current thriller rock star Brad Thor.

Rod works hard to ensure his plots are filled with a myriad of moving parts, lived out in characters with compelling blends of virtues and flaws. The characters have complex personalities and struggle to balance their hypocrisies and better selves.

When Rod isn't writing, he enjoys flyfishing, birding, and photography. He and his family spend as much time as possible at various campsites in their RV.

The author resides in a small north Texas town with his wife. Their daughter attends Purdue University on a Naval ROTC Scholarship.